The Circle of Duty

Book 2 in The Circle Series

Owen Elgie

*Rhys
Should we always do
our 'Duty'?*

Copyright © 2016 Owen Elgie

All rights reserved, including the right to reproduce this book, or portions thereof in any form. No part of this text may be reproduced, transmitted, downloaded, decompiled, reverse engineered, or stored, in any form or introduced into any information storage and retrieval system, in any form or by any means, whether electronic or mechanical without the express written permission of the author.

This is a work of fiction. Names and characters are the product of the author's imagination and any resemblance to actual persons, living or dead, is entirely coincidental.

The views expressed in this work are solely those of the author and do not necessarily reflect the views of the publisher, and the publisher hereby disclaims any responsibility for them.

ISBN: 978-1-326-63922-8

PublishNation
www.publishnation.co.uk

For family.

My parents, Marian and Fred. My wife, Jo. My sister Beth and brother-in-law Tom and my niece Lucy.

Oh the horror they've witnessed as I've worked on this book. I'll bet they can't wait for book three.

Also by this Author

The Circle of Fire

1

Staring out over rolling hills and craggy mountains, watching on casually as the sun set through the majesty of deep reds and buzzing oranges. All the while, a warm, drifting mountain breeze tugs ever so slightly at your clothes and your hair. On paper, that seems to be one of the most romantic ways to spend an evening with a beautiful woman. Six weeks ago I would have totally agreed with you.

That was six weeks ago.

As I looked out at the remarkable vista that was presenting itself to us, I could feel the thought of coming back here with Andrea at a later date lodging itself at the back of my mind. It was sat quite comfortably next to ideas about candle lit meals and walks along the beach. I really was getting quite soppy.

Six weeks on, however, and I was standing on a wide expanse of jagged rock looking out over the magically enhanced view coming from The Hive prison buried deep within the mountainous western border of Argentina. The Andes had never looked so beautiful. They had also never looked so terrifying. As I scanned all around me, the aforementioned beautiful woman appeared at my side.

"It's good to be back. Is everyone in place?" Andrea's rolling Russian accent was like a super charged purr, the barest hint of subtle suggestion layered over each syllable. Well, that's what I thought anyway. We had spent a great deal of time together over the last six weeks and I couldn't really help myself but see her as more than just my teacher in all things magical.

Since our first meeting where she had been part of my welcoming committee into The Circle, a supernatural force of age old power that stood guard over the prisons of the creatures that had been hell bent on the destruction of the human race, our relationship had been changing.

Where previously I was the pupil and she was the teacher imparting wisdom, now it felt more like we were stood together as almost equals. We had both been put in life threatening positions where we had had to rely on the other and as such we had grown closer.

"The teams are all ready, we're just waiting for Frederico to get to us," I replied without taking my eyes off the countryside before us. "He's still getting used to the finer points of bridge jumping." I didn't mean to puff out frustration with my comment but it seemed to rumble forward anyway.

Andrea nudged me gently in the side. "It does take a while to really finesse the process, doesn't it?" she said as she cocked an eyebrow. My habit for dealing with almost every situation with humour and Andrea's frustrated reaction had changed slightly so now she was starting to give as good as she got. Not every time mind, but enough for me to notice the change.

"Are you ever going to let me forget that?" I was starting to get a little tired of her always prodding me about what was a relatively minor mistake.

"Jumping us forty miles from our intended landing site, with no pressures of battle to cause the mistake, you are going to be hearing about that for a very long time. I'll never forget the look on your face when you hit the water. At least it taught you to be more focused on what you were doing rather than just assuming that everything you do is going to be right." I gave her a mock angry giggle and placed my arm around her, pulling her closer to my side. Pulling her to me, she settled into the nook of my shoulder and we leaned into each other. We had fit together like the interlocking pieces of a jigsaw, perfectly. Again, that's what I thought.

Andrea was stiff with apprehension. She felt like a wary cat that was being held against its will, still but looking for the moment of release. Despite her discomfort, we stood together and just let the evening wash over us.

I still couldn't work out why she was so 'off'. Every time I had tried to show any form of affection or at least familiar physical contact, she had barely been able to get away fast enough. I had seen her display very different behavior towards me during the weekend we first met and she seemed to be giving me positive signals all of the time so I thought that she must have had feelings of some kind developing. Maybe she just wasn't a big fan of public displays of affection?

We both stood watching the view before us, Andrea fighting against either my embrace or her own insecurities and me warring with the almost intoxicating need to pull her fully to me and kiss her. Who would have thought that standing on the edge of a violent conflict could be so tense?

Thankfully, the tension didn't last.

From behind us came the familiar sound of the crackle/hiss of the Cascade Bridge gateway opening up. A blue/white light spread out over the ground in every direction and the smell of ozone wafted all over the area we were stood in. We quickly jumped apart, the force of Andrea breaking clear sending me staggering in the other direction. We turned to face the ring of magical power that hung behind us. For people as strong in the supernatural arts as Andrea and myself, a Cascade Bridge is a relatively easy casting which can create a doorway between two points. I hadn't been fully involved in the control and use of magical energies for that long but I had been picking things up quickly. For people as powerful as the Elder, the oldest and most powerful member of The Circle, it was as simple a task as breathing. For The Mage, the central power which bound the whole Circle together, he could move the population of a city the size of London or New York in seconds, he was that powerful. It is a much easier way to travel over great distances without having to worry about booking flights or having to consider traveling time. All you do is concentrate on the ring construct and an image of where you want to end up, and boom! Through you go. It was a casting which needed a great deal of power to create and control so was something that only the creatures at the very top of the magical food chain could master. That translated to being only the Guardians of The Circle and the demons of The Hive. I'd heard that other creatures had been able to master it in the past but they were very much the exception rather than the rule. As far as I was aware, the Guardians were the only ones with the power to open the bridges.

For people who weren't as strong as Andrea and I, though, it could prove to be quite a challenge.

The ring stood before us and did nothing but hum, the thick band of magical energy which was holding the gateway looked to be both rigid and pliable. Then it flickered ever so slightly and looked like it was threatening to wink out. I took a step forward and began to focus my mind on the power that was floating before us, aiming to pour out some reinforcement of my own to the spell so it would stabilize. Andrea pushed at my arm and snapped my attention to her before I could do anything.

"What are you going to achieve by helping him?" she inquired in that tone that all parents seem to muster when they are attempting to educate their children in the errors of their ways. Maybe the teacher/pupil relationship wasn't quite finished with after all. I stood myself up a little straighter, just to emphasize how much more powerful and fearsome I was than her, and prepared to answer.

Andrea rolled her eyes at my display of bravado and raised her eyebrows. "Well?" She never took any of my posturing seriously and always seemed to have the ability to make me feel like a six year old who had been caught with his hand in the sweetie jar.

"We need to get him through sooner rather than later so we can get ourselves into position. We don't have the luxury of time for Frederico to make several thousand mistakes in the easy castings while we wait for his arrival." I was right, obviously, and as such turned back to the bridge gateway which was now flickering quite badly and started to draw my own power to bear on the ever weakening magical construct. Andrea kicked my leg. Not hard enough for it to really hurt but enough for me to have to swing my attention back to her.

I span round again and could feel my frustration starting to rise.

"What?!" I inquired in only just less than a shout, a wave of deep crimson passing over my vision as my instincts took over and I drew in power. I did have a reasonably short fuse and all the confusion around Andrea's behavior towards me was starting to get under my skin a little.

Andrea held her position but I could feel the temperature rising around her as she countered my display of power with one of her own.

"If we help him with the easy things now, how will he be able to rely on his own skills when he really needs them?" Her voice had taken on a slight hint of a growl as she spoke which made me take a firmer hold on my senses. We were both starting to get ready to fight over the most trivial of points so I needed to calm down before I did, or made her do, something stupid.

"We don't have the time," I told her as the building anger in me faded and I released my growing power. I straightened my shirt just to prove the point, and show that I was totally in control of my anger.

"He needs to have as much confidence in his abilities as we can muster in the short time we have available. If the Guardian feels they are ready, they can achieve a great deal more than if they have fear of what they are capable of. Remember, making someone think they are in control can go a very long way." With that, she placed one pale skinned hand on my arm and squeezed ever so slightly. I relaxed at her touch and smiled lopsidedly at her. She smiled back, and then turned to face the Cascade Bridge again. I turned with her and stared at the ring as it threatened to collapse under the weight of expectation which was being poured into it from this side. I didn't make any attempt to reinforce the power ring and just stood there on the rocky ground, hoping that the bridge would work.

For a very long minute, it seemed that the bridge was spending more time flickered off than it was on. We both willed that it work but I could feel the growing dread that it was doomed to failure. I would be proved right but that made me feel guilty.

Looking on with ever shrinking hope, I took another step forward and began to gather in my power. I could see that the bridge was doomed to failure and had given it more than enough of a chance to succeed. I pulled in my attention and prepared to shore up the construct before me but before I could do anything, the bridge suddenly snapped into life completely and hovered in place with all the requisite power coursing through it.

The sudden out pouring of energy from it took me by surprise and I stood stock still, with my eyes wide and my mouth open as a very young, gangly man with black hair burst through with an expression of both surprise and pride plastered all over his face. Dressed in ill-fitting black fatigues and heavy walking boots, he stumbled to a stop as he looked at the two of us. He frowned slightly as he looked at me and the strange expression I was wearing while the bridge snapped out of existence behind him.

"Anthony. Did I scare you?" His voice was ridiculously high pitched and almost sounded like an impression of an Argentinean accent.

"Did you scare…?" I mumbled under my breath as I re-gathered my composure and turned to face Andrea.

She was wearing a very smug expression which had been interlaced with barely contained giggles following Frederico's entrance. That made me angrier and the red flashes started to seep back into my vision.

"Come on Guardians," I growled to the pair of them. "Let's go and do what we do," and I started to stalk my way down the hillside towards the magically altered view of the countryside before us, expecting the others to follow me. They did and I could sense the fearful aim of Frederico to do what was expected of him and live up to what he was supposed to do, and the subtle happiness of being proved right coming from Andrea. That and the focus on doing what we do.

The breeze felt good as we strode down towards the bottom of the hillside but was taking the edge off what was stretching out before us, giving a false sense of comfort. Just to prove that I had some kind of control, I called over my shoulder as we descended,

"Let's go be Dragons!"

2

As we strode on down the hillside I could feel a very slight buzzing starting to develop on the edges of my mind. It felt like I was stood next to a very powerful electric generator but it was nothing more than an annoyance. My usual early warning system of mental gymnastics hadn't been triggered so I knew that I wasn't in any immediate danger, but the buzzing sensation grew with every step. The first time I had walked this path I had been on high alert and had misread what was in my head. I had mistakenly thought that this sensation was the spinning in my head which signaled an impending attack but now I was more familiar with the differences.

I looked over my shoulder as we descended to check on Andrea and Frederico. Andrea was wearing the blank expression of someone who was totally untroubled by the mental force pushing in at her or she was showing herself to be quite a bit stronger than I was. Frederico was a very different matter. He was looking worryingly pale and shook his head with almost every step as he tried to clear his thoughts.

"You OK Freddy?" I asked in as casual a tone as I could muster. I could understand what he was going through but Andrea's words stuck in my head. He needed confidence in his abilities or he was ultimately doomed to failure. He looked up at me and his expression hardened as he poured resolve over his features.

"I was born for this," he growled back as he puffed his chest out and scowled just to emphasize how tough he really was. On a heavy set man, that whole ensemble could have looked intimidating. On a seventeen year old who looked like the slightest breeze would knock him over; it came across as more comical.

I nodded and looked away as fast as I could before the smile spread across my face. He needed confidence.

"The barrier has been reinforced around the prison," Andrea added, "I can feel the power is much stronger than it has been in the past." I turned to start to tell her that it was exactly the same as it had ever been but my words didn't make it out. Frederico was now much straighter and he was more comfortable in his stride. Confidence is a wonderful thing. Andrea looked at me as we walked with the blankest of blank expressions but I could understand the sentiment perfectly.

This was the third time that we had been forced to defend this prison from attack in the last four weeks. On the two earlier occasions, the Hive forces had managed to score very damaging victories. We had managed to maintain the prison but on both occasions, the guardian had fallen. Frederico had lost his father and his sister in the last month and now he was directly in the firing line and very green with it. He had been training, practically since he was born, for this moment, the moment that he would be forced to stand as the sole force against the rancid hoards massing against his whole existence. No wonder he needed as much confidence as we could pump into him.

That said, he was handling it better than I would have done had I been in his position.

We continued our descent steadily, in silence and I let my mind drift back to my Awakening and how I had reacted. Looking back, I think that I had the easiest journey into the battle.

I had grown up without knowing any of the magical back stories that were draped around my family and was totally isolated from the supernatural war which was raging the world over. I had grown up in London and had what can only be described as a 'normal' life. When the power of the Fire Dragon Guardian was passed to me, I hadn't had any of the years of training to prepare me so I wasn't being weighed down by the knowledge of what was coming after me. I had just treated the whole thing as a challenge that I needed to overcome. Andrea had been chosen by the Mage to be the Guardian who would be best suited to the task of guiding me into my role as a Hive Prison Guardian. She was also handed the task of helping me to learn all of the details of magic and castings which I would need to master for my new role in life.

Leaning my senses back towards Frederico, I could make out his resolve stronger than ever but buried underneath all of his bravado was a very real terror. He may have had all of the training and skills drummed into him, and they do say that knowledge is power, but it was building to the point of paralyzing him utterly.

"Who are we bringing to the battle this time? These animals need to be hammered this time." My question was aimed at Andrea but was again meant as the start of a rousing speech for Frederico.

She looked at me with a questioning expression but quickly worked out what I was doing.

"We have the three of us as the Dragon force but we have massively increased the support groups. We have roughly two thousand troops spread out throughout the shielded perimeter; we doubled our force from the last attack."

As soon as the last part of the sentence left her lips we both knew that we had just undone our rousing and confidence fanning. We had just reminded Frederico that his family had been experiencing this same situation but with devastating results on more than one occasion. Damage control.

"We don't need any more Dragon help here Freddy and we've got enough muscle to demolish any army that they send our way." I stopped walking and turned to face the young Guardian.

"I know that we've been here doing the same thing over and over again but we will stop the attack and we are aiming to keep everyone alive. No-one is expendable."

Andrea added, seeing that he needed convincing "The prison will be maintained. Do not fear, we will all do our duty."

Frederico simply stared at us each in turn, blankly checking his feelings on everything we had to say.

"I don't want to lose the power of the Dragon but, more importantly, I need to protect my family. My sister is the next in line for the Guardianship. I don't want her to have to face this. There is more than The Circle to let down by failure." He hung his head at the thought of what was at stake. His mop of jet black hair was wafting gently in the breeze and it was easy to see him struggle with his own fears and the expectations that he was dealing with. I had met his sister. She was six.

"We will not let what happened before happen again. You are not going to die." I needed him to snap his attention back to what we were about to face rather than dwelling on the past and his loss and I was starting to get impatient.

He looked into my eyes and I could see the resolve climbing rapidly within him and a darkness climbed with it across his features.

"I will not let the fate of my family befall me. I will see them avenged." The final word was greeted by a shuddering within him, a blazing green light flared from both of his eyes, and he grew by roughly a foot. The Fire Dragon power within him was stirring as his anger grew and his transformation kicked into place. His rage was starting to drive him and he was still very young in terms of controlling his power. The temperature surrounding him fell by several degrees, covering the ground within a radius of about four feet in a slight sheen of frost. I could recognize what was happening. Andrea and I had been working with him over the last ten days to give him as much grounding in his abilities as we could but he was still very quick to get riled up. It reminded me of someone.

I reached an arm out to him and tried to calm him. The last thing we needed was an angry teenager with massive magical ability to lose it before the battle commenced and start torching his own troops. At least he wasn't scared anymore. I almost reached his shoulder before all hell broke loose.

Around us, explosions of greenish tinged power erupted and showered us in earth and debris which they had ripped from the ground. An odd smell of what can only be described as being somehow – cold, wafted through the air as the clouds of earth settled and we were left with a loud ringing in our ears from the impacts. Looking up and around the three of us all struggled for focus on to what had sent out the attack.

We all found them quickly.

3

Spearing through the air above us, their spindly bodies held aloft by gossamer thin wings, was a swarm of horrors which were all too familiar to both Andrea and I. They had made up a large portion of the enemy on the two previous occasions The Hive had attacked this site in the last six weeks. Andrea had called them the Tayne. They were creatures who were similar to the Wraiths that had attacked me in my own estate six weeks earlier but they were winged and didn't seem to have the ability to become living shadows. They all had the same emaciated bodies with stick thin bony arms protruding at angles which made them look pained just to exist but the Tayne had no legs. Instead they had a wisp of body which looked as if it was desperately trying to become a tail but had become stuck as a ghostly whisper of an appendage, more a stump than a limb.

The closely packed group of what appeared to be eight, maybe nine beasts shot through the air above us after unleashing their magical attack and speared onwards towards the edge of the shield perimeter surrounding the prison. We all watched them go and knew that the careful planning which had been put into the defence of this site was not totally useless but was certainly having to be massively rewritten.

"Now it's my turn," rumbled Frederico as the enemy powered on overhead.

The temperature plummeted and I could hear the tearing of fabric as Frederico burst from his clothes and became his Fire Dragon. His body grew and twisted, contorted by the change from human to mighty lizard, wings erupting from his back and his legs re-jointing themselves. In seconds, his transformation was complete and a mighty armored beast stood on the hillside where a once puny, gangly teenager had stood.

He may have been a Fire Dragon and shared the same magical grounding as I did, but his appearance was very different to me. Instead of the small scales of armor which covered my frame, Frederico was covered by much larger plates of what looked like bone. They were all coloured a very deep green and linked together over his crimson flesh which was visible at different points through the plates. He carried much larger slabs of protective shielding than I did and seemed to look slightly more aggressive for it. He did, though, still retain the same gangly dimensions in his Dragon form that he had as a human being. When he filled out he would look really imposing, but as it was he didn't look like he was quite finished. He looked exactly like what he was. A teenage Dragon, who'd a thunk!

His huge lizard frame orientated towards the departing squadron of enemy creatures and he unleashed a wide spray of flame from his mouth, somehow managing to release a full battle roar at the same time. His volley came nowhere near the Tayne who had fired on us but Frederico didn't seem to care. Without stopping his jet of flame, he spread his wings out to their fullest expanse and crouched down slightly as he prepared to soar after them.

Andrea and I moved quickly enough to transform ourselves and grab hold of Frederico before he could take off. In seconds, three terrifying monsters were occupying the space where three people had previously stood, one screaming at the departing attack while the other two held it down.

Frederico struggled and forced against both of us as he strained to break free and follow the enemy, his fire dying as he tried to claw his way from us. His young frame was no match for the combined strength of Andrea and I and we held him firmly in place. A second later, the enemies planned trap was sprung as a second, much larger group of Tayne hammered by overhead, raining down casting after casting at the three of us. In our Dragon forms, we were in no real danger from the magical attack which was pouring down after us from a great height. The power they were sending down at us would be easily deflected by our collective armour and would feel like a buffeting you might get when you're in the centre of an enthusiastic crowd at a concert, nothing life threatening but still something you need to concentrate on to control. If it had landed on one of us alone we would have probably been knocked over by it but the three of us were very close together so reinforced our collective strength. If they had managed to draw Frederico into the sky as they had planned then they could have done considerably more damage. Not by the power of their magics, but by the fall. The razor sharp jagged rocky outcroppings and uneven ground had been responsible for several injuries and a great deal of pain for me during the previous encounters here. I had fallen into the trap the Tayne had just tried to use during the last battle where Frederico's sister, Bethany, was lost.

After the fall, I had damaged my right wing badly enough to prevent me from being able to fly. It hadn't been the direct reason for Bethany's death but everyone was determined to make sure that all of the Dragons available to us were going to remain battle ready for as long as possible. I was feeling guilty anyway. When I was chosen as part of the defensive effort when this site was first attacked, there had been several raised eyebrows from other members of The Circle. Despite my natural deep red colour and huge self-belief, in magical ability and awareness terms, I was greener than Frederico. I had completed a massive victory over the enemy when the prison I had been charged with guarding had been breached and the evil demon entombed within had escaped. I had managed to put The Zarrulent, one of the original horrors, back in his box. I think, for a short time, I must have been viewed as being something of a star player. The power within The Circle must have thought it beneficial to have someone with a big win under his belt on the battlefield as a motivation to the other troops.

Frederico stopped struggling as he watched the enemy creatures surge towards the centre of the magically shielded valley. His control returned as he realized that he had very nearly fallen into the trap which had been set to play on his fiery nature. He breathed deeply as he stared after the winged creatures which had attempted to goad him towards his demise.

Andrea and I slowly released Frederico and we all stood scanning out over the valley before us. We weren't where we needed to be according to the information we had received from our intelligence forces but we seemed to have been exactly where the enemy had wanted us to be.

Before us, our waiting forces started to react to the appearance of three Dragons and a fly past of horrors from The Hive by opening up with magical volleys of their own.

From well hidden fortified positions on either side of the valley, blasts of energy lanced out towards the aerial forces as they headed on towards the edge of the shield perimeter which shrouded the prison. Reds, blues and greens poured out into the early evening air from various locations around the wide area we surveyed and started to tear members of the enemy from the sky.

Sparks flew in different colours as the impacts of magical energy ripped into the unlucky group. They had been used as simply cannon fodder to draw the youngest Guardian into the open, knowing that the Fire Dragon is prone to acting purely on impulse. The enemy had seen some success with the tactic of drawing their target into the open and had opted to use it again but when they failed with their initial objective, the Tayne were now horribly exposed to the defensive fire of the hundreds of hidden Circle forces.

One by one, members of the aerial attack were being picked off, their smoldering and flaming corpses tumbling from the sky to slam into the mountainous landscape below. The strategy that had been employed against us was being ripped apart and shown to be a failure.

I stood, still clutching onto Frederico and felt surges of pride as our previously hidden troops ripped through the enemy. Frederico stood next to me breathing deeply still, but with a violent pride much like my own radiating from him. I didn't have to use any magical skills to sense what he was feeling as he watched the demise of creatures that had been sent to kill him. He was intermittently growling and snorting as he watched the screaming animals fall to their death.

"Let them all fall," he snarled. His sentiments were painfully clear for all to see. He wanted to see the forces of The Hive defeated in the most painful way he could. He wanted to have the most awful revenge on those who were responsible for the death of his family. I could see that, when you drilled down through all of the duty and training, he wanted to make them pay for what they had done to his family. At that point, his duties towards The Circle had been completely forgotten.

For a second, I agreed with him.

My own loss of family was something that had been weighing on me for most of my life. I had seen both of my parents taken from me at an early age, in what I had been told, was a car crash. I had since found out that they had been killed in an attempt to destroy my own power line. They had been taken from me in an attempt to shatter the control over a demon of ancient power who could have been responsible for the deaths of millions of people had he broken free. The subsequent loss of my Uncle who raised me, and of my brother, to the same forces, would always be at the centre of a burning ball of hatred for the enemy that I knew would be alight for a very long time.

We stood watching as the opening skirmish of the latest battle here looked to be coming to a close firmly in our favour. There were only a small handful of the Tayne who had managed to evade the defensive fire from our hidden batteries but they were still heading onwards, spiraling through the beams of power coming from the surface and the falling mounds of their comrades coming from above and around them. I had to hand it to them, they were certainly committed.

I cast an eye around the newly formed battlefield, checking for any sign of another force making a move on us and watched the bright columns of light as they were being fired skywards. They all danced through the sky in a display of colour which I knew would be described away as a firework celebration in the press if and when anyone asked what had been going on.

We had brought in some seriously powerful magical artillery to make certain that the latest attack on this site would be dealt with swiftly and ruthlessly. It was plain for all to see that The Circle didn't like to lose. We had brought people in from almost every location around the globe, including a large number from my estate. As my eyes wandered over the valley before us, I could make out the familiar deep blue tone of Mark Howells' magic hammering upwards from what I knew was a magically shrouded, heavily fortified rocky location. Mark was the Head of the Kitchens at my estate, a title which meant he was responsible for the smooth operation of the kitchen and serving staff at the mansion. It also meant that he was second in command of the whole staff of the house in a military sense. He was very powerful in a great deal of the magics which were based around the use of sheer brute force and the manipulation of energies for strength. Mark gave off the feeling that he was more than ready to tear anyone he needed to, to pieces. He stood seven feet tall and was built like the side of a, very large, house. His jet black skin seemed to absorb all of the light around him and I swear it made him look even bigger. If I hadn't known him, he would have scared the life out of me, despite my inner Dragon. Like the Fire Dragon, not subtle, but very effective.

In the last six weeks, though, we had worked very closely together and had developed a very close bond as more than just lord of the manor and staff member. I would like to think that he was now my friend. He and Mike Christian, the Head of House, were my closest confidants and were helping guide me into the life of The Circle in ways Andrea couldn't match. They had been able to give me answers in a more user friendly way and weren't treating me like some kind of savior. I had needed someone to speak to me like a normal human being since I had entered this world of magic and monsters and that had been exactly what they provided. It was good to know that I had people around me who I could turn to, especially after Lloyd's death.

I shook the melancholy away.

"Come on Howells, there's only a few left," I muttered to myself as I watched the ever decreasing enemy force continue onwards. We all wanted the enemy to be brought down but my competitive edge was starting to poke at the surface. I wanted the monsters who were bent on the destruction of mankind to be vanquished, don't get me wrong, I just wanted my team to be the ones who did it.

"They're getting very close to the shielded area of the valley." Andrea had moved forward and had locked her eyes on the Tayne which remained. Her voice was still rolled thick with a Russian accent but it was now coming with a rumbling growl from her own Dragon form. The growl, though, couldn't disguise the hint of apprehension. I lifted my eyes from the ground positions and tried to establish where the line of invisible magical power was which was swirling around the South American prison.

"Let them hit the shield," boomed Frederico from my side, the purest violence coursing through his voice. I turned to face him and I was greeted by, not an unsure monster, but by a Dragon with hatred in his eyes. He was stood with his shoulders forced out squarely, his lips curled back in a vicious snarl and his teeth bared. He was really starting to feel the full terrifying beauty of vengeance.

I let my gaze wander over to Andrea, thinking silently to myself that Freddy was bang on with his desire to let the enemy burn on the boundaries of his power base. When my eyes finally landed on Andrea, though, I could see that she was truly concerned.

"Those little things are never going to damage the shield. Let them hit it if they want to, it'll save our troops power from having to take them out of the air." I couldn't see how there was anything we should need to be worried about. The Tayne were vast in numbers but they were also so fragile. We had broken them without any real trouble on more than one occasion and in every previous encounter, the outer shield was always far too powerful an obstacle for anything that The Hive had been able to throw at us. I looked on and couldn't see why Andrea was looking so worried.

"They have no real power and they have tipped their hand. Let them go. The shield we have in place is more than strong enough to burn away a swarm of barely solid, demonic ghosts like the Tayne. Don't panic." I meant every word of it, feeling supremely confident that what we had in place defensively was more than enough to stand against our foes. I faced Andrea and knew that we were in no real danger. I was already checking the surrounding area for other enemy troops hurriedly trying to work out what to do next.

Until the first Tayne hit the shield wall.

4

Over my shoulder, the leading Tayne had reached the domed boundary of the prison of the Hive beast we were trying to defend. One by one, they smashed into the invisible wall of power which was cast over the landscape which, in turn, surrounded the entrance to the stronghold. Their impact should have only been greeted by a small snap/hiss of incinerated flesh and the slightest ripple through the shell of the prison. After all, they were nothing to really worry about.

Instead, we were shown that the enemy hadn't been relying on the same tactic which had served them so well in the past.

A sound akin to a sonic boom crashed over the valley as each of the Tayne impacted with our defences, rattling off the age old stone of the surrounding area. The three of us blinked wildly in surprise as we were all forced to take a step backwards by the concussive force of what had just taken place. Frederico and I stood practically motionless as we attempted to take in what was taking place, stunned into a statue state by the sheer surprise of events unfolding before us.

Andrea, though, was already airborne.

With a single thunderous beat of her wings, she had surged skywards with the sound of the first concussive impact. She had instinctively known that there was something wrong, even before the Tayne had reached their apparent target.

"Come on Freddy, it's all kicking off. Let's move," I growled into Frederico's ear as I gripped him by both shoulders and shook him into action. I unfurled my own wings and readied myself for flight, still shaking Frederico as I did. He barely moved.

"Come on. We need to get airborne now. Something is going to happen and we need to be able to counter it. All of our weapons are inside the citadel." My voice carried the usual growl of the Dragon but the desperation I suddenly felt was clear enough to hear. The enemy hadn't made their move but their opening gambit was scary enough.

With one thunderous pulse of my wings, I surged up and back, watching Frederico and the ground vanish behind and below me. I turned myself to face forward, towards the edge of the shield and began to draw in my magical power in readiness. Whatever was taking place was going to need all of the muscle that I could muster, judging by the size of those opening explosions. Frederico was soon following.

Andrea had made a good start on her journey towards the centre of the valley but it didn't take me long to draw alongside her. From our elevated position, we could make out the different locations that our forces had been using as vantage points. Below us, I could make out people starting to get to their feet and shake off the effects of the explosions which had burst from the Tayne. There were still a great many lying motionless.

More tearing explosions boomed out as wave after wave of Tayne struck the shield. Each outpouring of energy and sound was getting more powerful as the three of us followed the enemy inwards towards the centre of the valley, closing the distance between us and their source.

"How are they doing that?" I was totally at a loss to explain how what was previously accepted as being the weakest of the enemy forces was suddenly able to create so much destruction. Andrea had known that there was something very wrong even before they had impacted so I needed to know what she did.

Andrea didn't turn her head to face me, instead keeping a watchful eye for attack from ahead, but she started to speak.

"This isn't the main attack. All of our forces opened fire on the Tayne when they were closed on the edge of our barrier. The Tayne had brought all of our troops into the open, made them all expose their previously shrouded positions. However they did it, their super charged attack from impact with our wall has managed to expose every faction of our troops and to leave them all vulnerable to their power. We need to get within the boundary and set our defences closer to the entry to the prison."

Without another word, she effortlessly accelerated and pulled away from me, spearing forwards towards her goal. Before she was too far from me to be heard, she twisted her long, elegant neck and called back an impassioned order,

"Get Frederico through the barrier. We need him." Her head snapped forward again and she powered on, leaving me to bank hard to my left to bring me back to his position. I settled into a cautious glide directly over him as he pushed onwards for all he was worth. From that position, I knew that I would be able to offer him protection from any threats from above by simply being between him and his would-be attackers. I was also now in the perfect position to see anything which was sent up at us.

"We need to get inside the boundary shield quickly. Our forces on the ground have been badly compromised so we need to pull our efforts closer."

Frederico nodded his agreement but I could feel a black anger pouring off him like an oil slick.

"We are all going to survive this but our first and most important task is to always hold the prison." I needed Frederico to hold is inner animal in check until he could use his soaring rage to its most devastating effect. He still didn't answer me but I could feel the chains around the violence of the Fire Dragon power pull a little tighter.

I continued to scan as much of the area I could, hoping that if there was going to be any fresh bombardment, and I would be able to see it coming well before it hit us. The first flash came from an area on the rocky lowlands almost directly behind us. A single spark of light burst out against the grey of the surrounding stone. I instinctively called out to Frederico and we both banked in opposite directions in an attempt to evade the shot.

As I leveled out, I checked back to the site of the flare to check for repeated fire. Instead of being greeted by the pop-pop-pop of magical artillery, I was greeted by the site of a small Cascade Bridge gateway. It wasn't the usual white/blue colour of the gateways I had seen previously. This one was more of a dirty yellow. It gave off the same kind of light you would find from a very heavily dust covered light bulb; you could see it was working but that it wasn't working in the right way. As I flew, more and more of these messy doorways were bursting into life all over the valley. They could only have been two or three feet in diameter but they were all clearly visible. Risking a look into the sky again, I found Frederico to my left and slightly below me. He was still heading in the right direction though. He too, was looking down at the gateways as they opened and floated in the gathering dusk. We both continued our journey towards the relative sanctuary of the boundary shield, still trying to work out what was happening all over the valley floor.

We hadn't come to a conclusion when the truth was revealed to us.

Each of these Cascade Bridges had been opened directly next to one of our troop's previously hidden bunkers. Accompanied by hissing and screaming, hundreds of small creatures began to pour out of the gateways and crash over the still reeling people below like the wave of an angry sea.

Crimson shards flashed across my vision as my own rage at the enemies attack on my people spiked. I wanted to drop from the sky and start torching every single thing that had dared to set foot on The Circle's ground. I prepared to help my allies but suddenly, and without warning, my rational mind gripped me tightly. The Tayne had been used as a diversion to draw a Dragon into a position where he would be vulnerable. Looking down, I could see that this was clearly the same situation. We needed to keep the Dragon force intact and, as Andrea had pointed out, we needed to protect the prison.

I turned back to Frederico to call him onwards but his rational mind had lost its grip some time ago.

All I could see was him fold his wings back into his body and set off towards the ground like an armour plated javelin, roaring all the way down.

I was left to roar out after him as he smashed down towards the shrieks and calls from the melee which had sprung into existence. Taking one last quick scan around the area for any other sites of enemy incursion, and making sure that there was no wild spinning in the back of my head which would have signaled impending danger to me, I took a deep breath, focused on the diving Guardian and growled to myself,

"In for a penny…"

I snapped my wings back with a slapping force that pressed them directly down to the length of my body. There was now a sudden lack of force holding me in the air and gravity was fast to make its presence felt. I started my rapid descent to the ground by piking my body and falling headfirst. The wind lashed at my face as I quickly gained speed. Ahead of me, I could make out Frederico reach the battle that was erupting around one of our artillery positions.

He wasn't slow to join the fray.

He waited until the very last moment before he deployed his wings as a natural parachute and hit the ground directly over the beleaguered encampment of our forces. It wasn't long before he had started defending the position.

The enemies' gateway was still burning and was still vomiting out swathes of the small creatures which had been attacking or forces. As I closed in on the action I could make out more and more detail of them. The outpost was being swarmed by what looked like thousands of two foot tall black, armored beetles. They had been overwhelming our small team of soldiers by sheer weight of numbers, doing God knew what as they poured onwards. When Frederico had landed though, each and every one of them swarmed up and onto him.

He started spewing out columns of green tinged orange flame, indiscriminately torching anything that was in his way. Our own troops seemed to become a distant memory in the blink of an eye and they were all forced to dive for cover, both physical and magical, as Frederico's immolation was cast all over the area.

A noise which can only be described as being 'wrong' floated up towards me as dozens of the beetle creatures screamed in agony as the full power of an angry Fire Dragon was brought to bear on them. Small bodies were turned to ash as all of Frederico's fury was given a free reign to exact what he must have seen as a divine retribution.

Frederico's efforts, though, hadn't gone unnoticed. More and more of the six legged creatures were bounding out of the gateway and into the fight as if it were the call for reinforcements that I had heard coming from them. It was hard to distinguish between them all as the numbers on the battlefield rapidly increased. All I could make out as I fell was that Frederico had been drawn into a very dangerous position where the enemy would have the advantage.

Again, The Hive had managed to draw a Dragon into a position where they would be vulnerable. Again, The Hive had shown themselves to have a stronger grasp on military planning and strategic forethought than any of us had given them credit for. As I neared the ground, I realized that I was crashing headlong into yet another fight at this prison that felt like I was being manipulated. The last time I had damaged my wings badly enough that I couldn't fly.

Mentally I crossed my fingers that I wasn't going to be on the receiving end of worse this time.

Steeling myself, I too waited for the last possible minute before throwing out my own wings and joining the fight. I smashed down far harder than I had intended and I could feel the waves of energy from my impact course through my frame, rattling against every part of me.

Shaking the stinging pain away, I risked a reviewing glance around the area. It was hard to make out the details of the enemy. They were all crawling over each other to be the first to attack the Dragon before them. They seemed to take on the appearance of a living liquid, ebbing and flowing as it crashed all over Frederico. He was doing his best up to now but the armored beetles were constantly replacing themselves. As Frederico burned away ever increasing numbers of them, more and more came scuttling out of the magical portal which floated at the edge of the skirmish. It was clear to me that my first focus had to be to try and stop the source of the enemy forces being spewed out at us.

As wave after wave of the midnight black creatures swarmed up towards me, I dug my claws deeply into the rocky ground beneath me and threw out as fierce a blast of searing flame as I could, aiming it through the corrupted Cascade Bridge.

Creature after creature was incinerated as my fire hammered into their magical construct. The screeching call that I had heard from the enemy earlier filled the air again as we fought back. This time, though, it was accompanied, from beyond the rim of the Cascade Bridge; by what can only be described as a collection of shouts from what sounded eerily like human voices. I stopped my beam of flame and tried to listen over the cacophony of clacking and screeching.

I thought I could make out garbled words, fragments of sentences and cries of pain as I focused all of my attention on the ring of power before us. I tried my hardest to focus enough of my mind on picking the details of the sounds that I thought were speech but the sound just hopped and flitted away from me amongst the battle. Who or what could have been on the other side of the construct?

My attention couldn't linger that much longer.

In a sudden collapse of energy, the Cascade ring winked once, and then fell back in on itself as the magical control governing it unraveled. One jerky lurch after another signaled the loss of control and the magical doorway, which had been held open by what can only be described as corrupt, broken power, was slammed shut, isolating the enemy from their support.

Swinging all of my attention back to the fight that was going on around me, I was quick to realize that the danger was far from being contained.

The remaining enemy creatures were still vast in numbers and were more than capable of causing serious damage to one or all of the Dragons and human forces they were attacking. They had split their attention between Frederico and the beleaguered soldiers who were still firing but who were now huddled together in a defensive position, looking they were making their last stand. They had also started to make a move on me.

I started to feel hundreds of grasping feet as they searched for grip on my scaled surface, all looking for the purchase as they scrambled for headway amongst their brothers and sisters in their mission to slay the Dragon. I tried to focus on all of the details of the little monsters as they moved all over me. They were new to me but I knew that Andrea or someone else in The Circle would be able to identify them.

I reached into the pool of broiling anger at me feet and held one aloft. Despite the battle which was raging around me, I reviewed its features and took in all of the details. It held equal parts humor and terror. They looked like they had come to being as a weird cross of a Pixar creature and the nightmares of H.R. Geiger, rounded edges and sharp points all rolled into one. A shiny black shroud of plate was draped around the whole frame of the beetle like creature but its head was far from being typical to that of your usual run of the mill black beetle. It carried flashing mandibles, each covered in thick, fibrous hairs which framed a mouth full of crooked yet steely sharp teeth. There were also no eyes to speak of at any point on the monsters face.

I turned it slowly before me, trying to ignore the sensation of its brothers and sisters crawling all over me, and took in all of the detail that I could afford. I could make out serrated blades all over its limbs and knew that this particular foe was going to be nothing for me to worry about on its own but that as part of a swarming group that they could probably have a very damaging effect.

My analysis was stopped there though.

Without looking up from the small creature in my grip, I was slapped in the face by a bolt of heated force. With a perfectly literal slap in the face, Frederico brought me back to the battle at hand.

I glanced up to see the young Guardian writhing around amongst an ever growing maelstrom of insectoid evil. The wave of Hive foot soldiers was looking like they were starting to develop the upper hand and Frederico was starting to throw his bursts of flame around in a very indiscriminate fashion. The slap in the face that I had been on the receiving end of had been a full blooded blast of Argentinean fire. There was no time left to study the enemy foot soldiers.

With the barest application of pressure between my massive clawed fingers, the beetle thing crumpled in on itself and stopped thrashing for freedom. A thick, yellow hued goo dribbled down my fingers and started to fall in heavy drops towards the seething ocean of The Hive forces. Slowly separating my fingers, I dropped the now crushed shell carcass to the floor and shook my hand free of the sticky substance. The first of the beetles had reached my head when I opened up with my own jets of flame.

With the maximum accuracy I could muster, I beamed out fire in as wide a jet as I could in Frederico's direction. The force of the flame was enough to knock him off his feet but it had a much harsher effect on the enemy which had been starting to overwhelm him. In an instant, there was nothing left but blackened ash covering the young guardian, all of the creatures which had been all over him now incinerated. Frederico was unharmed by the flaming blast. It wouldn't be the done thing for a Fire Dragon to be vulnerable to its own power.

He was quick to stand and start in on the others, again letting his hatred for The Hive drive his efforts. Roaring all of the time, he swung his head back and forth, spraying out fire in wide arcs through the on rushing hoards. Screaming and clacking clawed at the air as dozens and dozens of the small beasts perished.

I turned my attention back to my own situation and started to scorch off my own attackers. They were all resolute in their desire to kill the Dragon but without an unending supply of reinforcements, they were starting to run low on numbers. For a force that bases its entire strategy on overwhelming the opposition by the sheer weight of numbers, this meant that they were on a slippery slope.

But looking at the fight below me, they had thought of that as well.

The screaming sound which I had thought to be nothing more than the death throes of a mindless monster now appeared to be a more co-ordinated call to action, changing their orders on the battlefield. I was still partially covered but Frederico was no longer being rushed by the ever charging waves. The beetles had swiftly changed their attack focus and were all driving at the huddled band of soldiers who had been fighting for their lives. Up to now, they had been doing enough to stay sheltered but they were going to be overwhelmed in seconds if they had to see off the whole enemy force.

Frederico hadn't seen the change in tactics.

He was still spewing out column after column of molten hatred, despite the fact that the creatures were essentially running from him.

"Freddy! They're all aiming for the troops. The guys need help!" I roared out to Frederico trying to snap him from the glee of death while still scraping against the little beasts still surging all over me.

He didn't respond.

We didn't have time for this. I needed to get these troops to safety within the shielded perimeter of the prison and then work on the rest of the teams that were being swamped over the valley.

Focusing my mind, I took in as much of the detail around me and pictured in my head the landscape as I could make out, pinpointing the location of our forces. Closing my eyes to aid my concentration, just as Andrea had recommended, short tempered Fire Dragon after all, I built up my energy and pictured flame.

My stillness was seized upon by the force all over me and they were fast to bury me in a broiling mass of piercing jaws and slicing limbs.

I pushed the ever growing sensation away as much as I could and let the flaming image in my mind build and build. It climbed quickly to the point where it was struggling to be unleashed and I had to focus to hold everything in check. With one final mental review of the soldier's positions, I roared out as the power burst from me.

In an instant, I summoned as wide an area of fire as I could muster, torching anything and everything that was within its boundary. A wall of impenetrable heat burst to life and stood at least fifty feet from the ground. The searing heat and unnatural flash of brilliant orange/yellow filled all of my senses. Everything that had been moving around me had been incinerated in a split second. What little grass and foliage that had been scattered over the rocky surface of the valley was now a distant memory. Scorched earth and super-heated stone was all that was surrounding us. Frederico was laying flat on his back near the edge of the destruction, taking in massive gulps of air as he spluttered. The force of my magical outburst must have caught him by surprise and knocked the wind out of him. I knew that he was fire proof so wasn't really that worried about him being caught in the blast. All of the beetles, though, were a smoldering after thought. The warm breeze was still drifting through the air but it was now carrying ash fragments and the smell of, what most closely resembled, burning rubber. I stood up quickly and headed over to where the creatures had been aiming. There was one small area, though, which had escaped the fire.

A wobbly circle of untouched ground was visible with a huddled band of human soldiers looking equal parts surprised and terrified slap bang in the centre. I had managed to pinpoint their position and throw a small shield of my own around them to avoid burning them down with everything else. I sighed slightly to myself in relief. I had become pretty strong, magically speaking but my accuracy hadn't managed to keep pace with my strength. That casting had been a great deal more risky than I would ever let on to the team on the ground. They had just seen a wall of magical flame roar into existence around them and they had been untouched by its effects. They had had all of their power turned towards a defensive shield as they had seen the beetles swarming towards them. The combined efforts of their defence and my own shield for them had been more than strong enough to protect them from my explosion. I looked down at them, through the smoke, making sure that they were OK.

One by one, they all managed to look around them and re-gather their composure. From what I could make out, they were all pretty beat up but nothing truly life threatening. I was quickly noticed.

"Sir!" shouted the largest of the troop. He was a man of least fifty years, and roughly ten times as many good meals. His black fatigues and turtle neck jumper shrouded a heavy set frame which seemed to be carrying a beanbag round his middle. His graying hair was buzzed down to his scalp but he had the most flamboyant handlebar moustache that the world had ever seen. He may have looked a little out of practice shall we say, but you could easily tell that if push came to shove, he was more than a little capable of tearing things up, just for fun! I hadn't met him before but I kind of liked him.

Looking up to me with an earnest expression on his face, he performed a salute which must have been dipped in starch. The rest of his group was swift to follow his lead.

"At ease gents," I growled. I had been bowed, saluted, curtsied and groveled to since the very first day I had set foot in this life of magic and monsters. I had watched people endure pain in my name for no other reason than they had thought it was the appropriate response. This deference to the Dragon Lord was really wearing thin.

Back to business.

"Any injuries?" I boomed out.

"None too bad sir." He let me know with a hint of professional pride woven through his thick Australian accent.

"Good. We need to get everyone back inside the shield now. Has there been any contact from the other people out here?" I needed to know where we were in terms of the bigger picture.

"Nothing yet sir, but ..." he pulled a radio from his waist band and flicked it on. We were all greeted by a sound which chilled our blood.

Over the radio, on all channels as they were checked in turn, came the horrifying call of hundreds of people screaming for their lives. Snapping my head up and out into the valley, I focused on the nearest encampment to us and could just make out in the distance, the dirty Cascade ring of power and a maelstrom of black. The beetles had been driven away from this site but they were still fiercely attacking at what could have been thirty other locations.

Frederico and I couldn't help everyone but that wasn't going to stop us trying.

"Freddy." I surged over to where he was and shook him as he was getting to his feet. The impact of my magic had really knocked him sideways.

"We are still under attack. We need to move now." My voice was thick with rage and I could feel the effect rubbing off on Frederico. His eyes darkened and the wicked snarl he had been sporting earlier had returned. He was feeling the call of his blood lust again and I congratulated myself on getting him fired up again so quickly.

Turning back to the shell shocked troops, I called out instructions.

"I'm going to jump you guys back inside the shield. Get the word out to the field that the enemy Cascade Bridges are easy to bring down but let our reinforcements know that we need to rescue the forces outside, and we need to do it NOW!" The final syllable was almost lost in the snarl of the animal which was starting to climb to the surface of my mind.

I reached out my mind and a bridge gateway ring snapped into existence. Thrusting out one arm, I signaled for the men on the ground to get moving and turned to Frederico as they filed through the construct.

"We need to avoid landing in them all Freddy; they can swamp us if we do." I needed to get our tactics sorted quickly so Freddy could at least be aimed when he started to unleash his own brand of vengeance. "Also, we need to stay out of the air for long periods, The Tayne are still up there and they can bring us down." The final part of my pep talk hit me like a sledge hammer. If we couldn't land and we couldn't fly, where was left for us?

The penny dropped and I shackled my inner demon.

The enemy had again factored in the hot headed reaction of the Fire Dragon to its plans. If we simply tore into the enemy, we would be lost. There had to be another way.

"Freddy wait," I yelled but the young Dragon was already away from me. With one mighty thrust he had unfolded his wings and with massive effort, had sent him up and away towards the nearest fight, all thought of tactics utterly lost.

"FREDDY!"

I knew that any call after the departing Dragon would be useless but I tried anyway. His tail waved in the air as his body pulsed with effort sending him towards the next skirmish. I knew that if I followed him that I would be putting both of our lives in danger and risking the lives of everyone in the valley. The Dragon force was a central importance which I knew had to be maintained.

That said, we also couldn't afford to lose another of our number in the defence of the same prison. That meant that I couldn't leave him out here on his own.

Whipping my own wings out in a wild spray of leathery scarlet, I crouched down and prepared for the surge skywards. Before I heaved myself after the departed Guardian, I threw a final call to the departing Australian soldiers,

"Let Andrea know that I'm going after Frederico and have everyone who can help work on a way to get our forces inside the shield boundary. We need at least thirty bridges opened. And see if you can find out what the beetle-creatures are called and if they've been seen before. They're new to me."

I didn't check that he had understood or even heard. Pulse after massive pulse sent me after Frederico. My only hope was I would be able to get to him before he buried himself in more trouble than he could be dug from.

5

Lifting back into the sky was suddenly a much more perilous prospect. The Tayne were still intermittently crashing into the magical barrier on the edge of the prison in the centre of the bowl valley, and there was now widespread violence unfolding below me. This time, though, I was acutely aware of the huge gulf in the fortunes of the two opposing forces. In every battle which I had seen on this field before, despite experiencing heavy losses, we had always been giving at the very least, as good as we got. Today, it was far too clear to see that we had been utterly out thought from the very earliest point. We needed to change what was taking place right now or all of our troops were going to be massacred. The safety of the troops could not be overlooked as acceptable loses so long as the prison was maintained.

"FREDDY!" My call was lost in the noise of the enemy detonations and to the wind which whipped past me as I followed my young colleague. I needed to catch him fast before he did something really stupid.

"FREDDY! Keep flying! DO NOT land!" Please let him hear me.

I got my answer almost instantly. Frederico started to descend towards the next corrupted Cascade Bridge and the ever growing carnage which was still spewing from it.

"Christ Freddy, NO!" I pushed on with all I was worth. He was going to beat me to the fight but I could minimize the risk if I got there quickly. As he neared the ground, all I could do was brace myself for the impending impact that the latest Guardian was going to experience.

Frederico didn't hit the ground.

To my surprise and huge relief, he leveled off his flight path and instead released volley after volley of strafing fire from barely twenty feet from the ground. The effect was devastating.

A wide column of writhing insectoid foot soldiers was reduced to ashes as he passed overhead and with the minimum of effort he glided back on himself and unleashed again.

After what seemed like an age, I finally closed on this latest fight and entered the fray myself, duplicating what Frederico had started to do but aiming most of my attention towards the Cascade Bridge.

Our fire poured down onto the enemy creatures and the familiar high pitched screeching/clicking noise erupted everywhere. My first effort snapped the bridge construct shut and severed the supply of enemy reinforcements. Frederico was far less focused but no less effective for it. We were having an effect. I could make out groups of the creatures bunching together trying to huddle themselves to some kind of safety against our attack. That only served to urge me on and I could see that it was having the same effect on Frederico.

We completed multiple passes and continued to burn the enemy to ash from a position of relative safety. The Tayne had, so far, ignored us and had continued on their attack on the shield wall. The creatures below us were, as far as we could tell, flightless, and had been brought in solely as a ground force to over-whelm our own troops. We were practically free to attack at will.

As the threat of harm dropped slightly, I started to scan the ground for the remaining pocket of soldiers who had been defending this position for all they were worth. My eyes darted amongst the melee below as I tried to pick out any detail which would show me where we needed to go. Black ash intermingled with black armoured creatures which mixed with the black uniforms on our troops. It was proving difficult to pin point anything.

Frederico hammered past me and practically herded more of the creatures together into their ever growing mass. Wave after wave of flame forced the little monsters together and exposed more and more of the battle field. I could finally make out the troops we were rushing to save.

They were all lost.

I could make out shredded flesh and ever expanding pools of gore as it became terrifyingly clear that the entire group had met with an agonizing end. My flight faltered as I took in the detail and realized that I couldn't be certain how many bodies I was looking at, the damage was that extensive.

My mind raced. Was every battle site going to look the same? Had we already lost all of the troops we had placed around the valley? Was my own group of soldiers already gone? Had Mark, my giant warrior, been killed?

My feelings of fear weren't left hanging in the air for very long.

The violent spinning in my head dragged me back to the more immediate business below me. That was followed very quickly by the tickling sensation of small claws gripping onto my scales at several points. The beetles had managed to somehow swarm onto me. I started to swipe at myself at the points of sensation and I looked back to try to work out what they had done.

All over my body, I could make out patches of writhing black as the beetle creatures re-started their attack on me. Their small jaws and bladed limbs were nipping away all over my lizard form.

I tried to focus enough of my attention on the task of staying in the air while I continued to beat the creatures away. I needed to maintain the same level flight above the threat coming from below while simultaneously keeping out of the way of the Tayne and defending myself. Piece of cake.

As I batted at my assailants, I cast a quick glance over the view below me and saw how I had been boarded. Frederico was still swooping and diving as he poured down burst after burst of fire, each torrent scorching more and more of the ever huddling hoard. He was enjoying the clear shots at the enemy that he was getting so much that he wasn't paying full attention to what was going on around him. As we had both been forcing more and more of the little horrors into a central huddle by killing large numbers of their ranks, they had started to use this concentration to their advantage. What we had thought as being a sign of cowardice from them was actually a clever move to again overwhelm us. They hadn't been trying to huddle together to hide from the death we were raining down. Instead, they had been creating a massive living tower which a great many of their number had been able to climb and which had granted them much easier access to the flying Dragons that had previously been out of their reach. They had just waited for us to come to them. Another change in tactics from The Hive which showed that they were really learning fast.

I risked a sideways look at Frederico to check on his progress.

He was now in the same situation as I was. He had swooped in too low to the enemy in exactly the same way I had, drawn in by his ever growing desire to unveil his own brand of divine retribution. These creatures may not have been the most dangerous we had ever encountered but they were certainly now showing that they had the capability to out think us and as such they must be viewed as a serious threat. And now, legions of them were starting to seriously threaten the safety of two of the Guardians.

This cell of our forces had been wiped out and there was no guarantee that the scene here hadn't been replicated at each and every position around the valley. I needed to get us back inside the shield wall around the prison and started on our counter offensive before the beetle things worked out how they could do some real damage.

"Freddy!!" I roared as loudly as I could, hoping to attract his attention.

Nothing.

I tried again as I continued to edge towards him through the dusk sky.

Still nothing but this time I could see why.

He was still far from being fully in control of himself but his previous wild fury for the death and destruction of any and all of the creatures that had allied themselves against his family and his sacred oath had now been replaced by a scrabbling fear. As I closed the distance between us, I could make out a great deal more small beetles crawling over Frederico than I had to contend with. He must have flown much lower than I had, drawn down by the apparent terror in his enemy. Black spots were dotted all over his green armored frame but as I starred, it became clear that they were all moving in the same direction. They were all making a drive for his wings.

Having been downed by a tiny enemy who had focused their attack on my wings myself, it was not something that I was keen to see happen to my young charge. Aside from the pain which the young Guardian would experience if he was forced from the sky, I knew that he would feel terrible guilt at having let down the other members of his family and The Circle as a whole. The last thing he needed was to feel that thousands of years of history were wagging its collective finger at him for his failure to uphold the vaunted line that is The Circle.

I set myself quickly and drove onwards towards Frederico, my own feelings of resentment filling my head at what I felt was a dangerous character flaw in the group I was now a massive part of. The Young Dragon needed my help.

Frederico had lost his focus on the melee still broiling below him and was now smacking and scratching at himself as he started to falter in mid-air. The beetles had started to have an effect on his ability to fly as they had begun to reach his wings in ever growing numbers and he had slowly been sinking towards the rocky ground below.

I didn't try to attract his attention. I didn't need it. Checking my own rate of descent and my line of flight, I knew that all I needed to do was maintain a collision course.

The distance between us closed at a remarkable rate and I was quickly in the position to do what needed to be done. I emptied out a vast wave of flame directly at Frederico. There was no thought of controlled aiming or measured bursts, brute force was the order of the day. The searing jet splashed into him and set his assailants ablaze. The click/screams rang out again as they were all superheated in seconds but I didn't stop.

Forcing my mind to power down to a pin point of concentration, I willed a huge cascade bridge into existence directly behind the still flaming form of Frederico and flew directly into him, wasting no thought on finesse or comfort.

I gripped him tightly and forced us both through the ring of magical energy.

Through the whip-crack of white light which was the event horizon of the bridge construct, I heaved our reptilian forms away to as much safety as I could think of.

We smashed to the ground at the entrance to the ancient citadel which stood at the mouth of the prison that Frederico had been charged with guarding. Frederico shouted out and swatted at the last few beetles which were still able to scrabble around over his skin. Smoke lifted from his body at numerous sites but I knew that he would be safe from harm. Fire Dragon after all.

Before I could make any move to check my own attackers, I was shrouded in a cloud of white hot fire of my own. Any of the swarming mass of beetles who had survived the previous hits of flame were left with nowhere to go and they were all torched to a cinder.

After a minute of roasting heat, which created a feeling of equal parts fear and, strangely, comfort, the flame abruptly vanished.

I slowly pushed myself up to a standing position and stretched my back out, flashing out my wings to their full extent to dislodge any charred remains which may have still been lingering in the folds. I brushed the last vestiges of the burnt beetles from me and turned to focus on the details around me.

Andrea stood before me in her crystalline Ice Dragon form, her hands slowly lowering from directly in front of her at chest height so that they finally rested at her sides. She shook her head and forced her concentration against a sudden and all encompassing, fatigue. I was able to feel her discomfort as it washed out in all directions.

Staggering slightly, she fell to her knees and struggled against a dizziness and nausea. She was breathing deeply after the effort of drawing in the power to create enough fire to be able to clear both Freddy and myself of the enemy. An Ice Dragon summoning the full power of a fire casting that size would have been experiencing a mighty amount of discomfort at best. In my own training, I hadn't even been trusted with being instructed in the ways of calling the opposite powers of my line to my will.

By the look on her face, I really wasn't going to enjoy those lessons.

"Did you get my message?" I asked as I tried to keep the urgency of the situation to the forefront of the conversation. She tilted her head slightly and pushed her fatigue away as much as she could, then signaled towards a gathering of troops off to my right. The big Aussie I had spoken with earlier was now barking orders to a collection of very young soldiers. He nodded once at me as our eyes met and saluted quickly before turning back to his duties.

The message must have got through.

I turned my attention back to Andrea. "We're getting hammered out there. Have we heard anything from the troops still in the field?" I needed to know if our forces were still active but more than anything else, I needed to know that my friends were still alive.

"We have so far lost contact with twelve of the thirty troop positions." There was no emotion in her voice, just the cold hard facts.

"We can bring those people who are still alive back inside the shield but we will lose the valley. If they are still active they can still be affecting some kind of defence against the Tayne. Remember, this prisons security is our ultimate goal."

Our eyes locked together for a split second, emotion and opinion crashing against each other. Neither of us spoke, but for very different reasons.

Andrea blinked once. Her luminescent grey eyes bored into me. She looked at me as if she had just declared fact rather than opinion. She was absolutely certain of her own superiority.

In that instance, I realized that there was no reinforcement group on their way to our aid.

The temperature around me started to drop and small sparks started to crackle from my hands. My own superiority jutting out.

"We are not going to lose hundreds of people who could be saved just because they may be able to create a delay to a numerically superior force." I struggled to remember to use language that would sell my case.

"Those people are more valuable to us in here forming the basis of our counter attack than used as cannon fodder. The valley *is* lost and hundreds of extra deaths will not change that fact." I tried to gather myself. The last thing we needed was for me to lose control here. Aside from the physical damage I would do to all of the troops gathering around us, the damage I would do to my argument would be worse and that which would result in massive loss of life.

Before I could say anything else to strengthen my claim or Andrea could attempt to scientifically prove that she was right, Frederico joined the debate. The young Guardian strode forward and declared with the force of someone with true authority,

"I will not let my name be associated with the greatest massacre of troops we have seen in Argentina. How do we bring our people back?"

Smoke was starting to form plumes from both of his nostrils as he showed he was not going take no for an answer. My chest surged with pride for Frederico. He wasn't going to be just another member of The Circle; he was going to try to look after his people. He was going to spread the wealth, so to speak.

Andrea's eyes darted between us and I could make out the scenarios that were running through her mind, on her reptilian face.

Eventually, she looked at us each in turn, and rumbled,

"It is possible to retrieve all of the outstanding troops, but I will need both of your help." Her eyes danced between us.

"And there will be no guarantee of success."

I smiled and slapped Frederico a little too hard on the back,

"When is there a guarantee of anything?"

6

With only a hand full of well chosen words, delivered with just the right amount of growl from Andrea, the entry way to the citadel at the centre of the mighty magical shield over the Argentinean Hive prison was cleared of people and equipment in less than five minutes. Troops darted back and forth, attending to the tasks that had been assigned them, scuttling around in a fashion which was strangely similar to the insect creatures outside the shield.

The Tayne force was still crashing into the shield wall over the entrance to the prison but the number of impacts was starting to grow. They had gone from being an intermittent explosion to creating a steadily building percussion with each massive detonation ripping through the air around us all with ever growing menace.

None of us were sure how the ghost-like Tayne had managed to become such a potent threat to the magics we had deployed but, by the expressions of people as they completed tasks assigned to them, they were creating the very real concern that they were going to be able to bring down the shield.

I scanned the troops, then swung back to face Andrea and Frederico.

They had both reverted to their human forms and were pulling on loose clothing which had been rushed to them. A painfully young looking trooper was stood holding one more set of neatly folded field attire, obviously meant for me.

I took the hint and brought my form back to my human shape and quickly gathered myself into the on-hand uniform. Moving quickly to Andrea's' side, I looked on hoping to learn how we were going to proceed. She wasted no time in her explanation.

"I need to create a link between us to build a Cascade Bridge complex" Andrea stated matter-of-factly over the sound of enthusiastic troops and the still deafening pounding of the Tayne on the shield wall.

Frederico and I looked at her without any fragment of comprehension. Andrea rolled her eyes at me.

"We are going to combine our collective power to open multiple bridges to all of the remaining sites in the valley." Frederico and I took that information in much more readily. She continued without further interruption.

"We can create a group of bridges and open them wherever we need. We need to focus our magics together to be able to complete the task but Frederico has the tools to complete the task with us in the fortress." As she finished her last words she gestured over my shoulder.

I turned round to stare back in the direction she was indicating and noticed the large Aussie soldier we encountered earlier, making a bee line through the activity towards us, carrying a large wooden trunk. He made no attempt to avoid anyone who may have crossed his path and casually barreled through and over two shocked troopers.

He skidded to a halt before us and lowered the trunk down, trying his best to infuse the gesture with as much ceremonial reverence as he could manage despite the obviously heavy burden.

Andrea beckoned us all forward and continued her explanation.

"We have access to many weapons at each of our estates. This will allow us to maximize our efforts, both in the rescue of our soldiers and the repulsion of the enemy." Andrea's thick accent wrapped itself around the words and infused them with a strident feeling of anger and impending retribution. That same feeling rose within both Frederico and myself and we could practically touch the sensation. The temperature began to drop around us as the rage of our magic drew in power in preparation. This was going to be some weapon.

She reached forward and flipped open the heavy wooden lid of the trunk to reveal the weapon which was going to help us not only retrieve our surviving troops, but also climb back into the battle.

We crowded around the trunk with a growing feeling of awe and were greeted by the superpower that Andrea expected us to deploy to the maximum effect.

"Banus Stones??!!?" Boomed Frederico with blatant incredulity in his voice. Before us all, was a trunk full of rocks. There was no buzzing sensation of bridled power, no feeling of barely tethered force which we could unleash to devastating effect.

Just a trunk full of stones.

He crossed his arms across his chest and looked at Andrea without hiding his frustration. "This is a magical map. We know where everyone is already."

Andrea wasted no time trying to placate the young Guardian.

"You have listened far too much to the teachings of the newest of us," she nodded at me. "With this ancient tool, we will be able to pinpoint our people and channel our power exactly to launch our rescue. We will also be able to use this power to highlight the enemy energy focus points. We need the ability to deliver a surgical strike to all of the enemy forces and this "magical map" gives us just that ability."

For the length of a heartbeat she stared between both of us as forceful support to her point. She continued without further pause as our silence ceded the argument to her.

"Gentlemen, we need to move now to reclaim our people. I need you both to give me your power to drive what we need. Do what I say and we will be able to save the people we have in the field that you have both said are vital to what we are."

There were no more uncertainties for us. Frederico beat me to the sentiment we were both feeling,

"What do you need us to do?"

"We need to charge the map field with as much energy as we can so we clearly view our troops. We'll be adding our 'human' energy into the map to locate the other humans within the field of the map. After we picture them all, we can use the locator stones on the "map" we create to become a virtual locus to our combined Cascade castings."

"Doesn't sound that complicated," I said. Andrea stopped in mid-motion of unloading the smooth, dark stones. Her response left me in no doubt of what she was thinking.

"Creating a single Cascade Bridge requires focus and energy. We are going to attempt to create eighteen bridges over a very wide area. This has the potential to be lethal to all of the troops outside the barrier but also to the three of us. We are all going to be shoving every last vestige of energy we have into the working to attempt this rescue. If we are unable to create a stable enough conduit through the stones, none of the bridges will open and we will lose everyone outside. There is also the very real chance that we will exhaust our supply of power before we can draw the bridge complex into existence and our magical being, the power essence of what we are will be drawn into the map. In short, this process will draw all available power it can find, even if that kills everyone driving it."

Maybe it was a little complicated.

Frederico was looking a little pale at the revelation of the inherent dangers of what we about to try.

"How will we know if we are approaching that level?" he asked but instead of his voice trembling with the obvious fear he would be feeling, it instead strode on with a calm sense of purpose. I could see that he was battling with the internal dilemma he would have hanging over his head like the Sword of Damocles for the length of his 'service' as the Guardian. He was trying to weigh up the importance of the bigger picture against what his own demise would mean. He was thinking about his little sister.

That pricked at my own familial memories as those people who had had a direct effect on my life in bringing me to this point sprang to mind. Had they ever weighed up their own lives against the task they had faced? Probably.

Andrea continued her preparations as she spoke.

"We will know that the bridges are opening but," she closed her eyes momentarily "but, there is no signal that a caster is in danger. From what I can see, those who have tried something of this kind have simply fallen, they have just stopped." No emotion, just fact.

Great.

Before there was any further discussion, another Tayne hit the barrier but the concussive blast from the impact seemed to shake the ground all around us. Every eye in the compound swung up to see the small wisp of smoke that was the Tayne's scorched body, drifting skyward in the low dusk light. The tiny creatures were proving to be suddenly successful in the attack.

The singular plume of smoke, though, wasn't all that held every gaze transfixed as if locked in amber. High above the rushing troops, surrounded by a spreading crimson cloud within the power matrix, was a brightly lit, ragged edged crack.

For a split second, no-one moved or even seemed to acknowledge the image that they were staring at. Andrea broke the collective trance.

"WE ARE BREACHED! SEAL THAT CRACK NOW!" exploded into the eerie lack of action which had descended on the camp. Everyone was fast to react to Andrea and they moved to the repair of the damaged shield, and in a matter of only a handful of seconds since the order had been called out, at least ten beams of brightly coloured energy had shot towards the crack and were knitting it back together.

Andrea smacked Frederico and me, firmly, back to the task before us.

"We have no time to build into this. We need to complete this as fast as we can." She promptly sat on the floor, crossing her legs beneath her and began to draw in deep breath after deep breath, obviously pulling in all of the power she could muster.

Frederico was quickly down doing the same before I could move, determination draped fiercely over his expression as he copied the actions of the more experienced Guardian. I quickly joined them and began to pull in everything I could in preparation.

"Focus on the view of the valley. Picture the people we have on the field of battle and sense their locations." Andrea was calmly explaining what we needed to do despite the shouts and commotion spilling around her.

I lifted into my mind the faces of the team of soldiers who had been supplied from my own estate and started to feel for their presence outside the shield wall. It took me less than ten seconds to be able to find them and I was quickly confronted by the image of a huddled band of men and women fighting for all they were worth against the familiar beetle-like creatures which were still spilling out of the corrupt enemy bridge. I could feel the 'wrongness' which was coming off the yellowed ring as it lent on my view of the battle.

"Pass the image of the people into one of the stones on the map; let the stone lock as the location." Andrea was directing our movements.

I did without any further encouragement. Summoning a view of the stones in my mind's eye, I wrapped the still moving picture of my troops around it and willed it onto the map. I risked a snatched glimpse of what was happening between the three of us to see seven stones stood on their ends at different points round the map area marked as the valley around us. Looking at the map, I was able to feel that the one stone I had managed was sitting alongside six of Andrea's. Frederico was still working on his first and the beads of sweat on his face and the erratically pulsing veins in his neck showed that he was struggling. If he was doing the best he could, I would have to pick the pace up to reel in some of his slack.

Closing my eyes again, I returned to the task and with the two other Guardians, summoned up group after group until I couldn't feel anything else outside. I pushed to find anything I could but there was nothing more than what had already been found. Andrea spoke before I had opened my eyes.

"We have them all. Now push your power into the map working and we will open the bridges. Don't hold anything back. We need to use everything." The Russian accent still purred from Andrea and I could pick up a steady hint of deep frozen anger in her voice. I took one steadying look into the map and forced out all of the power I had to build the bridges just as Andrea and Frederico did.

The air within the map wavered and started to fizz and crackle as a mighty amount of focused energy washed into and through it. The stones all started to glow purest blue/white and within a heartbeat, I could feel the bridges opening up around the valley.

One by one, the familiar snap/hiss of power and the smell of ozone burst into being and the sense of relief from the people who had been near them quickly followed. The complex was active but we had to maintain it long enough to effect a rescue. A single bridge gateway was hovering in the main courtyard where we were based and it was soon acting as the funnel for all of the other bridges to pour their contents from.

At the edge of my mind, just swimming around the limits of my awareness as I held the magic as strongly as I could, I could start to make out the shouts of troops and the sensations of magical weaponry being loosed. People were calling for medical help, for more firepower, there was a bustle as more and more boots hit the ground and they were also intermingled with the shrieks and clicking of the enemy who must have followed the retreating troops through their salvation. The battle was going to be brought inside the barrier.

"No more left. Make them shut it down NOW!" The authority in that single command rang through my mind and I knew that we had completed what we had needed to. With a single effort, I forced my head back from the map and pulled all of my attention and power with it. The effort of will was required as the casting had been pulling against me, dragging me towards the map. I blinked my eyes open and drew in a huge gulp of air I hadn't noticed I had been missing and watched Andrea do the same, look slowly around her as our central Cascade Bridge collapsed in on itself, and she fell backwards to the floor, unconscious. She had been doing the majority of the heavy lifting so was feeling by far the most fatigue. Frederico sat slumped forward with his legs crossed and his arms hanging limply at his side. I tried to move but my head spun wildly. I couldn't be sure if this was a signal of impending danger or whether I was as fatigued as the others. I tried to focus on the nearest detail to give my mind something to grip to and looked hard at the map casting. The stones were all still stood upright and there was still a very faint glow leaking out. I scanned through the positions and counted up the number of stones that showed the locations of our battered soldiers. We had been looking for eighteen groups of survivors.

I finally fell onto my back with exhaustion after counting through the map. All the effort to locate our people had been aimed squarely at picking up the energy of those people still fighting. We had moved fast despite being pummeled by the enemy forces and as my eyes closed I could still hear the explosions of the still active Tayne hitting the shield, and the calls of the fighting forces as those beetle-things which had made their way through the bridges were dealt with. I held the number of lives saved in my mind and felt for the life force all around us. I could taste the conflicting emotions coming from the different people around me, relief and anger, fear and hope all vying for supremacy of the embattled troops.

We had only been able to find and save thirteen groups.

7

The relaxation of unconsciousness was short-lived.

Despite the supernatural warfare which was raging around me, I did feel that I was roused a little more roughly than was absolutely necessary.

My blurry concentration settled on the force that was shaking me awake. I could also make out the muffled sounds of a voice shouting for my attention. It sounded like the voice was coming to me through water and that that water was getting shallower.

Despite the almost over-whelming urge to swat the sound away and slip back into the welcome of a *very* deep sleep, I was still just about aware enough to realize that there was probably a very good reason behind the overly assertive attempt to bring me round.

That awareness was compounded when a flash of pain burst across my face. I was instantly rushed to full consciousness through a cloud of receding stars and tweeting birds. Looking up while I shook my head clear, I could see Mark standing over me with his long right arm held up at his side. He was shaping to bring his heavy hand down for a second slap to rouse me. At least that explained the stinging in my chops.

"I'm up, I'm up," was all I could muster as signal to stop another welt across my face. I must have sounded just like a bleary eyed teenager complaining about having to get up to go to school. Judging by the flicker of a smile on Marks face, he thought the same.

My big head chef was quick to pull me to my feet and had to steady me as my legs were still apparently made mainly of jelly.

"Thanks mate, still a bit light-headed." The last thing I needed was to fall on my face and knock myself out.

"No trouble. There's a lot of it going round." Marks voice was as deep as ever but there was a rough croak folded in there now. I looked up at him and shook the last of the fuzziness from my head and took in the detail around me.

Despite his easy demeanor, Mark was injured. Badly.

There were tears and rips in his clothing and almost all of them had the irregular staining of blood pools. I could make out several points of laceration where the little beetle creatures had been much more deadly to him than they had been on the armour-plated hide of my Dragon form. He was still standing proudly upright but the pain he was feeling was easy to see. Steady lines of blood were flowing down his arms and from the damage to his torso. At a rate that would never be acceptable, pools of the spilled crimson were steadily forming at his feet.

The last pieces of my woozy brain fell back into position and I realized what I was looking at. I had known that Mark and his team had been one of the troop teams who had been trapped by the waves of insects; my own anger at the possible loss of our troops had pushed Andrea to actually mount a rescue. Seeing him stood before me had made the very serious risks which were facing all of us fall more sharply into focus.

Since the beginning of this fight, he had been taking on a numerically superior force in a desperate defence. That he was part of one of the teams which survived the attack said as much about his group's ability in combat, both conventional and magical, as it did about the speed the Guardians had managed to open the bridge complex. By the looks of him, his survival hadn't been an easy one and there had still been a great cost paid.

"Jesus, Mark. You need a medic, now." I started looking round the area I was stood in; trying to pick out anyone I knew who could help. I scanned past the already roused forms of Andrea and Freddy, who noticed the frustration and worry in my movements, and my eyes fell on a group of our forces huddled around sporadic patches of people. The injured and dying lay around the courtyard and what medical help could be provided was being given.

"Come on, you need attention." I started to move towards the medical teams but Mark didn't follow. Andrea moved to my side as I had started to raise my voice. I turned to him and he looked down at me with steel in his eyes.

"There are more injured than me who need more help. I am needed as part of this fight." He stuck his jaw out to prove he was resolute as he looked down at me and finished his thought with, "This is my 'no' face".

"You are badly injured and need to be restored to, aside from full strength, to full health. I don't expect people to die for nothing." I tried to stop short of jutting out my own jaw. By the look on Marks face, I wasn't as successful as I had hoped.

"If I fall here today, if we all do, as long as we can maintain the prison, then we could never die for nothing". His jaw was still out, but now it was joined by his massive chest, all puffed full of pride.

This seemed to be the central pin to a difference of opinion I had been having since I was first introduced to the clandestine world of The Circle. Everyone I had met in 'my' estate and those of the other Guardians seemed far too keen to throw themselves off the nearest good cause. They all viewed themselves as having an almost divine calling to defend the world from the forces of darkness. To the point that everyone I spoke with looked at me with confusion and, what I interpreted as, pity for not wanting to dive into the jaws of doom at the first opportunity. Don't get me wrong, I believe that everyone in the world would happily give up their life for the right cause, whatever that may be for them, the protection of their family, defence of their country, to see Wales win the Rugby World Cup, the serious things.

The issue I had was that everyone who was involved in this world seemed to take virtuous sacrifice as being the correct move in any situation. From what I could see, Mark was willing to die from his injuries because he thought he was doing the 'right thing'. He viewed the cause as being bigger than himself. I could see his logic but he saw his position as that of Red Leader in the first Star Wars film (the proper ones, not the prequels). He was falling to his death after his engines had been destroyed but he knew that there was no more that could be done. He had given his all and he knew his ship was going to give one last poke in the eye as it crashed.

As far as I could see, Mark was simply refusing medical help so others could receive attention, regardless of whether they were in the same danger of death as he was. Saving others was the cause Mark was preparing to swan dive from. The only crumb of comfort I had was he was at least trying to joke about it.

I didn't have time for this.

"You are getting medical attention. NOW!" ordered Andrea.

My frustration at his lack of action to his own health was boiling over but Andrea beat me to the punch.

She had roared out at him that he needed medical help and despite her human form, her voice had been that of the Dragon she could become. She roared her position clearly and there was no mistaking that she was expecting her order to be followed.

In a gesture which would have manifested as a dive for cover in anyone else, Marks eyes twitched at the explosion of sound. Despite everything Mark was in terms of magical ability, elevated position in the estate back in Wales or sheer brute force, he was scared of Andrea. Not because of the Dragon element of who she was but because he saw her as being his superior and not because of any reason other than he seemed to be programmed to defer to the person who was socially above him.

There was the slightest nod from him and he started to move towards the medics.

I watched him go and sighed as he went.

The second big issue I had with The Circle as a group was that there were far too rigid boundaries between the different levels of the group. It smacked of "a place for every*one* and every*one* in their place". Mark, and indeed everyone, was duty bound to follow the orders of those people above them. Free thought was a very rare thing indeed. I had started to drill into that dogma from the very first day I had been welcomed into this group. I had seen some success too.

Mark, Mike Christian, my Head of House, and a few other senior members of the estate staff had started to call me Anthony rather than sir. Not all the time mind, just on random occasions. It did look they were all trying the new skill out for size, where and when to use it. None of them could ever be described as being comfortable with the situation but my hope was to make small changes which grew.

The down side to the first faltering steps into a new realm of perceived freedom was they were starting to get used to not doing what I told them all of the time.

I stood next to Andrea amidst the melee of people around the courtyard as we watched my giant general finally receive the medical attention he was so desperately in need of, thinking that maybe there was something to this obeying orders caper. Maybe The Circle was having an effect on me too?

That line of thought would have to wait.

We were both quickly snapped back to the danger of the continuing attack which was still raging around our position. Explosions of sound were still booming out as Tayne after Tayne blasted into our shield wall but now, as the sun had finally retreated below the horizon and pulled all of the daylight with it, we were all greeted by a diffuse burst of colour spreading through the magical shield to accompany each explosion.

Our own teams of troops were lending their own talents to the light show which was raging overhead. Our defenders were casting skywards, lance after lance of magical energy of all different colours to repair the cracks which were opening up. We were being bathed in a stunning showering rainbow of magical aura as the ebb and flow of defense and attack took place above us. Move and enchanted counter move flashed across the early night sky as more and more breaches of our defences opened up and were quickly sealed.

Despite the peril we were all in, there in the warm night air, under a screen of crackling fireworks of sorcery, I looked at Andrea and couldn't help myself. As the bright sparks of hue played across her face, despite the deep concern and palpable worry on her face, all I could feel was the need to whisk her away from everything. The thought of spending time with her in an environment where we wouldn't be in mortal danger every second was an appealing prospect, not only for the lack of danger but also for the chance to crack the puzzle that she was to me. She blew hot and cold with me all of the time so I would have loved to understand exactly what was going through her mind.

A particularly violent thunder crack broke that chain of thought.

Andrea and I, and all of the people who had been running around us, were forced to take a steadying step as the ground shook under the latest hammer blow that The Hive unleashed.

"How are they doing that?" I asked mainly to myself but also hoping that Andrea would have at least some idea. The Tayne had been such a miniscule threat in the past, I was at a loss to explain how they had suddenly become the potent threat they currently were.

Andrea closed her eyes and furrowed her brow in concentration. She tilted her head slightly and began to chew on the inside of her cheek. The effort of whatever she was doing was easy to see as she battled against some unseen foe.

Through clenched teeth she started her response.

"I can feel their *power*. They're coming." The sentence was forced as she continued to struggle but her emphasis on the word power showed that she was almost in awe of what was baring down on us. I tried to reach out with my own senses, fumbling mentally for the clues Andrea was picking up on.

I got nothing but a pain in my forehead. It would appear that I was still very inexperienced in terms of mental control. It was something I had only really started to use in the last three weeks. I could sense the broiling rage, confusion or determination in Freddy but other uses of my newest skill seemed to be beyond me.

Breaking my own attempts at expanding my senses and looking back to Andrea, I found her scanning the horizon beyond the shield wall. Her eyes were darting back and forth, hunting for any impending danger.

The expression on her face was enough to sell it to me. She looked truly worried.

"Freddy. We need to get everyone ready for the next attack. The shield will be coming down."

I'd barely finished my call when Frederico flashed to my side. He was breathing deeply and looked almost to be too ready for the attack. He was only just holding onto his transformation. He was still just in his human form, but he was currently stood at roughly fifteen feet tall and had the starting of armour plates forming all over his body. His skin was changing colour, his face was starting to distort, to widen his mouth and lengthen his snout and he had started to form the early shapes of his wings.

It was easy for me; it was pretty easy for anyone, to tell he was taking this attack personally.

"I'll kill them all! Bring them to me and I'll laugh as their forces break at my hand!" The basso roar as he spoke rattled our chests and his Dragon form burst into being, snarling wildly as he took up his stance for battle, planting his feet and digging his clawed feet into the stony ground while spreading his wings in much the same way as a cobra might spread its hood, a clear signal of impending danger.

He was still calling out his defiance to the darkness when the wild spinning in my head cranked up and almost knocked me off my feet.

I staggered to my left and fought for control over the huge sensation which was threatening to tip me from my feet. The dizziness had burst from nowhere with such a force that it made me forget where I was for a fraction of a second.

Freddy's call from above me maintained the grip on the here and now.

He was still booming out to the night, and the hordes of invaders who were massing within, that he would never stop resisting them when the spinning in my head made sense.

As early warning systems go, mine wasn't going to rank up there with best. Yes it could warn me of impending danger but it did so by putting my mind into a blender.

Andrea must have picked up on the sensation I was going through alongside what The Hive unleashed.

She wrapped a steel cable like grip around me to keep me controlled as she pulled me to the ground and started to call to Freddy to get down.

Everything was too late.

Above us, there came an almighty explosion as the latest Tayne suicide force smashed into the shield wall. The sound of the collision was accompanied by a sun-bright flash which must have spread throughout the valley and potentially beyond.

As we all blinked the flash burn from our eyes, we were greeted with the image of the shield wall being threaded through with tendrils of icy white fingers. The matrix of power which had been standing between the entry to the Argentinean Hive prison and those who would seek to breach it, was almost freezing before our eyes.

In the space of no more than five heartbeats, the whole dome of power was transformed into an icy shell.

The next Tayne impact laid us all open to attack.

With an almighty thunder clap, another impact hit the shield wall. The effect was instant.

The newly brittle surface of the magical boundary cracked and shattered.

As every member of The Circle forces who were gathered around the entrance to the ancient prison watched, the dome of supernatural energy which had stood above them for generations shattered into a billion small pieces and with an in rushing of warm air, cascaded slowly down around our ears.

Tiny pieces of crystalline energy floated down like the constituent parts of a bright snow storm and dissipated into nothing as they hit every surface below them, their energy fizzing away as a strangled whimper of light and sound.

Around us all, the faces of all of the troops gathered within the boundary shield became awash with looks of confusion and fear. Each and every face had written upon it the utter lack of comprehension of seeing something which was considered a constant, an unending force, a symbol of permanence, broken before their eyes and laid bare.

In all of the conflict which had been raging throughout the world between The Circle and The Hive, no-one had ever seen anything like this. Their faces said it all.

The Hive were winning.

But they didn't stop there. As our whole force caught its breath at the surprise of the attack, our enemies drove home their advantage.

Andrea and I hit the stone floor of the ancient citadel with her still calling out to Freddy to drop as the main cause of my sudden spinning head revealed itself.

From far beyond the fallen shield, there came a dim explosion of muddy yellow light which lasted for no more than five seconds before it collapsed back to nothing. The flakes of shield were still plentiful in the air around us so our view into the battlefield was being curtailed. Andrea and I could recognize the appearance of one of the enemies withered bridges but couldn't see why it had been deployed.

My head showed no signs of letting up the revs so I could l sense that there was more to be alert for.

There was no further warning as; from the curtains of night which were hanging all around us, three massive stone javelins, each measuring at least thirty feet in length and weighing God knows how much, slammed into Frederico.

The young Guardian had still been roaring out his defiance to the advancing enemy when the attack had struck. He had been stood in an undefended area, open to attack without cover.

His skewered body was sent crashing backwards, the stone projectiles protruding from either side of him, until he was slammed into the time weathered wall of the main building of the citadel.

Andrea called out once as the spears hit him but her voice was lost as shock and fear seemed to reach into even her and pull the sound from her.

Frederico's limp body hung from the wall like a trophy from a hunt. From the distance I was at, I couldn't even tell if he was still alive but the force of the impact was such that I couldn't imagine there being much hope for him despite his armoured Dragon form.

No-one in the area around us uttered a word. Everyone had been stuck like a prehistoric insect in amber with the ferocious nature of the enemies strike. We had been on the receiving end of Guardian deaths before, twice before here in the last month and a half but they had always been part of an ultimately victorious effort. I could feel from everywhere that the confidence in our ultimate victory was draining away.

It was then that we began to make out the first sounds of billions of enemy feet marching towards us.

"They're coming in now the shield is down." I hadn't noticed that Mark had made his way to my position and both Andrea and I were startled by his voice coming from so close by. He was still far from fixed, blood was seeping through the bandages and surgical dressings which covering at least half of his body, but any thought of not fighting was so far away from his mind, you'd swear that he hadn't ever even known the words. His eyes continued to scan through the gloom which surrounded us as he struggled to pick out any individual signs of the forces moving our way.

There was nothing to see but everyone knew that the hordes of beetle creatures that we had been facing earlier would now be streaming down the sides of the valley towards us. With the shield wall down, we would all be open to the massive force heading our way. Even with two Guardians at the centre of this fight, the odds weren't looking good.

"We need to bring in reinforcements immediately" said Andrea flatly. "Anthony, we must give care to Frederico to preserve his position and slow the enemy advance." Quickly turning to Mark she continued.

"Mr. Howells. I need you to take command of the troop effort within the boundary. Set up to receive incursions from all sides. Take those who are too wounded to contribute, down into the chamber below us and surround the obelisk with a defensive force to provide a last line. Instruct everyone there that should the enemy reach them, they are all to give their lives causing as much damage to The Hive and that they should be prepared to bring the cavern down around them to kill everyone and bury the creatures prison. Go."

With one barely perceptible nod, Mark agreed and turned to head off to complete his task.

Before I could make any kind of utterance, Andrea had started to move towards the prone form of Frederico, still pinned to the wall of the citadel. As she ran, she started to tear her clothing free and send it scattering. As the final garment was discarded she called over her shoulder, again in the same flat tone,

"Transform and help me get him down from there before we get over run." She then blurred up into her Crystal white Dragon form.

I didn't wait to argue or debate what she was doing, knowing that she had much more experience in these matters than I did. Despite what I may have felt about her treatment of my friend who was still in desperate need of medical help, I was big enough and ugly enough to realize that the time for recriminations wasn't now.

I didn't wait to get undressed before I drove my transformation to my own individual Guardian form. I knew that time was a serious issue to what we were doing but, deep down, everyone's got to love the old Incredible Hulk moment of shredding your clothes.

We reached the macabre form of our Guardian colleague and my mind was made to focus fully on the task at hand as we set about bringing him down. Despite what he had been the victim of, he was still alive. He was slumped forward unconscious, his body limp and his head lolling down almost lifeless. His chest was fluttering through shallow, rattling breathes as the damage to his torso caused blood to bubble through to areas it shouldn't be able to reach. There was a steady pulsing flow coming from the sites of the injuries but also from his mouth and there was already a huge puddle of crimson liquid pooling beneath his suspended legs.

The javelins had been driven through his chest and out the other side to force themselves through the wall behind him. His injuries must have been massive.

"Take his weight, I'll break the stone" Andrea was all business, not even a hint of human emotion filtering its way out of the reptilian form.

I did as I was told. Taking as firm a grip as I could manage around Freddy's waist, despite his blood making the grip treacherous, I heaved up and took as much of his weight as I could, relieving what pressure I could on the young Dragon. He moved slightly forward as I did and slid faintly along the stone columns which had skewered him. The movement must have been agony because he groaned slightly despite his unconscious state.

"Hold him there. Do not move him" spoke Andrea calmly. She reached past and behind him, and placed her hand flat on the wall behind him. With a concentration of will, she drove extreme cold through all of the stone of the wall and of the javelins within it. The rock of the wall and of the spears through Freddy creaked and moaned as the temperature within fell drastically.

"Change places. I need you to super heat the stone so we can shatter it" Andrea ordered, not even a hint of emotion to be found in her voice.

I did as instructed and drew together my own casting. The fire in my mind surged through the freezing stone and the effect was almost instant. Within a billowing cloud of steam, the stone shattered apart and Frederico dropped from his position. Andrea was strong enough to at least control his fall but the weight of the javelins through him toppled her backwards. They hit the ground in a crumpled heap.

"MEDIC!!!!" I knew I needed help from someone who actually knew what they were doing. I swept my eyes around the immediate area hunting for someone, anyone, who could bring Freddy some desperately needed help.

Andrea was at my side quickly and grabbed my face to look at hers.

"Do not lose focus of the defence of the site. FOCUS NOW!!!" There was absolute urgency in her reptilian face and the firmness of her grip forced me to look away from the issue of Frederico.

All around us were masses of scared people who would now be looking to us for leadership and protection. None of our assembled troops had ever had any experience of seeing the strongest magical barrier that had been created be so readily shattered under the force of a previously weak aggressor. In everyone's mind, our shield had been taken apart by the Tayne who had previously only ever shown themselves as being slightly more powerful, magically speaking, than a Guardian's fart. I had, literally, shit bigger than them!

They had all been taken into a realm of uncertainty by the unfolding carnage which had befallen our force and they were all looking for some kind of reassurance from the Dragon force that everything was going to be alright. All I had to do was make certain that I didn't let on that I was just as scared as all of them!

Taking a deep, steadying breath, I buried my own fears and turned out to face the situation ahead of us all.

It didn't look good!

The final glittering shards of the magically dismantled barrier fluttered to rest around us taking with them what remained of the illumination they had provided. The inky darkness pushed in at us all, leaning against the small light sources we had dotted around the courtyard. The medic group had quickly reached Frederico and had started to administer whatever power and potions they had to save his life. Elsewhere, there was a tangible feeling of fear bubbling amongst those soldiers of The Circle who were rushing about gathering supplies and creating some form of complex of defensible positions. Mark was stood in the centre of the space, directing the movements of everyone with a calm focus and steely determination in his voice despite the impending violence. His face was a blank mask of pure business – not a shred of apprehension or any other emotion for that matter to be seen.

As he casually yet forcefully gave the ringing orders that provided all of the other people around us something to focus their attention on and therefore something to occupy the space in their minds that abject terror was threatening to over run, it became obvious to me that he was truly built for the leadership of others. He was fully aware of what was happening around us all yet he was providing that solid rock that everyone else could cling to to escape the oncoming flood.

I could do a lot worse than look to my giant general for tips on leadership.

Beneath that most hurried layer of movement from our troops came the creeping train of the injured, snaking through the courtyard towards a large stone door frame which had been long parted from its door. To the casual observer, it made up nothing more than another ancient opening in the ruined citadel walls, another cracked view through the spyglass of history which led into a room or building which too was decayed into memory. I knew that Mark had followed Andrea's orders completely and that this shuffling line were those who were too seriously injured to provide a meaningful addition to the rearguard action which was being put together as we spoke.

They were being moved out of harm's way in the short term, the hope to protect them as they were too weak to stand up to the nightmare of battle which was about to befall this site, but, more tellingly, if the enemy did manage to breach the outer defences, they were to raze the prison to the ground, destroying everything that the enemy had thrown at them and all of them as well.

The line continued through the crowds without being impeded. Every member of the teams was working fluidly together without encroaching on the requirements of others. They were, despite everything, a well drilled and supremely organized fighting force.

Seeing that everything within our encampment was progressing in the way they should, I turned my attention outwards, beyond the veil of the night, to the surrounding enemy.

I couldn't see them. I couldn't hear them. Spreading out my magical power, I couldn't even feel their presence around us.

But they were there.

I knew that millions of the tiny raiders were pouring down the valley towards us, their mandibles clacking as they zeroed in on their objective.

Looking back to what Mark was doing, marveling at the smooth, well practiced activities of the people around me, fear crawled up my back and roared its own defiance in my ear. The familiarity of all of the movements made it clear to me that our defences were going to be over run in minutes when the beetle things actually hit the site from all sides.

We were all about to be massacred and we were all happily walking into the mincing machine and laying down, the collective familiarity of the tactics used by our troops worldwide looking like they were creating the blueprint for our own downfall.

"We're about to be slaughtered" slipped from my Dragon lips as they peeled back to bare my teeth, more on instinct that conscious effort. Andrea was quickly to my side and griped my arm tightly, spinning me to face her.

"Do not spread your own fears through the troops. Even if we must fall, you must NEVER allow those beneath you to know that you have been broken by fear." She had jabbed her face forward to such a degree that our noses were brushing together as she growled out the words, hard anger etched all over her face.

Her sudden movement had taken me by surprise and the level of pointed order in her voice had put me on the back foot. It didn't last long.

My fire nature took over and the anger within me surged upwards. Pushing my jaw out and squaring my shoulders, I straightened myself up to my full height and loomed ominously over Andrea, forcing her to take a small step backwards.

"I'm not an idiot!" rattled more from my chest than from my mouth. The sudden growl had startled Andrea enough to make her pause.

"They've worked out our calls." I rumbled to her as I took furtive glances around the courtyard. I wanted to make certain that all of the people milling around our feet through the courtyard weren't able to listen to the conversation we were having.

Andrea's expression said she had no idea what we were talking about. Since we had first met, she and I had been involved in a great many battles but also a great many normal situations. We had spent a great deal of time together which I had thought had been more than just trainer to trainee. I had learned a great deal about her and her family outside the realms of her duty to The Circle. I knew that her father's favorite colour was red and that she hated eating white meat. You'd have thought that she would have remembered that I was a rugby nut who used the metaphors from sport. Christ, aside from anything else, I was a man so sporting parlance was to be expected, surely.

"They know what we're going to do in our defence; they have done for a while." I thought back to the battles which had seen the loss of Frederico's father and sister in the last few weeks and started to think about the nature of the defeats we had all suffered. We had always been just lucky enough to be able to keep the advances of The Hive at bay but it always seemed to come at a very high cost. We had lost hundreds of troops and two Guardians in the last month and a half, defending a prison which had never once come under this kind of sustained attack.

"We've got to change our strategy."

That seemed to make more sense. I continued without waiting for any comment further.

"Everyone who is part of our group is fully prepared to die in order to protect the prisons. Everyone will happily see the total destruction of our forces if it means we can stop The Hives advances. That's our current problem."

Andrea's mouth dropped open.

"Our collective will to repel the enemy of the human race is not a problem!" Her vehement objection of my train of thought was clear for all to see. I needed to get this turned around fast.

"I mean that our forces have always behaved in the same way. Under every attack we've encountered all over the world and all the way through history, our forces have been either able to squash whatever attack has been mounted quickly or they have consistently fallen back towards the prison as they have fought, all with the final plan of bringing the prison down around their ears. Every person I've spoken to about previous battles has said the same thing."

The sound of the on rushing beetle creatures was starting to move beyond that of an approaching force and was beginning to resemble a broiling thunder clap. Looking around quickly, it was clear that I needed to accelerate.

"The point is that we have always done the same thing. The whole fight here today has felt like we have been running at least one step behind the enemy all of the time. The opening fly-by from the Tayne who would have been able to bring us down if we'd taken off, the enemy cascade bridges right on top of our forces, the Tayne smashing our shield. All of it says we're being worked out. We need to do something very different."

She narrowed her eyes at me but was quick to cede to my point despite her fears.

"What do you suggest?"

"How wide a ring of ice can you create? We need a wall between us and the outside world at least fifty feet high, ten to fifteen feet thick and angled out."

"That will be very hard to bring to. I will be exhausted after this effort and unable to provide any further support." Her voice showed no sign of any emotion. She was purely stating fact.

"Well, we may be able to reduce the size a bit. What do we need to do to get the shield back up?"

This time, even Andrea's icy calm exterior was unable to cover her resignation.

"We need much more powerful Guardians here to be able to rebuild the shield at all and even then that would take too long for us here on the ground. We need to fall back into the caverns below the citadel. We need to prepare to bottleneck the enemy and bring down the tomb for us all."

I looked in her eyes and could easily see that she had no other options available to her. She was out of possible responses to the battle which was rapidly being lost around us except the tried and tested mass suicide play which seemed to be the oddly preferred method of defence.

I couldn't accept that.

My frustration was crawling through me like an invading parasite. Second by second, it bored deeper and took more and more control until I roared out and turned to face back towards the on-rushing enemy.

"They want in and you want to kill everyone here to stop them." My humanity was gone and I could feel the same lust for violence that had boiled over in Frederico wildly boiling over in me.

"I don't give a shit about history or what you think you should be doing to defend this place. I am going to take the fight out there."

I dropped down onto all fours and charged out into the darkness beyond our encampment. I was going to burn so much of the surrounding land and anything that was stood on it, it would probably be seen from space!

I could hear the onrushing hoards ahead of me but before I could do anything in my own attack, an icy cold grip wrapped itself round my shoulders and legs and heaved me backwards towards the citadel, sending me across the ground before Andrea.

She stood looking directly ahead, rigidly tall and not flinching at the sight of a restrained Dragon.

"What are you doing?" I bellowed at her as I worked against the invisible bonds which she had entwined me with, struggling to get free to recommence my attack.

"She didn't do anything to you ignorant child." The voice was authoritative and hard edged. It had the natural resonance of someone who was supremely confident in what they were saying and who was used to getting their own way. A female voice I was very familiar with. One that, despite its reptilian origin, had retained its strong Chinese accent.

The Elder moved like black liquid from behind Andrea's statue-like form and thrust her snout into my face.

"I pulled you back before you could ensure the loss of a second Guardian today. You are showing me that you shouldn't have been let within five hundred miles of a newly called Guardian." She was very clear on her thoughts and didn't care about stepping on toes. Her absolute focus and certainty of her position was unnerving at that close range and took the fire of anger from me as easily as if she had reached in and pick-pocketed it from me.

"Shield collapse at each and every site around the world is closely monitored and should the event take place, it will be brought to my attention. You will come to understand that I have a connection to so many things in this group." She pulled away from my face and straightened up but she held my attention none the less.

"My forces are helping to organize our wounded and prepare for our retreat into the cavern. I am here to re-build the shield wall."

She was utterly matter of fact but I could see that her last comment was something to be surprised by, by looking at Andrea. She had turned her head to face The Elder. Not the biggest signal of shock the world had ever seen, but in context, massive.

The Elder swept past us and balled up her two clawed fists. I could hear the ever closing sounds of hundreds of thousands of armored limbs from beyond the limited light offered within the camp but The Elder made no sign she was either aware or interested in what they could potentially mean. She simply gathered herself facing out with the absolute air of being squarely in charge.

Millions of shards of gentle white light started to appear from the ground and ruins of the ancient citadel, hovering and dancing as if being toyed with by a gentle passing breeze. They all looped and wandered through the air and started slowly moving towards The Elder, beginning to collect around her, forming a shimmering shell of energetic light which hummed with restrained power.

Looking around, it became clear that the power of the casting being weaved ahead of us was building very quickly. Around The Elder, the light rapidly tore up in intensity and in a matter of seconds was reaching a blinding level akin to all the magical discharge which had been loosed by the gathered armies during the day's battle.

"Now understand what a Guardian who is fully in control of all of their powers is truly capable of." The Elder spat out to me, wrapping the words subtly around a metallic rod of effort. She may have been speaking to me but her comment was aimed at all within earshot – just showing that I didn't really know what I was doing. My stubborn streak responded without any thought.

"Better make this a good lesson, I'm not very bright." The situation was dire, there were dead and dying members of our teams scattered all over the valley but I had to have my say.

I could feel the disapproving glares from all who were gathered around us but I didn't care. I was used to always being the one who was blamed for all of the problems within this group, being seen as the weakest link in this magical chain and for being looked down on because I didn't share the same beliefs as everyone else here – including the benefits of mass suicide for the greater good.

The Elder, as was routine by now, ignored me.

She simply closed her eyes and with the barest hint of further effort, sent a rolling wave of energy away from her and out into the valley. There was a noticeable increase in speed the further it traveled from The Elder. It passed around all of the Circle team within the boundary of the old shield wall without the slightest effect and boomed out into the night.

The retreating light from the other worldly wave allowed us all to glimpse the surrounding areas in a sun-like clarity giving us a far too clear picture of the enemy which was surrounding us. The beetles were swelling and broiling towards us as one single mass. There was no singularity in their movements what so ever, each seamlessly becoming a constituent part of the whole. Even the shadows cast by the creatures took on malevolent forms of their own, my mind flashing back to the battle in my mansion where the unreal creatures had attacked me. I was seeing enemies growing from everywhere.

There were so many of them that there was no fear to be felt from anyone. I could feel pockets of utter acceptance in the face of the advancing wave. Before we could see what was coming and how close they were we had all been focusing on the hope of survival. With the illumination from The Elder, everyone around me had lost the drive to resist. There was nothing but acceptance.

I could still hear steady shuffling footsteps behind me as the seriously injured were being moved underground as the ultimate last line of defence but there was no longer the same force of will in any resistance. Everyone would continue to do their best but they all knew that the odds had just become insurmountable.

Out in the valley, the wave passed further out of site, obscuring areas of the enemy in shadow as it advanced. As the light continued, the previous chittering and chattering of the creatures began to die away until only an eerie silence remained in its place, holding within it the menace of the all too close attack.

Silence followed.

And followed.

I tried to reach my mind out into the valley night to sense the location of the advancing troops but more importantly, to register if there had been any effect of any kind from whatever the Elder had just worked.

I magically prodded in the dark and achieved nothing.

"As far as I can tell, *your importance*, the shield is still down so we're still very much in harm's way. Now what? Do you want me to start doing what I do best yet?" I tried to hide my own fears by politely inquiring as to the next strategy. I know perfectly well how to deal with people.

Andrea grasped my arm and squeezed. She didn't share my assessment of my interpersonal skills.

"Just wait Anthony; The Elder has more power than any of us. She is capable of a very great deal." Her words had been meant as a way of calming me down and of reassuring all around us but they just got under my skin. Even a creature as powerful as Andrea was being beaten into line by the threat of the history of The Circle.

I was about to give my feelings of the potential power of The Elder when whatever she had done had an effect.

At the farthest reaches of the valley, there was a low glowing pop of light. It was more felt than seen as a discharge of light but that sensation of energy was soon growing. Andrea, The Elder and I all staggered as we shared the sense of power from the edges of the vale.

"What was that?" was the best I could muster.

The Elder didn't even turn to face me as she responded, knowing that I was going to be hanging off her every word.

"I am using the enemy as our defence. Watch and learn child." She didn't add any further explanation but none was needed. From all around us, I could feel the change in energy. In seconds, I could hear the crackle and burn of thousands of armoured insect bodies being seared. This soon had screams added to the mix. Andrea and I just looked out at what had been a violent advancing army and stared as they seemed to be demolished by the casting of one Dragon.

"The shield will be in place in seconds. Return to your human forms now." The Elder hissed out at us. I had started to regain a sliver of my composure and was preparing a forceful response to what she had just ordered but she shimmered herself and her own Dragon form collapsed down to that of an upper middle aged Chinese woman. Looking at Andrea for some form of guidance, all I got was the validation of The Elders order, as she too transformed back.

One small effort of will and I followed them down.

We all stood stock still in the night air, naked, listening to the night and the approaching sounds of death which whispered through the wind. Whatever was going on, it was getting closer.

"Majesty" asked Andrea gingerly. "Should we be looking to find some form of cover before the enemy reaches us?"

"Or at least get some clothes on" I added, feeling that we were woefully under-dressed for fighting.

There was no time for any kind of response as from all around us there was a roar of wind and a surging light as The Elders returning magic reached its destination. All around us the light reared up and built upon itself, raising piece by piece skyward, building a brand new shield wall. Every member of the gathered forces who were still on the surface had stopped to watch in awe as the ancient magic which was being controlled by The Elder re-built our protective wall. I swear I heard at least one gasp. I also can't confirm that it came from me.

Brick by magical brick, the shell of power surrounding the gateway to the prison below was recreated until, with a slight thump of pressurized air, the keystone piece was placed atop the mighty shimmering dome and the spell was complete. The shield hovered in place for a second, and then vanished from sight as the transparency was returned.

The wall was back up, the advancing enemy hoards had had something done to them which had removed them as a serious threat to us and the fear and emptiness which had been spreading throughout our own encampment was rapidly being pushed aside, replaced by a burning defiance and a deep rooted pride.

I scanned the area around me and could feel the need for blowing out a very much deserved sigh of relief. The Elder had been called upon to do something vitally important for the group as a whole and she had done just that. Maybe she was worth giving a little more credit.

That thought was still buzzing around my head as I passed out.

8

Waking up and not being sure where you are is not a great experience. A great many of the human race will have had that experience due to the effects of drink or even drugs and they will no doubt back me up when I say it makes you feel lost, vulnerable and more than a little embarrassed.

Doing so knowing that you were nude when you collapsed is even worse.

Blinking a couple of times as I ran through my own inventory of sensations, I tried to work out the details as fast as I could. I wasn't hurt that I could tell and I couldn't not feel anything so I was hoping that meant I hadn't lost something important. I still checked the vital pieces just in case – its reflex after all.

That assessment complete, I eased myself up onto my elbows and, scratching an itch on the back of my neck, looked around wherever I was. The walls were tiled black, as was the floor and the ceiling. There was a low strength strip light overhead, mounted within a delicately ornate structure which was more artwork than light fitting. It was trying desperately to shed enough light around the room but the black surfaces seemed to be sucking in any and all light which rebounded around. There was a very strong smell of what appeared to be lavender or some other flower of which I wouldn't have any real knowledge being such a manly man. Lavender mixed with the barest hint of antiseptic.

I was laying on a very luxurious king sized bed which was positioned against one wall of a very spacious room which contained three other beds, exactly like mine. They all had deep purple sheets, mightily padded pillows and exuded wealth. Andrea lay in one, still unconscious with the covers pulled up tightly around her chin. Her white hair was falling in each and every direction and framed her face perfectly. I lingered while looking at her, I couldn't help it. She was an incredibly powerful Guardian who commanded the respect of all of the troops who fought for her. She was stunning in so many ways.

"What are you thinking when you look at her?" The sudden interjection of sound shocked me back into the here and now. In one of the other beds, the one to my left, lay the Elder.

Whipping my attention back towards the sound, I was confronted by her steely glaze. The Elder was sat up in her bed, her sheet wrapped strategically around her to protect her modesty. Within that large bed, her tiny human form was almost swamped. Her green eyes cast out an intensity that was deeply unnerving if you found yourself the focus of it at the best of times but when you're on your own in a relatively confined space as I was, it took on the piercing effect of an x-ray. My composure was lost ahead of those eyes and all I could muster was a mumbled stammer.

"I said," repeated The Elder, not showing any real emotion but somehow managing to convey it in her non anger, "what are you thinking when you look at her?" She brushed at something miniscule on her forearm, flicking whatever it was away with a calm contempt. I could see she was feeling much the same towards me.

I had been caught so off guard by her question I made the fatal mistake in this kind of situation. I answered truthfully.

"I think she's stunning. Why?" I had tried to take the combative edge out of my voice but I can't be certain that I was that successful.

The Elder just looked at me with the same withering gaze she had thrown my way on so many other occasions.

"You have no idea of who you are, do you? Who she is? Who any of us are? You are just reacting to the most basic level of yourself without thinking about the consequences. You Fires are all the same, driven by the primitive that you have to rely on others to control."

I mulled over what she had said, realised that I hadn't truly understood the majority of the context of what was said, assumed that she had been insulting me and proceeded accordingly.

"Look your angriness, I know that I still have a great deal to learn but will you please cut me some slack. I'm trying to learn on the go what everyone else in my position has a life time to master. And why shouldn't I think that Andrea is stunning? I think you've got that sultry older woman thing going on too."

That did make her angry.

Her features contorted into an animal snarl and she whipped the sheet away from her and in a flash was across the space between us, standing atop my bed, shaking with rage. Her small frame was covered in intricate tattoos, all showing reptilian forms of one kind or another. They wound around all of her limbs and formed a collection of restrained beasts around her body. Despite her advancing years, I'd estimate around sixty, she was in incredible shape and looked like she was more than able to take me on in a fight.

She was fast to assert herself.

"YOU ARE A STAIN ON THIS GROUP AND YOU WILL LEARN SELF CONTROL." Her voice rebounded from the tiled walls and each reflection of sound seemed to build on the others. I jumped with a mixture of shock at the speed of her movement and the pitch of her voice but was totally at her mercy.

The one door to the room opened before either of us was able to make any kind of movement beyond just blinking at each other.

No light accompanied the small procession of people who slowly trooped in to join us. There were six in total; the first two were tall, broad and covered in large swathes of metal. They carried vastly oversized Katana swords which looked as if they should weigh at least forty kilos but they handled them as if they were capable of handling a great deal more load. Their faces were covered by large metallic helms each moulded to show a demonic image, all snarling teeth and frowning eyes. They marched forcefully to stand on either side of the only doorway into the room and stood stiffly to attention.

The following group of four were all medical functionaries by the look of their clothing and the items they carried. None of them looked directly at the strange tableau that was being staged ahead of them but they all wore the expressions of utter discomfort, though not at The Elders nudity, more at the fact that they were looking upon her at all.

The Elder and I just remained motionless as the medics busied themselves with either checking on Andrea, who was still out cold despite the noise in the room, or waiting for us.

"My lady. Will you please return to your bed? After the exertions you have been forced through I very much doubt you are in a fit condition to be having any kind of disagreement, even one with *that*." The words came from outside the room. It was a male voice but not one which sounded comfortable in its maleness, the pitch was slightly too high, the handling of the words seemed forced. Even from just one sentence, I could feel a discomfort about the speaker. They wore an overly formal accent but that accent had been very well tailored. It carried the barest hint of at least five countries that I could make out. The owner of the accent slowly followed the words into the room and the medics all bowed their heads as he showed himself.

He stood about five foot seven inches tall and looked to be a lean man, weighing no more than one hundred and forty pounds. He was dressed in very formal attire of a suit which was more than just cloth and wore a black jeweled pin on his tie which he was straightening almost absent mindedly, and had at least three gold and crystal rings on his fingers, two rubies and a sapphire. Each decoration looked to be just too big for him, akin to a Super Bowl ring being worn by a child. The material of his suit seemed to shimmer in the low light of the room, as if changing colour as he moved from the doorway to the beds. It was more than any usual tailoring or fabric could manage. As he looked casually around the bowed heads, he smoothed down his jacket which was buttoned across him, showing that he was clothed in a magical construct, tidal forces of energy running all over him.

The Elder slithered back off the bed at his word and was across the room without making a sound. The medics remained rooted to the spot despite her passage, all looking intently at the floor.

"Thank you my lady," he cooed as she adjusted the sheets around her.

When she was settled, her turned back to me and took a step in my direction. He was a man of roughly forty but looked as if he could easily have passed for much older. His greasy red hair looked as if it had been styled to within an inch of its life, matching the rest of his image, but it was styled as what can only be described as 'cut by mum in a rush'.

"Hello Mr. Johns. My name is Visisamus Ward. I hold the rank of Head of House for her majesty The Elder. I would greatly appreciate it if you would refrain from causing my lady any further discomfort. She has been forced to expend a great deal of energy in the defence of the site in Argentina after you and your teams were so unable to defend the place. We must all really be more careful with what we do, don't you agree?" With the end of the sentence, he leaned forward towards me and a reptilian smile was cut across his face, baring his teeth in a gesture which was part grin, part threat.

I looked back at him as he smiled and tried to order my feelings on this new addition to The Circles upper tiers. I knew that he was, by definition, lower down the food chain than I was, but he carried with him the confidence of a man who was very used to getting his own way, and that included with Guardians.

Time for my own opening gambit in this exchange.

"You're Head of House for The Elder? You'd have thought I would have heard of you by now, wouldn't you?" I shifted my weight and forced myself to sit up as straight as I could muster, keeping my expression as flat as I could as I bared my torso to show him that I was a great deal bigger than him. If this character was used to getting his own way, used to throwing his weight around, then I needed to try and show him who the heavier hitter was.

There was no reaction from him except the smile spread even further and he took a step closer to me, leaning further forward as he did. It looked like a bow to the outside world but again felt very much like a gesture designed to invade the personal space of the person he was facing.

"Not at all sir. It is well known amongst every member of The Circle that you are very inexperienced so you must have been busying yourself with the basics up to now. At the ponderous pace you are going, you would have probably been ready to learn about me in about a century." Another step forward followed so his legs were now brushing the side of my bed. He held the same expression as he stood there despite the exertion it must have been placing on the masseter muscles in his jaws.

This close to me I could see more detail of him. His face was lined in an unnatural way, as if he had undergone some form of surgical procedure to reduce the wrinkles which hadn't quite managed to work correctly. His disturbing smile was populated by a collection of overly yellowed teeth which looked to each carry the slightest of points – almost harking back to a previous evolutionary trait.

His glimmering suit of magical power was the most confusing part of him. Up close, he looked to be a not quite polished version of himself. The sheen looked to be missing from his persona but the suit was immaculate. And he caught me looking.

"Do you admire my dress, sir?" Always the 'sir' despite what he was saying.

"This was a gift from The Elder herself," he looked down at his own magnificence and loved himself.

"A strip of skin from the beast she is guarding was flayed free when they first fought all those centuries ago. She made me this suit as a way of expressing her gratitude for my services. She had kept this pelt for thousands of years but gifted it to me. Please, feel free to admire the quality."

With that he proffered an arm for me to inspect. It smelt of nothing more than run of the mill leather but there was a massive significance behind the garment. This suit was a symbol of his power, bestowed on him by The Elder in much the same way as my own Guardianship had been on me. He viewed himself, and perhaps he was viewed by others as well, as a supremely powerful man and that power was shown by his supreme suit of Hive skin. I needed to show him that I wasn't going to be pushed around by him.

"OK Leatherpants. Go attend to your Master. I'm feeling pretty good at the mo. Don't you worry though, I'll let you know if I need you to get me something."

That comment made his carefully controlled exterior crack just slightly. The barest suggestion of something crossed his face but it was hidden almost as fast as it had been created. That carefully rehearsed smile back firmly in place, Leatherpants straightened up and turned back towards The Elder without another word, floating back to her bedside while throwing withering gazes at all of the gathered medical personnel who immediately resumed their deep study of the flooring around them.

The next ten minutes became a very uncomfortable silence.

The medical staff passed around all of us in turn, reviewing and assessing what our individual conditions were and addressing them as they deemed necessary while The Elder and I did our best to avoid the others eyes and Leatherpants did his best to always meet mine, that almost painful smile coming with him.

I had a collection of prods and pokes and the laying on of hands was performed with some dexterity by two of the 'nurses'. After a short time I was told that I was fine and that my passing out had been caused by the effect of The Elders casting. I would need rest to recover but there would be no long term effects of what had happened.

"What did you do to all of us?" I asked The Elder. This time I had worked out that I didn't need to be confrontational with what I was saying as I truly wanted to know. The Elder simply looked at me as Leatherpants answered for her.

"Her majesty cast a leeching spell which stole the power and energy from anything it came into contact with. She used the combined strength of those creatures in the area to drive the working to re-build the shield." The same painful smile remained rigid across his face as he spoke.

"She sent her power to the edges of the valley and ordered the magic to return to her, bringing with it all the strength of those in the area to complete the spell. The three of you all gave power to the casting, which is why you were rendered unconscious. As always, her magnificence saved you from any further pain by encouraging you back to your human form. Had you been still as Guardians, the power taken could have been a great deal more dangerous."

The information that he had given to me seemed to be reasonable. I was still pretty green in terms of casting ability and the power to call the forces of nature to my will but everything did stack up. It still felt like sand in your swimming shorts that he should have this understanding and I didn't.

Time to get his unending font of knowledge working for me.

"Thank you for your help providing me with the mechanisms behind our current position. Do you know the fate of the soldiers who were fighting alongside us? How many of our people are safe and well?" I tried my best to inject a measure of decorum into what I was saying but I wasn't very effective by the expression which spread across both The Elders and Leatherpants' face.

He slithered across the floor between the beds and took up station next to me, again leaning over me with the same forced smile. "Are you not concerned with the condition of the shield that my mistress risked so much to re-build? Do you take your ancient responsibility so lightly that you concern yourself with the fate of a group of *nobodies* rather than the reason we are all here?"

It was his stressing of the word nobodies which did the damage.

I could feel the fire behind my eyes. His words were like daggers to me and I wouldn't, I couldn't, let him continue to think that he could place the value of human life below that of some magical shield.

My anger whipped up like a violent tropical storm and I was powerless before its force.

The covers to my bed were still floating gently towards the floor of the room by the time I had burst from my bed, picked the simpering Leatherpants from the floor and slammed him into the opposite wall.

"HOW DARE YOU CALL THESE PEOPLE NOBODIES? THESE ARE THE REASON WE DO WHAT WE DO."

I held him pinned to the wall as he took in what I had said. I was breathing deeply and becoming more and more aware of the fact that I was naked again. I wasn't too sure if this would enhance or diminish the point I was making but I could only keep going forward.

Leatherpants hadn't even registered my explosion of emotion.

He dangled before me, me with handfuls of his magically tailored suit bunched under his chin and him with his spindly legs hanging limply beneath him. He regarded me with the same overstretched rictus grin still plastered onto his face with no signs of it slipping in the slightest.

"None of us who have been called into this most noble and worthwhile cause are anybody."

His words came out with no force at all, just a certainty of the message they were conveying.

"All of the blessed few who have chosen to be a part of what The Circle have to offer, are nothing. None of us amount to anything more than the sum of what we do. You are concerned for the well-being of the few you have met or are aware of. I am concerned for the whole human race. I am concerned for the seven billion people on this planet who don't know we are here but who are utterly dependent on what we do. Shouldn't we all just be glad that we are able to provide the protection we can? Isn't it just your vanity which is making you look beyond the calling to protect the masses?"

Silence hung between us as my own heavy breath was the only sound I was aware of.

The same smile stretched even wider as he continued to speak.

"Look at yourself. You are one of the mightiest creatures on the face of the planet but you are not allowing yourself to look at what is truly important. You are no longer a human being, one of the herd but you still cling to that irrelevance. You are a slave to the most basic urges of yourself and that is why you are on the verge of becoming your Dragon form within the confines of this hospital. If we lose fifty thousand people here shouldn't we rejoice if we save fifty million or more?"

He continued to stare at me and maintained the question even in the silence.

I tried to think about the details of what he had just said and I became aware of the fact that I had been letting my inner monster drive what had been going on. I was indeed starting to transform into my red Dragon form as he had pointed out. Leatherpants hung in the air only three or four inches from the ceiling of the room we were in which meant I was holding him at roughly twenty feet from the floor.

Looking down at myself, I could see that I had grown in size and that my skin had started to transform into the armoured surface of the mighty Dragon and with that realization, I could feel a great deal of the fire draining from me. His words had made me think about what had been happening and my Dragon was being slowly put back into his box.

I slowly returned to what I should have been and Leatherpants was gradually returned to the floor. I did my best to maintain the feeling of some superiority and dignity despite the fact that he had openly shown my arguments to be floored and he had done so while I was pinning him to the wall. Whilst I was naked.

Returning to my bed without making it look as if I was in any way slinking, I slowly got myself comfortable and settled back to look upon everyone who was in the room.

The medical staff all maintained the steadfast view of the tiled floor as they busied themselves all around the beds, righting objects that I had managed to upset in my latest outburst. Leatherpants had smoothed out his prized suit and had floated to the side of his master. The Elder, in turn, was settling herself back under the covers. She had apparently stood as I had boomed across the room at her servant. By the feel of the magical energy in the room slowly deflating, she had been readying herself to react against me had Leatherpants not been able to talk me down.

My eyes continued around the room and alighted on Andrea's bed. There was no sign that she had reacted at all to any of the commotion I had been making but now her eyes were open and she was awake.

She looked at me intently, the covers of the bed still pulled up tight around her chin. There was no movement in her eyes but that seemed to make her attention seem more heavily weighted. Despite her blank expression, and the only sign that she was conscious being her open eyes, I could still feel a mighty level of disappointment coming from her.

We just stared at each other through the silence of the room.

Leatherpants was quick to flow to Andrea's side as soon as he was aware she was awake. She didn't move as he did but her eyes flicked in his direction.

"There is no need to trouble yourself my lady. The youngster is calm again so there is no more danger. He will learn to show some level of self-control in the future I have no doubt." The last portion of the sentence was accompanied by a turning glance in my direction, just to prove who he was talking about, in case there had been any doubt.

Andrea didn't move.

Leatherpants turned back to face her and looked into her eyes. By his body language, he wasn't welcomed by what he was facing. He shrugged back away from Andrea and quickly made his way back to The Elders bedside.

The three Guardians in the room remained silent from then on as we all simply laid still. I let my attention run over the various points of my body which hurt in whatever delightful way they could, taking a more detailed list of what I had done to myself. Judging by the way I'd moved when I'd got angry and how the pains I had at present were more annoyance that bone shattering agony, I mustn't have been that badly damaged in the fight. Yay team.

It was roughly another hour of silence as different medical types flitted in and out, before anyone I knew came in and thankfully it was Mike.

He moved quickly but steadily across the room, bowing his respect to The Elder and Andrea as he went. Leatherpants seemed to take his signal of deference to The Elder as somehow being aimed at him as well. That man was taking smug to another level.

"How you doing bach?" said Mike as he approached me. He tried his best to keep his tone low but by the reaction from Leatherpants he hadn't kept it low enough. Another example of the outsider Guardian doing his best to corrupt the purity of what The Circle was all about. It was good to see a friendly face though.

"Just epic Mike. Absolutely epic. Do you know anything about what happened out there?"

Mike hadn't been involved in the battle. He had remained back at my estate to ensure everything was safe back home. The Head of House in each of the estates is a very powerful magical being and is very useful in any fight but you would leave your own estate open to attack if you send away all of your biggest guns to each and every fight around the world. Those Guardians who are involved in any fighting will leave a very strong force back home which is always led by the Head of House to protect against being caught by a sucker punch. The Circle insisted upon it but that order did seem to make sense.

"The Elder took power from all of you to bring the wall back up but she was able to use energy from whatever was gathered in the valley as well. She killed everything and used their magical power to rebuild the shield wall. It would appear that you lost a great deal of power but thankfully not too much, hence the long sleep."

"Long sleep? How long have I been asleep?" I didn't think that I'd been out that long but you can't help your mind wandering towards the Aliens end of the spectrum. The sound of *'57 years'* drifted through my head before Mike responded.

"Three weeks, give or take a day or two. There had been a fear that you had all given too much to the spell The Elder cast and that you'd never come out of it but Mr. Ward was on hand to assuage any fear we had."

I looked at him blankly.

"Mr. Ward?"

"My counterpoint in the house of The Elder," responded Mike with a flick of his head towards Leatherpants.

I nodded my understanding and was quick to realise that I had already lost his real name in favour of the nickname Leatherpants. Don't call him Leatherpants for God's sake, I reminded myself. Mike continued.

"He said that you all had a portion of your reservoirs of life power siphoned off to augment what The Elder had done. All you needed to do was rest and build up your strength again."

"Sounds OK but just building up my reserves doesn't take three weeks surely. You're making it sound like it was a very matter of fact event but if the three of us have been unconscious here for almost a month, I'm willing to bet that there was nothing simple about it."

Mike considered my words but his only response was that Leatherpants – damn it, Mr. Ward – had given him all of the information and there was no chance of him questioning him. "Indeed, none of the Heads of House for any of the fallen Guardians had been called here until you had woken up. We've all been marooned at our estates waiting on word." Mike gripped my arm and squeezed gently, showing me that he was glad I was awake and apparently unharmed. That small gesture made me feel good.

"What about the other people in the valley? What were our causalities like?" I still wanted, well more needed, to know what had happened to all of the other people who had been involved in this latest skirmish.

Mike straitened and stiffly started to reel off statistics about the fall-out from the battle. There had been a total loss of one hundred and thirty three people from the shared force, four of which had been people who had come from my house. I listened intently to the names as Mike ran through who was no longer with us and I felt a confusing surge of happiness as there was no mention of Mark amongst the fallen. There was at least that small comfort amongst the death. The four who had fallen were only barely known to me. I thought that I recognized one of the names but I couldn't be sure.

"The troops swept through the valley after The Elder had finished her working and there was no sign of any of the beetle creatures, the Tayne or anything else. You were picked up and transported here as fast we could. There hasn't been any further activity from The Hive here or anywhere else, since." Mike was still standing at my bedside but now that he had recounted the story he seemed to relax and was practically sat next to me on the mattress.

I mulled over the details he had given me and tried my best to put them into some kind of order. The Elder had managed to sweep in at the last possible minute and save the day, we had experienced a large loss of personnel but we could have been hit a great deal harder, the shield wall was solidly in place and the prison we all guarded was still intact. All things considered, this was a good win in comparison to what we had seen before. This was the first battle in long enough to count where a Guardian Dragon hadn't died. Whatever else had happened, The Elder had made sure that there wasn't going to be further need to perform the Awakening ceremony to call a new Guardian, and so she had done well.

But had she been that successful?

"What about Freddy?" I shot at Mike as the thought hit me, shuffling myself up on the pillows as I did.

Mike looked blank. There was no emotion in his face as he regarded my face.

"Frederico wasn't as lucky as the rest of you. His injuries were much more severe. Indeed some think too severe to survive."

That lack of anything emotional remained bolted to each and every syllable as he spoke and he continued to speak as if there was nothing more to be added to his original statement. I wasn't looking for him to give me a grisly breakdown of the exact extent of his injuries but surely there needed to be more than just 'he will most likely die'. Freddy had been a very green (in terms of experience and colour) member of our team and he had been under my command – roughly at least. I slumped back into the bed.

The Elder broke the silence.

"Frederico understood all of the expectations he had on his shoulders. He, as a Guardian of The Circle, was more than willing to make the ultimate sacrifice to be able to protect the prison that he was charged with defending."

Her voice carried no forceful aggression, no need to dominate, only a granite surety. Looking at her, I could see that she had her eyes closed and she was relaxed back into the voluminous pillows of her hospital bed. She continued with her eyes closed.

"We are all links in a great chain. None of us is more valuable than the next and all of us are gifted the chance to be a saviour to the human race. Not one of us would turn away from the chance to be the saviour of the human race – not even you." Her last syllable was accompanied by a weighty silence. Looking around the room, I could see that each and every person within was transfixed by her words. Andrea, who was still in the same position she had been when she regained consciousness, looked on intently with only her eyeballs showing the level of attention she was paying. All of the medical staff stood spellbound by her words, not moving in any way.

This time, Leatherpants broke the silence.

"Indeed my lady. Soon enough we will know if our Guardian has survived or if we are required to re-forge the strength of what The Circle truly is." He nodded deeply towards the bed bound form of The Elder. She, with her eyes still closed, made a shallow nod and the point seemed to have been ratified.

I nudged Mike and as he turned to me I asked in the most efficient / erudite manner I could muster, "Huh?"

"The next Awakening." he informed me, again in a very matter of fact fashion.

Of course. If Freddy did die there would be a weakness in who we all were. With the latest Guardian fallen, the power of the Dragon would pass to the next person in line. Despite my best efforts to keep the whole issue business like in my mind it still meant that the previous Guardian had died. That of course meant that I would have to return here to take part in another ceremony I could truly do without, all the time being reminded that I was the one responsible for failures which had led us to this point.

Suddenly being the one that everyone knew was a 'winner' seemed to be the weightiest part of my position. I'd seen nothing but losses since I had completed my first fight.

Laying back in my bed, I happily let the pillows and soft blankets absorb me. I wanted to be enveloped by the welcoming feel and smell of warm bedding and push all of the death away. I wanted to pull the covers over my head and shut myself away from everything.

I was tired and I wanted to go home.

9

Thankfully, I didn't have to wait much longer to get my wish.

The three of us were quickly deemed fit to be discharged by whoever was the head of the medical facility we were staying in. Leatherpants had been doing his best to hurry things along so he could take The Elder home and away from the presence of such low creatures as Mike and I. I don't think his efforts were responsible for the decision to let us all leave but you can never be sure with people like him, can you? The Elder was the first of us to leave but we were soon all making our way from the shared infirmary, surrounded in turn by the gathered throng of our personal retinues.

The Elder travelled amidst a bristling cloud of fabrics and metals. All of her armed and armoured guards locked into a protective shell surrounding her and the tiny woman was spirited from the facility under maximum security.

Andrea had a fraction of the people to see to her but still seemed to exude the same level of almost royal concern. Through all of her preparations she didn't once look in my direction, instead feeling content to give me a solid view of her back. Looks like everything that had happened had even made Andrea wary of me. Soon, she too was whisked from the infirmary and back to her estate in northern Russia. She did, though, flick a single glance at me through the gathered troops as she left.

Or at least I think she did.

I deliberately took the longest to prepare myself for my departure. Indeed, I didn't start gathering together my belongings until all of the others had left. It took me roughly three minutes to put together my possessions in a leather case which had been left at the side of the bed. I hadn't brought any change of clothes or toothbrush when I'd brought my forces down from Wales. I'd just opened up a bridge and we had all trooped through. Everything I had used up to now had been a loaner from Freddy's estate. I couldn't even leave any of it there. Everyone had looked aghast when I'd suggested it and Mike had had to politely explain the requirements of etiquette. Again.

Finally we were set and the least impressive of the Guardians supporters groups, just Mike and I, left the infirmary where I had been recovering and headed out towards the exterior of the estate.

Before we left, a bustling nurse gave us a rundown of important points to remember. It was the last piece of information which threw a spanner in the works somewhat.

"We can't use a Cascade Bridge? How are we supposed to get home if we can't open a way there?" I tried to prevent the petulant child tone from touching my voice but there was no way of being sure I was successful.

The nurse looked up at me, trying to hold the tough professional expression on his face but he wasn't having much luck. Fear of his perceived superior wasn't so much bleeding out as it was gushing around the edges of the poorly applied mask. In fact, I think he was actually shaking a little.

"I'm very sorry sir, but following on from the effects of the working that was the cause of your stay with us here, heavy magics of the kind which will bring the Cascade into existence are likely to be violently unstable at best but potentially fatal at worst. The Elder was very certain that it would be too dangerous for someone as inexperienced as yourself. I can only apologise again my Lord but you will have to take a plane back to your estate."

He was definitely shaking now. His brown eyes pleaded with me to accept what he was saying. I thought about the need to travel back to Wales 'the old fashioned way' and the out and out pain in the bum that was going to be but I couldn't leave him panicking any longer, he looked like he was going to have a heart attack. Besides, it was The Elder who'd pushed the importance of my slow travelling to him. Infusing my voice with all the regal authority I could muster I gripped him lightly on the shoulder and let him relax.

"Thank you for your help and advice. My team and I are in your debt for the information which will have probably saved our lives. Until the next time."

Mike also thanked the young nurse who, judging by his expression, hadn't been expecting anything as positive as that for the knowledge that it was going to take hours instead of seconds to return home. He looked back and forth between us for a handful of startled seconds and then, straightening his posture, he puffed himself up as large as he could.

"It is my honour to serve my Lord," he stated forcefully and bowed theatrically at the waist, sweeping down to the floor before he stood tall, turned and strode from the corridor we had been holding the conversation in.

"You see? Correct decorum can have a very strong effect on people. Just be glad we have planes these days, travelling back from here by sailing ship would have been just a little bit worse," Mike whispered as the nurse vanished from sight.

"Decorum nothing Mike. The important part of what I said to him wasn't the fancy bit; it was the bit where I thanked him for what he'd told me. He now feels valued for what he said and he is. No-one should feel that they are simply there to be shouted at."

Mike just looked at me but he was working it through in his mind. I'd been trying to encourage the feeling in the people in my estate that there wasn't the raging need to bow and scrape all of the time but it was a slow job of getting them to remember what I was saying on that topic. The requirements to treat all your 'colleagues' as being human beings first was a tough skill to learn. Everyone was having to untie years of social knotting regarding the way to treat people but I would not have everyone scared of me simply because I was the one with the wings.

"Hang on." I stopped Mike as we were turning to walk down the corridor.

"Why can't any one of the other Guardians just open up a bridge for us? Surely they can do that?"

Mike shrugged ever so slightly.

"Because The Elder has instructed everyone not to."

My mouth dropped open but luckily I was so surprised by the detail that I didn't erupt immediately. Mike was quick to recognize that he had to carry on with his explanation fast.

"She told everyone that it was a part of your on-going training but with a very clear understanding that there was no reprieve for anyone who did help."

I hated her but listening to that detail made perfect sense of the situation. That must have been why the nurse had been so utterly terrified of speaking with me concerning my travel arrangements.

He'd thought that he was going to get both barrels from a Fire Dragon.

Looks like I'd barely started to unpick that social knotting.

"Come on then," I sighed, rubbing at my neck as a tension began to tighten the muscles, all the while knowing that we had to get going. "Let's see if we can arrange a flight back to the UK in the next week."

Mike walked steadily along beside me. "Week? We'll be airborne within the hour."

Apparently, I'm not the only one with wings.

It hadn't ever occurred to me that without me being at the estate back in Wales, there had been no-one to actually open the bridge to bring Mike here quickly. I'd seen too often that members of my mighty order are a little 'funny' about offering help to the servants. I think Andrea was probably the only one who would have come to Mike's aid but she was unconscious with me. As I'd been lying unconscious in Argentina, he'd been forced to make his way to the other end of the world another way.

The small airfield was located roughly twenty miles from the estate and we had been driven there by a man whose neck was wider than his head. He'd sat in the driver's seat of the giant Mercedes Benz and waited for us to climb in. He hadn't acknowledged us in any way for the duration of the journey.

In no time at all he had brought us smoothly onto the tarmac of the runway, past gated checkpoints and barriered roadways without even slowing down. The car swung steadily up to the ladder which led up to the open hatch and stopped perfectly to allow me to simply step from the interior of the car onto the bottom rung of the ladder. My last contact with terra firma in Argentina seems to have been back in the estate.

The door was coolly opened from the outside by a uniformed member of the ground crew and my path was clear before me.

Before I left I aimed a comment towards the driver.

"Thank you for getting us here so quickly Mr...?" Again, I wanted to make sure the person who had been working for me didn't carry that feeling of terror just because of my perceived elevated station. Ahead of me he shrugged and looked like he was trying to turn slightly, though I could only imagine that his massive neck was making that an almost impossible task.

"Perez, Sir." His voice was much more high pitched that I had been expecting.

"Thank you Mr. Perez. Until next time." I left no more preamble and climbed from the car and into the plane with Mike following closely behind.

Climbing aboard your very own private jet is a very strange event. Especially when you didn't know that you had your very own private jet.

As I climbed on board I was amazed by the sheer opulence of the interior of the plane. The dark wood and beautiful smell of leather. The plush carpeting and antique looking fixtures and fittings. The plane looked like it was similar to something Tony Stark would be flying around in but this one was the truly top of the line version. Iron Man wishes his plane was this good.

Ahead of us was a retinue of immaculately dressed cabin crew, waiting to answer the calls of their passengers no matter how severe or outlandish. The three women and two men were standing as if they had been starched at least twice as much as their uniforms.

Not sure what to do next, I nodded to them all and declared into the silence, "Carry on," and made my way to the nearest seat available.

My words were apparently the key for the starch team to burst into life. They almost behaved like pieces of shrapnel from within an explosion, each rushing forwards in slightly different directions to attend to my each and every need.

Mike allowed himself to be settled fluidly into his seat and looked perfectly at ease with the whole situation of being waited on hand and foot. I was not so receptive.

I was surrounded by three fluttering people who seemed to be hell bent on making me comfortable, regardless if I wanted them to do it or not. I had pillows being tucked behind my head and under my legs by one as another adjusted my seat to have it fall into a half recline while the third placed a drink in one hand and a TV remote control in the other.

"Is this pillow to your liking my Lord?"

"Is this the correct drink for you my Lord?"

"Would you like us to adjust the cabin temperature for you my Lord?"

"Which channel would you like to watch on the flight my Lord?"

"We also have DVD's and Blu-rays should you so desire. You do like Start Wars do you not?"

"Would you like to change seat?"

"Is there anything we can do for you before take-off?"

All of these questions and it felt like a hundred more that I didn't catch washed over me in a tsunami of good intentions. Their good wishes were quickly translated to being a stifling wave of cloying sweetness.

Fingers were pulling at me and each face seemed to be leaning closer and closer, each trying to make certain that every whim or wish of mine could be dealt with, potentially even before I had recognized that I had had it. The ever crowding group of rictus grins became forcefully claustrophobic as the seconds dragged by.

Eventually, it was all too much for me.

"PLEASE, WILL YOU ALL LEAVE ME ALONE!" boomed through the cabin in a growling rumble and startled every single person into both stillness and silence, including Mike.

Each and every one of the faces which surrounded me looked as if they would shatter and crack due to the force of the rebuke. They all swayed before me with such a deep fear carved onto their features that it immediately started to cool me down.

Everyone slowly edged away from me, all looking as if they were trying to put as much distance between themselves and a very angry animal. That thought was quick to have all of the previous flash of anger drain away from me. But no-one else knew that.

Amidst the almost palpable atmosphere, Mike slowly but purposefully stood and easily addressed the cabin.

"I believe that my Lord has had a very taxing day and wishes us to all return to Wales as soon as possible. He is tired and would like the journey to take as little time as possible. Please see to it that we are delayed no longer than we have to be."

His words rang with the confidence and authority of someone who was perfectly at ease within the confines of his position. It made me feel worse.

"I have had a very hard time that I wish to return home from. I am eager to be at my own estate. Please understand that I am not angry with you." I was trying to repair the damage that my outburst had done but judging by the looks on the faces of the cabin crew, even the ones who hadn't been dealing with me directly, my efforts had fallen a long way short of the mark.

"Please leave us and let us know when we are about to take off. We will call for you when we need you." Mike's voice again had the calm authority ringing through it that seemed to fit the situation that all of the crew were expecting. They each nodded toward him in a curt and worried fashion and hurried away towards the cockpit or the tail of the plane and seemed to vanish into the very seems of the vehicle.

Mike and I were quickly left alone in our outrageously comfortable leather seats within the confines of the flying mansion. The only sound that accompanied us was that of the idling aircraft, clicks and cracks as it sat waiting on the runway.

Mike spoke first.

"Just relax bach. We'll be home soon."

I shook my head at what had just happened.

Mike watched and waited. He didn't have to wait long.

"This whole lifestyle seems to be designed to brutalise someone. I'm just tired of being the one who doesn't understand where I'm supposed to be." Mike said nothing and let me continue.

"I don't want to be the one who is feared just because. I also don't want to fear just because either. Everyone I speak with seems to be either expecting me to tear them apart for smelling a certain way or expecting to tear me apart because I had the sheer brass effrontery to look them in the eye." I stared straight ahead as I spoke without focusing on any of the details of what was around me.

Mike answered my frustrations.

"Everyone in our whole group, the world over, acts in a very certain way as is expected depending on their station. Since the very beginning of the conflicts, there have been so many different strata to who and what we all are. That has allowed us to be able to give and take orders and not have any weakness in our ranks."

He leaned forwards and gripped my arm and in an almost conspiratorial tone added, "Can't have armies disobeying their orders can you?"

"That's true but the attitude I'm talking about is wound up through everyday life. Every single person we've come into contact with since I came round in Freddy's estate has been on edge when they've had to be in the same room as me let alone actually speaking with me. I've told you before that I will treat everyone with the respect that any normal human being deserves." I sighed and fell back into the comfort of the chair, staring blankly out of one of the windows.

Beneath me I could feel the subtly building vibrations of the plane's engines as they were being wound up to push us into the air. There was barely any noise leaking into the cabin as we started to move quickly down the runway. Mike continued.

"Did you treat the cabin crew of this plane with the respect that any normal human being deserves? Just because you don't want anything of what they were trying to offer, does that give you the right to scream at them to leave you be?"

Silence hung in the air as the plane surged skywards.

"I am very sorry for my behavior sir" said Mike straightening his posture in his seat. "If you so wish I will deliver a very serious punishment when we return to the estate.

I shook my head as I considered his words. Talk about shining a bright light on someone.

"That won't be called for Michael," I told him. "You've done exactly what I asked you to do when I did exactly what I was fighting against. It looks like you've listened to me even if I was too pig-headed to listen to myself."

We reached out and shook hands.

"Please continue to tell me to act like a person not Lord of the manor."

We both leant back into our seats and started to relax. I then half twisted around and shouted to the cabin,

"Everyone. Please all come here."

The attendants were all in position at my side in seconds but they were all on edge.

"Anyone fancy watching a film? It's a long journey."

10

Hours later we touched down in Cardiff airport. I took in a deep breath of the air of home before I eased down the steps of the plane and boarded the sleek Aston Martin which was waiting for us on the runway. We sped through checkpoints and hastily opened gates without stopping and were soon out onto the open road, accelerating through the traffic without the barest hint of slowing. No passport control or customs for us. I was sure that I needed to be more 'anti' the ease of our passage from the plane to the open roads but I was just too tired to summon up that much anger.

I sat in the back of the car and relaxed as Mike coolly pushed the car through the empty night roads and made short work of the tarmac between us and the estate. I felt drained of all energy from the journey we had just completed so was glad that I had someone else to do the driving back 'home'. I was more surprised that Mike felt he would be able to do the driving despite him having been on the same journey as me.

"Don't worry bach. I'll get us home. Just means we won't have to drive our chauffeur back after he's dropped us off. Good sense all around." He then slapped me on the arm a little too hard as way of encouragement and gave me a big grin.

After that, the decision had been made and as I sat in the back of the luxury car I was confronted by the pure white pony-tail that Mike wore as the only one of his features I could see, his gaze steadfastly on the road ahead.

We moved without hindrance down the transportation veins of the country. I let my gaze tumble hazily out of the car as we sped past night shrouded details of the countryside. I could comprehend the position of the passing towns and villages but didn't let my attention focus on any of the details. I saw them as just being singular entities rather than collections. Each was sat resting during the night, waiting for the onset of the new day. We continued our journey and every place we passed seemed to watch me go past in return. I sleepily watched them and I swear they all looked at me with trepidation and regarded me with the suspicious sideways glance of those watching the man they know to be guilty of an unspoken crime.

I hadn't even registered that I had fallen asleep until Mike turned onto the small track rather than road which led through the tightly knitted mass of trees which created the vast natural wall around the whole estate. I had felt a little exposed when I had first had the details of the estate described to me. No solid brick walls or castle architecture at all despite the threat which was massed against us. Instead, just a magical shield and an enchanted wood. Despite the fairytale connotations, there was more defensive power coursing through the environment around us than could be bettered by a huge stone structure. Lloyd had almost been proud of the fact that no-one even knew that there was a mansion inside the woods. The stone wall would have announced our presence, the woods were naturally camouflaging. I smiled sleepily to myself as I remembered my former Head of House. He'd helped me into the madness of what I was a part of but he had done it with the same casual feeling about life that I enjoyed.

Every member of the house had liked Lloyd a great deal.

So had I.

Now, though, he was just a memory. He had fallen during the battle at the mansion a few months earlier, making sure that the Guardian of, not only the estate but also of the whole human race, had been able to fight back the creature which had broken free of the prison it guarded.

He had done this by passing what life force he had left to me when it looked like I was going to be bested by The Zarrulent, the creature I was guarding. That transaction had resulted in a huge surge of power for me which helped me push the beast back into its prison and survive the conflict but it had meant that there was nothing left for him.

He'd been dead before he had fallen to the ground.

I sat up straighter and rubbed at my eyes.

"Are we back?" My voice was that croaky version of itself we all get when we first come to. Mike's ponytail didn't move as he replied.

"Almost there bach. Another ten minutes and we'll be pulling up at the front door. I've called ahead and there will be someone to meet us.

I relaxed back into the seat and blinked my eyes in an attempt to complete my waking. I wasn't sure I needed to have anyone actually receive us as we arrived but was also barely awake. Whatever time it was I'm sure anything that could be done to minimize the amount of work that Mike had to do was a bonus. That said, it wasn't like we were carrying hundreds of bags were we?

After several more minutes the car emerged from the oppression of the wooded driveway out into the open air of the estate courtyard and grounds. The night was draped over the entire open area with what little light there was fighting a battle of its own. There was a huge tidal wave of illumination spilling out of the mansion itself, casting a yellowing glow over the steps to the door, the gravel driveway and the surrounding flower beds and planting. It also covered a fair proportion of the front of the house. The shadows were still there trying to push back against the light but it looked that, up to this point, the light was winning. Beyond the immediate façade of the building, the lights strength was waning.

The gravel of the courtyard area before the house snaked back and away, moving deep into the darkness and towards us. The individual lights of the driveway took on an almost runway-esque appearance as we approached the house. The roadway we had to maintain was clearly marked and Mike was able to keep a swift speed through the night towards the house.

The final piece of illumination which was within the boundary of the trees could be seen off to the right as we travelled. Smaller lights than lined the driveway were gathered around the base of a huge grey obelisk of stone. That stone was in stark contrast to everything else within the lifestyle of the master of the house. Every other detail of the location was one of wealth and station but not that. It had been blasted from the ground during the battle we had all fought here and was all rough edges and random angles. It was bathed in light but I knew without looking what it symbolized and had engraved on it. I had carved a single word into the surface of the stone, REMEMBER.

It was my thanks to those who had fought alongside me when they had been called to but it was also my way of thanking everyone who had fallen in support of the Guardian throughout time. I had been shown how members of The Circle had honoured the fallen Dragons but also how they had never honoured anyone else.

Thousands upon thousands of people would have fallen in service to this cause over the years and they had all been ignored.

I had always wanted there to be a feeling that there was no-more value in the Guardians death in battle as anyone else's. The stone and the crater it loomed over, was my memorial to everyone who had fallen in service, Guardian or not. Each person who had died in that battle had had their name carved into a stone coin which had been cast into the pool at the base of the crater to mirror the memorial of the Guardians.

There was a coin in there with Lloyds name on it.

I missed him.

Mike hadn't turned to look at me but he spoke as if he had.

"Get some sleep when you get in bach. Rest up and we'll be able to take stock tomorrow. We'll give them all a good send off." He'd known what I was thinking about.

I let my head rest against the window as we covered the last few yards towards the front of the house. I let my eyes focus on nothing as we travelled. More names were going to be carved for the pool. We may have only lost four people in the latest battle but those four still hurt.

"Does it get easier?" I asked the question almost of no-one and didn't really expect an answer. Mike returned one anyway.

"You've lost more than a handful of staff since you were welcomed into The Circle. From what I've heard of the past Guardians, they all viewed us underlings as being expendable so they wouldn't have cared about how many people they lost. I think it means that the more pain you feel for the fallen troops you have commanded, the closer you are to being an actual human being."

I smiled at the thought but also at the fact that Mike had agreed with me, been holding the same feelings as me. Equality rather than bowing and scraping.

Pulling up outside the house I could hear the crunching sound of the gravel under the tyres of the car. It immediately snapped me back to the here and now.

Spread around the entrance way to the house were five people who were all dressed in immaculate business attire. Four of them rushed forwards and practically attacked the car as we came to a halt. There was one to open the boot and retrieve the bags, two to open the doors and aid Mike and I as we disembarked the car and another was hovering around the driver's side, apparently waiting to take over from Mike and take the car back whence we had come. The final member of the greeting party still stood at the top of the stairway at the main door, casually watching over the activity. I could recognize Mark's silhouette even before I had left the car.

Mike and I were quickly ushered towards the house.

"Welcome back to the house, sir," rumbled Mark as we climbed the stairs. He gave us both a bow that was uncalled for and, even if it had been, was far too deep. He straightened and stared out into the middle distance as he waited for the correct response from me.

I rolled my eyes and tried to remember what I had to say. Protocol was expected but I was tired.

"*Thank you for receiving me. It is good to be back,*" coughed Mike under his breath as he cleared his throat. I nodded and he smiled to himself as I repeated the phrase, doing my best to infuse it with as much power and authority as I could.

The rest of our welcoming committee quickly hurried into the house and vanished from sight.

"Are you well sir? We have all been very concerned about your health," continued Mark. He nodded a bow towards me as he completed his sentence. The official tone and ordered demeanor remained.

"I'm all good, don't panic. A little jet lagged but nothing major wrong. You?"

"I am well sir. My injuries were dealt with and I was able to return quickly to service." Mark stood stock still as he spoke and showed no emotion on his face.

Odd. I hadn't seen him this uptight since we'd first met.

"How is everything here? No problems with me away?" I asked the second question with as healthy a dose of sarcasm as I could muster, the house and estate would probably do better without me about.

"Every member of the house has performed well in your absence but we are very glad of your return sir."

Mark had been learning to be less official around me and had been starting to show signs of treating me more as a person rather than just a member of his ruling class. His lack of emotion and

93

adherence to the 'correct' wording for each question and response now was more than a little strange.

Time for some subtle probing to get to the bottom of things.

"Are you sure you're OK? You seem a little tense. What have I missed?" See, subtlety and hidden meaning.

If anything, Mark straightened even further, practically shaking all of the muscles in his body as he held himself rigid. "We are very glad you have returned sir and I must only apologise for the extra demands of your time but we have guests who have requested your presence when you arrived."

"Who are they?" I didn't have the first idea of who was here but they were obviously causing a fair amount of stress in my staff.

Mark remained statue still but dropped the very slightest pleading glance down at us both.

Guests? It was daft o'clock in the morning at a secret magical fortress. Who wanted to see me? Looking at the obvious discomfort being exuded by my giant general and getting nothing more than a slight shrug from Mike, I didn't have a great many options.

"Right then. Lead on so I can speak to whoever it is so we can all get some sleep."

11

Mike and I were led quickly down corridor after corridor, passing by various rooms which had a full complement of people hurriedly trying to look both busy yet invisible. Furtive sideways glances greeted me wherever I looked and we were keeping far too fast a pace to have anything good waiting at the other end.

"This is looking a little serious," I whispered to Mike as we both worked to keep up with Mark.

"Indeed. Just act like the Lord of the manor until we know any different. This could be very serious." Mikes response made the situation even worse. What was going on?

Mark silently led us through the estate but I could feel that he was taking us towards the library that I had had my first magical training in with Lloyd. I had had the door to the power at my disposal opened to me in that room. It was all rich woods and leather, every square inch of it was a clear show of wealth and power which had nothing to do with magic or spells.

I think that's why I hadn't been in there since that very first night.

I could feel something strange though as we closed on the room. Any tiredness I had been feeling was quickly being replaced by apprehension.

With each hurried step I could just make out a feeling of 'something' as I went. There was just something, off, like that nebulous sensation in a pitch black room that you get when you know that there is someone in there with you. And we were moving towards it.

Rounding the final corner, the weight of perceived awareness had grown to quite uncomfortable levels but I was given some explanation of why. Ahead of us were two armoured guards who made Mark look something akin to a Munchkin extra from The Wizard of Oz. They both scraped their heavy helmets against the ceiling of the corridor outside the library which I could estimate was roughly twice my height. Twelve feet plus then. They were covered in a similar form of armour as the guards that had accompanied

Leatherpants in Argentina. Heavy chain mail, luxurious fabrics and highly polished metal were all over them and they looked like they were bursting at the seams, slabs of barely controlled muscle forcing against the battle dress.

We closed the distance to the door to the library and they both snapped their gazes onto us. They made us all stop in our tracks just with that withering look and I just knew that my usual brand of greeting and humour would not be appreciated. Mark introduced us.

"The Lord of the Estate, Master of Fire, Anthony Johns and his Head of House for the attention of the Messenger."

They both inspected us silently for an eternal five or six seconds until they had deemed us to be acceptable, then one leaned down and gripped the handle of the door in one of his giant hands and pushed the door open to bid us entry.

Easing past him I could only estimate that my own fifty inch chest was only a third of what he was, even without the armour. His biceps looked to be a better match to my chest. Whoever was inside my house wanting to speak to me was incredibly well guarded. Trying to maintain what little of my composure I had left, I hesitantly made my way into the library. The feeling of unease grew with each step.

Ahead of us, the large stone fireplace was filled with a welcoming fire. It popped and crackled in a way that conjured up feelings of Christmas and cozy nights in log cabins. The other features of the room were as I remembered them. Wood and leather, wealth and luxury. The leather chair that I had managed to bridge jump out into the depths of the wood had never been recovered; instead it had been replaced by a new chair. The match of leather was perfect, of course.

The door was pulled shut behind us and Mike and I had been left alone in the room. Who were we supposed to be meeting?

Looking around quickly I couldn't see any sign of there being anyone with us but the sensation of gathered awareness was stronger than before. Now we were inside the room, I could feel the prickling sensation even more powerfully. My head wasn't spinning in warning of some impending attack but that didn't mean that I wasn't in danger. I hadn't had a spinning mind when Leatherpants had come close to me either but after our meeting I knew he was trouble.

"Show yourself now," I boomed into the room with all of the authority I could muster. Don't show fear, never show fear.

Silence followed.

And followed.

"Come on. I'm not going to stand here all night waiting." I could feel the wince from Mike as I said it but my instincts took over, Fire Dragon after all.

There was no signal of activity but there were suddenly three more people in the room. They were just there. No bridge jumping in through a construct of any kind or closing of another door as they had come in. They were just there.

Two of them were mirror images of the guards who had greeted us outside, towering over everything in the room and making both Mike and I look both tiny and insignificant. The third stood between them, just staring ahead at me. The third person was much smaller than me but the way she carried herself she could never be described as being tiny. Certainly nothing insignificant there.

And she didn't look happy.

12

"Messenger. Welcome to the house. I hope you have not been waiting for too long." Mike had stepped before me in such a liquid movement I wouldn't have been able to make a comment before he greeted our guest. There also appeared to be a new tone of utter deference in his voice.

The Messenger regarded him casually with an expression fixed into a frown, more of boredom than anger. She was dressed head to toe in what looked like a shimmering velvet cat suit of the deepest purple. The attire made subtle emphasis of her shape and it was easy to see that she was very physically imposing. She was possessed of a frame which showed that she had spent a great deal of time taking part in very strenuous physical activity. Looking at the giants who had accompanied her I could only assume that that activity wasn't just confined to a gym and involved a great deal of fighting. She was certainly Xena rather than supermodel.

Her gaze remained on Mike and I could feel the quiet ferocity coming from her. She was obviously the cause of the unease I had been feeling on our way through the house. Whoever she was she had a great deal of power at her disposal.

Then she turned her gaze on me.

It was only now that I was under her gaze that I truly saw her features. Her short red hair sat in a functional rather than showy style and her slightly too large green eyes somehow made her attention seem both welcoming and terrifying. Looking at her I couldn't decide which emotion was winning.

"Guardian. Thou art needed in Egypt. Bring thine retinue and attend in three moons hence." She had a deeper voice that I had expected but it sounded like warm honey as she spoke, no, commanded. Seemed like welcoming was taking the lead.

"Very well Messenger. We will be there as ordered," squeaked Mike from next to me.

Both The Messenger and I turned to face him. I wanted to know more about what was going on and didn't really feel like being ordered about by random people in the middle of the night. I hoped Mike would be able to recognize what I meant in the single look. In the end it was irrelevant. The Messenger had a much stronger effect on him.

Her frown deepened and shadows crawled over her every feature. There was a noticeable increase in the uneasy pressure which had been in the room since we entered and it leaned very hard against my senses. Mike could obviously feel it as well.

He was down to his knees in a flash with his arms outstretched before him, burbling into the carpet.

"Please accept my apologies Messenger, Master. It was not my place to speak as the Guardian. I offer my most humble apologies." His voice was shaking as he spoke and it was easy to see he was fighting against something which was making it difficult for him to speak.Now that did it.

Mike may have done something he shouldn't have done but he hadn't killed someone in a public place. He hadn't defrauded millions from the banking system. He hadn't spoken ill of the Welsh rugby team. So therefore he didn't deserve to be face down on the floor begging for forgiveness from someone I was still undecided as to whether or not deserved this veritable display of worship.

My back straightened and without turning my eyes from the prostrate Mike, I stepped between the Messenger and my Head of House.

Mike gasped from his position on the floor. It was a gasp of pain as whatever was taking place started to squeeze him tighter.

Turning steadily to face the Messenger I could see a mixture of surprise and fury fluttering across her face. The whirling shadows which moved over her like a living thing, all rushed in and around her eyes, creating an almost tangible mask of inky blankness.

"Whatever you're doing, my dear, please release my associate. He didn't mean to do anything wrong but he was acting to help me." I looked through my eyebrows at her in an attempt to create my own feeling of menace but it didn't look like it was having much effect.

She made no movement, but I could feel the pressure building against my head of whatever she was exerting. And there was a better than average chance that if I was feeling the force of it, Mike was really suffering.

"Thine cattle must be shown his station. Would thou allow dishonour to thine guests?" The Messenger didn't turn her head from me as she spoke but I could feel the continuing burning force coming from her.

"Beast, you must know your place," she spat out and the feeling of pressure grew painfully behind my eyes.

Mike screamed at the pain.

Now that, I wasn't going to stand for.

"Release him," I bellowed at the Messenger and took what I was hoping was a mildly reproachful step towards her. I don't think I was that successful.

Her two guards barreled forwards creating a living wall between the two of us. The pressure didn't ease though.

"I said, Release him. NOW!" This was not going to be someone else coming into my house and pushing me and mine around with the minimum amount of fuss. This is my house.

I took another step forwards this time making no attempt to hide the threat within the gesture. The guards reacted in kind. The brute standing on my left hand side reached out one giant arm and gripped tightly around my throat. His gloved hand smelled strangely of wild flowers and it seemed very much at odds with the crushing sensation he was placing on my neck. Time for the Guardian to assert himself.

Without any move to counter the actions of the guard, I pulled my focus together and made my own move.

The Cascade Bridge snapped into existence immediately behind the Messenger and her protection. Even as the guard who held me squeezed, I could see the flickering bolts of power leak from the magical construct I had called into being. I needed the power to be at my disposal and hadn't even thought about the issues of being able to do the deed. I'd just pushed for the power. Looks like I'd re-charged after Argentina.

For an instant, no-one moved. There was no sign of recognition on the face of the Messenger and the two guards who had accompanied her hadn't even flinched at the appearance of the crackling ring of power which was pulling against them.

Their cloaks snapped out horizontally behind them, pulled by the force of the bridge, and both guards started to lean forwards against the force centre of the magic, working hard to maintain the exterior of control.

"I will not have the people of this house treated like slaves just because someone has the power to do so. Everyone in this house is a member of the human race so is therefore under my protection."

Looking at them all I couldn't see any sign of fear or any other emotion creeping into their postures so I pushed harder.

Calling up the power of my transformation, I felt the waves of energy that was the foundation of the Dragon I was, pooling through me. I could make out the sound of my clothes starting to rip and tear as my body changed.

I was soon staring eye to eye with the guards as the mighty monster crawled from me. Despite the full face coverage of the helmets they wore I could make out the fear as I became that monster.

Spreading my arms wide I gave no further signal of what I was doing and surged forwards, forcing the Messenger and her hired help through the bridge.

By the time the bridge construct collapsed in on itself, I was fully in my Dragon guise and I had landed in an almost stereotypical stance of the three point landing, my right arm curled up underneath me as a way to prepare magic if needed.

The guards who had looked so utterly terrifying in the mansion had now lost the aura of menacing brutality. They may have been at least twice my size as humans but now I was the Guardian, I'd managed to trump their strengths. The two of them had been flung backwards by my original thrust and they had smashed into the ground at least fifty feet from our entry point to the grounds of the estate.

They both struggled to stand up amidst the cloying mud of the furrows they had just created, their armour and ceremonial dress now caked in the extra heavy weight of mud. Seeing them both struggle against the horror of physics as the ground seemed to be working against them, took the edge off any fear they may have been able to inspire.

Looking around the scene of chaos before me, I could feel a level of satisfaction growing as I regarded the ones who had been happy to try and throw their weight around in my house. The two guards were still flopping around on the floor like stranded fish marooned so far from the water.

The Messenger, though, was a different story.

She was stood a little further back from her two bodyguards but seemed to be utterly untroubled by the effects of my magical retort.

Straightening myself up to reach my full forty feet in height, I took a single step towards her by way of reinforcing my point. This was my house.

"I hope I've made my point clear. My people will not be treated as slaves by you or anyone. Do you understand?" The boom of my voice was carried across the whole expanse of the grounds of the estate and probably beyond.

The Messenger still didn't move. She just stared back at me with an expression etched onto her face which seemed to convey both anger and disappointment. Well, that's what it looked like to me anyway.

"You attack the Messenger of The Circle, Brute? Know you not, what I am? What I represent?" she narrowed her eyes, "The power I wield?"

"I was always bottom of my class at school, especially at History." Good thinking, diplomacy of the highest order. "No-one will be able to do what they want with the people of this estate just because they can. This is my house."

The Messengers stance didn't change but she gently smoothed down the fabric of her clothing and starred relentlessly at me.

"Thou art Fire. Fire will always fight. If thou dost need demonstration, I shall fight."

The next thing I was aware of was the hammer blow that smashed into my jaw and sent waves of pain flooding through my whole head as it snapped wildly to the right, forcing me backwards and to the floor so quickly that, for a split second, I thought that I'd been hit by a meteor. Stars swam before my eyes and my jaw quickly took on the lolling appearance of any number of fallen prize fighters. There hadn't been any kind of sign from my dizzying early warning system. I was just hit.

I tried to ease myself back to my feet but all I managed to achieve was to send my majestically powerful Dragon form staggering drunkenly across the open ground until it lurched over and crashed into a nearby pool of water. Through the stars and darkness which were both fighting for the control of my vision, I could make out the gentle, almost caring, sound of a female voice drifting through the sky.

"Thou art a Fire. I understand the Fire. Accept my apologies for offending you. The values which you hold will be kept." I was still more than a little woozy but I could recognize the tone of the Messenger. I tried again to get up but met with the same sprawling failure. Out there at the edges of my consciousness, that same female voice continued, but this time the change of tone was clear enough that even I could make it out.

"I will uphold that which you hold dear, but should thy attack my forces or myself, you will be dealt with in a more forward fashion. Thou must view my actions here as a demonstration."

I felt bad already but those words made me feel worse. She'd just 'demonstrated' that she could smash lumps out of me at the drop of a hat. In fact, she could do it ten or twenty times before that hat had even hit the floor. She continued speaking through the haze my attention had become.

"Remain still, my Lord. My guard will attend to your injury. Dost thou require further assistance from thine own estate?"

She rested a hand on the side of my head by way of reassurance and I could just make out the approach of armoured figures through the mud. Her guard I assumed.

There was a succession of odd noises from around me but I made no attempt to identify them or try and see what was happening. All the time this was taking place, the Messenger kept her hand on my head and ensured that I was calm. I'm not sure how she did it but it worked. She just didn't let any worry or concern form in my head, as if she was keeping the would-be normal reactions away from my mind. Eventually, I could make out words from the side of my head. A low whispering chant or words I couldn't recognize but knew were part of a healers casting.

It made me think of another healer I'd known. I missed Lloyd.

The pain and disorientation drained out of me and my mind cleared enough for me to open my eyes and try to look around.

"Remain still, my Lord," spoke the Messenger again, this time with all of the authority and serious edge to her voice removed, this time replaced with a melodious thrum of persuasion. It reminded me of the way Andrea spoke to me when she was at her most alluring. Any burning anger at the indignity of being leveled by the Messenger was quickly burning away as I listened to her speak now.

"You seem to be a good teacher of history," I said as I opened my eyes, thinking hard about the thoughts running through my head concerning the people I'd known.

Looking at the Messenger, I could see that she had no understanding of what I'd just said.

"Don't worry. This whole situation just triggered a few memories that's all." She looked at the ground in a sweeping gesture of old fashioned deference but I'd swear that she had turned a little red.

I sat up gingerly and looked down at the people next to me.

The Messenger was stood rigidly tall and seemed to be totally unruffled by the events which had just unfolded. It appeared that she was utterly untouched by the mud and water surrounding us, her clothing as pristine as it had been when we first met. The two mud covered guards were not in the same condition though. They were both sprawled on the ground next to me, face down. Neither of them moved.

"Did these guys do the healing?"

She nodded in affirmation.

"Are they OK?" I enquired, reaching out to gently nudge the nearest of the two to make certain.

He didn't move.

"Dost thou feel healed?" she asked without acknowledging the guards.

"I feel fine but what about these two?" I nudged him again and still elicited no response. Until his helmet fell from his head and rolled away from him.

"They have given what force of themselves that they must to be able to repair your pain. If they survive, they will be able to do so again."

Looking at the fallen guard without his helmet, I could see that his face was sunken and grey. The long flowing hair which had been hidden under the helmet was spread wildly about, obscuring much of the features of his face. He carried the pallor of a corpse and was just as active. The formally intimidating giants had been rendered nothing more than inert lumps of meat.

Is that what had happened to Lloyd?

I heaved myself to my feet and scooped the two guards up, concentrating my attention on as much magic as I could pull together. With a final push of concentration, I dragged a Cascade Bridge together and thrust my arms through, depositing the two motionless guards in the infirmary of the estate. Withdrawing my grip, I dropped my own shape back to my human self and started to run through.

Turning to the Messenger as I entered the bridge, I gave her my opinion of the situation.

"No-one will give everything to anyone because they feel they have to. I will not be viewed as having the right to everything. Like I said before, this is my house."

The following few hours became a very uncomfortable time to be the Messenger of The Circle. I had my medical staff working on the two guards who had been affected so badly by the healing they had given to me. I also made sure that Mike was treated for any ill effects of the Messengers treatment. This, I'd made certain, had taken place so the Messenger could see everything. Her own guards who were still mobile stood rigidly by her sides all the time as their comrades were treated but I swear I could make out barely perceptible tilts of the head or gentle sways of the body to ensure they always had a view of their fallen fellows. Maybe under all the ceremony and armour there was a being that cared more for friends than for perceived rules of etiquette?

Eventually, my medical director, a mountain of a man called Llewellyn who I'd made it my business to get to know better following the events surrounding my Awakening, declared that everyone he and his people had been working on were going to recover. He said that Mike was likely to be fine after a good night's sleep, the effect of the psychic attack from the Messenger being quite minor but the two guards were much more seriously injured.

"They'll never serve again. They have had a massive amount of their life force removed and they'll probably only live for a further five to ten years. They gave a huge amount of their energies to you."

How hard had she hit me?

I hung my head and contemplated what he was telling me.

Here we go again. More lives handed to me because they had to be.

Turning to the Messenger and her remaining guards, I had emotion burbling around my head but this time it wasn't the usual fire that both the Messenger and I had been expecting. This time it was a resigned sadness.

"I will always do my best to help everyone I can, that's what I am, surely. As far as I can see, the whole purpose of The Circle is to act as the ultimate protection for the human race. We are all charged with one purpose. It seems a little too easy to throw people at a problem rather than looking beyond."

The two guards remained rigidly at the Messengers side but I could make out, thanks to the stark lighting of the room we stood within, that their eyes were flashing back between me, the Messenger and the fallen forms of the other guards.

The Messenger spoke now but without any anger of her own. The deep voice was threaded through with that same steadfast attention to the rules she lived by but also with the barest hint of long past sadness.

"I have passed mine message to thee my Guardian. My role here has been completed. Thou hast been summoned to Egypt and thou must attend."

Without further comment, she bowed her head ever so slightly and she and the two guards were just, gone. Whatever veiling technique she had used had just snapped up and cloaked the three of them. I assume it was a veil rather than any kind of teleport but you never know do you?

I turned back to Llewellyn and was about to thank him and his people when a massive shape reappeared in the room.

Turning to face the presence, I was again facing one of the Messengers guards.

There was nothing spoken by either of us as we stood as statues within the antiseptic surroundings of the infirmary. Our eyes met and there was nothing more for the longest time. Eventually, the giant form leaned forward to stand eye to eye with me. My first thought was this must be how other people feel when they are confronted by the anciently terrifying form of the Dragon that I could become. It was not a very comfortable place to find yourself.

Eventually, the lone guard spoke.

"My gratitude for helping my friends."

Before I was able to answer or indeed, show any kind of response to what had just been said, the guard simply vanished before my eyes.

I turned slowly to look at the other people who had been in the room to acknowledge the shared nature of what had just happened. I knew that this was unheard of. A lowly guard, a military functionary, thanking a Guardian for their actions was a massive deal.

That said, what surprised me more than anything else was the fact that, judging by the voice, and a million other non-verbal signals, under all the armour and the terror of the guard of the Messenger, I'd been speaking to a twelve foot tall woman.

13

The days passed quickly before the allotted appointment. Mike had healed quickly as the doctors had said he would and Mark was back to the usual level of appreciation of the rules of decorum.

I had spent the days just relaxing. This I did because I was incredibly tired.

Despite my best efforts, Mike and Mark made sure that I was waited on hand and foot and ensured that my time was spent comfortably.

The house had been remodeled following the effects of my welcoming to the activities of The Circle.

Gone was the original room which had been the master suite and therefore, mine. After it had been smashed and torn to pieces, I'd made sure that the decoration was now much more to my style, or at least what Andrea thought was more my style. The walls were all a tasteful off white and the flooring had been changed from stone tile to a thick beige carpet. The massive tapestries had gone as well but I had wanted to keep the same message that they had been showing. Instead, there was a small area on the left hand side of the room which held a small photograph of every member of the staff here at the estate. They weren't passport photos or anything quite so staged but they each showed the person at a time when they were having fun. Images of family and friends were spread over a very wide area as everyone I came into contact with had given me a picture.

They all served to remind me of the position that I held as part of The Circle but it also served perfectly as being an impromptu album of my newest family. I'd missed out on my own tight knit family thanks to the actions of our enemies, The Hive, but now I was in a position to create new bonds and feel that sense of belonging I'd always felt was just out of reach.

The wide windows were back at the front of the house but now the entire roof area had been replaced by glass. The individual areas of glass skylights had been removed as I made certain of a clear view of the sky. There were also sprinkled about, several pieces from my own collection. I'd relocated several nuggets of my own from my flat back in London which included framed movie posters (Star Wars and Hellraiser being the highlights), a stash of sci-fi box sets to be watched whenever the mood took me and assorted other bits and pieces that made me, me. I also had a Hulk figurine smashing something heavy next to my bed. The connections to the creature losing control were too cool not to highlight.

The building work had taken no time at all. It hadn't even needed to be transferred to outside contractors. Instead, a vast force of people from within the staff had been able to get everything done in a matter of days. I'd offered to do some of the heavy lifting myself but had been told that that just wouldn't have been acceptable. My protestations of the availability of a Dragon to lift materials and truly do the heavy lifting were quickly swept aside so I let everyone get stuck in on their own.

There was even a little extra security incorporated into the structure. Mike had been keen to avoid any further chance of the Guardian of the estate being attacked in his room as he slept so had insisted that a few extra 'safeguards' as he called them, be installed. I hadn't ever been able to get a straight answer from him concerning the exact details of what he'd actually had put in but he always smiled when I asked for details, saying I'd have to just enjoy the show if all of the other defences fail.

The majority of the time since the visit of the Messenger I'd spent just lazing about between the master bedroom and a TV room I'd managed to put together. It was basically the same room as it had been before but I'd thrown in a comfy chair which didn't scream lord of the manor and a small fridge to hold a few well-earned beers. All it meant was I had one of the best places to watch films and sports you could possibly imagine.

I had, though, spent a great deal of time discussing with Mike, just what was likely to be happening in Egypt and why I was being called there.

"Anything to do with Egypt is a massive deal," Mike offered by way of explanation.

"Why? Strategic pyramid purposes?" I just couldn't help myself.

Mike shook his head and took a deep breath, maybe stifling a laugh? Unlikely.

"The site in Egypt is where the Mage is truly based. I've never seen a need for the Guardians to be called to Egypt in my lifetime." Mike and I were sat in my TV room, both relaxing as much as we could; me slumped back in my comfy chair with highlights of the last Wales 6 Nations Championship win playing on the eighty inch TV. I didn't even know you could get an eighty inch TV.

Mike was sat at my side in a slightly less comfortable chair and he even made it look like that was causing him some form of discomfort. Too much of a good thing?

"The Guardians? Plural? This call is given out to more than one of us?"

"It is indeed. I was told of the process that calls The Messenger into service and it only happens when there is the gravest calling from the Mage. The Messenger being brought out has always signaled the fact that The Circle is facing something very serious." Mike explained without letting a vast amount of emotion spill into his words.

This did sound serious.

"Why did this happen in the past? If you've just been told the stories then it doesn't happen that often?"

Mike ran his hand over his white hair.

"I'm not that old you know?"

We both chuckled briefly. The feeling of growing closeness was a huge benefit between the Guardian and the Head of House. There was no way that I wanted my closest adviser in all of this to be feeling like he's only there because he has to be. That and it was good to have a friend.

Mike continued after the laughter between us had drained away.

"The Guardians are kept apart as much as possible. The fewer connections between them the better."

"Why? That makes no sense at all." All I could see was the benefits of working together and Mike's point made little sense to me.

"You watch lots of TV don't you?" Mike suddenly changed direction with what he was saying and I could feel the familiar crease of ignorance spreading across my forehead.

"You've seen Friends, haven't you?" He continued, noticing that I was showing minimum comprehension.

110

"Imagine all six members of the Friends cast had come to work together in the same minibus. What would have happened if the bus had crashed on the way to the studio and everyone on it had been killed? How would the show have been able to continue without the whole cast?"

I looked at him and the frown deepened.

"If Friends had lost one of the stars because of an accident like that, they would have been able to continue to make the show. If they'd lost all six of them then the show would have stopped dead. The Circle is the same. There is no way that there could be any risk of having all of the Guardians together in one place unless there was the utmost need. We lose one Guardian, we can go on. We lose them all, well, you can imagine."

I let that fact sink in.

Despite the Friends analogy, it made sense. If you brought all of The Circle into one place there was going to be a massive risk that any attack which could affect one could affect all of them. Thinking back to my own Awakening I was able to start picking out the number of suspicious glances and concerned groups from my memories.

I'd always thought that there had been a level of mistrust from everyone concerned with The Circle because I was the new kid on the block, outside what was usually done and unknowing of what was expected, but it would appear that my initial fears had been misplaced. Well some of them anyway.

Maybe the suspicion had been truly down to the fear of having all of these mighty forces together at one time?

"So what was the reason everyone was gathered together last time? Is there any chance that's happening again?"

Mike chuckled quietly to himself.

"The last time was just before the start of the Second World War. To be fair though, the meeting lasted for less than a minute when everyone was told what they were there for. No-one saw the war as being anything to do with them and the feeling was that each and every site we oversaw was safe from the effects of the fighting to come. I was told that Mr. Ward had been pointing out to The Elder that there could be some issues caused by such a wide reaching conflict and that was why the meeting was called but the rest of The Circle quickly put him in his place."

The thought that Leatherpants was given a very public dressing down put a smile on my face. He really did see himself as being above everyone else.

"What about before that? What was it that got everyone together before that?"

Mike mulled it over.

"The plague. There was widespread death and disease in the fourteenth century which killed close to two hundred million people. It was put down to being just a nasty strain of disease which happened to flourish but it actually came from a biological attempt to destroy The Circle. Some bright spark in The Hive had been stockpiling the venom of one of their masters and used it as a chemical weapon. The creature is the one that The Elder is guarding. The attack started in China and spread throughout the world from there."

I sipped steadily on my beer as he spoke, all the time considering what was being said, hoping that a small kernel of insight would leap out and help me start to put the whole picture together.

Nothing came.

"So everyone was called together in Egypt to discuss what to do next. What happened?"

"You were there. Have a look and see." There wasn't any frustration in Mikes tone but he was pointing out something I should have known. Realising what he meant, I closed my eyes and started to let my mind wander to the shared memories of the previous Guardians of my line. I was still a little wary of looking at them all too often. The one thing that they always had was the quick temper of the Fire Dragon as the main emotion. What I needed more than anger was perspective so the memories were only called on should there be no other options.

Picking through the images which floated before my mind's eye was harder than I had first thought. I tried to aim for the appropriate time period but kept getting lost at the last moment, ending up reviewing any number of castle scenes, banquets or battles. This was getting more than a little frustrating.

"Michael. Can you give me a few clues as to where I need to be looking? I'm doing my best but I can't pick it out."

I must have looked very odd with my eyes partially closed, frowning deeply as I asked for help navigating my own mind. Mike helped without complaint.

"You'll be able to see a dark cavern filled with all the Dragons. It should be quite a singular memory."

The gentle insult of his answer made me slightly angry but also made me smile. Maybe he was starting to learn a great deal about the need to treat everyone as a person no matter where they come from?

I looked inwards again, aiming for the largest number of scales that I could find, but again, each effort sent me to the wrong areas again and again.

This was getting annoying.

"The definition of insanity is doing the same thing over and over and expecting different results."

This wonderfully mocking sentence was delivered with a different voice. One that hadn't been in the room when I had closed my eyes, but which I was very happy was there now.

I kept my eyes closed but let the images floating before my mind slip away to nothing. As they disappeared, the smile spread lopsidedly across my face.

"You know, it really is rude to insult The Guardian of the estate in his home. I will have to make sure my people deal with you in the appropriate fashion. Michael?"

Even with my eyes closed I could sense the fact that Michael was still on edge with the thought of being this relaxed around what he still perceived as his superiors.

I hadn't seen Andrea since she had been motionless in the hospital bed in Federico's estate in Argentina. She had watched as I had a small disagreement with Leatherpants and had been silent throughout the entire exchange with The Elder. Thinking back, I wondered if she'd been awake when I'd explained my feelings about her to The Elder.

Andrea broke the silence and I was quickly back into the here and now.

"All Guardians must be able to withstand a wide range of attacks. Can't you defend yourself against mere words?" Her voice was its usual cultured tone and carried the accent wonderfully as it always did. Opening my eyes I found that Andrea was stood directly ahead of me, dressed casually in perfectly fitting jeans and a pure white shirt. She was nonchalantly leaning her weight on one hip as she stood with her arms folded. She also carried a very playful expression on her face.

Mike nodded to both of us and excused himself. He too had a smile on his face but it wasn't the same as Andreas.

As the door clicked shut behind him, Andrea made her way to a leather sofa which resided against the left most wall. She practically melted into position and stared at me, her eyes smoldering so much that they practically had smoke coming from them.

"My lady. What brings you to my humble abode?" I climbed from my seat and started to make my way towards her.

"I felt that you may be in need of some explanation about what was happening around you. I assume you've met the Messenger by now?" She remained recumbent on the sofa, oozing an animal sense of passion. For a creature of ice she was showing a very strong grasp of all things fiery.

"Mike told me all about what's coming and yes, I have met the Messenger. We had a small disagreement but I think I've turned her around."

I slipped onto the sofa next to Andrea and tried to return her sultry gaze with something similar of my own but I swear that I fell very short.

Andrea froze as I sat down. She remained in the same languid position but her 'heat' had gone totally.

"Mike has told you everything has he? So you don't need me to help you?"

"I didn't say that. Mike's been giving me a run-down of what's happening. If you know anything else, I'd be more than happy to hear what you've got to tell me." I knew that I was suddenly walking a very high tightrope but I didn't know why.

Andrea seemed to take this onboard and continued.

"You were looking to passed memories for information concerning the specifics of the content of the meetings we are being summoned to, yes? You do need to know but that won't give you what you need. Word of mouth is the only way to make certain that the correct information is passed down the line of time."

She was still laying over the arm of the sofa but now some of her enthusiasm was returning.

"Of course I need as much help as I can find. We've got to be in Egypt tomorrow so can you give me the breakdown of what I'm likely to be confronted by? As you've pointed out already, I'm flying blind in my studies."

Andrea seemed to think about this and her posture relaxed somewhat.

"Good. The reason you can't see these memories is that the site in Egypt is soul bound to reality."

I looked at her blankly.

"The whole site is kept in the present for all those who experience it. Everyone who is called will be able to take part in the groupings which take place but there is no way that anyone involved will be able to take memories from the room where we all meet. The meeting will only take place in reality. There is no way a memory of the event, therefore something from the past, will be able to escape the meeting."

"Well that makes no sense. How is everyone expected to be able to carry out the orders of the meeting? If everyone forgets what they talked about, how do they get anything done?"

"We have a large group of scribes who record all of the details we need. The records are sealed for the view of the senior members of the house only. The scribes themselves reside at the site but they never retain any of details of any gathering. At least that means we can trust them never to divulge our secrets. Having to kill, find and re-train scribes every time the Guardians gather would be a wholly unproductive situation."

This time it was my turn to lose the heat.

Her last comments had again highlighted the difference between us. Despite everything I had been saying to her since I had entered her world; she still hung tightly to the dogmatic expectations which had always been thrown around. People lower down the ladder than her were seen as disposable.

She noticed the change in me quickly.

"I was trying to make a joke you petulant fool. You've got to try to remember that the whole world isn't out to get you. Stop looking for faults in everything that's said around you."

I tried to hold on to my righteous indignation but my grip just wasn't strong enough. Maybe Andrea was right? Did I always fall to the default setting of wanting to rage against the machine? Was I looking for perceived slights when there was just conversation? Granted, there was still a massive amount of the way The Circle as a whole, and individual members (cough, Leatherpants, cough), did things but their methods had been working that way for thousands of years and up to this point seemed to have done a bang up job. There was also no way that I'd be able to get everyone to suddenly change their behaviors overnight. It was a minor miracle to have made the changes that I had already, Andrea making her joke now being a sign that things were different for her.

I relaxed my own posture and nodded my understanding.

Andrea maintained her blank expression but showed that she was pleased that I'd calmed down. Maybe that meant that I was changing too?

She continued with her lesson.

"When we all enter the bastion which is the Mage's domain, we are expected to lead our retinue to the correct area."

"Our retinue? Our eyes are going somewhere without us?" I tried to inject a shot of my own humour into the dialogue. By the expression on Andrea's face, now really wasn't the time. She continued after casting me in the full force of one of her icy gazes.

"The retinue will be made up of the senior members of the house force. The Head of House, your general, a healer and an honour guard of at least three of your most able warriors. The stronger the force you should be able to present will be seen as a show that you are willing to protect the whole with your best if needed."

Mulling over what she had said, the group I was expected to take practically picked itself. Mike, Mark and my medic Llewellyn were the named members of the team and the strongest and most able fighters would be easy to round up. Mark had seen every one of the 'team' up close so he would be able to help me find those most to The Circle's tastes. That just left where I was supposed to be taking them.

"How will I know where I've got to take them all when I'm in the memory-less room? What's the correct area?" Andrea looked at me like I had wild squeaky panic in my voice but I swear I'd managed to hit casual curiosity.

"Within the hall, all The Guardian seating is evenly spaced around the edges of a vast space. You'll be able to recognize exactly where you've got to go, probably more than most, trust me. Behind each Guardian Throne is the stone carving of the horror that we stand guard over. You should be able to recognize the form very easily."

Well that was a positive. I could picture the face of The Zarrulent, the brute which was imprisoned in the prison I was charged with guarding without any effort. I'd had a few nightmares after the fighting of what Mark had been calling the Mighty Restraining. It sounded a little strange to say the least but it made him happy. That said, there was a level of pride involved in my decision. In a thousand years, it would sound really cool on a tapestry of some kind.

I took all of the information in and turned it all over in my mind. It seemed to be a very basic set up in terms of pomp and ceremony and that fact threw me off a little. There appeared to have been a huge amount of importance placed on the correct protocol being used in the correct situation from all levels of The Circle. Each and every member of the houses had a rigid expectation that if one thing happened, then they must respond in another set way. Deviation from the prescribed pathways was almost viewed as being the most heinous of crimes. I say almost, but I bet that Leatherpants would have people strung up for not using the correct fork at the dinner table.

Calming myself from my usual anger, I got back on track with my tutorial.

"What happens in the meeting proper? Is there anything I'm expected to do or say?"

Andrea adjusted herself in the sofa and continued what she had to say. There was now no hint of her previous levels of interest in me. She had moved completely on to a teaching session rather than anything else. I was again the student that needed her to show me the correct way to behave.

"The issues affecting The Circle will be discussed and a course of action will be decided upon. The Mage will chair the meeting and any decisions will be made quickly in line with previous precedents. From what I've been told and what I've read, these gatherings are rarely extended beyond what is absolutely necessary so it should be over quickly, allowing us all to move on with what needs to be done to combat what is affecting us."

That sounded positive. The last thing I needed after the succession of battles in Argentina was for there to be long, drawn out discussions which would most likely be more treacherous to navigate than the fighting. That meant that I didn't have a great deal of homework to occupy my mind. And Andrea was here and had been showing signs of warming to me again. Sliding up close to her, I thought I'd see how she felt.

"So you came all the way here, just to make certain that I was up to speed on the expectations of this meeting we've all been called to. Thank you for your concern but it would appear that you've given me all the information I could have needed very quickly. Maybe your fears about my welfare have been somewhat misplaced?" I tried to hold my expression of cloaked animal suggestion as I spoke and waited now as she pondered how to respond.

That response was not slow in coming.

"You think that everything is easy, don't you? I have come here to be able to show what is expected of you, in line with the task given me by The Mage at your Awakening, and all you see is that you already knew what needs to be done." She stood up quickly and threw me backwards on the sofa so I landed prone, much like an over-turned tortoise, staring back at her.

"The gifts of my knowledge and insight are not to be taken lightly. If you feel that you are able to survive the deep waters of what you are about to enter, then I bid you success at their navigation."

With that, she turned on her heels and marched towards the big screen which was still showing rugby highlights. Before she hit the wall, a blazing cascade bridge ring snapped into being, and she was through and away from me.

I sat there on the sofa, staring after the spot she had vanished through. The hanging T.V. screen rocked gently as if hit by an unseen breeze as it settled back to the calm it had before. I wasn't entirely sure what had just happened but I was pretty certain that I'd made a massive mistake.

"It was just a joke," I said after the collapsed ring, almost pleading that Andrea would hear me, but she didn't. We'd both made the same mistake during our conversation but at least she'd had the chance to explain herself.

Settling myself into a comfortable seated position, I was left to consider what was going to happen in Egypt. Thanks to today's little effort, now I had something else to worry about.

14

Despite my best efforts, sleep didn't come easily to me that night and I was left to lay staring up through the vast skylights at the clouds of the night sky. The unknown of this gathering was playing on my mind but also the need to speak with Andrea again. Add in the knowledge that I wouldn't be able to remember a single detail of what was being discussed during what I was being summoned to made the whole state of affairs develop into something which had more sharp horns covering its body than I did. Eventually, the sun crept above the horizon and the new day was beginning.

Resigning myself to the fact that there was going to be no more sleep, I heaved myself up and out of my bed, hoping that my mood would improve as I stood up. It didn't. Through the early dawn light, all I could think of was the fact that I was again going to be thrust into a place where I was woefully under prepared for what was awaiting me. I did know that there was likely only going to be a relatively small amount of expectations on what I was saying or doing but I was still nervous. Add to that the knowledge that I would soon have to be speaking with Andrea again, and I was really in trouble. Showering quickly and dressing as appropriately as I could think, in a black suit and deep maroon shirt, I made my way down the stairs and headed towards the kitchens.

Since I'd first been welcomed into this house, the kitchens had always been a great comfort to me. Not because I felt a strong kinship with the people who worked there, although I had got to know them all very well, but because this was where I could usually find Mark and Mike. These men had been my closest confidantes since I'd started out as the Guardian and as such were the two that I trusted beyond all others in my house. Wandering casually into the kitchens, it still blew my mind the level of activity that could be found in here at any time of day or night.

Today was the carbon copy of any number of days as white clad staff members hustled and bustled around the space, all with a very determined focus on the purpose of their movement. Looking around

I was struggling to be able to pinpoint anything as there was steam and all manner of other gases emanating from the various foods which were being prepared. Taking a deep breath through my nose, I was able to bombard my sense of smell with a startling range of smells, all of which were connected to a wonderful taste. Working my way through the cacophony of aromas, I could make out the expected bacon, sausage and egg of the full English but there was also the more subtle hint of laver bread and cockles floating about, component parts of the full Welsh. These and fish, curries and other roasted meats were smells all trying to take ownership of my nostrils.

Looking around the room, sifting through the smells and sounds which were jumping up at me like an excited puppy, I was able to eventually pick out Mark at the back of the room, casting a severe eye over everything which was going on before him. He looked every inch the hard task master, dressed still in his chef's uniform, but his expression was that of a man who was equally at home on the battlefield. He expected the best from his people because that was what he would be expecting of himself.

Straightening myself up as tall as I could manage and pushing as much lordly authority into my stride, I worked my way through the melee to stand at his side. The other people in the kitchen carried on their duties but were all very careful to give me a clear path as I walked.

"Morning sir." Mark greeted me in his usual deep tone without releasing the kitchen as a whole from his gaze. Everyone else knew the eye of expectation was on them and I could already sense the extra starching of postures in reaction to my appearance.

"Morning Mark. You're up early? What's going on?"

"Just preparation for the day sir. I want to make certain that this event passes correctly. The Guardian must be fully alert for what is expected today and I will make sure that you are."

I smiled to myself at his words. I thought I'd been getting a little on edge about the day. At least I was the boss. They were pretty much stuck with me. If anyone else did something unforgivable they could expect a great deal more than just a scowling put down. Suddenly all of the fears I'd had for the day started to drain away as I thought about everyone else in this room and I was quickly very tired, a massive weight of nervous energy leaving me with the realization that it wasn't only me who was going to be under the microscope.

My need to be active and up and about was rapidly draining away and seeing what was happening in the kitchen showed me that my presence was going to be viewed as yet more pressure being added to a situation which really didn't need it.

"Thanks mate. Will you bring me up the full works please? That's exactly what I'll need at this awful time of the day."

I slapped him once on the back as I left as a way of showing that we were more than just master and servant. I'd been aiming at slightly too hard which seemed to be the only way anyone seemed to do it to me but judging by Marks utter lack of reaction, I'd feel confident in saying that I'd missed what I'd been aiming for.

Heading back into the hallway, towards the stairs which would take me back to my room, my mind was drifting to all corners of everywhere rather than being focused on the here and now. The formally elusive sleep was now circling me like an unseen predator and it was just at that point that I absent mindedly walked into the hurrying form of Mike.

"Sorry Michael. Was in my own little world there. You're up early? Nervous about today?" I could see from the deep creases which were etched over his forehead that he was feeling the weight of worry. Coupled to that the slightly mussed condition of his hair and the twitching glances and it looked like he'd been up all night working.

"Indeed sir," he breathed and started to ease his way passed me, obviously in a rush to complete whatever task he had before the events of the day could begin in earnest. I let him go but called after him.

"Don't beat yourself up too much. Whatever fun and games we've got waiting for us can't be that bad. If in doubt, blame me."

He carried on out of view without acknowledging the comment, so I was left alone again. If Mike was feeling the stresses of expectation to the level that he obviously was, this gathering of Guardians *really* must be a big deal. Locking that thought away, I headed back to my room to await the allotted hour.

The food was brought up and I was quickly through all of it. As far as I could place, I had a few hours before I was due to bridge jump my selected team of staff to Egypt. Even before the decision was made, I was laying on the bed, asleep.

My dreams ran through the usual collection of mismatched images, like my memory had been shuffled and dealt out in a new and exciting hand. Images from my life and from the Guardians who had preceded me wafted around, giving the whole feel of a very poorly made action film. I let the images swim and made no attempt to truly watch them. I knew that whatever was going to happen today, it wouldn't hold any place in my mind. If anything, this made the sleep even more relaxing.

I was eventually woken with a very gentle nudge.

Forcing my bleary eyes to peel open against the wonderful effects of sleep, I could make out Mike standing over me, a serious smile on his face.

"Sorry bach. We've left you here as long as we could but it's time to get underway." His tone was apologetic but there remained that familiar hint of humour. Propping myself up on my elbows I tried again to get my eyes fully open and my brain fully engaged. Still wasn't looking that good.

"You get all your jobs done? You don't seem quite so stressed as you did earlier."

Mike's smile grew wider at that. He still held the expression of concern but he was looking happier at me asking after him. He offered me his hand and helped me to my feet.

"You'll need to change your attire sir," he continued. "I'm afraid your current choice has reacted badly to your rest."

Looking down as he directed, it was easy to see that my previous choice of lordly apparel was now looking far from lordly. Creases had been allowed to roam freely over every area of my clothing and there seemed to be at least two different stains from the food which had been brought in.

"Right. I'll go change. Get everyone together and I'll meet you all out the front of the house in twenty minutes."

Without further discussion I was across the room, heading for the bathroom and hopping out of my clothes. I heard the heavy wooden door whisper closed as Mike left me and knew that I had to put my mind together quickly for what was already shaping to be one of the most vitally important days of my life.

I was down the stairs and at the arranged spot a full five minutes faster than I had told the others. They were all stood waiting for me anyway. Casually stepping down to meet them I was again back trying to exude the maximum amount of power and authority. Judging from the reactions from most of the assembled group, I'd managed to have a little success. Maybe I was growing into the role as the leader of this estate?

"Good choice sir," Mike offered as I approached them. I straightened my grey jacket and thanked him.

"You guys all look a little swish. Suddenly I feel a little under dressed." Mike and Mark smirked ever so slightly but not that the others with us would have seen. Mike had selected three members of the staff here to act as the honour guard and they had a very creepy quality about all of them. They were triplets so were identical. Reviewing the assembled crowd, I did my best to push the ceremonial review posture forward but I don't think I was that successful. The three guards all worked in the estate as the maintenance crew. I'd seen them in action when they had been doing a startling amount of work on the re-building of the house following my attempts to knock it down. The three men were of average height, average build with average faces. They all had the same average haircut and stood in such a manner as to make your eyes just pass right over them. Indeed, it was only the memory of them being so massively active during the building work that I was able to really pay them any heed at all. Thinking about it, that bland, magnolia averageness could be a very useful trait where we were going.

All of the people I was having accompany me were dressed ready for battle. They all wore the full tactical regalia I'd seen on so many of the people who fought with us. There were pieces of worked armour covering arms, shoulders, chest and back. It was all polished to within an inch of its life and I could see six reflections of myself looking equal parts amused and intimidated. They all wore a black undershirt, black combat trousers and combat boots and looked like they were just ready to take part in the most well-presented fight you could imagine.

"Are we all ready to go?" was all I could think to ask and I was greeted by six curt nods.

"Whenever you are sir," Mark bellowed and the inference was clear. Concentrating my mind, I summoned the power in my head to bring a Cascade Bridge into being and linked it with the desired spot in Egypt. You don't have to have an exact image of where you're going, or be able to see where you want to land. Instead, you create the details of the jump point by the 'feel' of your intended target. The ring of crackling energy snapped into existence as I held a crude picture of the Mage sat on a pyramid in my head. Not really the most inventive but that never stopped me being effective before.

"I'm ready now team. Shall we?" and I gestured through the magical construct with one arm as I bowed slightly.

"Stay between us all sir," Mark pointed out as the people he'd selected for this task fell into position around me. I felt comforted by the close protection but was still worried by what may be waiting for us on the other side of this bridge.

15

The gateway snapped shut behind us with the barest hint of a breath of air. The first thing that hit me was a sweeping blanket of unbelievable heat. It was like being punched in the chest as each inhalation had become at least forty percent harder. I could feel the beads of sweat forming all over my body in seconds. Maybe the grey suit wasn't such a good idea? Squinting my eyes against the blazing sun, I looked around my surroundings, trying to work out where we were.

My first instinct was that it was nothing like the films. In every film I've ever seen which included a trip to see the pyramids, everyone always ends up in the middle of the desert, surrounded by sand dunes. For everyone's future reference, the pyramids that everyone sees on the TV are actually in Cairo proper, not the middle of nowhere. Looking around us, I could see the vastly commanding forms of the pyramids of Giza practically kicking sand in our faces as they loomed over all of us, but as I turned I was confronted by the Sphinx and then Burger King, McDonalds and at least half a dozen other company brands which can be found in any city around the world. For that delightful moment, I must have looked a picture of power and authority as I stood there with my mouth open and a slightly confused expression on my face.

"This way please."

The voice had come from behind everyone, which had been some feat considering we had all been facing in different directions. Mark was the first to reach the owner of the voice, both his ham like fists burning with an angry blue fire as he slammed into the small, dark skinned man in white robes and hammered him to the ground.

"I mean no harm to my Lord Guardian or his retinue. I am merely here as a welcome to bring you to the Mage." His accent lilted over the words and he was almost begging for forgiveness as he spoke, never once taking his eyes off me as he pleaded, the hulking form of Mark over him giving him no concern at all.

The other members of the group had immediately encircled me as an act of protection but it had been clear, even to me, that if this person had wanted to hurt me in any way he would have been able to do so without announcing his presence. Besides, he'd used the word retinue.

I walked up to Mark and placed a calming hand on his shoulder.

"Let him go. He's one of us. Besides, we don't want to anger everyone around here with the flaming hands and armored presence."

Mark remained rigidly atop our welcoming committee, crouched with one hand poised to hurl who knew what at him, but the fire slowly started to die away. After another handful of breaths, Mark stood up and practically threw the tiny man to his feet. Dusting him off a little too roughly, Mark returned to his position amongst our group and we all waited.

Our welcome finished straightening himself and bowed deeply to me.

"My name is Ashraf and I am here to bring you to the audience of the Mage. You also don't have to concern yourself with others seeing us. We are within the shield of the prison site so we are all quite invisible and intangible to the tourists and locals. Please, follow me." He gestured towards the heavy stone wall of the pyramid next to us and started to move away.

We all followed after him, my armoured bodyguards looking in every direction as they fanned around me, trying to create a living wall between me and any would-be assassin.

We made our way quickly towards the nearest of the pyramids which happened to be the smallest of the three, and Ashraf reached out a hand and ahead of us a small doorway appeared in the stone and the blackness of the space ahead of us stood as both a welcome and a threat. Ashraf headed into the darkness without waiting to see if we were following him. Leaning in to speak with Mike, I gave him a breakdown of my fears.

"Keep your eyes open will you. I think this could quickly become a very unpleasant meeting if we let it. We need to be sure we don't end up in any more trouble than we're likely to be."

Mike nodded and whispered back to me without breaking step or turning to face me.

"Don't worry bach, we'll be fine in here but if things do start to go in an odd direction, we'll be OK."

I decided that what he was telling me was reassuring despite not really feeling the level of reassurance I thought I should.

We all passed beyond the threshold of the mighty stone wall and started into the boundless black ahead. No sooner had we all crossed through the opening, did the wall begin to reform in on itself, filling the space we had just used to gain entry. The deep sound of grating stone and tumbling sand was all we could hear as the last remaining sunlight was blocked from view. We all stood motionless in the dark. I'd been forcing myself to remain totally still as the magic worked behind us, fighting my natural instinct to run screaming for the outside world. Listening to the breathing which was coming from around me, I was the only one who was in this situation.

All the others who were around me hadn't even reacted as far as I could make out. I could pick out everyone's breathing as it was uniformly calm and I could feel nothing more than a subtle curiosity as to the details of what was going to be ahead of us.

Just at the edge of my senses I could pick out the mind of Ashraf. It was the only unfamiliar mind in the darkness, all the others being the group I'd come in with. There was no hint of any kind of duplicity or subterfuge in him, which was something I supposed. All I could make out was a slightly hurried focus, as if he was trying in vain to complete what should have been an easy task but was finding it harder and harder as the seconds passed by.

Eventually I could make out a level of relaxation as he managed to complete whatever task had been proving so troublesome, and there was a flash of light as he called into being a diffuse glow from a small stone which rested on his outstretched hand.

We were all stood in a small, non-descript cave more than a room of any kind, and there was nothing but bland stone making up the surrounding walls and ceiling. The floor was covered with a deep layer of sand. Looking around the space, I was reminded of the simple appearance of the opening of the tunnels down to my own underground fortress. This area wouldn't be indicative of what I was about to find as we continued.

"This way gentlemen, please. Follow me if you will."

Without further ado, he turned and headed down the tunnel which was directly behind him and started to make his way into the depths of the pyramid, the circle of his illumination radiating around the tunnel.

The journey down was without further incident as we made our way, led by the constant pleading of Ashraf. I could feel the decline of the tunnel and, despite my best efforts, I started to feel a little more on edge with every step deeper we took. Images of ambushes or assorted attacks filled my mind. I may have been a mighty force of supernatural horror but within the confines of the tunnel we were in, my Dragon would be useless. There was no spinning in the back of my head. I couldn't feel anything beyond the casual, almost bored, sensations coming from the team around me so there was no rational reason for my fear but when you get down to it, I was in the dark underground. Eventually, it became too much.

"Ashraf. How many others are here already? Are we the first to arrive? The last?" I had to make some kind of conversation to break the silence.

"I believe that there have been several arrivals already, master." Ashraf managed to reply in the most perfunctory fashion while still moving down the tunnel as he bowed to me.

"So are we the last to arrive?" Please let there be others still to get here.

"I do believe that you are the final Guardian to attend this day. I will direct you through to the audience chamber immediately. Mr. Ward was very keen that the ceremony commence at the earliest convenience."

Wonderful. Everyone was already here and now Leatherpants was throwing his weight around. What a fantastic start to the day.

All I managed to say to Ashraf was a curt "Thank you" but I think that Mike and Mark could read that I hadn't liked what I'd been told.

Mike was fast to speak into my ear.

"Someone had to be last in, don't panic."

"That's easy for you to say. I'm the one who is in the sights of his Leatherness. He's got a bad impression of me as it is without me adding fuel to the fire."

"Don't worry bach" said Mike. "Whatever happens, remember, I'm here to protect you," and with that he slapped me with that familiar, just too hard clap, on the arm.

He was right. Concentrate on what I was able to address.

"If I'm the last one in, what have I got to do? Is this just an overblown board meeting?"

Mike looked sideways at me.

"From what I've read, the Guardian must be seated in their official point within The Circle to form the link between everyone. Their honour guard is expected to sit at their feet in readiness should they be needed. After that, it's just pomp and ceremony as everyone discusses what the issue of the day is. Simple."

It certainly sounded simple. Sit in special chair, talk about issue at hand, and leave. My mood began to lift slightly. Then Ashraf stopped, turned to face us and spoke.

"We have arrived at the Great Audience Chamber my lord. Will you all please take your places and I will signal that all is in order."

Walking through the small opening which was the end of the tunnel, we all entered into a massive subterranean space which was similar to the one under Neath Abbey back in Wales. The fact that this was a huge underground room was where the similarity ended though.

Whereas the cavern in Wales was a very basic space where the glyph decorated obelisk which was the magical lock for my own magical captive, sat alone in the centre of the room; this was at least five times the size and carried the presence more of concert hall than ancient prison. On the walls all around the cavern were huge stone carvings of Dragons of all shapes and sizes, all depicting heroic battles of a bygone age. Taking in as much of the detail as I could, I was able to see carvings of my own Dragon form fighting at different points. There were also other Dragons I could recognise so it must have shown all of the monsters who were part of The Circle. There were flaming torches to provide light at strategic points around the walls. No encroachment of modern technology in this room. Each of these torches was more the size of a double decker bus so was pulsing out a great deal of light. Despite the massive scale of the space we were in, they seemed able to pump out more than enough light so I was able to see clearly every detail around me.

I had no idea how deeply we had travelled beneath the surface but the oppressive heat which had greeted us as we had stepped from the Cascade Bridge had been held at bay. It had been replaced by a very temperate climate which was immediately calming. I could also make out the smell of burning wood coupled with burning something else coming from the torches.

At the centre of the room was a large ring of huge thrones carved from the very stone of the cavern. I could see, even from this distance, they were so much more than just functional seats. They all carried the same beautifully detailed carving work that was adorning the rest of the cavern and each had the feel of a seat of huge magical power, exactly what was called for a meeting of the most powerful creatures on Earth.

The thrones formed a ring which included at the far end of the cavern, a large block dais with carved runes and glyphs all over its surface. There was a much smaller chair at the centre of the dais and it was flanked by the two largest thrones of the massive ring. That smaller chair was still to receive its occupant.

From our vantage point, we all stood dumfounded. It was clear that we were on the edge of the walkway which led down to the floor of the space and on to where the events of the day were going to take place. This really was more than I had expected to see by several orders of magnitude. For that delightful second, I was utterly lost.

That was until the realization that all of the thrones bar one were occupied by the Dragon forms of The Guardians of The Circle. They were all looking at me and none of them looked happy.

That collective stare was all I needed to be able to snap back to the here and now. It seemed obvious to me what was needed so I cracked on with it.

We all made our way down to the floor of the cavern and approached the final empty throne. Looking at it at this close range, I was able to pick out the intricate detail which had been worked through the stone. I could recognize the huge reptilian shape of my own Dragon and that of The Zarrulent, the creature of legend I had to stand guard over. We'd both been depicted in a herculean battle of some kind which I was no doubt winning. Next to the throne was a small set of stone benches which didn't carry any of the same care or detail. This was what Mike must have meant by the honour guard sitting at the Guardians feet.

"If you would be so kind as to take your place we will be able to begin."

Turning to face the originator of the comment, I knew who I would be facing but there was still the barest hope that I would be wrong.

I wasn't.

Leatherpants leaned towards me from his position at the right hand of The Elder and kept that same fixed grin of his plastered onto his face. Despite the smile it was easy to see that he was as contemptuous of me as he had been before, his smile still didn't reach his eyes. I hoped it couldn't. Bad plastic surgery or something.

"We are all waiting on you." He leaned and smiled just that little bit further to go with the last comment. He was still wearing his gifted skin suit, colours writhing over its surface as he moved ever so slightly. He really must have felt himself to be untouchable if he thought he could speak to a Guardian in this fashion, in front of all of the others. I didn't get the chance to respond.

To my right came a very familiar voice. One I'd been missing to a much larger degree than I would have first thought.

"Mr. Ward. Do not forget your station here. You will address every member of this great order with the reverence they deserve. Never presume to think you are at the same standing as those who are your betters." Andrea's reptilian Russian accent did what it always did to me and lit the fires of my animal self. It also seemed to be able to carry the ice cold threat to one of the subordinates at the same time. Looking over to her throne I was greeted by her huge Dragon form locking its grey/white eyes onto Leatherpants and holding him fixed. He responded without the barest hint of ego.

"My humble apologies my lady. I simply wished to convey the importance of the issue of time. I live to serve The Circle, as do we all." Another huge bow and he seemed to melt back to his station at the side of The Elder, that same smile still plastered all over his face.

Watching him retreat I was struck by the fact that he was still dressed in his demonic skin suit where everyone else in the gathered retinues was decked out in their finest ceremonial armoured dress. He did have a very high opinion of himself.

I nodded and smiled to Andrea to show my thanks, feeling that the details of our parting would be smoothed somewhat. Her Dragon face gave no signal that she had noticed my gesture. Whatever I'd done to wind her up would still need some figuring out.

I wasn't given the time to be able to do anything more on the subject then.

"We are still waiting."

This time as I turned to face the owner of the voice who was admonishing me, I knew that there was going to be no easy exit. This time it was The Elder herself who was speaking out.

"The Circle as a whole is in enough danger that we are all required to be here yet we are still waiting on the last member of our group to deliver himself to attendance. Is there some reason you don't wish these sacred proceedings to commence or are you just ignorant of the situation you find yourself?"

Andrea may have saved me from the attack of The Elders little dog but she was helpless to do anything against the questions of another Guardian. It all rested on me to stand my own corner.

Turning to face The Elder I called together as much of my booming voice of authority as I could. I call it that but really it's just the ability to project your voice so lots of people can hear you. I'd taught exercise classes in my former life as a fitness trainer where I'd needed to practically scream over the music we had been working out to.

I addressed the whole room and made certain to include a glance at all of the other Guardians as I spoke.

"Accept my apologies fellow Guardians. I meant no delay in my actions and I attend to allow The Circle to resolve the pressing issue before us. Let us commence."

Turning back towards my own throne I could see Mike sitting casually on the stone benches set aside for my honour guard. He nodded approval for what I'd just said and gave an ever so subtle thumbs up.

Hurrying out of my clothes as fast as I could, I drew in all of the power I needed and my body contorted and grew until the final mighty Red Dragon of The Circle stood in the centre of the ring of Guardians. Stretching out my wings to their full extension just to show the gathered crowd just how terrifying I was, I turned and settled myself into the final throne in the ring.

The second I got myself settled, things began in earnest.

There was more of a feeling than seeing what was taking place to begin with. As I took my place on the throne, a magical circuit was completed and there was a huge onrushing of power. It wasn't like a wind passing through the cavern, more like a shared sensation of an electric current, like those experiments where you can shock the person on the end of a chain of people thanks to the wonders of conductivity.

Looking around the cavern I could see that all of the other Guardians could feel the same sensation. Each and every Dragon was sat just that little bit straighter, had just a little more serious an expression on their faces. The collected groups with each of the Guardians gave no hint that they were aware of the experience which was passing through the room, instead all sitting respectfully still, waiting for who knew what.

Then as fast as it had started, the current of power stopped.

Whatever it had been, I could only assume that it had been what would make certain no-one could remember any of the details of what was to take place to allow them to take the memories out of the chamber.

Taking in a steadying breath, I looked around the cavern and tried to take in the details of what had just happened. From the dais, there were now signs that the power which had passed through the cavern was doing something.

All of the carved glyphs covering the surface of the giant structure had started to emit a very low light. Nothing like the glowing beams I'd seen come from the runes around the obelisk in my own prison, instead they were more like a glowing ember from a dying fire. A small hint of what the fire had once been rather than a view of what it was. They all just glowed gently over every available area of the dais' surface.

That seemed all they were going to do for the longest time but that low light was soon building in intensity as the power within the stone grew. From all around the cavern, flecks of light started to drift down and towards the dais. It was quite a beautiful sight to behold as they slowly danced their way from whatever random points of the space we were all in and were absorbed by the dais, adding to the building power being emitted from the carvings.

I risked another look over to Andrea as the light show continued, hoping to catch her eye and give her some signal of placation. She, like everyone else in the room, was transfixed by what was going on ahead of us and gave no indication that she was even aware that there was anyone looking in her direction.

Great.

Turning my attention back to the light show at the head of the ring of thrones, I could make out a shape beginning to form around the lone chair on the rock stage. A shimmering sphere was slowly taking shape, made of glowing rune symbols of various sizes.

That sphere steadily grew in density as more and more power was poured into it until it eventually took on the appearance of a solid, golden ball bearing. It encircled the chair on the dais and gave the impression of being impervious to any and all power which was in the room.

Before there was any further movement of any kind, on either side of the sphere, appeared ten of the giant armoured guards who I'd met at my estate. They were just there. It again made me think that there must be one hell of a trick to get them all in front of that many magical beings without there being any sign they were there. The final appearance on the dais was that of the Messenger. She appeared in exactly the same fashion as her hulking guards, as if she stopped time to position herself and then started it off again to show herself to the rest of the world. There was no overt sensation of pressure to accompany her arrival as it had done when she had visited Wales to give me my invite to this party but it was still apparent that she had a great deal of power here, magical or just political.

She was still wearing the same clothing she had on the night we'd met. I couldn't help myself but admire her very powerful form but it also made my jaw ache with the memory of our short skirmish. Still, she was a very, striking young woman.

All those on stage finally stopped moving about and all was still. I'd already worked out what was going to happen next but I hadn't expected it to happen in quite the way it did. It had to be the entrance of The Mage to the proceedings.

It was, but I'd been expecting a huge collection of explosions, flashing lights and booming thunderclaps to herald the arrival of the most powerful of our number to this gathering but instead, the sphere just melted down to run through the nearest carvings around the top of the dais, leaving behind the serene looking shape of the Mage, sat casually casting his glance over the room before him.

Everyone in the cavern, Guardians and retinue alike, all sat bolt upright, practically straining, to show the correct deference or respect to the head of our order. He on the other hand, just sat still and looked around the room.

It was The Messenger who broke the silence.

"WE ARE ASSEMBLED LORD MAGE. THINE CIRCLE IS AT THE READY."

Her booming voice was akin to a detonation rather than a call to the area and it made every single one of us jump, including The Elder. It made my own attempt at a call to the group seem very anemic in comparison.

The Mage slowly moved from his throne and purposefully paced towards the front edge of the dais. When he reached the edge, his toes practically curling over the lip of the stone, he asked to the assembled group, "Why are we called to this gathering?" without really trying yet still managed to cast his voice wide enough for everyone to hear clearly. The Messenger replied.

"WE HAVE BEEN CALLED TOGETHER BY THE ELDER. IT IS SHE WHO HAS REASON."

All the gazes in the room passed to The Elder as everyone looked for an explanation. Now it was Leatherpants who spoke.

"My gathered Guardians. Please accept my thanks and apologies. The Elder would only have evoked this requirement at the most dangerous situation and she feels that we are all found at that point." He'd slowly walked to the centre of the ring of seated Dragons and was speaking in a calm and authoritative tone. He was familiar with the waters he was swimming in at the moment and it was plain to see for all those who were looking on that he was grandstanding and enjoying every second of it.

"All the mighty Guardians who find themselves gathered here today have been grouped together far too regularly in the recent past. There has been regular reason to all travel to the estate of one of your number over the last months as one Guardian after another has fallen to the attacks of The Hive."

He stopped speaking to really let the point sink in and, looking around the gathered Dragons, I could see a variety of postures, nodded agreement, bowed heads, no movement at all, which all showed that Leatherpants' words had had the desired effect. He slowly surveyed what was going on around him and waited an extra heartbeat before continuing.

"My master, The Elder of this mighty force, has seen for herself what has taken place during the fighting at the prison site in Argentina and has borne witness to the continuous failure which has blighted that once mighty house."

I just knew that this wasn't going to end well.

Leatherpants continued with a steadily raising volume and fervor.

"There has been a continuous falling of our Guardians from one family line despite the expertise and training each of the members of the line have had. At the same time the enemy have been able to exert more force on our defences than they have ever been able to do before. Why have they been suddenly able to find ways of destroying our defences now when before they have been utterly incapable of breaching those defences? Why have they now been able to group together their efforts to be able to stand against our troops on an equal footing?"

Again, he let the words drift around to everyone and waited for the seeds he was planting to take hold in the minds of those looking on. Looking at the expressions on the faces of a great number of the surrounding Dragons, it was easy to see that Leatherpants had been able to make his point without actually making his point. The fertile soil of suspicion doing all of the work for those well placed seeds.

"My Lords and Ladies. Guardians of The Circle. I have been a humble servant of this most vital and honourable of groups for almost a thousand years and I have seen a great many problems come and go as the might and force of this order has stood resolute against all who would seek to break it apart. The strength of The Circle has never been in doubt over all of the years I have been involved and I believe that many of you will feel the same."

More nodding from some of the gathered Dragons. Still hung heads from others.

"The one factor which has been altered in the recent past preceded all of the current issues we are experiencing and that factor has been present at each of the most recent attacks from The Hive in Argentina. My master has been forced to conclude that our latest Guardian from Wales has either been causing these issues because of his lack of training and skill in the matters into which he has been thrust or he has been making deliberate attempts to undermine everything we as a group have been working to maintain." Another perfectly timed pause as all the eyes of the assembled war force turned to face me. Even Andrea was looking on worriedly.

This really wasn't going to end well.

Growls and rumbles of anger and shock rippled around the thrones as all of the Dragons made their feelings known. The Messenger was quick to step into the void left by Leatherpants to be able to snap all attention back to the expected ceremony of what was supposed to happen here.

"QUIET! THIS IS A MOST SERIOUS CLAIM. ELDER. STEP FORWARD AND MAKE THINE CASE."

There was a new silence which fell over the assembled group but this time there was no mistaking the fear and anger which was sat squarely at its centre. The Elder practically uncoiled herself from her throne, her black scaled skin giving more the impression of a liquid.

"My fellow Guardians. I have served for the longest of us all and have seen as each of you has made your first steps into the world of what we all are. I have been able to watch on as each and every Guardian has taken their place amongst our order and has done what is expected of them in defence of the whole world." Now she paused and let her words hang before the others. This double team effort did seem like it was going to be able to make me guilty of everything they wanted and possibly any other crime they could wish to throw into the mix. I could see it now, my fault that Marathon bars became Snickers.

"We are all though, my brothers and sisters, only as strong as the weakest link in our Circle." She turned and fixed me with her all too familiar withering gaze.

"Our latest Dragon from Wales has been woefully under trained and has shown nothing but arrogance and disdain towards the expectations placed upon him. He has allowed his own estate to be overrun by the enemy and was supremely fortunate to be able to prevent a wider catastrophe by getting his demon charge returned to its prison. At best, what this Guardian was able to do resulted in the release of his charge, the one thing we are all here to prevent came to pass, merely days after his Awakening." Another pause.

"Since he has then been involved in the actions which have been taking place in Argentina, we have all seen how The Hive have been able to make much deeper inroads into our forces than they have ever previously been able."

Now she was turning to face each and every sitting member of the Circle, all of whom were now staring intently at her, hanging on her every word in response to the fervour she had been able to whip up. I'd felt the frustration building inside me from the very first utterance from Leatherpants but to hear The Elder heaping on the accusations was taking things beyond what even I thought was possible. All I could do was sit and take whatever was being thrown around regardless of the truth behind the claims. I just knew that me losing it and making a lunge for my accusers would do me no good at all.

"It is not unheard of that we should lose a Guardian during an attack from the enemy. We all assumed the position we currently hold through the sacrifice put forward by our predecessors so we know that the role of Guardian is one that has so many dreadful risks. But. We have all seen how one Guardian after another has fallen at the same site despite what has been done in defence by our latest would be savior."

Now she turned back to me and fixed me again with her blazing hatred, bringing with her each and every set of eyes there.

"The Hive were never able to do what they have done. They have been able to undo everything we have at our disposal for the defence of the prison in Argentina and have been able to destroy our Guardians far too easily. You have been deeply involved in the defensive effort each time following your 'would be success' and now we see a sudden and large increase in our enemies abilities. I witnessed myself the almost limitless supply of creatures they had at their disposal during the last battle, of a kind not ever seen by any of us before. Aside from that fact, somehow, The Hive have also been able to find the power to create their own Cascade Bridges, something only the highest members of this order have the ability to do."

Her expression began to show the building emotion behind what she was saying.

"I say that you are responsible for the weaknesses we have in our group. You are either just so incapable of doing what is needed that you have been making mistakes to create these issues or you are directly working with the enemy to bring down this respected force. You've shown that you have little or no respect for any of us and the role we fulfill, indeed thinking as a beast when you look at another one of our number."

I knew that she was referring back to our conversation about Andrea when we were in the infirmary but I was only barely holding onto the last vestiges of my self-control. Looking around the other Guardians in the ceremonial ring, I could see that there were a great many of them who were looking on in a fashion which suggested that they believed the worst of me. There were others who were less inclined to believe that one of their number would be willing to throw the entire line of protection to the enemy. At least that was something.

I clamped my hands down on the carved arms of my quarried throne and could feel the cracks spreading out through the frame as I took out my frustrations at what was being leveled at me. This was another attempt from someone to try and put me in my place despite the truth or sense of what was happening not warranting it.

Growling and with smoke curling up from the sides of my mouth, I eased myself up and out of my throne and took two measured steps towards the centre of the ring of thrones and The Elder.

The entire cavern could feel the winding up of the tension as I prepared for my response. The Elder didn't retreat as I approached her but her posture did alter subtly to put her on a battle ready footing. I could also see members of her retinue cracking their power into being as a readied glow of magical power crawled upon each of them. I knew that Mark and the others would be doing the same in response.

This really had the potential to fall apart fast.

The Messenger had obviously reached the same conclusion I had and was the one to break the silence.

"THERE WILL NOT BE BLOODSHED IN THIS CITADEL. THERE WILL BE DISCUSSION AND ACTION SHOULD THERE NEED BE BUT IT WILL HAPPEN IN ACCORDANCE WITH THE CODES OF WHO WE ALL ARE."

She had the same massive boom to her voice but I could barely make it out above the fury in me. I'd watched as different members of the group who had been connected to me had been killed for doing nothing other than follow the rules laid down by those above them. All I'd done was to try and follow those rules as best I could without giving myself over to the seemingly ritual suicide the group as a whole seemed to lean towards.

I would not have someone pass the blame for an event onto me just because I was potentially the easiest target. Blasting plumes of smoke from my nostrils and fixing The Elder with as strong a version of her own withering gaze, I made my response. Through an effort of will I tried my best to keep my voice both loud enough for all to hear but also quiet enough to get my feeling of violence across.

"I am not responsible for the demise of the Guardians during the fighting. I have not been conspiring with the enemy and have not been giving away what we need to be doing." I looked slowly around the ring of thrones and fixed each of the Guardians who were looking at me with my own force of will.

"I have been fighting alongside so many of the people I now stand amongst and have done so without giving death to any of them. The Hive have shown that they can adapt to what we have been doing, that's all. They worked out our systems. We as a group have been doing the same thing for so long that everyone knows exactly what's coming. If you keep doing the same thing, the opposition will know where you're going at every point of your defence."

There seemed to be a few nods of understanding but not many. Maybe the sporting analogy was a little too far.

"I've watched as there have been deaths from so many of our number, not just the Guardians. I've stood as part of the Awakenings of each new Dragon as they were called and have been involved in their training but I will not be held responsible for every loss this group suffers just because I'm the new kid on the block."

I huffed a little roar onto the last syllable by way of emphasis and judging by the reactions from around the ring, it did have some effect. If that was a good effect was still to be seen. I also kept the fact that I wasn't choosing myself to be involved in the conflicts each time quiet. I may have been present at each of the battles but I had been chosen to fight rather than just turning up. Blamed for someone else's mistake again.

The Elder still hadn't broken her stance but was quick to step back into the exchange.

"You have pointed out here that you have been to the Awakenings of Guardians following the fall of the former to hold the rank and you were quick to highlight the fact you have worked with the Dragons as part of their training. Surely these facts will highlight perfectly that you had been placed in a position of power over the latest to answer the call, making you directly responsible for the knowledge and skills they possessed?"

Again she was silent for that extra heartbeat as she let the point sink in to everyone. I opened my mouth to respond quickly but found myself struck dumb as I considered her point. She let my silence hang that extra beat as a validation of her point then continued where I should have been speaking.

"You have continuously shown that you haven't been given the requisite skills to be able to truly be effective in the role of Guardian and all it entails. You were brought into this world without any training or schooling and expected to perform in the same way as anyone else." Now she softened her voice and spoke with a tone that of a caring parent.

"How could we expect you to be able to do the same things we are when you have had none of the training involved? As you said, you were the, what was the phrase? The new kid on the block."

There were low rumbles of agreement coming from more than one point in the ring around us now as The Elder again let the silence do more damage than any words she could have used. I couldn't argue with her logic at this point without looking like I was just being petulant, just as she said I was. Instead I was forced to remain silent which gave the impression of acknowledged guilt.

This time the silence lasted for much longer than a heartbeat.

The Elder continued to pace the ring around me, this time looking studiously at the floor as she paced. Now when she spoke she didn't look up or indeed aim her attention in any direction other than at the space of bare stone floor just ahead of her feet.

"The new kid on the block. Such an interesting way to describe yourself, don't you think? The newest member of the group is probably as close as I can see your meaning. Am I right in my thinking of how you used that phrase?" She tilted her head up to me as she passed and I could feel more than just her eyes on me as she waited for me to respond, every other person in the cavern, Guardian or retinue alike was waiting on what I was about to say.

I gave the only answer open to me.

"You are correct. The newest or youngest member." I'd hoped for there to be at least a fragment of a barb attached to the comment about age but it would appear that she was either unfazed by the advancement of years or she just missed what I was saying.

"But you're not the new kid on the block are you? Not anymore. Indeed, your greatest success came when you were the most recently called Guardian so, if anything, you've deteriorated since you became a Guardian." She stopped walking and whipped herself round to face me squarely, jabbing out an accusing finger as she did.

"The new kid on the block has fallen more than once at your hands recently and that has brought us to the second part of the reason I called this most holy of gatherings. I request that The Circle conduct the ancient rite of Bridging to bring this weakness in our ranks to an end. There are two calls for it."

The place erupted.

There were roars of agreement, dissent, fury, enjoyment all mixed together and there was no real way of being able to pick out who was saying what.

That said, I didn't even know what Bridging was.

16

Even the Messenger wasn't having an effect on the cacophony of noise swirling round the cavern like a hurricane in a jam jar. She boomed out to the assembled group but even her words were lost amidst the sound. There was an ululating mass of reptilian voices, roars and howls forming the main blanket of sound which was riding over the few human voices adding to the soup.

As the cacophony continued, The Elder slowly, deliberately returned to her throne and settled herself back to review the situation she had just created. I sat, lost for words, in the centre of the sound and just stared at her. There really wasn't a great deal I could do.

I'd had my own monster about to climb into a display of unbridled violence but The Elder had walked me into a position that would have me set upon by every other member of The Circle. My Dragon nature was to kick off if something was going wrong and she had known that. I'd been lucky enough to have at least some level of awareness which had stopped me from going off the deep end and proving the worst point. The trouble was that I hadn't been prepared to have to defend myself against claims which appealed to the fears of the other members of the group – regardless of the truth.

Looking at The Elder I knew that she had created an enemy which The Circle could have a true effect on, someone she could single out who they could all take action against rather than just leave us all with the gnawing fear we were starting to lose our conflict.

She sat in her throne and gave no hint of emotion. There was no smug grin. No pompous expression of superiority, just a blank expression, as if she had done nothing more than her duty in this situation. Leatherpants, on the other hand, was a very different matter. He was now on his feet waving his arms wildly in all directions as he screamed into the mass of noise. He was doing all of this with an expression of the wildest glee twisting his face almost to the point of euphoria.

Whatever the Bridging was, it couldn't be good.

I was brought back out of my own thoughts at the same time the rest of the gathered Circle were silenced.

The only way to even begin to describe what happened was to say that there was a sound we could all see accompanied by a flash of light we could all hear. It was beyond the senses and seemed to just be more than anything any of us could describe. And it had come from The Mage.

He was still sitting in his own throne but he now had his left hand raised above his head. He passed his gaze over everyone before him in the same fashion as a scalding teacher to their unruly class. Everyone stopped and just focused their attention on him. As he lowered his hand slowly, The Messenger filled the silence.

"THERE ARE STEPS WE MUST TAKE SHOULD THERE BE A CALL FOR THIS RITE TO BE CONDUCTED. WE MUST ALL REMEMBER OUR STATIONS AND NOT DECEND INTO CHAOS. ELDER. WHY DO YOU CALL FOR THE BRIDGING?"

Leatherpants stepped forward from his place in the seating next to his master.

"Gathered Lords and Ladies of The Circle. My master has shown that the latest bearer of the mantle of power from our stronghold in Wales is unable to deliver what is expected of him. We have all seen as Guardian after Guardian has fallen when he has been involved in the defence of the prison. This level of failure hasn't been seen since the very earliest days of the struggle between The Circle and The Hive. My lady has shown that we need to have a more capable Guardian in position to allow us to have the strength we have all come to expect."

"Sorry shorty, I'm the last in my line. Nowhere for the power to go if I die so you're pretty much stuck with me." I couldn't help myself. The words were out before I'd even thought about them and by the look on Leatherpants's face, I'd just done him a favour.

"We have a perfect example of how this young pup is ignorant of the expectations placed upon him. He will act without thinking. We all understand that the natures of the Guardian power will affect the carrier of that power but he seems to be totally unable to curtail his impulses. Indeed, he has been lusting after another Guardian without consideration for what consequences that could precipitate."

Now that comment really caught the room by the short and curlies. There was a palpable weight smashing into me as all of the eyes in the room were cast firmly in my direction. I could see that everyone was trying to work out who was on the other end of my attentions and it didn't take long for the whole room to work out that Leatherpants was talking about Andrea. She had, after all been the one who had trained me and had been present at all of the battles in Argentina. I risked a furtive glance in her direction but found that she was unmoved. She was sat utterly still and had lowered a mask of casual indifference over her features.

Leatherpants continued as the emotion was buffeted around the room.

"There has been no denial so he has confirmed the point. He has been focusing on his animal attraction rather than on what he needs to be doing as part of this order. We need Guardians who will give everything to the cause of the defence of our prisons rather than just following the calling of his animal self."

He was about to continue but I stopped him. There was no way I could let him continue this character assassination and expect to get out of here in one piece. I still didn't know what this Bridging procedure was but by the way it was being teed up, it really wasn't going to be something I'd encourage my friends to have done. Standing up again, I tried to give a reasoned response and make it look like I knew what was going on.

"Is it wrong to have feelings for another person? If the enemy is successful against us, should we jump on the easiest explanation or look for the right one? How could my feelings for anyone be cause for making me the scapegoat for what is going on here?" I tried to look as sincere as possible as I spoke, using wide arm gestures to aid my point but I'm not sure that the pleading part came through the armoured Dragon exterior. Leatherpants continued.

"Is it wrong to have feelings for another person? No, but you are a Guardian of The Circle and as such are expected to dedicate yourself to all things geared towards the protection of the human race. You must suspend your pursuit of a mate. You can't think beyond yourself can you? As for picking on the easiest explanation, I do hope you've heard of Occam's Razor. Of course you haven't. That the simplest explanation is usually the right one. The power of logic is your undoing young fool."

There was another intake of breath at that last comment and even I could see that Leatherpants had just done something he shouldn't have done. I risked another look at Andrea but she was still as calm as a glacier.

"My lord Mage," I said while turning to the dais at the head of the room. "I am being accused of crimes for which there is no proof other than I was close by. I am being told that what I think is wrong so I should be sanctioned for it," now for the big risk, "and I am being disrespected by a mere functionary. As I see, a great deal of the call for my Bridging is that I do not follow the prescribed paths of The Guardians in thought or action yet I am being insulted by a servant. Do you not see the hypocrisy of this? Can't I be allowed to prove my own innocence of what I am being accused?"

Fingers crossed.

Looking at Leatherpants as we all waited on a response from The Mage, I could see that I'd just caught him with a very sneaky shot. He knew that he'd pushed just a little too far with the young fool comment and he could see the issue he'd just created. If The Mage was to uphold the rule of everything within The Circle and have me 'Bridged' he would have to do something unpleasant to Leatherpants and I could see that Leatherpants knew it. If he let Leatherpants off the hook, then how could he hold me to the same laws?

The Elder was utterly unmoved by this situation though.

The anticipation in the room was growing by the heartbeat and I could sense around me that everyone was practically pleading with The Mage to give an answer to show The Circle what it was expected to believe. Eventually he spoke.

"Gathered Guardians. We have indeed found ourselves in a situation where the enemy has been able to exert a great deal of pressure on all of us and our forces."

His voice was like a mixture of warm honey and chocolate but cut through with razorblades and fish hooks. He was able to project both the caring love of a parent while holding the implicit horror of what he was able to do. I imagined it felt like being an insect drawn towards that deadly blue light, only with knowledge of what that light could do to you. It just highlighted how serious this whole mess had become if the Mage was as angry as he was showing himself to be.

"Mr. Ward has made a well-balanced case but he has not shown that there is any proof of his claims. In much the same way, Mr. Johns has been accused of a great many things which do fit the accusations but he, as a Guardian of The Circle, is subject to a great many different forces that the servants of this group must be unaware. Elder, had you made the fullness of this claim yourself, I would have ruled for you, but My Johns is correct that he is being insulted by a mere servant, even one with the length of service as Mr. Ward, so I am forced to decline the call for Bridging in this case."

The Elder remained motionless and her expression gave no hint of any inner emotion, positive or negative. Leatherpants on the other hand, was less able to hold his emotions in check and I could see that he was more than a little angry with the word of The Mage. He quickly turned and sat down next to the throne of his master, carrying the demeanor of the spoilt child who hasn't gotten their way.

The relief I felt was quite remarkable. I'd been able to talk my way out of trouble without there being the need to demolish the location afterwards. I'd prevented myself being 'Bridged', which I still had no idea about, and had been able to make The Elder and Leatherpants lose face before all of the gathered Guardians. Not bad at all.

"ELDER. WHAT WAS THE SECOND CALL FOR BRIDGING?" boomed The Messenger as I was turning to sit down again.

She, again, purposefully stood up and made her way toward the centre of the ring of thrones.

"Gathered Guardians. My second call for a Bridging is also linked to the actions of this Guardian from Wales and I call for a swift action. The actions of this member of our group have resulted in the outcome we must rectify here. I call for a new Guardian to be called for the fallen."

As she said the final word of her sentence she waved out an arm in a theatrical flourish and aimed it towards one of the thrones. All eyes followed her arm and I was confronted by a hideous reality.

Up to this point, I'd been utterly concerned with the situation I had found myself and it had seemed that every single action which had been taking place had been aimed at making me aware that I had been responsible for the problems which had befallen The Circle. At no time had I even really looked at the detail of what was going on around me. I'd seen Andrea as I had looked at her for guidance or comfort but I hadn't looked beyond her and the direction of The Elders arm proved it to me.

She was signaling at one of the thrones at the back of the ring in relation to the dais the Mage was sat upon. The Dragon sat upon it had had their head bowed as Leatherpants and I had been making our points and The Elder had said what she had but I'd not ever really paid any true attention to the detail. It was only now that I could see what was happening. The head was still bowed but I could now see the detail of the Dragon. The large plates of armour over the slightly thin, adolescent frame were far too familiar to me as I finally worked out that Frederico's Dragon body was slumped in the throne.

17

I just sat dumfounded.

There was nothing more for me to add.

I'd been told that Freddy had been killed but that detail seemed to have gotten lost in the mix. I'd been so focused on what was happening to me that maybe I hadn't thought about what was happening to everyone else. Looking at the slumped form of the young Guardian I'd been working with I realized that he had been nothing more than a boy and I had been asked to give him the training he needed to be the Guardian. My efforts had brought us to this point.

Taking in the details of his empty form now, I could see the draining of the colour from his skin and how his musculature had sagged following his passing. The body had been arranged with as much reverential care as could be mustered for the giant frame but it was easy for anyone with the slightest awareness to see that he was dead.

I felt sick that I'd missed it.

I tried to hold my expression together without letting my own horror seep out. I don't think it worked.

The Elder continued to speak into the cavern but there was no orchestrated pausing or movements. She just ran through the points.

"This is the Dragon form of our latest Guardian victim. He fell in the defence of the prison in Argentina and understood the need for sacrifice his position called for. He was happy to give his life for the good of the protection of the human race but he was also wise enough to notice that there was an ever shrinking pool of people to choose from behind him."

The silence in the cavern was almost too much to bare as I sat and listened to what The Elder had to say.

"He is survived by a sister, Maria, who is the next in line for his mantle but we are forced to re-consider our position." There was a heavy resignation in her voice as she spoke about Freddy's sister.

Now I could remember all the most painful of the details. I could recall now, in all too clear resolution, the conversation I'd had with Freddy on the eve of the final battle he would see. He'd been resolute in his understanding of what it was he was expected to do. He'd been sure he must protect the human race, but he'd also been sure he must protect his family first. He'd known that he had to make certain he didn't fall, not for the good of the population of the planet as a whole but because he knew if he did, it would be his sister who would have to take up the mantle and she was still a six year old child.

The thought of a small child being given the power and responsibility of one of the Guardians of The Circle was terrifying. I could remember the pain and discomfort I'd felt prior to my own Awakening and the horrors I'd seen since then. I'd been woefully underprepared for what was coming but at least I had been an adult. At least I'd had enough faculty to understand what was happening. This was no world for a child.

"Which brings us to the request for Bridging." The Elder had turned to face The Mage now and was speaking directly to him.

"I have asked that the child Maria be brought here so we will be able to complete the process as quickly as possible to restore the full power of The Circle. I've selected a member of the household in Argentina who will be able to take her place and their family line will continue to serve as Guardians from this day onwards."

There was movement from the base of Freddy's throne as his assembled retinue made their way forward, carrying the crying form of Maria. They were being followed by a tall, heavy set man with dark skin and beady black eyes. He was stripped to the waist but looked like he was wearing a fur coat thanks to the swirling black hair which covered his entire upper body. He must have been the replacement The Elder had spoken of. As he moved forward with the rest of the group, I decided purely on instinct that I didn't like him.

I tried to be as covert as I could manage but I'm not certain that the results quite reached the heights I'd been aiming for. Leaning down as much as I could without drawing attention to myself, I whispered down to Mike.

"What's going to happen to her?"

Mike looked up and gave me a curt shrug. If he didn't know, what hope did I have of finding out without re-establishing the fact that I was still no more than the petulant child that Leatherpants had been painting me as. Surely Mike knew something.

"You don't know anything? At all?"

This time it was obvious that others had heard. The Messenger responded so there was no chance of me escaping the finger pointing because of my lack of knowledge.

"THE CHILD WILL HAVE THE POWER OF THE DRAGON REMOVED FROM HER BODY AND FROM HER FAMILY LINE. THAT POWER WILL BE GIVEN TO HER REPLACEMENT AND THE CIRCLES STRENGTH WILL BE RESTORED."

I could feel the level of petty frustration which was being casually thrown in my direction but I didn't care. I wanted answers. In for a penny...

"Thank you Messenger." Keep the decorum in place. "But I'd come to that conclusion on my own. What will happen to her after this has been done? What will happen to Maria?"

The Messenger looked at me quizzically.

"SHE WILL DIE, OF COURSE."

I was on my feet and across the space in the centre of the cavern in a fraction of a heartbeat. I stopped astride the group of soldiers from Argentina and roared down at them, showing them and anyone who would listen that I was in no mood for games.

Snorting out a small jet of flame from each nostril, I thrust out my right hand.

"Give her to me. Now."

The guards beneath me stood petrified as I bore down on them, unsure what they were expected to do. Huge roars and screams were erupting around me as the other Guardians took my movement as being the insult to their customs I had intended it to be. It was bad enough for me to have to stand by and watch as Dragons or soldiers died in huge numbers because of what we were all doing but there was no way I was going to let a small child simply be killed because of the needs of the Circle. It was practically a sacrifice.

"QUIET!" The Messenger boomed into the noise but this time everyone did as they were told. Silence returned but I kept my attention on the people below me. I wasn't going to let this happen.

"What do you intend to do? How do you intend to resolve this situation where everyone wins?" It was the first time Andrea had spoken to me in what felt like an eternity. I still hadn't moved but now my attention was being split between the people beneath me and the pale Dragon which was edging its way towards me across the stone floor. She continued to speak, her voice pitched low as if she was trying to soothe an angry dog.

"This is a very rare process which hasn't been performed in generations. None of us in The Circle would want this process to be conducted unless in the gravest of circumstances. What is it you are planning on doing to help her?"

I still hadn't moved but Andrea was now directly in front of me.

"Anthony. If she is taken from here without us acting in some way to resolve this problem she will be driven mad from the energies trying to take hold in her. If we perform the Awakening for her, she will become the next Guardian and will be expected to fight in the protection of everything."

She lightly touched my face and I could feel a familiar cooling strength there. It really was the other half of me, Fire and Ice. Andrea lifted my face away from the gathering below and we stared into each other's eyes.

"Both of these options will leave the Circle much weaker and we will be less likely to be able to defend what we must. Would you see this child torn apart by madness or sent into battle against the horrors we have all seen? And in doing so, risk the entire population we are all sworn to protect?"

We stood still looking at each other and the conflicting thoughts swirled in my mind as I tried desperately to find a way that we could get out of this situation without destroying The Circle or a small child. I knew that Andrea was speaking with dispassionate logic and she was right in everything she said but I also knew that she was still wrong. Despite the logic and reason she was able to call on I could see that there was still a flaw in what she was saying.

Speaking directly to her, not the rest of the room, I answered.

"You're planning your actions with the starting point of The Circle and the protection of the human race as a whole. Surely the protection of the human race should start with one child?"

I blinked and lightly touched Andreas face, feeling safe that I was that close to her again.

I leaned closer and, from this distance, could finally see through the armoured exterior of Andreas Dragon to the pain and conflict she was feeling. Her glacial surface was covering a turmoil which was similar to my own. The only difference was she was held so strongly by the dogma of obedience to The Circle that she was trying to argue for a point she had a doubt about.

I had to continue now that I could see that there was even the barest of hints that I could stop this horror. Raising my voice, now was the time to speak directly to each and every other Dragon in the cavern.

"We can't just play the game of numbers can we? We are all in a position to be able to protect something which is pure and good. We cannot just cast aside what we are trying to protect just because it is getting inconvenient. There has to be another way to resolve this situation."

There was silence from the other Guardians, broken only by the occasional shifting of weight across the stone thrones. I had had an effect on everyone, now all I had to hope for was that it was the effect I'd been aiming for.

The Mage raised his arms above his head and the attention in the room was pulled from me and to him. From behind me, Andrea gave my arm a gentle squeeze and I could hear her backing away to resume her place on her throne. I didn't turn to look at her. I just stared on at The Mage, still keeping myself between him and the group bringing Maria.

The silence continued. And continued. Around us all, I could feel the expectations of all of the gathered members of The Circle, Dragon or not.

And still The Mage waited. His eyes slowly worked their way around the people in the cavern, as if taking in the details of everyone one at a time.

Finally his eyes fell on mine and didn't move off to anyone else.

"Young Guardian." His voice was calm and gentle as if speaking just to soothe me.

"The great order has existed for millennia and has seen so many things which should never come to pass. If you search through your own shared memories you will no doubt be able to find any number of atrocities which have been committed to enable the whole to continue." His shoulders sagged as he considered his words, possibly remembering more terrors done in the name of the good of humanity.

"We are all here to maintain the whole of the human race and that indeed does start with just one child." He was looking down at Maria now and his face showed that he too was feeling sick at the road the events of the day had taken him.

He shrugged slightly and continued.

"But what is to say that this is that one child? We are here to safeguard all the children who don't even know we are here. To protect all of the families, all the people who make up this world of ours, from the brutality of what The Hive masters and their forces will do to them should they gain strength over us. We must at no point forget that this mighty force must be maintained or we risk the end of the human race. I'm sorry, but The Bridging will take place now."

I roared at him with all the frustration I could muster and hunched down to prepare for the inevitable attack he was going to unleash.

But it never came.

Instead he just looked down at me with an expression of concern on his face.

"Would you kill me to protect this child? Do you really believe that your actions will help to deliver what is best for the whole?"

"I will not let anyone just kill someone because it is inconvenient to what they want to do. We have to be more than that surely."

The Mage at least seemed to consider what I was saying, and nodded once. Was he going to back down?

The slithering cold force which wrapped itself around me and pinned my arms and wings to my body and my legs together instantly rendered me immobile. I could also feel the most gentle of tendrils creeping up and around my snout, forcing my mouth closed.

The speed of the attack had caught me utterly by surprise but I could recognize the power which was gripping me tightly. It was the same as had pulled me back from a suicide run of my own at the last battle in Argentina.

The Elder was out of her throne and was casually weaving her arms ahead of her as she controlled the power which was keeping me prisoner. He face was an emotionless mask as she made certain that I wouldn't stop the proceedings any longer and inch by inch she nudged me back towards my own throne, eventually depositing me back there and securing my arms and legs to the stone with a power which was far too strong for me to break. I did thrash a little to test the magical strength but it soon became clear that brute force really wasn't going to do the business. The Elder looked at me as I finally subsided against the futility of what gripped me and instead of the expected contempt, this time I swear that I could see, just for a second, the barest hint of regret in her eyes.

From behind The Elder, the small group of people from Freddy's estate started to hurriedly move forwards again. Hairy was still staring at me as he moved on, shepherded by the Head of House. I don't think that he was expecting to have to fight his way through warring Guardians on his way to taking up power.

They all bowed as they reached the designated spot and The Elder spoke again as order returned to what was happening.

"After this outburst my lord, I bring to your attention the child in question and the man who I have chosen to replace her and her line in everything we are. What is your ruling in the matter of the Bridging before you?"

Again, there were no flourishes or grandstanding as she spoke. There was no well-rehearsed stage craft as she delivered her question. There was still just the bare facts presented to The Mage and the group of Guardians around her.

The Mage looked over both Maria and the newly chosen Guardian. He seemed to consider the details of each of them before he spoke, his eyes lingering on Hairy.

"Present yourself to this gathering of The Circle. Are you prepared to stand as one of this mighty order in the defence of the entire human race?"

Hairy wasted no time in giving his answer.

"I am Franco Morales Blanco and I am ready to accept the mantle of power which I have been chosen to bare."

His voice was a rolling deep and heavily accented but already carried all of the immediate authority that a Guardian should have. He was obviously familiar with the details of what was going to be expected of him and he would be more able to control the forces which he was going to be the master of but, through all of the detail and the power he was already able to wield in this place, I still didn't like him. And he was called Franco Blanco.

The Mage considered his words and took three seconds to make his decision.

"The Bridging will be granted and will happen immediately."

There was no chorus of roars to greet this decision.

None of the other Guardians made any more fuss at the seriousness of what had been decided than a brief agreement and a nodding of heads.

I had been returned to my throne which had become a great deal more uncomfortable since I'd last sat in it. I could feel that I was being shown another level of what the Guardians are expected to do and where I sat in the pecking order of the group. The collective power plays disgusted me and it was nothing I wanted to be involved in. I couldn't shake the taste of rot from my mouth and my stomach felt like there was something very sharp and angry trying to crawl its way out and it didn't seem interested in using my mouth. I wasn't looking at anything in particular but Mike finally started to speak to me.

"They're right you know." His voice was as cooling as could be expected and I could sense a level of apprehension despite his best efforts to conceal it. He obviously thought that his words were likely to set me off again and he wasn't keen on being the focus of my anger. As the ceremony had moved on, at least The Elder had released the bonds holding my mouth closed.

"They think they are." My response was meant to show that I was under control and my monster was contained but I could feel that my grip still wasn't as good as it could have been.

"I can understand what has to be done. I can see that, at first glance, there isn't another way out of this issue but there has to be more available than just we kill her. There has to be more thought to options rather than just doing what has always been done."

Mike continued, "Every single decision is based purely on what is best for The Circle. None of us are anything more than parts of the whole so if we need to be replaced for the good of the group, then so be it."

His words were the absolute truth and with a purely clinical mind, they made perfect sense. The removal of a weak or broken part was needed to maintain the whole. But it still meant that people were being treated as nothing more than machine parts. It was the clearest example of someone being discarded without the thought which should have been reserved for a human being.

I felt sick.

I needed to get out of here fast.

"What have they got to do to finish the Bridging? Are we likely to be out of here quickly so we can go home? I can't be here anymore."

Mike looked up at me and shrugged again.

"I have no idea but I think that it will be done quickly. The Mage did say it would happen immediately so fingers crossed."

I shrugged back, feeling a numbness of my very soul creeping out to touch every part of me. The life of Maria was going to end and all I could think of was my own need to go and hide in my estate. The sheer functionality of what was going to take place was all that was left.

"Fingers crossed indeed".

18

It turned out that Mike was right.

For a mighty casting which was only enacted in the direst of circumstances, there was precious little which appeared to be needed to get things moving.

The Messenger and The Elder had arranged those people required into a very misshapen triangle at the base of the dais. The massive corpse of Freddy was laid out at the very base of the dais, directly below where the feet of The Mage would be as he stood surveying what was taking place. As the elements of the ceremony were arranged, he had returned to his own throne to await the commencement of events. At two points roughly twenty metres from the dais and from each other were stationed the proudly ram-rod straight form of the Guardian elect, still with his shirt off and his body hair sweater on display, and the shuddering shape of Maria, curled into the fetal position as she tried to protect herself from the unseen forces attacking her.

Around the cavern, all of the other Guardians simply sat and watched as the ceremony took place.

The Messenger called us all to order.

"GUARDIANS. THE MAGE REQUESTS THINE POWER AS PART OF THIS ANCIENT RITE AS WE PROTECT OURSELVES FROM WEAKNESS. DO THY DUTY AS CALLED BY THE MAGE AND WE WILL BE REFORGED."

A solemn silence remained as she finished speaking and all of the gathered Dragons prepared themselves for whatever was about to be asked of us all.

The Mage stood from his throne, straightened his robes and took paces enough to take him to the edge of the dais, looking down on the forms gathered beneath him. Raising his arms to shoulder height he started.

"Guardians. I require a sample of your powers to be able to open the locks of what is needed. Give to create a shared power."

His voice was more serious this time, carrying an increased threat but also an increased care. He was able to make sure people did what he asked them.

From his outstretched arms launched a wobbly glowing triangle. A gentle yellow glow was emanating from it as it drunkenly drifted towards the centre of the cavern, holding its position before all of us, bobbing like a willow the wisp. Everyone looked on and stared as there was the briefest of seconds where everyone stopped, unsure of what they had to do next. People may have read up on the event before they'd come to Egypt but when something like this actually takes place, no-one wants to be the one to make the mistake.

The two Dragons on either side of the dais were the first to stand up. They had just vacated the two largest thrones in the cavern and they both looked as if they were supremely confident that they were doing exactly what was expected. That said, they also looked as if they were supremely confident that if they had made some form of error in the correct procedure, they wouldn't be called to task about it. The two giants were covered in all manner of horns and spines, plating and absolutely implicit menace that anyone with a different opinion than them would think twice before bringing their thoughts to the table.

"My lord Mage." The Guardian on the right of the dais spoke first and sounded like his voice was an explosion rather than a sound which should come from a person or animal.

"Let Thunder be the first to answer your call."

There was another dramatic pause as everyone else in the room digested what had been said. Looking around as quickly as I could, I could see that there were a few others looking on to see what was actually going to take place with the same kind of interest I had, born out of not wanting to admit to not knowing already.

I'd met these two at my own Awakening and had seen them during the following ceremonies in Argentina but this was the first time I'd seen them in action so to speak.

Thunder lifted his massive right arm, and offered his open hand towards the wobbly shape before him. The shape reacted immediately to the gesture by lurching at him and wrapping itself around his hand, making him look very much like he was wearing a luminous bandage. Thunder grimaced slightly as the shape covering his hand contorted and shifted, moving as a living being.

Everyone else in the room stood and looked on with curiosity all over their faces. Those people who had no ideas about what was going to happen (like me) were taking in all of the detail as it unfolded and no doubt wondering if it hurt. All those who had some prior knowledge of the event would have read about the details but seeing them in reality would be a very different proposition. Even The Elder was in a state of shock as what took place unfolded.

With a small grunt, Thunder was freed from the glowing binding and it returned to its previous point in the centre of the room, this time glowing slightly more brightly. Thunder returned to his throne and sat back, cradling his arm in his lap. The next Dragon, this time identifying themselves as Lightening, raised their hand and the process was repeated.

As Lightning sat back down, the rest of the Guardians all stood up and we all proffered our arms to the magical construct. I did so begrudgingly. I may have been released to be able to take my part in this ceremony but it was far too clear that if I so much as grimaced in the wrong direction that I was surrounded by more than one creature who was able to make me take part by force. The longer I was free from any form of magical binding meant that I was still able to stop this before we all killed one of our number.

One by one, it attached itself to each of us, fed and then disengaged. It reached me after six others had taken their turn.

As it engulfed my hand with quite astonishing speed, I was struck by the all-encompassing strength of the grip which went from simply being tight to being a smothering pain, like my hand was rapidly being taken to vast depths underwater and the pressure threatened to crush all of the life from my appendage.

It continued to build and moved relentlessly past very uncomfortable to agony. I kept quiet, not wanting to show weakness in front of the others but I was sure that this must have been easier for all of them. How much longer would this go on for? It must have been happening for almost an hour by now.

Then, before the pain became too much to handle, the sensation was released and the magical shape had floated away in preparation of crushing the next willing victim.

Looking my hand over for the inevitable damage, I was relieved to find everything intact but the pain was still very real. I did as all the other donors had done and settled myself back in my throne to await the completion of the process. Looking at my little team of personal soldiers, I was greeted by expressions of both concern and confusion. Mark asked the question they all had in mind.

"Are you alright? What was that?"

It made me feel better that he'd asked after my health first but you could see that he was desperate for the information on the magic of it all. It was all too familiar to me in a strange way.

"Not a clue but it would appear that there will be a great deal of power required to achieve it. It would definitely suggest something big."

They all looked at me as they mulled over what I'd told them.

"You don't know either then." Mike had never been fooled.

I shrugged down at them and gave them the only reassurance I could.

"We'll just have to see what happens when that thing has had a nibble from all of us. Just stay switched on, all of you."

The gathered group all nodded and turned back to watch as the process was continued. I just settled back and hoped that nothing bad was coming.

The remainder of The Circle were dealt with in the same way I was and we all waited on the next step.

The magical triangle was still floating in the centre of the space of the cavern but it had changed from the barely tangible, drunken looking shape it had been to be something of striking edges and with brightly glowing power coursing through it. The expectation in the room was almost palpable.

Throughout the entire procedure, The Mage had maintained his stance at the edge of the dais, watching on as each of the Guardians before him had taken their turn to give a little of themselves to the goal of whatever it may be. There was a whisper at the edge of my mind of the reliance the group had on the constituent parts. The Awakening, the Bridging. The strength of the group was dependent on the strength of the group. Any single weakness could damage the whole.

Eventually satisfied that everything was in order, he again raised both his arms towards the construct he had sent out and it flashed back to him. Stopping at his fingertips, the shape began to shrink down from the huge glowing mass it had been to something only two feet in height. As it did, the light being emitted from it seemed to double and double and double again, indicating that the power was being contained in the much smaller shape, so was becoming much more densely packed.

There was a palpable intake of breath from everyone in the cavern, all watching with awe and fear fighting for the right to be the dominant emotion, as The Mage simply thrust his arm into the centre of the shape and leaned forward to sink up to his shoulder in the magic.

"Now we see what happens" muttered Mike as much under his breath as could be managed and still let me hear what was said.

I couldn't take my eyes off the activity before us but I agreed with him with a covert grunt.

Ahead of us all, the centre of attention to all who were in the cavern, The Mage looked less like he was manipulating ancient powers of magic and more like he was reaching into a very deep and over stocked cupboard. I swear I could see him grimace as he reached for something which was proving to be unnaturally elusive. Whatever he was after, it looked like it didn't want to be taken from wherever it was.

The seconds ticked by.

The Mage continued to reach through the construct before him and everyone else watching on waited. The sniveling shape of Maria remained huddled on the ground where she had been left and the giant form of her replacement looked on in raptures, no doubt keen to receive the energies which had been earmarked for him.

The minutes ticked by.

The Mage continued to reach but now the expression of serene calm which had been his mask since this whole ceremony commenced, had slipped and he was now wearing a much more furrowed brow atop the look of worried surprise.

Something was wrong and by a quick glance around the room, I could see that I wasn't the only one who'd noticed. Andrea and The Elder, as well as Eugene and Wagdi, also had concerned expressions on their faces but they seemed to be coming at the issue from different angles.

Andrea was as mystified as I was but she was far more scared by the events unfolding before her eyes than I was. Whatever was happening, it would appear that it was a great deal more concerning than I was aware. The Elder on the other hand was staring directly at me with a portion of worry but that was blended heavily with at least ten parts anger. It was easy to see that The Elder, somehow, thought that whatever was taking place was actually my fault.

Great.

Trying to ignore the disapproving glare of the black form of The Elder, I turned my eyes back on The Mage as he slowly removed his arm from the construct and he theatrically shook his sleeve back down to his wrist. It was clear that he was concerned by whatever had just happened by the creases in his forehead.

There was silence as everyone waited on him. Some of the gathered Guardians were blissfully unaware of what was happening and waited happily, seeing nothing more than what was expected while others knew what the next step should have been and were waiting for The Mage to deliver the required line.

The Mage raised his arms and spoke.

"Guardians. We are broken."

Everyone else started to catch on to the problem.

"I have discovered a great loss in The Circle and there will be no Bridging. Ever."

If I'd thought the roars from the gathered crowds had been deafening before, this took things on to a far distant dimension. The Elder was on her feet and was across the open space of the centre of the cavern to stand before my throne, jabbing out an arm with murderous intention.

"You took it. Give it back now and only have your own life ended, or is it your aim to have your entire estate sacrificed at your side?"

Her actions made me jerk back into the throne and all I could do was simply stare at her with my mouth slightly open. I'd been able to keep up with everything that had been taking place up to this point but The Elder had completely lost me now.

What did they all think I'd done now?

19

"GATHERED MEMBERS OF THE CIRCLE, GIVE THY SILENCE NOW."

The Messengers words detonated into the soup of sound and everyone snapped to her voice. The Elder didn't move and I could see that she was broiling over with fury.

Silence drifted down over the assembled group like a gossamer thin sheet thrown over raging fire but somehow, the silence won out.

The Messenger continued.

"ELDER, PLEASE TAKE THINE SEAT AS THE MAGE ADDRESSES US ALL."

The words rebounded through the heavy atmosphere of fear, battering at the lack of understanding which was trying to overwhelm the whole group. The Elder nodded ever so slightly and stalked backwards towards her own throne but she never removed her gaze from me, her intention painfully clear for all to see.

The Mage looked out over the throng of worried expressions which beamed back at him. Maria and her replacement remained in their positions, each dealing with their own pressures as the regimented process around them seemed to be falling apart.

The heavy silence of expectation was held further by The Mage until he finally uttered the words we were all waiting on.

"Guardians. Our power has been stolen. The Drake Stone has been taken from us and with it has been taken the power we have had to be able to control our destinies."

There was a collective intake of breath and growls coming from all corners of the group, even those I knew had no idea what they were being shocked about.

The Mage continued to explain but as he did there was a wave a nausea which crashed over my mind and images began to float before my eyes.

"There are a great many sources of power we have in our possession around the world and beyond, which have allowed us to control our own lives and maintain the dominance over the enemy and The Drake Stone is one of them." Disembodied calls of battle filled my head with the description and pictures of flame, ice, wind and earth filled my head, images of a thousand battles fought over several thousand years.

"It is that which holds the massive energies of each and every Dragon in our order in check, allowing them to be harnessed and given to the next Guardian. It is that stone which gathers the power from a fallen Guardian and keeps it safe before it can be transferred to the next in the line." All of the sounds of warfare from across the ages remained but now the only image which remained was a hazy, almost ethereal painting of a mighty jewel. It was smooth but so deep that it felt as if it was looking back at you as you stared. It was utterly compelling in its simple beauty that I could feel myself being drawn towards it, looking beyond the mere physical boundaries it was contained within to see the ocean of swirling power which was held at its core.

"Without it, we are now in a position where we are without the power to complete the Bridging which has been called for." The stone suddenly vanished and I could feel more than see the hole that it had created in who we all were. Despite all of the mistrust I had for the road we were now travelling down, deep within something which was far greater than just my own consciousness, I could feel that this was something I just must have back.

"We must reclaim this mighty source of power or we will be forced to put this child through the Awakening and let her take her family place as a Guardian of The Circle. This will create a grave weakness in who we are."

I couldn't think anymore. All I could do was feel. The Mages voice was still drifting across all of our awareness as the shared images he was pushing forward dissipated, leaving behind only a hollow emptiness which made me feel a loss down at the root of who I was.

This information wasn't greeted by a tidal wave of emotional outburst from the gathered masses as would have been expected having seen how they had reacted to previous events. This time, with potentially the most damaging detail for The Circle as a whole laid before the Guardians, no one uttered a sound.

All of the histrionics had been replaced with a terrified uncertainty. None of the gathered Guardians had any idea how they should react to the information that one of the most powerful of artifacts they as a group were in possession of had been stolen. Everyone was now feeling the same sense of loss that I was following the mental images cast by The Mage. Everyone knew that The Drake Stone was of a vital importance beyond that of anything they may have seen before.

That and it would appear that the majority of the gathered group didn't know of the Drake Stone in the first place.

The Mage continued to speak into the group, sensing quite rightly that this sudden revelation had the potential to cause a panic. This group had been built on the knowledge that they were practically omnipotent so news of The Circle not knowing something, and indeed, something so vitally important, could be incredibly dangerous.

"Gathered members of The Circle." The Mage maintained that same even tone to his voice as he spoke and reached his arms forwards in a placating and calming gesture.

"We have seen a great deal of warfare over the thousands of years we have stood as the guards of the world, this is something which has been seen in the past and is something we as an order have the power to rectify. Do not fear that the resolution of this issue is beyond us."

Just that small trinket of information was all the salve that the guardians needed and there was a palpable release of the tension which was knotting into the Dragons surrounding me. Everyone around us had just been told that they were actually facing a very mundane problem which had been solved in the past and would be solved again. Everyone was quickly reassured that they were still a part of the powerful group they had originally thought and that they shouldn't worry.

They had all believed every word they had just been told.

The only problem that I could see was, I didn't believe The Mage.

"Guardians. We have a situation which has presented itself which requires our best efforts to resolve as quickly as we can. We have had The Drake Stone stolen from its holding and we have to complete The Circle with a new guardian for the estate and prison charge in

Argentina. We must understand how our enemies were able to remove the Drake Stone and what it is they intend to do with such an artifact."

The Elder was quick to inject her opinion into the dialogue.

"It is painfully clear to see that the Drake Stone has been taken by the forces working in league with the Welsh Guardian. As I have declared prior to this, he is responsible for the weakness we have seen in every part of who we are during the consistent incursions in Argentina. Our first order must be to remove him from the position of gravest responsibility he holds so we can repair all of the damage he has done. Without him to putrefy the heart of what we are I will be able to track and retrieve the Drake Stone before it can be used for anything other than the most sacred of callings."

"Sacred callings?" I just couldn't help myself. There were still so many of the gathered Dragons who hadn't even offered a comment on what was going on around them, including the apparent death of a child which seemed to be still on the table. I was getting far too comfortable with the feeling of being in the firing line but at least I was able to defend myself. I couldn't see beyond the pain that Maria was going through and I just wouldn't let her be written off as merely an acceptable loss.

I remained in my throne as I spoke.

"I have been accused of some awful things here today and it would appear that wanting to protect the life of a little girl is amongst them. Killing her," I jabbed out a taloned finger towards Maria by way of emphasis, "is not a sacred calling of any kind. Does anyone else think that just blaming the nearest person isn't the best way to go about conducting an investigation?"

Silence was again cast over the room and there was an all too familiar feeling of being the odd one out as the Dragons considered my position and seemed to be falling on the side of The Elder.

"I believe that we need to see the truth of everything we have presented to us."

The Elder and I were still staring intently at each other as those words were added to the argument. We both held our positions, waiting for the other to blink and turn to see who had dared to come down on the side of the accused man.

After a heartbeat, The Elder broke our gaze and turned to face Andrea but it was Leatherpants who spoke.

"You would side with someone who has been accused of the most heinous of crimes against the Circle?" His words carried with them the frozen cold venom of a calculating mind, wrapped effortlessly in the cloak of deferent servitude. There was no fire in his voice as he answered from his seat, instead he met the Ice Dragon with the most subtle ice of his own.

"I would side with the truth of any situation Mighty Elder." Andrea spoke to The Elder despite Leatherpants asking the question. "I can fully understand the position of seeing our Guardian from Wales as being the cause of our weakness but all of the evidence you have presented to us has been circumstantial at best. Wouldn't you rather have the real culprit accused rather than just the most convenient?"

All the other eyes in the cavern passed onto The Elder and waited. Leatherpants continued.

"And why would you feel the need to support someone who is so blatantly incapable of delivering what is expected of him? We are all in service of The Circle in our different ways. We have all been given a role to play in the performance of our lives but we all rely on the fact that we are all pulling in the same direction. Should there be someone who is undermining what we are doing, shouldn't we purge them from our system?"

"I wholeheartedly agree mighty Elder but are you certain that it is Anthony who is the one working against the best interests of us all? Is it not possible that another within our number was capable of betraying us? Surely it is more likely that someone of great power and experience is more likely to have been the traitor?" Andrea dropped her gaze pointedly towards Leatherpants at the last point and everyone in the cavern saw it.

Maintaining her focus on Leatherpants now, she continued.

"Our Welsh Guardian is far too inexperienced to be the only suspect in this matter, do you not agree?"

The Elder said nothing. She levelled her mask of indifference back over her features and practically turned to stone before our eyes. Leatherpants on the other hand, turned and slinked back to his position back at the side of his master. He knew that he couldn't respond in the way he must now be burning to. He'd already been slapped back into his place so couldn't risk opening his mouth. He had also had his master remain silent when he was being signaled out as a potential threat. In terms of honour and protocol, he'd just had his trousers pulled down and been given a very public spanking.

I grinned at that image in my head.

"Gathered Guardians," called The Mage. "We require a team of you to go forth and reclaim The Drake Stone from those who have taken it from us."

Thunder and Lightning shot from their thrones in unison.

"I will go for The Circle," boomed from the pair of them, in a very odd stereo effect.

The Mage seemed to consider the two of them as options, weighing up the possibilities of having them questing and gave his answer.

"My most loyal servants. I thank you for being so eager to volunteer for this most important of causes but I must refuse your offer. If The Hive are truly capable of damaging us as has been suggested here today, I cannot take the risk that the charge that the two of you have here could be released in your absence. You must remain on guard here."

The two giants bowed to their master and settled back into their respective thrones. The Mage turned his gaze back to the group at large.

"I'll go Lord Mage."

Everyone, Guardian and retinue member alike, looked at me agog. No-one had been expecting that obviously.

"You must want to go. You probably already know the location of The Drake Stone having been responsible for its taking." The Elder was now using the tone of a petulant teenager rather than that of a leader of armies.

Taking yet another steadying breath, I gave my reasons.

"I've been set up as the bad guy in this whole situation despite not being involved in anything which has been levelled at me. How else can I prove to everyone that I'm not part of a big conspiracy?"

The split second of understanding from the other Dragons was enough for The Mage to give his feelings of my offer.

"I agree with your logic Mr. Johns. You do indeed need to show you are not responsible for this but also to find who the real enemy is. I accept you as volunteer to this cause, both to retrieve that which has been taken but to put you to the test as well."

"I will also go Lord Mage." The Elder was out of her throne as she spoke to the crowd. "There must be someone to oversee this one to ensure he is not passing further secrets to the enemy. I will go to ensure that our true destination is not lost."

She bowed and returned to her throne.

"Very well my friend. You will accompany Mr. Johns."

Great.

Now I was stuck with the one person who was out to get me being able to work next to me as we went into who knew what. She'd already tried to have me bridged, and as far as I could work out, there was still a chance that it could still happen. Now she was going to be at my side if we got caught in a fight with nothing to stop her killing me herself and then returning my body as a terrible loss. There was no way I was going to be left alone with her.

"I request that there be another to attend this task my lord. I would request that Andrea be allowed to be a part of this quest."

I flicked a furtive glance between Andrea and The Elder and hoped that The Mage would agree. Andrea looked back in much the same way but The Elder could see what I was trying to do. She simply narrowed her eyes and gave the barest hint of a nod of acknowledgement.

"Agreed." The Mages voice had taken on an almost casual tone with the last word. "Assemble a handful of soldiers who will be able to assist you in this undertaking and begin when you are ready. You will take the child and her replacement, Mr. Blanco, with you as well to ensure you are able perform the bridging quickly when you retrieve the stone."

Everyone nodded and stood as The Mage made his way back towards his throne, content that they had all the information that they could require and that they had been dismissed.

I didn't share their feeling of calm.

"My lord. Won't we have to bring the stone here to let you do the business of bridging?"

Everyone looked at me with the all too familiar expression of casual pity they reserved for the mentally infirm member of their group. It didn't worry me, I just hoped I'd be able to buy the maximum amount of time to find another way for this awful situation to play out. I was still clinging to the hope that I could find a way to remove the power from Maria without it killing her.

"Do not worry my Guardian. The Messenger will be able to perform the rite. She will be accompanying you to ensure everyone is able to remain focused on the task at hand," explained the Mage as he regarded The Elder and then Andrea before turning back to me. He could see what I'd done and why I'd called for Andrea to be a part of the group. He frowned down at me and I could see his mouth open slightly, as if to say something vital, but it closed slowly before anything was uttered. His eyes remain fixed on me and the frown deepened.

It was official. That was, of all the awful claims and events which had taken place in this mighty cavern, the most unsettling. It would appear from what he hadn't said, that The Mage was also aware of what The Elder had been talking about earlier on when she was recounting my feelings towards another member of the group.

The Mage returned to sit on his throne and all of the gathered Guardians bowed their heads to him. He gently returned their bow and without any form of summoning, the shards of light which had formed the sphere of power he had been called from began to reform around him, rebuilding the shell which enclosed him.

After less than a minute it had been totally reformed and without there being any kind of ceremonial effort, it simply faded before our eyes, to reveal the now empty throne.

Immediately he had disappeared, the magical circuit connecting all of the Guardians was broken and everyone took a deep breath as a response to the release of the invisible force none of us had been aware had been leaning on us.

And we all looked around at each other and scrabbled against the memories which were starting to become hazy already. Whatever had just taken place had begun the process of emptying our heads of the activities of the morning. Guardians and staff alike looked around at the other members of the teams gathered for the meeting and it was clear that everyone had just had their minds infiltrated and all of the details of what had just taken place were slowly being extracted.

We all knew that we'd been called to Egypt for a vital gathering but the whys were being plucked away. Opposite me, The Elder and Leatherpants were both sat stock still with smooth expressions where everyone else had confusion of varying depths. Did they remember anything? Were they just familiar with the sensation?

"Now what?" I growled down to Mike as quietly as I could. The holes in my recollection were growing as they sucked in more of the details. By the looks of things around the chamber, everyone was doing much the same. Surely this couldn't be the best way to conduct business of this seriousness?

"Not really sure. From what I've read, we get given the records of the meeting and then we can leave."

That didn't sound too bad. I could recall bits but there were already too many gaps to create a clear image. Whatever it was that had just happened here, I was reasonably certain that it couldn't have been good.

For the longest second imaginable I just stared around at the others in the cavern and fished through the empty spaces which was the full recollection of the time in the cavern. There was nothing of coherence there. No shards of sound or pictures for me to be able to start trying to reassemble the events of the day. It truly was as if there had been someone cast into the room with an editor's scissors who had laid out the film of the experiences and had swiftly snip, snip snipped them all away. Pretty soon, there was going to be nothing left at all.

From behind the mighty stone dais at the head of the assembled stone thrones, there came a briskly marching column of red robed individuals, all with their hoods covering their faces, all carrying a rolled piece of parchment. Reaching the head of the gathering, they began to split away from the column and each member started towards a specified Guardian.

One by one, they approached the Head of House in each group and passed over the scrolls with a ceremonial bow. Mike accepted his with a bow of his own, as did most of the others. Leatherpants just snatched the scroll from the person delivering it, casting out a withering gaze which left no doubt what so ever as to the meaning. I swear he didn't even look at what was written on it, just tossing it aside to one of his minions.

Mike cracked the wax seal and opened out the paper, scanning quickly through the details that were enclosed within. Looking down at him, I willed him to finish quickly so he could tell me what had happened.

"I think that you may be in a little trouble." He was still reading but he'd obviously read enough.

"What have I done this time?" This really was getting far too familiar.

"You may be in a lot of trouble." He was still reading but the details were clearly getting much worse.

Looking at the other people in the cavern it was quick to see that they had started to come to the same conclusion as Mike had. Sideways glances of suspicion and mistrust were all that I could see from everyone. At least Andrea looked ice calm as normal. That was something I suppose.

Mike finished reading and ran through the highlights. Accusation of treason, magical neutering and the mission to save the world. All things considered sounded about right.

Around me, the other members of The Circle had begun to revert back to their human forms from their Guardian Dragons and were making their way back to the tunnel I'd used to get in here, and the surface above. Shrinking myself back down, I took the scroll from Mike and ran through what was written on it.

"Is this it?" I asked while I read through the writing before me.

"Indeed sir. Were you expecting to have something else?" Mike was maintaining the language of the dutiful servant.

"I was expecting to see a complete record of every word, like a court record. This is just a list of the highlights. Granted, it points out that I threatened people, but still."

"It gets the point across though doesn't it? We'll get back to the estate and gets things under way for the arrival of our 'guests'." His tone was more conversational again and it was very relaxing. Even though I was facing what was a barely disguised death sentence, at least I wasn't going to be marooned to resolve this on my own.

Looking around, all I could do was take stock of the mess I now found myself. The Mage had vanished to wherever he'd come from and I'd been left in a situation where I just knew that nothing good was going to happen, even if I was successful in what we were about to do.

"In for a penny..."

20

The gathering of Guardians were quick to leave the cavern as soon as the meeting was declared over. The Messenger and her guards all vanished the same way they always did after confirming to The Elder, Andrea and myself that we would all be meeting at my estate to start out on our quest to retrieve The Drake Stone.

The Elder was quick to leave after them all and headed directly back to her estate to, as she put it, prepare what would be needed for such a task. Andrea and I both opened Cascade Bridges to our own estates and sent our teams back to start preparations of their own. Mike had reassured me that he would make certain everything was in readiness for the arrival of everyone else and that I shouldn't worry myself. He also took the still whimpering form of Maria and her gathered people, including Franco the Hairy, back to Wales with him. He'd worked out immediately that I'd want to have her as close to me as I could manage. The thought of her being 'cared for' by The Elder before we started out was, quite frankly, a terrifying thought.

Finally, everyone had headed out to their destinations, leaving Andrea and I as the only two still within the mighty pyramid. We stood in the low light of the tunnel mouth and the awkward silence returned.

All memories from the gathering below us were now gone completely. We had utterly lost all of the detail of the cavern as well as the meeting we'd been involved in. Functionally speaking, I felt that I'd just arrived and hadn't moved beyond the tunnel mouth.

Looking at her face it was clear, even to me, that whatever it had been that had been winding her up was still there despite all of the fun and games from the cavern below. At least it looked as if she wasn't quite as angry as she had been.

She eventually went first.

"You still have a great deal to learn." He voice was one of the disappointed teacher after the pupil had done something wildly ridiculous despite knowing they shouldn't. Just the tone I wouldn't appreciate.

"What do you mean by that? I must have been the picture of restraint in there. No-one died did they?" I had tried to keep the belligerent tone out of my voice but, again, I'd missed by some distance. Andrea folded her arms and squared her stance towards me.

"You just never stop and think do you? All you see is the effect that any set of circumstances will have on you. You don't, for a second think how anything you do or say will affect anyone else. It's always just about you."

Her tone built in ferocity as she crashed through the sentence until, when she finished, there was a deep chill to the air and, I swear, it was snowing a little. She quickly re-gathered her composure and stared at me. It looked like she was preparing herself for a fight.

That made me stop and think.

Did I just go off the deep end when the mood took me and to hell with the consequences? I had to keep calmer. Let people notice just how controlled I was.

"From what I read, I tried to get my point across in there when I was being attacked by people who I thought were a part of the same struggle as I was." Temper still in check.

"Besides, it would appear that we were ending up with the slaughter of a child as a viable option. That will never be acceptable to me." My own temperature had risen through the sentence as well until I'd snarled the final word and the temperature in the cavern had been taken well above the searing heat we had felt when we had first arrived in Egypt. Any frost, snow or ice which Andrea had created as a physical effect of her anger, was quickly melted away.

I straightened my own countenance and quickly gathered in my own flapping feelings.

We both looked at each other, then at the floor.

"Anthony." Andrea was speaking to me but didn't take her gaze from the sand covered floor beneath us.

"We are a part of a massive machine which controls the enemy leaders and fights off attacks around the world." She raised her gaze and met mine.

"I know, I know" was all I could think to say. I was getting very tired of being reminded of the position I held in The Circle, how vitally important we all were and how we must put the strength of the whole above all else. Andrea could see that in my face.

"You have been told the same point over and over again and by the look on your face you've heard it more times than you'd care to think about." She reached out and touched my hand. "The problem is you don't seem to be listening to what is being said. All you seem to want to do is rage against the machine. Haven't you ever stopped to think that the only reason you keep hearing the same comments is that you keep doing the same things which creates the need to remind you of who you are."

We both looked at each other and I tried to think clearly about what kept happening to me. I was always butting my head up against the processes that were built all around me. I'd been so obsessed with making sure that everything happened in the way I thought was acceptable I'd not been paying attention to what was actually going on around me.

"You have to be more subtle with how you go about your dealings with the other members of The Circle. We are a very strong, good group but strength can also cause rigidity. You've fought within the confines of us before but this mission will be as much a test of your ability as a soldier, but also as a member of The Circle. We will both be judged by the outcome of this mission so you must be more careful. Trying to smash through obstacles won't work. You have to be more, persuasive."

She'd made sense, as always. Yet again I'd been a little too enthusiastic in my comments. I nodded to her and showed my understanding, accepting that I was going to be under the microscope even more than usual.

"Is that all I need to do to keep safe? Just make certain I say the right thing to the right people?" I nudged her in an attempt to lighten the mood.

It didn't work.

She folded her arms and stared at me, standing with her weight on one hip.

"You need to pay attention to so many other things as well." Her Russian accent was both threatening and alluring. I couldn't have whatever it was that was angering Andrea remain unresolved. Especially as it was on the brink of what was bearing all of the hallmarks of being my final endeavor within The Circle.

"What?" If in doubt, the direct approach. Showing that I'd listened to every word she'd said about the importance of always being more subtle.

"What is it that I did that you're holding against me? Believe me, I didn't do it on purpose, whatever it was and I'm really sorry if I've offended you."

She swayed ever so slightly as she listened but by the look on her face now, what I was saying was having a positive effect. Made a change.

I moved closer to her, feeling that the symbolic freeze between us was beginning to abate. She took a step back and scowled at me, the expression whipping upon her face at a terrifying pace.

"We will return to your estate to continue this conversation. There is a great deal that we have to prepare before we commence our journey to reclaim the Drake Stone." Her voice was oddly loud and booming in the stone tunnel under the pyramid but it left me in no doubt as to the meaning of her tone. Looking into her eyes as she raised her left arm, I could feel the Cascade Bridge crackle into form behind me and the gentle tidal tug of the power within the construct pulled on my senses like a magnet.

Andrea didn't let me say another word before she strode purposefully past me and through the bridge. I didn't let her get wholly past me before I turned and walked with her.

The gateway snapped shut behind us.

Walking from the sauna like temperatures of Egypt into the temperature of South Wales, even during what is considered summer-ish, was a shock to say the least. The only way I can describe the sensation is akin to walking into one of those industrial walk in freezers you get in restaurant kitchens. The feeling of walking between rooms of massive temperature differences isn't something you get a great deal of practice at.

We both walked through the Cascade Bridge together but our reactions were quite different. I felt like I'd been punched in the chest and couldn't help myself but cough as we stepped back onto the steps of my mansion in Wales. Andrea on the other hand, took in a deep breath of air and there was a level of tension which left her body at the completion of it.

"It feels good to be out of the heat." Andrea stretched as she spoke and started to form some very interesting forms with her body. I was looking purely with the eye of the personal trainer you understand. You can't just turn all that training off, you know.

She turned round slowly and faced me. My chest still felt like I had a lead weight pressing down on me and I swear I could feel every single alveoli in my lungs, each of them shocked by the sudden drop in temperature.

"Are you alright?" She asked with genuine concern.

"I'm fine, wasn't expecting such a huge temperature change that's all. Took me by surprise." I smiled/grimaced at her and straightened up, trying to keep everything all business, just like her.

She rolled her eyes at me.

"We are at your estate, yes?" She was at my side.

"Yes." Looking around we were stood at the top of the stairs by the front door. The door was shut and there was no sign of there being anyone around us.

"Then you can relax." What followed next was almost as shocking as any other detail which had come out of the day so far, including the frown from The Mage. She lunged forward, wrapping her arms around my neck and hugged me.

I didn't know what to do.

I'd been thinking all manner of things could take place but that wasn't one of them.

I was still stood with my mouth open and in a partial hug/poop stance when she snapped away from me, a fraction of a second before the front door to the estate swung open and Mark and the three members of my honour guard from the Mages cavern marched forward and stood to attention, waiting on the word from me.

I looked at Andrea and then back to Mark. She stood casually ready for anything and wore the expression of casual awareness that someone who hadn't just been hugging would have. Mark and his band of troops just looked like Mark and his band troops, bound in officialdom but utterly lethal.

In the middle of everyone, I carried the aura of the perpetually lost.

"We will be ready shortly my lord. When can we expect the other Guardian and the remainder of our party to arrive?"

"They will all be here shortly." Everyone just looked at me with the casual blank expressions of those who aren't aware that there may be anything else going on. Andrea wore the same expression despite herself.

"Have our other guests been given appropriate accommodation?" I was back to the purely business.

"Yes sir, they have. If you would like, I can take you to see the child."

"Yes please Mark. We'd both like to make sure she is comfortable."

Andrea just looked straight at Mark but I could feel that familiar tension return in her from next to me. She obviously wasn't as keen as I was to see Maria.

"Certainly sir. Please, will you follow me? I believe Llewellyn is still with her." Mark nodded curtly and turned to dismiss the other guards. Andrea and I casually followed him into the house and we made our way through corridor after corridor, into the guest wing to find Maria. I was slightly reassured that my mighty medic was on hand, especially after what he had done for the fallen guard a few days previous.

As we arrived outside the allotted room, I was struck by the memory I had of my stay in this part of the building. Lloyd had let me sleep here before my own Awakening when I was being pulled apart by the power raging inside me. Maria was going through the same thing but she was a small child. The discomfort must have been almost unbearable.

Mark slowly opened the door and stood to attention as both Andrea and I padded inside as quietly as we could.

Mark pulled the door to behind us and there was barely even a click of the lock as it closed.

Llewellyn was trying to hold a damp cloth to her fevered brow but by the look on his face, he had been fighting a losing battle. Our arrival must have been the last straw in terms of him continuing the task so he instead placed the cloth gently down on the table next to the bed and silently eased his way towards us.

"I'm sorry to report my lord and lady, that I am unable to help her condition in any way. All I can suggest is I give her a massive sedative so at least she'll be able to sleep through what's happening to her."

"She'll be dreaming and she won't be able to wake up." I could remember what it felt like.

"But at least her body will have some much needed rest. I'm sorry but it's all that I have open to me."

There was no more said between us and Llewellyn left silently, obviously headed for the infirmary to acquire the sedative.

We were alone with her.

Maria was still mainly in the fetal position but she was writhing and squirming on top of the bed. The covers were a distant memory for her and lay strewn in various heaps all over the floor. She was burning up and the droplets of sweat were very clear to see, matting her hair to her forehead and face. The hair plastered to her face did little to hide the expression of agony she was wearing. It gave her sweet features an almost demonic visage, as if the Dragon itself was pushing its way out against the flesh above it.

She grunted and squeaked, barked and wheezed. There was no doubt to anyone that she had to be helped quickly.

We'd both read the details of what had taken place during the gathering in Egypt and of what must be happening to the poor child but seeing the reality of her condition was something no-one could have been prepared for.

Andrea was hovering back by the door as I sat down slowly on the bed next to Maria. I tried to smooth her hair back away from her face, attempting to do something that may be able to have some kind of beneficial effect on her, to show even the barest hint of human concern. Looking down at her twisted body, it re-doubled my feelings on the importance of politics. Turning back to face my Guardian colleague, I repeated my stance.

"This is the reason we do what we do. Yes we have to look at the big picture. Yes we have to consider the population of the world in every choice we make but we can't look beyond the individual."

Andrea just stared at Maria, her own pained expression suddenly making me feel that I'd pushed too hard. She must feel more about this situation than I'd thought. Her own Awakening possibly?

I stood and joined Andrea by the door. Her eyes didn't move from Maria as I stood before her but I spoke to her softly anyway.

"We cannot overlook the pain of one person as an irrelevance. Next it becomes two people, then ten and then a hundred. The Hive think like that don't they? Caring is what makes us who we are. I think that The Circle has forgotten that."

She looked up and met my eyes. The conflicted expression remained on her face but the barriers which had for so long held back her emotions finally cracked. One tear fell from her left eye. It streaked down her cheek, leaving a trail on her porcelain skin. A second longer, and the water froze to ice and cracked from her face.

She made no attempt to hide it as she spoke to me. "You are a great quandary to me Anthony. I've been working with you for some time and there are so many things about you that make no sense at all. You seem to be permanently at odds with the actions of The Circle but you agree with what we're doing."

I considered that for a second but she continued before I could interject.

"I have watched you act in the defence of people no-one expects you to and you seem to want to pick a fight with almost every member of The Circle that you have contact with. You are a man of undisciplined thought."

I frowned at that but let her continue. She seemed to be ready to give me a huge insight into her character and I didn't want to break the mood.

"Despite everything that you do being an exercise in heart over head, I've found that I've started to question if you aren't in fact correct in the way you are choosing what you do."

My frown was replaced by an expression of confusion.

"What are you saying? That you don't believe in what we're doing, you're doing, or what I'm doing?" On the ball as ever but this needed to have the details spelled out to prevent even the tiniest of misunderstandings.

Andrea continued.

"I mean that I am looking at the actions of The Circle in this case here but also in so many that I have been dealing with over the years and, because of you, I'm starting to question. I've been in this life for so long there has just been the knowledge that things just happen in a certain way because they do, that they always have. I'm no longer sure that what you are saying is wrong because you don't understand who and what we are."

She stopped and pushed herself away from me, turning her eyes back to Maria as she continued her own struggle.

"I need to be away from here. I can feel so much power coming from the child, it's making my mind swim. I need to be away from the surrounds of The Circle, just for a short time but I don't know where to go. Where can we have some space from this?" Her voice was now far from that of the powerful woman I was used to dealing with. She now sounded unsure where previously there had been certainty. She had been forced to really look at the choices being made. And I knew that I had to do my best to resolve her uncertainty. Her admission to me could have highlighted to anyone perfectly, that she, along with all of the members of The Circle, Guardian or otherwise, was just as important an individual as anyone else.

"I've got the perfect place" I said and, reaching out my hand behind me, summoned as gentle a Cascade Bridge as I could. The last thing I wanted to do was cause Maria any further pain or to alert anyone in the estate to what was going on. I knew that when Llewellyn returned that he'd just assume that we had made our way to prepare for the quest at hand so we wouldn't be missed for some time.

I led us both through the construct. As it snapped shut behind us, Andrea looked around trying to gather some kind of understanding of where I'd just jumped us.

"Where are we? I don't know this place." Her emotions were hurriedly being brought back under control as she was trying to discover the details.

We were stood in an alleyway between two buildings, bin bags and litter strewn carelessly about. There was a light drizzle of rain falling on us from the bruised sky above but we were being afforded some level of protection from the tall buildings to either side of us. There was the sound of cars drifting on the air and the hustle and bustle of a city was bubbling along under that.

"I've brought you to my home." I smiled and started to walk away from her, aiming to the end of the alley to my left.

"Your home?" Her confusion was almost amusing but I knew she was hurting so kept the chiding to a minimum. She followed behind me as we exited the alley onto the roadway next to the building housing my flat in London.

We made our way round to the front doors of the building and were inside and out of the rain in no time. Both of us were still wearing the rather official ceremonial dress we had been in Egypt. My grey suit and Andrea's deep green business attire at least didn't stand out as much as they would have done to anyone in the Egyptian desert but I knew that the building I lived in wasn't populated by bankers or business people. I knew that my neighbors would be more used to seeing people in jeans rather than business dress and me specifically in sportswear in my day job as a personal trainer.

We were quick to climb the stairs to my flat and I fumbled around behind the name plate next to the door displaying my flat number, hunting out the spare key I'd squirrelled away. Pushing the door open, it swung smoothly until it heaved against the mound of post which had been building up over the intervening weeks. A small mountain of paperwork, letters, flyers, newspapers and other communications were swept aside as my door became the cow-catcher of the flat. I mounded everything up in one spectacular bundle as close to the wall as I could and beckoned for Andrea to come in. As she stepped gingerly over the threshold, her eyes fell to the pile of papers I was stood before. Perfectly framed on the front of a free newspaper was a picture taken from the Millennium Stadium in Cardiff, of a red Dragon swooping in on its white enemy, all under the heading proclaiming 'I'LL PROVE DRAGONS REAL SAYS EXPERT'.

I dropped the last few papers and menus behind the open door and just smiled at her.

Eventually we were inside and I shut the door against the world with as much ceremonial finality as I could muster.

The place smelled musty and there was a gathering of dust at far too many points around the rooms to be healthy. I'd never been the most fastidious cleaner but this was taking things a bit far. I hadn't managed to come back here following my almost continuous involvement in the fighting in Argentina and the flats appearance was far too clear an indication of it. Looking back into my bedroom as Andrea passed me I could see that my work phone was flashing to say I had messages. Professionally speaking, I think I was in trouble. All I could do was shrug and return my attention to my guest. One catastrophe at a time.

Andrea had walked into the main room of the flat and just stood staring at me, her face a mixture of emotions.

"You don't like it?"

"Why do you still have this place? Don't you have enough from the estate in Wales?" She asked the question but she was unsure of what the answer could mean. Taking my jacket off, I casually wandered back into the comfort of my *home*.

"I kept this place for just this reason. This is my home, my Fortress of Solitude. You said to me that you needed to get away from The Circle for a short time. So do I. I'll bet that every Guardian feels exactly the same from time to time."

Andrea nodded along with me, understanding what I'd said as it related to me but still fighting with the thought that any of the other Guardians could have ever felt the same way. She even got the Fortress of Solitude comment. Progress?

I lowered myself into the angle of my corner sofa and relaxed back into the comfortably familiar seat. Andrea just stared at me. She needed more explanation.

"This is where I feel like a human being. I lived here for years before the exciting life of The Circle came knocking on my door. I had a life which was mundanely enjoyable. I worked and then relaxed. The toughest thing that I had to be worried about was the mortgage each month or keeping my business going. No-one was trying to kill me every day."

Andrea considered the detail of what I was saying but it was clear to see that she wasn't fully understanding what I was trying to get across. She probably didn't even understand the concept of a mortgage.

Leaning forward out of the sofa, I reached out and took her hand.

"This is where I feel like I'm not a part of The Circle. This is where I feel that I'm not the barer of the power of a Dragon. This is where I'm normal."

Looking down at her hand and then to me, I could see the change in her posture as she knew that she was within a safe environment. She lunged forward to me and kissed me deeply, passionately.

That second was something that has had songs sung for it. That was the fraction of time you see in films where the object of his desire suddenly breaks from the normal routine and gives, in the most wonderful display of affection, proof that they have been feeling the same way. For a heartbeat I was rendered motionless as a statue, frozen by the sheer surprise of her actions. I could just imagine the expression on my face, all wide eyes and squashed lips. Finally I caught up with what was happening and began to kiss her back. There was no further awkwardness involved in what we were doing, we both just *knew* what the other was going to do and what they wanted. There was no further thought of anything which may have been between us. The fears and stresses of The Circle were gone and all that mattered was that we were together.

We broke apart after an eternity and just stared into each other's eyes, our heads resting gently against each other.

"I've never been normal. Show me normal." Andrea's voice was low and there was no confusion over what she had meant.

We melted into each other and there was nothing on Earth that was going to come between us.

21

Now despite what some people will say, I'm a gentleman.

I'm not going to give you any sordid details of what took place but just know that Andrea and I worked out so many of the issues that we'd been dealing with. I had been given the knowledge that Andrea thought more of me that just being another member of The Circle and she was given the first chance in her life to be more than just the mighty Guardian of The Circle.

We both lay on the sofa, clasped in each other's arms and breathing deeply. We both had a feeling of utter relaxation and contentment and I felt fantastic.

The relaxation didn't last long.

Andrea was still breathing hard when she leapt away from me and stood up, hurriedly adjusting her clothes and straightening herself.

"What's wrong?" I was less inclined to scrabble to my feet but I still did my best to protect my modesty.

"We are expected back at your estate. The Elder will be arriving soon, if she hasn't already, and we cannot be absent when she presents herself." She was still re-building the organized exterior as she spoke and it was easy to see that she was suddenly very nervous.

"What's the matter? You can't be scared that I won't call?" I began to re-adjust my own clothing and struggle out of the sofa. Andrea had by now backed away from me and had found herself with her back pressed up against the far wall of my living room. She stood rigidly straight and her eyes flicked nervously around, as if trying to pinpoint an unseen enemy.

"What's wrong?" I matched my own tone to the fear she was clearly feeling.

"It is forbidden to do what we have just done. We have just broken a very deep code of The Circle by giving in to the animal instincts. The Circle will know what we have done and they will punish us." Her eyes were still moving around the room but she was starting to tremble as she looked at every point at once.

I had to reassure her in some way. Stepping forward to meet her, I reached out my arms to hold her but she flinched away, as if they would infect her with the merest touch.

"What we did wasn't the end of the world. Every Guardian has had a family so The Circle can't be that bothered by the thought of Guardians being intimate." I reached for her again to soothe away her fear but she moved away again, resolutely keeping a space between the two of us.

"We can have families but we have to engage only in relationships sanctioned by The Circle. It is highly unusual to not do what is expected." I thought about my own mother and how her own choices of partner could be described as being highly unusual. That still didn't explain this level of terror.

"My own parents were together because my mother didn't do what was expected of her in her personal life. There were no reprisals because of what she was doing." She still didn't look any happier.

"Your mother chose her partner from outside The Circle but she chose what could be described as being with someone who was lesser than her. It is expressly forbidden that Guardians become involved. The threat that would imply to The Circle as a whole would be too much to accept." The tears had been clinging to her eyes but they started to fall as the threat that Andrea could see grew beyond what she was able to process.

"The penalty for such fraternization between Guardians is Bridging. We will be unmade and our power given for another to carry." She broke down into sobs and I just couldn't leave her. I scooped her up into my arms and just held her as she cried.

"Who told you that?" I needed to work out where the threat was coming from so I didn't accidentally reveal any details to the wrong person.

"My father always told me that there would be consequences to any acts of the flesh. It has been very clear that I was only allowed to have a relationship with someone who was deemed appropriate by The Circle. He said the punishment would be to have my power taken away. Having read what happened today, that means Bridging." She continued to hold her head down, not risking meeting my eyes as she was.

"No-one will bridge us." Deal with each point one at a time.

"The Drake Stone is missing. Besides, how will anyone know that anything has happened? It's a private matter between us, nothing for The Circle to know. I won't tell them and neither will you?" I held her to me and just breathed in the smell of her hair.

"The Circle always know. We have so many ways of knowing everything, we will be discovered."

"Only if we tell everyone. You've just got to work on your poker face. Just treat me the same way that you have been doing since we met and no-one will be the wiser. We both wanted this so it can't be wrong. All we'll need to do is behave in a normal fashion and the strength of The Circle will go on without a hitch."

Looking down at the top of her head, I could practically make out the gears whirring as she considered what I'd just said.

"We cannot afford to be discovered. This can never happen again and we will never speak about it. We will continue in our roles and there will be no further reference to any of this. Do you understand?"

She was now staring directly at me, her reddened eyes highlighting the process going on inside her. The fear she had been feeling was slowly being replaced by a hard brick determination.

I nodded my agreement but couldn't feel anything like the certainty she was currently channeling. Why shouldn't we continue to see each other? What damage could it really do? We were both adults and by the looks of things, it was time that The Circle updated their ideas to bring them into the twenty first century.

Andrea sighed slightly as she registered the relief that she felt the problem at hand settled. I knew that this was going to be something that we still had to resolve in the future but for now, I was glad the terror was gone. I just held her and stared into her eyes. We held each other that way for both a long time and no time, all at once. Following the decision we'd just made, there was now that all too familiar feeling brewing between us where I was just desperate to kiss her and I could see that she was feeling the same, despite herself.

That tension was wrapping itself around us tighter, and tighter as the seconds ticked slowly by and I could feel myself leaning in to kiss her, it was practically a natural reflex. As our lips closed on each other's, Andrea's eyes changed as she broke from the grip of her animal instinct and broke away from our embrace.

"This is a clear indication that we must be supremely careful in what we do. This will never happen again."

I was about to reply to her when the Cascade Bridge opened behind her. She took a step further away and pulled the construct in after her, repeating the single word "Never" as she left me behind.

I stood in the living room of my flat and knew that something massive had just changed in who we both were. Andrea had gone against the very fabric of who she was and everything she believed in to do what she had just done and it had been me who she had chosen to break those rules with. If the power players of The Circle ever discovered what we'd just done, we'd both be ended.

I hadn't even started out on the mission and I'd found another way for my own people to want me dead.

Great!

I left it twenty minutes before I opened my own bridge and returned to the estate in Wales. I wanted to make certain that Andrea was back and away from wherever I could possibly go, letting everyone see that we weren't together, even if we had been.

I decided to jump back into my own suite rather than risk anywhere else. I knew that there would be the chance of someone realizing that I hadn't been seen leaving Marias room but it was just too risky.

The gateway snapped shut behind me and the smell of ozone which accompanied the magic began to waft throughout the room, dissipating quickly. There was still a faint hint still in the air as the door opened and Mike came striding in, all ceremony and ritual poise. He started sniffing the air ever so subtly as he approached me, obviously picking up the hint of the magic still in the atmosphere.

"Didn't fancy walking back through the house did you bach?" He was maintaining his important pose and stood practically ram rod straight as he looked at me. His face, though, told a different story. He wore a very conspiratorial grin as he spoke, all the while keeping his voice low and his back to the door. Looks like he knew what was going on already, or at least part of it.

He raised his voice before I was able to give any form of response, official or otherwise.

"I present the arrival of The Elder of The Circle to the estate my lord." He tacked on a theatrical bow as a final flourish and stepped to one side, clearing my view of the door.

The Elder flowed into the room. There was barely any hint of her locomotion as she entered. It almost looked as if she was on roller skates and someone had just pushed her in, allowing her to roll effortlessly to a stop before me.

She looked to be wearing a version of ancient ceremonial armour from China, preparing herself for combat in a time long past. The black of the armour was decorated with astonishing detail to depict Dragon faces and beasts in various poses of authority, all rendered in what looked like gold leaf. She was truly familiar with being in a position of power.

"Thank you for the hospitality you have shown in allowing our shelter. My forces stand ready for our departure. Let us adjourn to discuss our opening move."

Her voice was her usual mix of hostility and contempt and she held a very loose hold on her emotions, allowing a great many of her feelings to leak through onto her face. She must have been forcing herself to wade through the platitudes which were so demanded by the time honoured traditions of The Circle.

"You are most welcome fellow Guardian. Michael. Would you please escort The Elder to the Library and I will join you there shortly." I had no idea what the correct response was supposed to be but I knew that I had to show at least some kind of understanding of what was taking place.

Mike bowed with just a little too much ceremonial starch and gestured for The Elder to follow him. She, in turn, nodded slightly in recognition and turned to follow. She didn't even acknowledge me, obviously keen to show me what she thought of me.

"And Michael." He stopped abruptly and turned to me.

"Would you please ensure that Miss Thomich is also called, there really is no time to lose."

Mike nodded in agreement and tried to hide his smile. "I will my lord." I think he tried to hide his smile.

After a hurried shower and a short but fruitless attempt to decide on the most appropriate clothing to wear for my very first war council, I entered my library dressed in jeans and a T-shirt, prepared for the worst.

Andrea and the Elder were the only two people in the room and they both turned to face me as the doors opened. The Elder was stood, still dressed in her armour and looking every inch the commanding officer of a feudal dispute. Andrea, though, was seated. She was dressed in more contemporary tactical gear but there were still areas of plate metal and some form of mail in her uniform. She cast her eyes towards me with no more concern than if any staff member of the house had entered. She didn't give even the barest hint that she was going through anything other than the mundane waiting before an important meeting.

I did my best to accept this as the actions of someone who had the strongest poker face you could imagine, someone who was keeping her end of the agreement to keep the actions of the pair of us a secret. I don't think that I was all that successful in transferring the same emotion to my face.

Her casual indifference to my arrival was a great deal more painful than I had bargained for. Despite knowing that there was a greater reason to how she was behaving, all I could feel from the very first second of the encounter, was a feeling of failure. I wasn't good enough for her to even register anything of me other than the most cursory of glances. My rational mind told me everything I needed to know, everything I already knew, but my internal fears screamed at me. Doubt and anger expanded in my chest and spread throughout my limbs. The power of the fire Dragon was making me worry no doubt.

"Please enter and close the door. We have precious little time to waste just staring at space."

The Elders voice cut through the fog of my internal torment and dragged me back to the here and now. Keep it together Anthony, for crying out loud.

I shut the door behind me and took a steadying breath before marching into the room.

"Just one more person to arrive and we can get started. Has there been any word from The Messenger?" Andrea and The Elder gave no indication of any prior knowledge before The Messenger herself announced her arrival.

"I have been here for some time my lord and ladies."

Each of us did our best to conceal the undoubted surprise that her words had caused. She had again just appeared before us from beneath whatever type of concealment or veil she had been working. Personally, the worst part of the situation had been that the first half of her sentence had been delivered from beneath the shroud. Her voice had been cast into the room with nothing to show as its source until she materialized. She simply stood in the room and waited on a response or action from anyone else.

The first thing which went through my mind was she had been amongst us without our knowledge. She'd been able to listen to everything which was being said in a room without the people in it being any the wiser. Andrea's words from my flat in London rang in my ears like the deep tolling of an ominous bell, *"The Circle always know. We have so many ways of knowing everything."*

If I'd thought of this as a potential threat, so would Andrea. I didn't dare look at her for fear of my own resolution collapsing before the pressure wall I could see rising before me. All I could do was keep my focus on the job at hand and try not to let paranoia get the better of me.

"Shall we begin?" I said as I strode in and aimed for the table at the far end of the room. The Elder watched me pass her with the intense gaze of a predator waiting to strike, but followed after me, her focus not wavering from me for a second. The Messenger and Andrea followed her.

I sat myself at the table and the three ladies joined me.

"Should we wait on the arrival of our pending Guardian? Mr. Blanco is here within this house so should be called to be a part of this discussion." The Elder had decided that her man Hairy was needed at this meeting and no matter what we were going to do, he was going to end up as the new man in charge in Argentina.

"Lady Elder. Only the most senior members of The Circle are to be in attendance in this meeting. You must know that fact?" The Messengers voice carried no malice or disappointment; it was just statements of fact that we should have all know.

I felt good that The Elder was coming up against someone who was happy to put her in her place but a small voice in the back of my head still whispered that Mark or Mike could have some vital input to the proceedings. Why was it that only the supposed big wigs got to sit in?

Nothing more was said on that point as The Elder made no further attempt to push her feelings forward. The silence draped itself over the room and waited for the meeting to remove it.

Back to business then.

"Where are we going to begin this hunt? We currently know nothing about the Drake Stone so we're a little at a loss." I hadn't meant to sound quite so negative but it just seemed to tumble out of me.

"We know a great deal about the Drake Stone, child." The Elder gave her opening salvo and the battle lines were drawn instantly. As she spoke, she gestured with her hands to give extra description to what she was saying.

"The Messenger knows everything which we will need." She may not have had all of the information herself but she was confident that someone on her team did, so by extension, she had the knowledge at her fingertips. Again, The Elder showed that she was completely certain of the infallibility of The Circle and everything it had at its disposal. All eyes passed to The Messenger and waited for her to shed some much needed light onto the subject.

"It is a deep purple, ovoid object, similar in shape to a chicken's egg, roughly the same size as a rugby ball."

I swear my mouth dropped open. Her voices pitch and intonation remained the same but it was only now that I realized that her vocabulary had lost all the thee's and thou's from our first meeting. The cadence was different as well. She was sounding more like one of any number of people who we've all spoken with over the years. The difference here was she didn't sound as if she was used to speaking in this fashion. On top of all that, she'd talked about a rugby ball? How did she know about a rugby ball?

The Elder noticed my surprise, as did the Messenger. Andrea kept her poker face intact.

"I have spent a great deal of time learning about you Mr. Johns. I do not understand a great many of the details related to you but I learn of everyone. You are to be a part of who I am within The Circle therefore you need to be fathomed."

There was a pause before she continued. "Did I use the sporting analogy correctly?"

My mouth dropped open again, though this time not solely because of the shock. I could hear more than just knowledge in her voice. The question carried a real concern for the accuracy of the information. I just nodded in the affirmative. I just didn't know what else to do. Considering how our previous encounter had unfolded, I hadn't expected to have anything less than snarls and aggression. To think that the Messenger had been learning about me? She was probably just readying herself for the arrival of a new Guardian and comrade but knowing that she had started to dig into the detail of who I was, was more than a little unsettling. Was she preparing a plan to lull me into a false sense of security?

She continued speaking without showing any further emotion, again in the more modern words of today's societies.

"The Stone was housed in a maze of wonders." Andrea and I looked on waiting for the follow up description but nothing was forthcoming. The Elder kept the same neutral expression on her face all of the time, showing nothing of any understanding she may or may not have.

"It was kept safe but in plain sight. It was part of the great private art collection of Bress Tal."

"Who?"

"Where, you fool." The Elder must have already known at least some of the details judging by that reaction.

The Messenger continued to hold the same expression despite another outburst from the floor. She made no sound but cast her hand out before her, causing the surface of the giant table we sat at to glow and buck. In seconds, a miniature city had grown from the wood to form a visual representation of what was being discussed.

"Bress Tal was an ancient seat of learning and antiquity in the long days before the total rise of mankind. Races of the wide Southern Empire kept everything of their wealth and knowledge in a shared city of wonders. People would come from all over the worlds to witness the wonders of the artwork, the knowledge held in the scrolls, the music, and the architecture."

The miniature city rotated as she spoke, highlighting specific images and creating stunning enchanted wood depictions of those wonders, all infused with a subtle yellow glow of animating power.

"There were objects of amazing power and unrivalled beauty in the collection, of which the Drake Stone was just one. The city was surrounded by walls of stone over a hundred feet high and half that thick to protect what was inside. The city was a beacon of harmony and was curated by only the wisest and most revered members of the races who made up the Empire, but above all things, it was a place of learning, meditation and peace."

Giant magical walls reared up around the edges of the miniature as she described them before folding back on themselves to hold the image of a beautifully smooth stone. I could only assume it to be The Drake Stone.

She took a breath and waited in the silence before she continued her history lesson. I swear it was just to create tension.

"When the war rose up between The Circle and The Hive, it was decided that it would be safer for the collection to be moved from Bress Tal to prevent it being destroyed or perverted. The Circle were able to divide the works into much smaller groups and have them spirited from the city before the enemy came for them. The majority of the artifacts were removed before the city fell but almost a quarter of what was held in the city was either destroyed or taken by The Hive when they over-ran the walls."

She took another breath, but this time there was no hint of there being a staged pause. This time the beat of recollection carried a much stronger air of reverence. When she started again, there was a new ring to her tone, that of resolution. It almost sounded personal.

"It was deemed by The Circle that to hold every artifact, artwork and weapon in one location would be unwise in the path of the oncoming conflict so everything was divided to allow us to protect the collection but also to prevent there being any possible way that The Hive would be able to acquire everything together in the future."

"What's so important about the Drake Stone? I read what was written on my scroll but that was pretty sparing with the details. Is there anything else we need to know about it? It's power? Other uses?" I could feel Andrea looking at me as I spoke and, maybe it was just wishful thinking, I could recognize an expression of appreciation. That was obviously the right thing to ask The Messenger. She, in turn, cocked her head slightly to one side before she spoke and her vision disappeared into the middle distance, her losing focus as her mind searching for the details.

"The stone was ancient even before the oldest races of this world were young. It was discovered by a Tromin party as the earth cracked apart as the lands shifted. I believe that you will have known of this occurrence as the continents breaking and moving apart." Another attempt to put the situation into words I could understand. "They witnessed a chasm open under the weight of the changing planet and found the Drake Stone, perfectly smooth and finished, within the rocky heart of the land they travelled over." I could feel a slight pull in my chest at the mention of the Tromin race. Lloyd had come from their line and I still missed his counsel.

"The Tromin had no idea what they had discovered but they recognized it as something of great value. It was taken with them wherever they travelled, passed down through their families until the earliest civilizations grew up. It was eventually taken to Bress Tal to be studied and it was there that the discovery was made of its ability to store the energy of the Guardian."

"Lady Messenger. Is that it's only power? Is it able to do anything else? Can it be used in any other ways?" The Elder spoke with a level of deference in her voice, no doubt aware that The Messenger was incredibly powerful so not someone to insult, but she was thirsty for knowledge.

The Messenger faced The Elder and cocked her head to the other side this time, again letting her mind wander her memories in search of the required details.

"The Stone is thought to have the power to focus and store power. It is believed that this ability comes from the properties of the stones crystal constituents rather any form of magical involvement but there has been no conclusive study done on this point. When The Mage discovered how he could store the power of a Dragon within the stone for a time, other uses and strengths of the stone were never found as study was stopped and it was dubbed The Drake Stone from that point on. Does this answer your question Elder?"

Our Chinese Guardian nodded her head curtly and there was no more said on the point. The Elder looked as if there were still questions she had that remained unanswered but she made no further attempt to push the point.

After a dragging heartbeat, Andrea was the next person to speak.

"Lady Messenger. Why did The Mage stop all study on the power and potential uses of the stone when he discovered the abilities to store a Guardians power?"

I flashed her my own expression of appreciation at her line of query. She wanted to know what I did. Why would you just stop when you could have been on the cusp of so much more? It really did look like we had both been having an effect on the thought processes of the other.

The Messenger regarded Andrea with a casual indifference and cocked her head again, delving back into the details she had stored in her mind.

"There were no details ever stored on the reasoning of The Mage. As leader of our order, he has made decisions for the whole population of this planet. There must only be the one conclusion drawn for all of The Mages actions. He saw that our cause would be advanced by the cessation of study and further comment would be superfluous."

Now that was an interesting answer.

"Does this answer your question Miss Thomich?"

Andrea nodded her answer but it was clear for me to see that despite her submissiveness, she was far from content with the answer.

"All this is good to know so far but that doesn't really advance us a huge amount. We're still no closer to working out where the stone is." We needed to get back on track.

"I think it may be a good idea that we examine the site the stone was taken from, see if we can find some clues or pointers as to the who's and why's of this whole situation. Agreed?"

The three ladies all looked at me in silence but each wore a very different expression. Andrea seemed to be the only one who was reacting like I'd just had a good idea. The Elder still looked like she was barely keeping her desire to have my flayed alive under control and The Messenger just looked at me with nothing showing on her stark features.

"That would be an appropriate place to begin." The Messenger gave a small bow and the decision was made.

"Excellent. Where have we got to go and dust for prints?" A little positivity leaked out as someone agreed with me openly. No-one got the reference.

Try again.

"Where was the Drake Stone held?"

Again, The Messenger delved inside herself to retrieve the details.

"The Drake Stone was hidden in the fraction of the collection saved from Bress Tal which has been watched over by one of our very Guardians. It was held in The Circle Mansion in Argentina."

22

We all moved very quickly.

The Elder, Andrea and I told The Messenger to wait where she was for the next twenty minutes while we put our forces together in preparation and we would meet her on the steps at the front of the house ready to depart. She just had her own honour guard of giant warriors and I somehow doubted that they'd be anything less than at the highest alert. She agreed with nothing further added and, nodding tightly, simply disappeared, concealed under her impenetrable shroud. She'd said she was going to stay there but there was no way of knowing if she was going to.

The twenty minutes passed in roughly six amidst a flurry of hurried activity and rushing about. Mike and Mark screamed around the mansion pulling together the people that we would need should there be a sudden call for an armed response while Andrea and The Elder headed to the rooms we had billeted their people in readiness.

As they pulled the people together, I waited in the reception of the mansion, doing my best to look regal and as if I was thoroughly in control of what was going on around me. Looking around as people busied themselves around me, I was joined by Leatherpants who sidled up and stood next to me, still clad in his magical skin suit and finery. Always classy.

"My lord. Are you having trouble assembling your force? I would be most willing to offer you my services as a facilitator to expedite the gathering of the people you seem unable to pull together."

He spoke looking at the activity before him. As he finished though, he leant forward in a bow of sorts and eased himself into my field of vision. I had been doing my best to ignore him but he was determined to elicit some kind of response.

Deep breath Anthony. Keep calm.

"Thank you Mr. Ward, but I think that we will be fine without your help." I kept my eyes focused resolutely ahead, picking out the details of the turned wood in the staircase rather than looking at him. He didn't leave it there.

"Lord Guardian. Is there anything else I could offer you to be able to help the mission get underway? It does seem, to a lowly functionary such as myself, that you are experiencing problems. I am, of course, only judging you against the standards that The Elder sets of me and that I then set of my people. I am more than willing to offer my considerable experience to help order your staff. I have been involved in the activities of The Circle for a great deal longer than you after all."

Again he leant forwards and practically dared me to look him in the eyes. He was starting to get under my skin.

Deep breath again.

It didn't work. I'd just had enough of him wanting to prove how great he was. He needed to be put in his place.

"Your help would be wonderfully received, thank you." Leatherpants could barely hide his smugness at the apparent tacit agreement that he was more able than me. Ahead of us Mike was marching with a rod straight back and a determined expression on his face. He was ready.

I continued to Leatherpants as Mike stood before us both.

"Will you please go and get my black leather coat from the cupboard in the main hall? It would appear that my staff have forgotten it."

I'll give him credit, he didn't show anywhere near the level of anger I would have if our positions had been reversed. He did though, harrumph and stride away on his mission grumbling as he went. Probably didn't help that I was already wearing another jacket.

Mike smiled ever so slightly.

"You've got to be careful of him. He carries a great deal of power within The Circle. Don't just antagonize him, you may need him soon."

"I know, I know. It's childish and I should be above such things but he needs to be reminded of his station. I will not have someone like him thinking he can push me around. I will keep him in his place."

Mike frowned and nodded slightly, "As you wish my lord."

That hurt.

An awkward silence fell between us and I couldn't look him in the eye. I'd just done exactly what I had been straining against from the first day in the fight. I'd thrown my weight around and there hadn't really been any cause for it. If I'd used my position of power to change some great injustice or defend someone weaker than myself I could at least defend my actions as being for the good of one or many. What I'd just done was make fun of someone who, despite being a world class knob about it, was only trying to help. I'd probably just antagonized him even further so he'd probably just take it out on the people below him. Excellent work Anthony. The hot head of the Fire Dragon doing something that seems like a good idea at the time which will do nothing but hurt people around you.

"Look ..." I started to apologise but Mike spoke first.

"Come on bach. I know what you meant." A broad grin creased his face as he slapped me too hard on the arm. "If I was in your shoes I'd have done worse to him by now."

I didn't add anything. I didn't need to. I just smiled back at him, relieved that I hadn't broken something between us. It was at that moment that Leatherpants re-joined us, my leather jacket casually slung over his arm. Our smiles faded back to the blanks of all business.

"Was this what you required my Lord?" His tone was back to his syrupy servile best as he proffered my jacket. Any anger or frustration had been utterly smoothed over.

I reached out and lifted the jacket from him to give it a cursory look before discarding it (in as respectful a manner as I could, Mikes words still ringing in my ears) but got no further than taking it from Leatherpants.

I couldn't believe my eyes.

Both of the sleeves remained on his arm, both severed from the jacket as a whole. Whatever he'd used to make the cut hadn't been that sharp judging by the ragged ends.

Leatherpants and I just stared at each other.

"Is your jacket to your liking my Lord?" That sticky voice of his was pouring all over me, threatening to swamp me in saccharine deference.

I could feel from Mike next to me and, despite his best efforts, from Leatherpants as well, the subtle fear of anticipation. Both knew that the Fire Dragon would behave in a very set fashion after such a slap in the face so they were readying themselves for the inevitable.

"HA! Fair enough." You had to admire what he was risking. Standing up to a much more powerful adversary who was pushing weaker people about. It was so easy to become the bully. Somehow, I'd found myself on the wrong side of the equation.

Mikes words were truly still in my mind as I responded. I'd given him a dressing down before my 'staff' despite his elevated position within this group and he'd just repaid the favour. He wasn't at my level in the hierarchy of The Circle but he was as close as anyone could be without them being an actual Guardian and he'd pushed back.

Mike was right. I needed to keep him on side despite my dislike of him. That and I had to treat everyone like the human being they were. I'd been happy to talk the talk, now I was being put into a position to walk the walk.

Mike and Leatherpants flicked glances back and forth between themselves and me, both uncertain what my reaction could ultimately mean.

"Touché. Come on then team, let's get amongst it." I grabbed all of the ruined coat and threw it at the nearest wall before slapping Leatherpants on the arm, more than just a bit too hard, and made my way out of the main door.

Outside, everyone was gathered ready to fight. Each member of the task force who had been brought together were armed to the teeth with all manner of medieval weaponry and they all looked like they were standing on the edge of a very violent and potentially fatal battle.

Andrea stood with her group and was speaking quietly to a couple of her guards who were clad in what can only be described as an Elvish interpretation of the Snow Storm troopers uniform from The Empire Strikes Back. The armour was all white except for the small eye slits in the blank faced helms. Whereas the Empire had been very functional concerning their uniform, these looked as if they had been fashioned with the greatest of care in every detail. The most subtle of designs could just be seen on the various surfaces, none wishing to truly scream to be looked at but exquisite in their design none the less. Her whole guard looked ethereally beautiful, almost as if they were designed to be nothing more than works of art.

They weren't the only armoured troops.

The troops who joined us from the estate in China all stood stiffly to attention in ordered lines. They wore a similar uniform to the Elder but they were far less ornate. I cast my eye over the assembled battalion and could pick out different designs and pictures on their armour which no doubt signified the different ranks within their army. Each had worn a helmet with the full face guard designed into the traditional demon design. As Andrea's troops, the only feature of their faces that I was able to see was their eyes.

My soldiers were still to join the group. All I could do was just stare on and do my best to keep my mouth from dropping open. I had to cling to the knowledge that Mike had said everything was under control.

Each and every member of the guard who waited for the off was attired in a way that called back to a long past time when there was no mass production of materials. Each soldier's uniform had been created with the future wearer in mind. Everything about the group was bespoke, I suspected, even down to the weapons.

Andrea though was able to outshine all of them.

She had finished speaking with her lieutenants and had turned to face me. When I'd last seen her she had been wearing a great deal of more modern tactical gear along with areas of more 'olde worlde' plate armour but she'd obviously been busy completing her dress since we had finished our meeting. She was now stood in what can only be called Angel Armour.

She was now covered in what looked like full ceremonial battle dress taken from the pages of so many graphic novels or from computer games. She was practically glowing as she strode towards me, her simple protective wear catching the sunlight and wreathing her to perfectly highlight that she was so much more than human. Her white hair had been pulled back into a tight braid giving her a severe expression which left no room for argument.

Her glare could scare a man perfectly well without her even having to consider the helmet she carried under her left arm.

"Why are you not in your suit of armour?" She asked me with the familiar tone of the teacher addressing a particularly slow student.

"No one said anything about armour. Don't we just need to have everyone prepped and ready if we need them? We're going to the estate in Argentina, we're not jumping into an enemy stronghold are we? We were both there a few days ago and there was no threat of doom from the staff there, was there?" I understood the need to be prepared but come on.

"The Drake Stone was stolen from the estate. The item is of huge importance to The Circle and there was no sign of there having been an attack to remove the item." Andrea began to lay out points which, to her, seemed to be obvious to everyone. The Elder arrived next to her as she continued.

"None of us knew where the stone was kept prior to the knowledge coming from the Messenger. The Hive were able to attack us regularly in Argentina and not allow us the knowledge of what their true goal was. They obviously had prior knowledge of the location of the stone so will more than likely be watching that location to be certain of how long we are unaware of the theft."

Both ladies folded their arms as Andrea spoke in a startlingly similar way. Now The Elder joined in.

"If the site in Argentina is compromised by The Hive, we need to show a swift and violent response, proving to the enemy that we are not to be crossed. A full out assault on the estate is the only option here." The words came from The Elder but there was no anger behind them this time.

"Why?" It was all I could ask.

Andrea picked up again.

"Because in this situation, when there is an on-going threat of one of our bases being infiltrated by any creature from The Hive, we advance on it and make certain that if there had been any form of breach, it is neutralized in the clearest way we can muster, thereby sending a message to anyone who is aligned against us that we will stop at nothing to defend our duty."

I just stood dumfounded. If in doubt, nuclear option. At least they hadn't done that to my estate after what happened when I was brought into this conflict.

But they probably thought about it.

Just in case.

"Do you doubt the tactics we are to use here?"

The voice came from nowhere but I knew that she would show herself soon enough. The veil shimmered away and The Messenger was left standing at my side.

"Yes I doubt the tactics. Are you insane? Why is it a good idea to just level the estate?" I still had that flicker in my stomach at the knowledge that they were probably readying themselves to do the same to everyone around me only a matter of months ago.

Now all three women just put their hands on their hips and stared at me.

The Elder was the one who spoke.

"Look back through your memories. This has been done for years if there had been a threat anywhere near this kind. A swift and decisive strike to cleanse everything we are and send a message to our foes." She added, again with the calmly modulated tone, "Look through your experiences to see the truth. We aren't lying to you."

I was so unnerved by her more calming tone that I just delved directly back, hoping to be able to prove her at least partly wrong.

The pictures swap before my eyes and I looked into each of them in turn. One by one, long past recollections of the horror that was the Dragon Guardian line beamed out in the most perfect immersive experience. Sights sounds and smells all crashed into the wall of my mind, illuminating to me what had happened before. And they all showed the same thing. The other members of this party had been telling the truth. I watched on as estate after estate was demolished before the power of the advancing army. I recognized several sites from South Wales and watched on as Neath Abbey and Neath Castle were both ripped apart by magic and Dragon alike.

But none of this made the decision the right one.

"You see that we have done this before? We as a group understand what we have to do." Andrea's voice was cool and business like but there was still a glimmer of calming power in it. She was speaking as The Circle but at least she was showing some level of compassion. It wasn't just a matter of levelling the sites.

The Elder continued, and matched her tone with Andreas. There was no anger in her voice but there was still a level disappointment to her tone.

That was even worse despite my opinion of her and everything she was talking about.

"We have been doing this in this way for thousands of generations. This has given us the peace of mind to continue, knowing that we have done everything in our power to stop any weakness which may have afflicted us."

"But there are other options which need to be discussed, surely. Messenger, is this tactically the best move we have available to us or is there just the reliance on what has been done in the past? Can't we at least have a discussion about a course of action before we ruin a perfectly good mansion?"

All eyes turned to The Messenger, the two ladies looking on with expectation that she would back up their opinion, me with a shred of hope she'd at least listen to mine.

"Everything that Mr. Johns has said is accurate. This may be an unusual course of action but the logic that has been delivered is sound."

The Messenger had been beaten to the punch and whatever opinion she had been about to provide had been still-born.

This time we all turned to face the owner of the voice who had leapt to my defence. We had all been so focused on the discussion that we hadn't even noticed anyone else approaching to listen to what was being said. Leatherpants just stood with his hands behind his back, rod straight with his familiar expression of casual certainty fixed in place.

The Elder looked at him with a mixture of surprise, pride, horror and anger all warring for control of her. She wasn't the only one who was caught off guard by his comment. My own mouth must have been swinging open judging by the expression that Leatherpants flashed back at me, the barest frown coming my way.

"Why do you feel that this deviation from our recognized course of action is such a positive move?" Andrea was angry, judging by the clipped tones which were wrapped around what she was saying. Maybe my influence was starting to rub off on Leatherpants if he felt that it was appropriate to butt in on the conversation of the Guardians. Either that or he was just trying to push my idea forward to trip it up later. Having him agree with me was already more problematic than having him against me.

I'll say this for him, he reacted very quickly to placate any anger which was clearly rising in the group.

"My Lord and Ladies, I did not intend to cause any offence at all. I merely wished to offer my view on the issue at hand. My Lady

Elder had asked me to look into the behaviors and tactics shown by Mr. Johns in an attempt to better work with him in the mission and in my studies, I have been able to identify that, despite his unconventional attitude and complete lack of understanding of what he is doing, he does have a very singular way of reading situations that present themselves."

The ladies looked at him, carefully weighing up what was being said while I tried to work out if he'd just insulted me or not. He continued.

"Mr. Johns has claimed that our recent failures in battle have been caused by, what did you call it? 'Our calls being worked out?'"

Him saying that just seemed to make the phrase sound ridiculous.

"Looking at the detail of what has been happening to The Circle as a whole and to Mr. Johns as an individual since he was given the great gift of the Guardian power, it would appear that his childish appraisal of the situation is accurate. Even if he is the one who has been giving our plans to The Hive, following his suggestion here will either uncover his treachery as The Hive will be forced to show themselves or we will be able to gather much needed information. Either way, The Circle will be advanced by deviating from what has always been the usual course of action."

He finished speaking and bowed with a modicum of subdued ceremony.

The silence seemed to squat on the group, an angry creature almost daring someone to be the one to speak and set off a storm of fury.

But that storm was blown out before it could take hold. He really was very comfortable dealing with the Dragon powers who were his superiors. Over the generations he had been at The Elders side, he'd learnt his skills exceptionally well.

"Mr. Ward is correct. Only the Guardians shall travel to Argentina in the first instance but all of our forces will be prepared should they need to be called to deliver our more accustomed solution."

The Messenger was as emotionless as ever as she spoke and the decision was made. The Elder flitted her eyes from Leatherpants to me and back again but also kept the mask of blankness she always wore, firmly in place. Andrea was the only one of the group who was showing any kind of emotion.

She was trying her best to maintain that strong glacial mask of her own but there was fire building behind it. Without any real effort I'd found myself on her bad side again. Was she taking this personally?

I didn't have the time to find out.

Leatherpants had already melted from the group to re-join the soldiers of The Elder, knowing that there was nothing more to be said by him. The Elder was already half way out of her armour, piece by piece just floating from her as she magically dismantled her ceremonial dress. Andrea slowly closed her eyes and began the same process herself. Both women's battle dress gathered together before them until it had been totally removed from their bodies, then briskly drifted towards a member of their war force. It was a relatively basic use of magical power but it was impressive this close, none the less.

Their armour removed, The Elder and Andrea were left wearing a garment which was almost exactly the same as the Messengers. All three women were now stood in very form fitting suits which I could see now were actually vital pieces of the armour they had been wearing. The Elder and Andrea had metallic discs and hooks spaced evenly all over their suits, showing how the armour had been fastened but also how it could have been removed so easily. Looking closer still I was able to make out miniscule flecks of colour glinting like tiny river courses all over the fabric.

My studies of the detail of this level of what was being worn was interrupted by an angry sounding cough. Andrea had made the sound but by the expression on all three faces, my attempt to gather information had been misunderstood. Typical.

"Right" I stammered and clapped my hands together to try and break the mood which was now standing with us and laughing at me.

"It really only needs the four of us to travel to Argentina doesn't it? There's no point being anything other than relaxed about all this."

"Agreed" said The Messenger, immediately adding more weight to my argument. "Mr. Johns and I will follow behind Miss Thomich and The Elder as they infiltrate the site and gather information. We will act as your support and protection whilst in the estate but gather information ourselves but in a more covert fashion."

"Acceptable." The Elder was switching to business mode as she took orders from The Messenger.

"One question." I just needed one point cleared up first.

"How are we going to be more covert and act as their support? I think we'll need to have some serious thought about what it is we'll be walking into."

The Messenger just held that slightly confused expression of hers, just dealing with that familiar slow mind of mine. Until the penny dropped and she could see on my face that I'd caught up.

"We're going in under that cloak of invisibility of yours aren't we?"

She smiled as I worked it out. She smiled cutely and showed off her dimples.

"You will have to remain close to me as we move through the estate to prevent there being any risk of you stepping outside of my control. Are you ready for that Mr. Johns? The closer the better."

The smile remained on her face as she spoke.

What the hell did that mean? Was I mis-reading the whole situation or was she coming on to me? The crackle of anger which crawled over my skin suggested that Andrea had noticed and thought the same thing.

Covert mission to infiltrate a potential enemy stronghold with three people who all seem keen on keeping an eye on me for one reason or another.

Why can't anything be easy?

23

The Elder opened the Cascade Bridge and we all stepped through from the gravel driveway of my estate in South Wales to the comparable position at the estate in Argentina. The Elder and Andrea lead the way, walking with a casual confidence which came from the knowledge that they were going to be fawned over and shown utter deference by all of the staff at this estate or that they were going to be walking into the belly of a newly minted Hive fortress. Either way, it wouldn't be the done thing to show anything other than absolute confidence. The Messenger and I followed close by, veiled by a magical wall which made us utterly unseen.

The sensation within the veil was kind of like being in one of those massive balls you can either walk on water or roll down hills. There was a tangible weight to what we were surrounded by, like it had mass that we had to move along with us. The Messenger had said that it would be able to completely remove us from the awareness of the site, meaning we could speak normally and no-one would hear us but also that we could traverse any surface without there being any tell-tale signs. You could just imagine all the effort being for nothing because of muddy footprints on carpet. That would certainly have me hung, drawn and quartered.

The Messenger was holding a constant pulse of power as we moved to be able to hold the construct. The effort wasn't enough to be able to slow her down or cause her any stress but the strands of colour through her suit were glowing a subtle purple to highlight the magical effort.

Our magical ball rolled along behind The Elder and Andrea, our senses only slightly dulled due to the power of it and I tried to keep my eyes open for any chance to be able to work out how The Hive had been able to do what they had. I needed to be able to prove that I wasn't the monster that everyone else thought I was. Even though I can be a monster. A real monster, not a metaphorical one. But a good one. Not evil. You know what I mean.

Our collective pace slowed as The Elder and Andrea approached the imposing doorway at the front of the estate.

The design of this mansion was very similar to my own, all heavy stone and intimidation wrapped up in implied poise and decorum. The gravel driveway of this mansion had been dead straight rather than the weaving route of my own but the effect had been the same. The crunching of the stones beneath feet had been enough to alert the staff to the arrival of guests aside from the undoubted power shift of our arrival.

The huge doors were swung open with equal measures control and panic and a group of very nervous people made their way towards us. The woman at the front of the approaching group, a tall, lean woman whose age could have passed comfortably for anything between thirty and fifty, was the first to speak.

"My ladies, I must apologise for not greeting you in the appropriate fashion, we were not told that anyone would be attending this site other than our returning personnel and our new Guardian."

She bowed deeply and gestured that everyone around her do the same. They all did.

As one they straightened and the worry was clear to see even from within this magical veil. They had been expecting a new Guardian. They'd known that Maria was next in line so would need to be replaced. Was I being paranoid or was that knowledge jumping the gun? I'd have to look into that.

The Elder was responding as I pondered.

"You have been mis-informed. We are here to review the site in readiness for the next Guardian. The Circle knows that you have all been under such pressure recently that we wish to ensure you are all still able to do your jobs."

Everyone in the group went pale. The easiest way to wander the house freely wasn't to threaten the abilities of those in said house. Now everyone would be doubly on edge.

"What my fellow Guardian means is that we want to assist you all in the correct preparations. You have all been dealing with so much with the recent losses at this site. We want to safeguard the health and well-being of every member of the Circle." Andrea's words softened the blow somewhat but it was clear that there was still a fair amount of apprehension.

"Interesting that Miss Thomich should use such a tactic to elicit obedience from the staff here. Everyone within The Circle, at every level of service, understands that they must obey the commands of their superiors." The Messenger spoke almost absent mindedly, not taking her eyes from the people ahead of us.

"Maybe you have had an effect on our Siberian Guardian?" She turned to look at me. "What do you think Mr. Johns?"

"She's just trying to get the best response in the quickest time, nothing else." That comment made it very clear that I was going to be watched just as closely as everyone else in the Argentinian estate. I shrugged in response but kept my gaze ahead, showing her that I would rather just concentrate on the relatively easy task of the potentially violent mission ahead. She didn't push the point, instead returning to what was taking place before us.

The lead woman bowed deeply again and gestured that she would direct her guests to whatever location within the estate that they may desire. The remainder of the welcoming committee surged back into the house and, no doubt, back to their respective departments to do their best to prepare for the scrutiny of the visiting Guardians. The Messenger and I silently started moving again.

As we approached the main doorway we were confronted with a choice. Should we just follow behind our colleagues or should we separate and go exploring on our own? Both options had merits but they also had potential flaws. Fatal ones at that. We really should have done more planning before we'd got underway. The Elder and Andrea had stopped as they were being introduced to a small pocket of people giving me time to check on the preferred course of action.

Turning to The Messenger to vent my concerns I caught myself. I couldn't spend the whole time calling her The Messenger?

"What's your name?" Back to the direct approach.

She gave that same canine head tilt, considering my special brand of nonsense.

"Are you well? Have you forgotten that I am The Messenger of The Circle?" At least she had a level of concern in her voice for me, that was something.

"Not your title, your name. I know that there seems to be a real need to have everyone saddled with a title with begins with 'The' but what should I call you? I'm Anthony and you are?"

This time she dropped her line of sight to the floor and made no sound for a handful of seconds.

"I have no name. I am The Messenger of The Circle and that is all I am. I am to serve at the hand of The Mage and act as his hand in roles beyond his reach." The deep voice which had been the barer of such authority had now shrunk. Not to a squeak but it had certainly deflated.

Watching her actions, I could sense that this wasn't how she would have answered that question when we had first met. Her diction had changed since then but so had she. She was concerned that I might have been having an effect on Andrea but had I already had an effect on her just by being a part of The Circle?

"How about, rather than the full The Messenger, I just call you Em from now on? Shorthand rather than the full title might make more sense if we get into any trouble."

She tilted her head again as she met my eyes with her own and agreed with a short nod. Her expression was back to the usual blank visage showing no signs of any emotions lingering and the confidence was back in her posture. I think she thought that was acceptable.

Outside the bubble, Andrea and The Elder (what should I call her for shorthand?) were moving off down the corridor towards the back of the house, leaving us still to decide a course of action

"Follow them or make our own way? Any preference?" I wanted to get to wherever The Drake Stone had been stored before doing anything else but I was still wary of making any choice for fear of how it may be interpreted.

"We should explore the estate on our own. The Guardians are more than capable of defending themselves against attack should it present itself and we will be more likely to discover something if we are not surrounded by servants." Her logic was sound, I'd been leaning that way myself, but to hear her call all the people in the estate servants still grated a little.

We made our way from the entrance hallway and Em sent us to the right.

"Where are we headed? Are we just going to wander about or do you have a specific destination in mind?"

"I am aware of where The Drake Stone was located so I feel we should start our investigation there. She may not have known it, but it felt good to know that we had at least agreed on this first course of action.

Moving at a brisk pace through the labyrinthine corridors of the Argentinian mansion, we soon found ourselves stood before a massive pair of heavy wooden double doors. Black metal studs were everywhere over the surface and there was a definite air of medieval castle to the whole affair. There were even genuine burning torches either side, complete with the smoke staining on the walls and ceiling, truly selling that we were before an ancient stronghold. The massive locks on the door were the icing on the cake.

"We'd better be careful opening the door. We haven't passed many people but the last thing we need is to have a stray member of the team here wander by and witness the door magically opening and closing with no help from us."

"Not a concern."

I hadn't even had time to respond before Em simple grabbed my arm and marched us both forwards into the closed door. And through and out of the other side.

I collapsed. My head was spinning in the same way that it does when my danger spidey sense goes off but this time it was dragging around at least a ton of broken glass. I couldn't open my eyes and was using all of what strength I had left to be able to just hold onto the hard stone floor. The seconds dragged on and the spinning calmed, first losing the extra material it was dragging and then dialing down on the revolutions. It left behind a fuzziness in my mind and a squirming nausea in my stomach.

"What the hell was that?" I was breathing hard but I was at least able to ease myself back to my feet. Em, as it seemed with every question I asked her, just looked at me.

"We have passed through the doorway, nothing more."

"So we can just walk through things now?"

"The fields surrounding each of our prisons and estates is of the same magic. It has the ability to remove that which is inside from the same reality of everything which is on the outside. Depending on the type of casting, the size and form, it is possible that a smaller, denser field can carry the occupants through anything which comes in their way."

That made sense. It shocked me that she would be so forthcoming with the answers I'd requested though. It did lead to another question though.

"Why didn't I feel like I'd been kicked in the mind when I crossed the shield line the first time I entered the mansion in Wales? If this is all the same power, why did it hammer me now?"

"You are built entirely to function at the site in Wales. All of your powers are woven through every aspect of everything that happens there magically. In this estate you are not the main power so you would have felt a tingle as we came through. The hammer blow you referred to comes from the fact that we have just traversed a great shield wall. It is much more concentrated than the main defences around our various sites. This is a vault which needs to be defended. Also, the entrance way in Wales is designed to allow the smooth passage of people without them feeling any effect." Em smiled somewhat uncomfortably at me with the last comment. It obviously wasn't something she was used to doing, the attempt at humour or the smile. I didn't know what to say in return.

Em took my sudden silence the wrong way.

"Did I answer the question to your satisfaction? Have I said something wrong?"

The spinning in my head was receding to nothing again but that question knocked me off balance again. I wish she'd make her mind up. Was I someone she was keeping a close eye on with the potential of ripping me apart or was she trying to gain my approval as a potential senior member of the group she was serving?

"Thank you, yes. Everything was good. Where are we?"

Looking around the room we were now stood in I was surrounded by all manner of artifacts and objects of so many different sizes, shapes and materials that it gave the impression of the most densely packed museum of priceless wonder the world had ever seen. The room was more akin to something which would house an indoor tennis court, large but also at least triple height. On all of the available wall space were hanging all manner of paintings and weapons, tapestries and clothing.

But the contents didn't stop at just the wall hangings.

There were so many pieces on display of every imaginable kind and then so many more I couldn't have ever imagined, that lounged and crouched and stood proudly, it became difficult for your eyes to focus on any one detail in particular. There was just so much here. Huge panels of deep wood surrounded the room in the same way my own estate was decorated. Opulent function to always envelop the estate. Ragged towers of all kinds of precious objects surged up towards the far away ceiling and their respective bases sprawled out into any and all space which they could find. The way everything was wedged together reminded me of the way ancient trees burst their roots through concrete and just expand to fill the available area around them, no order, just use of the emptiness they could find.

Em exhaled in a sigh which was equal parts magical release and pleasure and stretched her back, the spell of her veiling collapsing and draining around us. That stretch reminded me of Andrea. All tight muscle and suggestion.

I didn't dare let my mind linger on that thought. The last thing I could afford was to let Em know anything about Andrea and I. Pushing the thoughts away as Em relaxed her posture, all I could do was try to keep things focused on the task at hand.

"This is a fragment of the collection from Bress Tal?" It was almost too much to believe that what we were looking at, stretching into every available piece of space in the room, including stretching up and reaching to the ornately decorated ceiling, was just a fragment of the repository of wonder which had been held in the fabled mighty city. It was like discovering that King Solomon's Mines were nothing more than a gift shop and this was the main attraction.

I made to step forward into the mass of precious everything but Em thrust out an arm and stopped me in my tracks, just as the spinning in my head returned but this time caused by my own early warning system.

"We must disarm the more subtle defences before we continue." Her voice was low and she flicked her eyes skywards, directly at the top of the mighty statue which was stood directly in the centre of a pool of golden coins.

Sat atop the marble column was an exquisite rendering of a lion, carved from the same marble as its perch and sat rigidly at attention. The artwork sat a proud foot in height but had all of the regal wonder of a true lion. The concern for us was it was staring directly at us with a sullen red fire burning in each eye.

"What is that and why is it looking at us?" Insightful.

"That is an enchantment of the carving. It is a guard of the room which can just be left once it has been cast. It will attack anything which comes into this room which isn't coming in in the correct manner." I took a slow step backwards and the things attention followed me, its marble neck grating ever so slightly as it tracked its target. That meant us.

"Enchantment of the carving eh? What does it mean to us practically? How are we going to get past it?" I was starting to feel like a mouse who was being watched by an ever so scary owl, trying to edge away without making myself seem like a viable option for dinner. As my wary eyes moved away from the lion for as long as I dared, I could make out several other statues of the same design, some cracked, some whole, some missing the lion altogether and others with much larger lions. Just so you'd never be sure where the attack was coming from.

My Dragon could squash this thing without a second thought but I couldn't risk becoming my beast in this enclosed space. We'd have to do this another way.

"It is quite simple to destroy. It is, after all, just marble. Crack it in half."

This time, Em took a step forward, but hers was a forceful incursion rather than my own stuttering effort. The lion leapt from his perch and hurtled directly at Em, its jaws spreading much wider than any real creature would have been able to. Em casually reached out and caught the falling animal by the throat, and with a deft swish of her wrist, wrenched its head clean from its body.

The two pieces of the creature fell to the floor and lay still, nothing more than the inanimate material, all life effortlessly removed.

"Not much of a guard." I was at Em's side and looked down at the broken statue.

"It is the perfect guard. The shielding on this room and the strength of the door are such that should someone breach them, they would expect the defences to be at an end. This is nothing more than a surprise for someone who ventures into the room. It does not attack immediately. Instead it is designed to wait until someone has reached a certain point. Even the most basic of weapons can be deadly if you're not looking for the attack."

I was taken back to the memory of our first meeting and being knocked unconscious by a single punch from Em. It certainly was the shots you don't see that do the most damage.

"But won't one of the others attack after we kill that one?" Again, I did my best to keep my focus on the realities of the task at hand.

"If I had employed magic in my defences, then yes, a further attack would have come but by just using my physical strength, the others haven't been alerted to the potential threat. To get here, you would have to use magic freely and heavily. Again, using what could be called a simple weapon is the most effective."

Em casually stepped over the dusty heap the lion now was and headed into the depths of the collection. I followed behind determined to find out as much as I could as we went, but also to try to build some kind of relationship with Em. She'd have to be conflicted about doing to me what she'd done to that lion if she actually knew me.

We squeezed through makeshift pathways, edging carefully past gilded weapons and sharpened curiosities and edged deeper towards the centre of the room.

"This is some collection. This must be almost the sum total of the wealth of the ancient world." Engaging in gentle conversation, the hallmark of any relationship/friendship.

She didn't turn to me as she replied, still struggling deeper into the forest of riches.

"Such a small part of the whole. The knowledge, wealth and value within Bress Tal was staggering. This is a poor reminder of all that was lost."

Really?

"All of this? How much did they leave behind?"

This time she did turn to face me.

"The value of any item is relative. Do you feel that a ruby the size of your fist is valuable? People would pay millions for such an object, yes? If you were marooned in a desert with that same ruby, wouldn't you exchange it for a glass of water?"

Her head tilted and it was clear that the would-be rhetorical question, was waiting to be answered.

"Possibly, depends on the details." Not the most deeply considered answer.

"The value of what was lost was vast, so far beyond the comprehension of most, but that which was saved is so much more." Then she added almost as an afterthought, "Any normal person would take the water but you are not normal. You would refuse it in so many scenarios, would you not?"

I just shrugged back at her and repeated my earlier comment, "Depends on the details."

Em frowned and turned her back on me again, resuming our progress into the vault.

The remainder of the journey was just ridiculous. The pathway we had been following petered out at the base of a mighty statue of what looked like a jade rendering of Freddy's Dragon form. I couldn't be sure as there was only a very limited amount of the statue I could actually make out with the surrounding wealth draping over and around it at so many places that it again gave me the idea of the objects being of nature, growing in, on and around anything and everything they came into contact with. From there Em had simply started to clamber over the piles of gold and jewels which had formed at its base and headed onwards and upwards.

Behind the statue of the Dragon the landscape changed from the gold and precious stones which had been making up so much of the area we had seen up to now, into craggy cliffs of ancient books. Underneath a canopy of what looked like a huge black sail but could have been practically anything else, we climbed over the treasures. Thousands, if not millions of tomes bound in almost every conceivable material sat in steepling piles, just set rigid against the march of time. They were obviously of great worth to be in this place at all but as I strained for sturdy enough grips and footholds, all I could think of was the question, when was the last time anyone ever actually read from one of these things?

Shaking my mind back into the here and now, I looked back ahead of me to find that Em was nowhere to be seen. My first thought was 'great, where has she gone?' but that was quickly followed by the more worrying thought of 'how the hell do I get out of here on my own?' My stomach tightened as I cast my gaze left and right, up and down in a vain attempt to locate my companion but also to pinpoint the best way down from the cliffs of knowledge I found myself on.

"If you've veiled yourself to try to be funny, you've picked a very odd time to do it?" I called into the air and waited on the response, should there be one. There wasn't a sound. Instead, from about ten feet above me, Em poked her head out from beyond an outcropping of darkly bound volumes which were showing their age a little more raggedly than the other books we were surrounded by.

"I would not veil myself without you being with me. Why would you think I would do that?" She spoke with a sullen fire in her voice.

I breathed a relieved breath and started my way to her. From her tone, it appeared that she wanted to know why I'd thought what I'd thought. Had I hurt her feelings? As I clambered onto the ledge she was already perched on with far less grace than I imagined she had managed, I started to respond.

"Sorry, just hadn't seen you climb in here. Thought you were playing a trick on me that's all." I smiled as casually as I could and waited. She cocked her head again in that canine fashion, assessing what I had just said. What little emotion that was in her features drained out to return her blank, business-like expression.

"We have arrived at our destination. Would you like to see?" Em sounded like my explanation had been enough. Crawling back through the small opening in the books ahead of us, she led me to our intended destination. I followed and did my best not to just stare at her backside as I went. Good God what's wrong with me?

Em stopped and crouched on her haunches, waiting for me. I joined her and sat down as comfortably as I could. I was in good condition but I knew my knees were going to thank me for not trying to copy her position. It was surprisingly warm in the tunnel, humid and sticky and the air felt thick on my lips.

"This is where The Drake Stone was stored to keep it safe. This is where The Mage was reaching from Egypt." Em was looking directly towards what looked like a beaten and worn old suitcase which had been incorporated into the rear wall of the cramped tunnel. Reaching out she gently eased the hinged front open to expose the interior. Inside it was more of a trunk in size than a suitcase. Tattered cloth lining a very bland box. Aside from a few small blue pebbles in the back right hand corner it was empty and thoroughly unremarkable. Certainly not the place to store a mystical object of supreme power. Maybe that was the point.

"Interesting" said Em as she looked over every detail of the space.

"What is?" I asked in reply. I'd been functioning on a reassuring level of fear up to this point but my curiosity was starting to get peaked as we progressed.

"The stones in the case. They haven't gone off." Em quickly picked up a little pebble and closed her fist around it, turning away from me as she did. The tiny strands of power which ran over her suit flared an angry purple as she did and I could feel a wave of power pulse from her back.

We both held fixed.

Nothing further happened. She slowly returned to face me and opened her hand. The pebble sat there, blue and innocuous.

"Doesn't look like it's that dangerous. What do you mean didn't go off?" The understanding had just caught up with me and I suddenly felt far less confident about being in an enclosed space with whatever it was.

"It is the very last line of defence for the Drake Stone. It is nothing more than an explosive really but it creates just a small tear in the fabric of all that is our reality, to what is outside the event horizon of the Cascade Bridges. The Yondah. Anything that sets this off is pulled into that tear and is sealed on the other side. Just an easy way to safeguard the stone."

"The Cascade Bridges? Where to? Couldn't we just jump there and retrieve whatever was sucked through?"

Em waited before responding, possibly trying to find the appropriate words.

"The Yondah is that which surrounds all of who and where we are. Energy and so much emptiness entomb our whole existence and we are able to use the Cascade Bridges to pass through the Yondah to another place in this plain."

She may have taken her time and chosen her words with the utmost care but they still left the hollow uncertainty of ignorance in their wake. This suddenly put a shadow of threat over what I was stepping through when I used a bridge. She noticed my furrowed brow.

"The Bridges that are created have never failed. Ever. Travel through the Cascade system has never resulted in accidents or losses. Do not worry. If you are strong enough to create the opening at all, then you are in no danger from its use." She smiled at me by way of reassurance but I still didn't feel that comfortable at what she'd just said.

Shaking my head free of the spectres of doubt, and a very real concern at what I was actually doing when I used one of the Bridges, I returned to information gathering.

"Wouldn't the stone just go with whoever set the trap off?" The last line of defence being that you lose the object you're defending did seem a little extreme. If I can't have it, no one can.

"The stone is locked to this side of our reality. You could detonate ten thousand of these devices around it and The Drake Stone would be the only thing left at the bottom of the crater. Think of it as a Cascade Bridge that only goes to one place but is also a one way ticket."

Cheery thought.

"So you risked setting it off and protected me to do it?" More realization kept coming.

"Indeed. You are a Guardian of The Circle. My life is forfeit in the protection of yours. I am able to exert some level of control on the power within the device but there would be no guarantee that I would have survived its detonation."

And despite all of the time we had spent together, all of the conversations we had had and whatever bonding I may have thought had taken place, when it really came down to things, Em was still a very strong result of her training and life experiences. She may have changed the way she spoke around me but if the time came, that correct thing to do in her eyes was to kill me, she would do it without a second thought. The image of her standing over my expired form with that familiar head tilt of hers was all I could imagine. The ice I was walking on was still as thin as ever and I was going to be viewed as the monster of the piece until I could prove someone else was.

I needed to be out of the tunnel in the relative open air of the rest of the vault. I started out without another word.

Em noticed the change in my demeanor but let me leave her. She did follow me, but a beat later.

Out of the mouth of the tunnel, we both straightened up and released tightened muscles. Em probed me for answers.

"What are you thinking about Mr. Johns?"

"I'm wondering why everyone wants to see me as the bad guy. All I've tried to do since this whole situation was dropped in my lap was the right thing but somehow that's just kept putting me on the wrong end of so many arguments. Why'd you ask?"

Em remained silent for several seconds as she just took in all of the details of where she was, as if they would have a bearing on what response she would give. Closing her hand on the pebble and then placing it in a pouch in her uniform I hadn't seen, she responded.

"I am The Circle. I am The Messenger of The Mage and as such I need to understand every detail and facet of everyone who is a part of who and what we are. You are a great change in The Circle. Your actions and behavior have the power to change The Circle as a whole and I wish to have an understanding of who you are and what your intentions are."

"Don't worry, we're going to get married before we live together."

Em tilted her head in that familiar way of hers. She was still struggling with my attempts at humour. The image of me dead came back into focus and as it did I swear the air got thicker and the temperature rose perceptibly. It did to me anyway.

We continued to stare at each other as the silence stretched on.

"I want to be a part of this group and do something good with my life. We're trying to keep the world safe aren't we? Why would I try to put the human race, myself included, at risk from the hoards of The Hive?"

"Why indeed? But you act in a way which is opposite to the long held ideals of The Circle. Why do you do the things you do?"

This was quickly becoming the same conversation I'd had when I'd been speaking with Andrea as we stood watching Maria's trembling form back in Wales. The light was being shined in my eyes every time I had a conversation it seemed. This couldn't go on. This mission was going to be bad enough without there being a veritable collection of Swords of Damocles swinging above me just waiting for someone from The Circle or The Hive to wander by with a pair of scissors. I had to try to get The Messenger to at least trust me enough to not have to be watching over my shoulder all of the time.

I stopped our forward movement and turned to face her. She gave away nothing despite my abrupt action.

"I am a part of the same group you are. The only differences between me and everyone else working on the defence of the human race is I'm not utterly bound by the ropes of history. I don't see everyone as just pieces of the machine."

There was no anger in my voice, at least I thought there wasn't but I couldn't really be sure when you really get down to it. The Messenger still didn't give anything away but at least she hadn't made a lunge for me.

I continued.

"What is it you want to see from me? Are you looking to see if I'm a traitor or if I can be trusted or just that I'm following all of the rules that you all from The Circle seem to be so obsessed about?"

"I am here to do nothing more than ensure that the mission is a success, as are you. As The Messenger of The Circle, I am just a servant of the human race, albeit one with a title. Do you see me as anything more?"

"Just trying to make sure that no-one's going to tear my head off just because I don't bow in the right direction, that's all."

"Mr. Johns, all I have in mind is the security of the world. Any decision on what will be your fate will be left in the hands of the Guardians. Besides, I know that should you attempt to move against me, you would pose no real threat, I've seen what you have to offer."

I knew it and that put me back under the titular sword. I hated Damocles. There was nothing more to be said. The only path open to me was to solve the riddle of the how's and who's and show these people that I'm on their side.

"Come on then. Let's go find the others and see what they've found out." I rolled my shoulders and gathered my power and started to call together a Cascade Bridge. I may have learnt that this method of transport was something so very much more than I'd originally expected but I couldn't let that stop me from using it. I had to get back on the horse as fast as I could.

The familiar tug of power and smell of ozone didn't come. Instead there was a thunder clap of sound, deep and angry, akin to having a jet engine roar poured all over you while someone sprinkled in a far too big helping of static energy. There was a pull of power but it was far more urgent than any Cascade Bridge I'd ever encountered before. Underneath the boom, I could make out the equally angry scream of Em fighting for space. I tried to turn, not understanding what was happening but needing to see what was taking place, all manner of hideous possibilities flooding my head.

Behind me, Em was stood with her feet spread wide to provide her with as sure a stance as she could manage as she fought against the hugely violent forces which broiled and howled between us. Her face was twisted in exertion as she held her arms out at the sphere of twisting blue fury which had appeared as if from nowhere. Her body was criss-crossed with flaring purple as the power coursing through her showed itself in her suit. That same purple flickered and flashed around the orb which was threatening to pull us both to it, indicating that she was holding tight on the control of whatever that thing was.

I just stood and watched. I had no idea what I could add to this situation and I doubt I'd have been able to move even if I had.

It lasted for roughly ten more seconds before it folded in on itself, collapsing away to nothing and released the pull it had been exerting.

Em's expression relaxed back to her usual relative blankness before she altered her stance. Eventually she slowly dropped her arms down to her side and shifted her feet back to a normal standing pose.

"Em are you alright? What the hell was that? Another trap?" I was beyond stunned. I knew I'd been left with nothing more than a gaping mouth and a startled expression. My knees were weak from sheer fright.

"That was the result of your Cascade Bridge," Em replied and by the sound of her slightly gasped breaths, she had just been given a very severe workout. I still didn't know what she'd meant but at least Em recognized that fact quickly.

"When you called the Cascade Bridge, it set off the stone. I managed to contain its power but it was not an easy task. Please do not attempt to open another Bridge. If there are further devices, I feel that I wouldn't be able to complete the task a second time."

Gulp.

I didn't know what to say. I just held her gaze as long as I could and the fluttering sensation in my stomach grew as my fear and embarrassment jumped up and down. Em took confident strides past me and started to ready herself for the descent and return journey through the vault. She stopped just over the edge of the book cliffs of Argentina and looked at me.

"Hadn't wondered why we hadn't jumped in originally rather than walk around the artifacts? You don't think like everyone else do you?" As she continued down, she shook her head but was smiling as she descended. Not a blank smile, stuck on imitation, she was actually smiling up at me, showing honest humour. It had creased her eyes and her lips were parted to expose her teeth. That smile was the truth.

Had she just made light of what had happened? Had she just made a joke? At my expense?

Just keep focused on what's going on and try to avoid getting killed, that's always the best advice. With that thought ringing in my mind, I started my own way down, not sure that the information I'd discovered had actually made anything easier.

I was still alive though so that was always a plus.

24

Em and I had been sat on a stone bench in as secluded a spot as we could locate in the gardens of the mansion as we waited for Andrea and The Elder to complete their journey through the various rooms and corridors. We'd had a general scout around the mansion within the all powerful veil but hadn't really seen anything which was anything more than normal for where it was. Eventually, we'd both come to the conclusion that we would just be wandering about aimlessly, hoping to bump into the correct information, especially as the mere presence of the other Guardians in the house would have put everyone on their guard.

We remained under the cover of our magical seclusion to ensure that no-one was able to see us but we were so far out of the way that no-one would have been looking for us anyway. I'd found this little out of the way spot on one of the many visits I'd been forced to make to this site during the myriad battles The Circle had been involved in. It had started out as being an excuse to get away from the constant pressure of expectation coming from all areas of the garrison here, other Guardians expecting me to live up to the sweepingly grandiose role which they all seemed so keen to play and then also from everyone else who was looking to me to have some kind of added level of insight or wisdom. I was the one who'd felled one of The Hive masters when it had broken free. I could just feel the weight of every glance as I'd walked.

As I'd sat here, on a stone bench set back in the edge of a wooded area of wild growth, my mind had taken an all too familiar turn to imagine time with Andrea. With each and every subsequent visit I'd developed more thought on the importance of bringing her to see this spot, secluded and away from prying eyes and maybe we would have been able to talk without there always being the fear of The Circle over hearing.

I never had managed it though.

We waited and waited for the others to join us. I'd hidden myself in a cleaning cupboard of some description and called Andrea on my mobile. I'd tried from within the veil but got nowhere, Em eventually telling me that with the amount of power being packed around us I had no chance of being able to get through from inside. We'd arranged where to meet and Em and I had just been left to wait on their arrival.

We sat in silence and waited, the gentle aroma of wild flowers filling the air and forming the relaxing atmosphere which was so utterly at odds with what was happening in the big picture. There wasn't a great deal to add to the investigation and I was no closer to proving anything to Em which would show my innocence. She'd been somewhat hot and cold and the image of her regarding my crushed form was still too fresh an image for me to ever really be at ease around her. That all too familiar uncomfortable silence settled in between us as we sat and waited, both willing the seconds to pass a little faster.

They didn't. They got slower.

I was about to give in to the dragging need to break the silence when, finally, the familiar tug of power, crackle of light and sound and the pungent tang of ozone filled the air and a Cascade Bridge burst into life a little ahead of where we were. Andrea hopped through first but was quickly followed by The Elder. It winked out before The Elder had hit the ground, showing that there had been a level of urgency in the creation and subsequent closure.

Both women headed directly towards us but I could make out the wary flickering eyes of two people who weren't aware of our presence. Em stood from her position on the bench and started towards them. I followed. Closing the distance, Em raised an arm and pulled in the leading edge of the veil, akin to someone pulling the wall of a balloon inwards, creating a hollow in the front wall and therefore exposing our position. The image of an apple with a bite taken out of it seemed appropriate. The Elder betrayed no emotion but Andrea did start a little.

"Please join us my Guardians." Em greeted them and invited them in, returning effortlessly to her ceremonial deference to her superiors. They both moved briskly. In seconds, they were stood next to us and the veil was raised into position again.

"We must be quick in this discussion, our presence will be missed." The Elder was down to business without there being the need or desire for her to check if we were OK. Obviously clear where she still thought the guilt of the situation lay. The Elder didn't wait for anyone else to start their report, instead barreling directly into her own.

"We have been shown to over half of the estate but there has yet to be anything which has been anything other than expected considering the position we have presented to the people here."

"You mean they're all on edge to have two Guardians walking around their home, looking like they're going to pass judgment on them any second?" I couldn't help myself. The Elder was waving her rigidity of thought around as a virtue, practically taking pleasure in the fear which was no doubt spread throughout the building.

Everyone just looked at me. The Elder with her usual mix of disgust and anger, Em just with her blank expression, giving nothing away, but Andrea looked pleadingly at me, I knew, just willing me to keep my mouth in check and not help everyone who wanted me killed achieve their goal.

I nodded and dropped my gaze to the floor, in as much a show of submissive deference as I could muster. The Elder considered the action and continued her appraisal of the situation.

"All of the staff members we have seen have been happy to help in any way they could, as should be expected. When we asked to veer from the route they were preparing to take us on they were content to be directed. There was no agitation from anyone beyond what is expected from the arrival of Miss Thomich and myself. We were able to explore huge areas of the building and inspect the staff without there being any hint of subterfuge. I would suggest that the staff here are either unaware of the plot that is being undertaken in this mansion or there is no plot in the mansion. We would need to explore the final parts of the building to confirm but they have all performed impeccably to our requests."

She folded her arms across her chest and stared at me with hard eyes. I could feel the unseen edges of the trap she had just laid. She wanted me to make a snide remark about her assessment of the people, that I was surprised that she could recognize good performance much less admit that she had witnessed it from anyone. She was trying to bait me into further showing myself to be against her. It really was that simple for her. You were either with her or against her. It would appear that a great many of the members of The Circle shared her need to deal with that false dichotomy.

"How long will you require to complete said investigation my lady?" Em asked the next logical question without seeming to register that there had been anything happening beyond the face value of the words spoken. The Elder didn't remove her attention from me as she replied.

"It will not be long. An hour at the most to be able to reach everywhere that needs to be reached."

Sounded good. We should be able to leave and at least get me out from under the business end of a very heavy hammer.

"Actually. There is a third option we haven't considered." The Elder was still looking at me but her hard glare had become much sharper.

"We are not considering the fact that Mr. Johns was able to warn his co-conspirators of our arrival and any incriminating evidence or behavior could be effectively concealed. It would appear that we are no further from seeing you as the traitor of the piece. Unless of course, you've found out something which contradicts this point of view?" She was getting angrier as she spoke. Having a conclusion which you then get the facts to fit was the hallmark of the zealot. It was going to take the ultimate silver bullet to defeat the image of me she had in her head.

Andrea was silent all of the way through the discussion but it was evident that she was feeling the tension keenly. She frowned as she listened and chewed the inside of her cheek in a nervous gesture which ruined the image of the war hardened Guardian she had always exuded. She was looking much more like a person concerned for a friend.

"We have explored the vault where The Drake Stone was stored and found that there had been no disarming of the counter measures which were in place but there was also no understanding of those counter measures by Mr. Johns. Indeed, Mr. Johns was almost killed by the items in play to guard the vault but he was also without knowledge of the power in the room. He attempted to open a Cascade Bridge while we were inside. All of these facts point to him having no knowledge of what was in the vault, what was arranged in its defence or how to remove anything from it. In this case Mr. Johns, your ignorance of the wider tactics of The Circle has shown that you would have been woefully unprepared to complete this theft. I find it unlikely that he is responsible."

Ems words were a soothing balm on the ever present fear of demise but she didn't have to be quite so derogatory about me to make her point.

"Explain please Messenger." The Elder wasn't going to let this go.

Em tilted her head to consider the request, then expanded on what she'd said.

"Firstly, the doors to the vault were still locked in place when we arrived. They would have needed to be unlocked to gain entry to the vault but the re-locking would have taken a Guardian or myself to complete. Should we suspect all of the Guardians as the thieves? Secondly, Mr. Johns triggered the Golem which was placed guard at the main door. He made no attempt to protect himself as he walked towards it and was unable to recognize what he was faced by. Thirdly, as we inspected The Drake Stone case, he had no recognition of the stone in the case. He had no understanding of what it was and what it did. Finally, when he attempted to open a Cascade Bridge in the vault, he showed that he had no knowledge of what was likely to happen. Is this sufficient for you my lady?"

The Elder seemed to mull over the details, her eyes narrowed.

"Can you be sure that he was truly without knowledge of these points or was he feigning stupidity?" As much as I hated to admit it, she did have a point.

Em remained as calm as ever as she responded.

"I am certain my lady. I am The Circle and as such, the Guardians are unable to keep such things from me."

The Elder's shoulders dropped so very slightly at that. She nodded abruptly and said, "Thank you Messenger. What are your conclusions?"

Was that it? Em just says that I didn't do it and The Elder just agrees? Surely it couldn't be that easy? Could it? Taking a deep breath, I rolled the dice and took a leap of faith.

"Am I off the hook? Does that mean that I'm not the thief?"

"We could return you to Egypt in Doomsday Braces if you would prefer?" The Elder spat the words at me, showing that she wasn't going to let a tiny detail like my innocence get in the way of her hate.

"Look, I'm not the thief but even I could pretend not to know all of these things if I had prior knowledge. All it would need is a good startled face and away you go." Turning to face Em, "How do you know that I didn't just pretend and you fell for it? Why can't I keep things from you?" I had to ask. I needed to remove all of the potential grey areas in my acquittal. It was Andreas turn to speak now.

"She is The Messenger of The Circle. She is The Circle. She has deemed that the evidence shows that you are not responsible for the theft. That is the end of the matter."

Her words were calming, soothing to the point of relaxation. There was nothing further to be added apparently and everyone just seemed to accept what Em had said. We needed to move on despite the fact that I felt like I was missing a vital detail of what had just taken place. I still felt that there was a piece of the puzzle missing.

"While we may have been able to remove our Guardian from Wales as the one responsible for this betrayal, there still remains the fact that we have had our security breached and one of our most important artifacts stolen. Have we found any information which could give us the identities of those responsible?" The Elder was clearly not pleased with the news that she had been blaming the wrong person. She needed to resolve the mystery of the theft, not only for the benefit of The Circle as a whole but also so she could save face and tear the real culprits to pieces. That, I could help her with.

"All we need to do now is start drawing up lists." Now I was in the clear, ish, I felt that I could start taking more positive action.

"Firstly, Em, you said that it would have taken either a Guardian or yourself to open and re-lock the doors. Are you sure that there isn't anyone else who would have been able to complete the task?" She didn't have any time to give an answer before The Elder bellowed into the veiled area, a concussive "WHAT DID YOU CALL HER?"

Shocked to silence by the explosion of sound, I was pondering what I'd done now.

"I called her Em." My tone sheepish as I spoke, The Elder had managed to turn me into the scared schoolboy caught doing something he shouldn't have been. The power of surprise.

"She is The Messenger of The Circle. She holds a sacred position within our group and is to be revered as a holy member of who we are. No-one will ever dismiss her or diminish her by reducing her to nothing more than a grunt. Do you understand me boy?" She was breathing deeply as she spoke and her posture shifted to highlight that she was far from calm. Her skin tone changing to include the first hints of her Dragon hue proved beyond doubt she was serious.

"I'm sorry Elder. I meant no disrespect to anyone, certainly not The Messenger. I found that by shortening her name it would allow for an improved way of communicating, less time to highlight any problem." I may have been taking more positive action but that didn't include nudging The Elder over the edge of the precipice of violence. Looking at her face, it wasn't going to take that much of a nudge at all.

"He made a valid point lady Elder. We spoke before he started doing this. I see no insult or lessening of myself from his actions." Em had spoken clearly, her voice ringing like a bell tolling the truth of time. She had shown, in what she had been saying during our time in the veil, that she had fallen down firmly on my side in every difference of opinion. It wasn't a massive point. She hadn't blatantly slapped The Elder in the face but she had pointed out that the stance she was holding was wrong. Whatever power or position that Em held in The Circle, it was strong enough to keep a Guardian in check. My jaw ached just a little at that thought. She could keep a Guardian in check easily.

Em continued to lay out her points as if there had been no interruption.

"All of the security measures which were deployed within the vault were still in place and active. The list of people who are able to complete this is thankfully very small. As I said earlier, the Guardians, myself and possibly one or two of the longer serving Heads of House. Elder, I would think Mr. Ward possibly capable of such a thing although this is by no means certain."

That was interesting to say the least. There could have been others who had had their sticky fingers on this and Leatherpants was in that group. He'd been nothing but a pain since we'd met so this news painted our previous meetings in a very different light. Very interesting indeed.

"We also need to assess what use The Hive have found for The Drake Stone beyond how we are able to use it" added Andrea, her face serious. "Just because we have only been using it in one way doesn't mean that The Hive haven't found another way."

Everyone looked at each other as we shared glances of understanding and agreement. Andrea and Em both looked calm but hard at what needed to be done and I was just glad to be doing anything now I wasn't public enemy number one. Even The Elder was in agreement, forced to admit that the line of thought she had been following so relentlessly needed to be re-evaluated. Finally she took in a deep yet resolute breath, as if both drumming up courage to say something dangerous but also forcing herself to do something she hadn't ever considered. She was having to think on the hoof as to what to do next. Every second that passed was taking her deeper into the unknown. She, as all of The Circle as well, had always done things a certain way. Now she was having to do something else and she wasn't confident of the results.

"We will return to the mansion and complete the tour." She kept the authority in her voice despite any reservations she may have been having.

"Lady Messenger and Mr. Johns will return to his estate in Wales and wait for our arrival. When we return, we will update you with any important information we were able to find and you will have drawn up a route of action to resolve this issue. Miss Thomich."

Without further effort or word, The Elder turned and marched from the veil of concealment, snapping a compact cascade bridge into existence as soon as her foot hit the grass on the other side of the boundary. Andrea held position a breath longer, just looking at me. There was so much I wanted to say to her and her to me it appeared but we couldn't risk even the simplest gesture.

Another breath slipped past and she then turned and marched from the veil, following The Elder into the Cascade Bridge. With a muffled thump, the bridge gateway collapsed down and was gone, leaving Em and I together to make our way back to Wales and to start trying to work out what was going on now everyone had accepted that I wasn't the bad guy.

"Come on then Em. Bring down the veil and I'll get us a way home. No use us just sitting here."

Em replied but she had a wistful tone to her voice and was gazing ahead, looking into the middle distance. "This is a very beautiful spot Mr. Johns. I have never been one to consider such things but I find myself considering now. This is quiet and secluded. If someone of the right mind were to see this place, they could easily call it romantic."

I stopped rigid with fear.

I couldn't hear myself think due to the sound of my mind screaming at me to run for the hills. Did Em know about Andrea and me? Had she been putting the facts together, the little glances, the time we spent together? Just play it cool.

"Could be," I replied, doing my level best to keep the inevitable tremble out of my voice. "I stumbled across this place when I was out for a walk to clear my head. You're right, it certainly is secluded. Pity I haven't got anyone 'of the right mind' to see it." Keep relaxed. Don't act any different. I could feel a bead of sweat run down my back, highlighting clearly that my body wasn't finding that task to be that easy. Em seemed to consider what I'd said, turning lazily to face me, still looking untroubled by any of the events of the day.

"Mr. Johns, I think you would be able to find someone who would be willing to spend time with you. Don't you think?"

That was it. That was the threat I'd been waiting for. Andrea had said from the beginning that The Circle always knew and that we couldn't and we shouldn't then that we mustn't, but we had anyway. And Em knew it somehow. She'd said that I couldn't keep things from her.

My heart thundered in my chest and I started to scan around for any way I could see that would get me away from the impending doom I would no doubt be on the receiving end of. Nothing presented itself as my eyes nervously flickered here and there, hunting for any and all options I may have. Looking at Em, she'd closed her eyes and had drawn in a short breath. She was obviously setting herself to be able to subdue me with the minimal effort.

I couldn't defeat her in a straight fight, she'd shown that far too easily and I doubted there would be any way I could get away from her. Even if I did manage to jump away and back to my home in Wales, she'd still be able to find me. I certainly couldn't go on the run. Even with my limited experience of The Circle, I'm sure they'd be more than able of tracking down a fleeing Guardian. Hell, even I knew how to use Banus Stones. No-one would even be able to witness what was taking place, inside the veil.

In the nanosecond which had passed as I made my choice, I was left with Dragon surprise attack. That was it. That was all I would be able to do to at least give me a chance of surviving. Just pull the power together fast enough and maybe I could survive.

Yet again, Em showed she was so far beyond what I considered her abilities. I hadn't been able to commence building my own power before she acted.

That was it. My Dragon was going to fall here.

25

Em opened her glittering eyes and released the power she'd drawn in. There was no other sign of her casting heaving its way at me. Nothing cut through flesh, broke bones or did any number of other terrible things I'd been preparing myself for. There was just nothing and I was rigidly helpless before her.

And her veil dropped calmly down around us like a sheet falling from a table.

"If you please. The Elder will expect us to have something to discuss when she and Miss Thomich arrive." She held her right arm out to emphasise her desire to move.

I had nothing. Not a thing.

"What?" was all I could muster.

"Give us a way home. I brought my veil down now you give us a way home. We are returning to your home, yes? Did I not hear you correctly?" Her head tilted again and I couldn't be sure which one of us was more confused. Probably me.

"Uh, OK" I stumbled and did my best to put my mind back in the right place.

"Excellent. Please open the bridge." She smiled and turned away from me to signal where she thought or recommended the bridge would appear. I just did as I was told. Had I mis-read what had just happened? Had I thought she had worked out my secret? Had I been jumping at shadows, assuming her to be aware of everything simply because I'd been told she was practically a mind reader? Was she just having me take us away from this estate so she could kill me somewhere else? If that was the case, why choose to go to my home? Ceremonial importance?

Whatever the answer was, it looked very much like I was going to have to stay on my guard around Em. The last thing I fancied was being sucker punched and getting stabbed in the back.

The Cascade Bridge crackled to life and I gestured for her to step through first.

"Thank you gallant sir Guardian" she replied at my apparent display of chivalry. Whatever was happening, all of us were making it up as we were going along and it would appear that no-one was reacting well to the unsure footings.

In seconds we were back on the driveway in Wales and heading up the steps.

It felt good to be back on home turf. Not only was there the feeling that I was somehow amongst friends just by being here but that I could feel a tangible weight being lifted from my shoulders as I breathed in the power infused air from my home. Any little aches and pains I'd felt in Argentina were now gone. I could walk taller with my back straighter. That said, there was still a bit of a kick from the cooler air. It had been a little more humid in Freddy's estate and I was getting a similar sensation from when I walked back here from Egypt. Didn't think it was that cold.

All of the gathered soldiers had dispersed now and had obviously been returned to the guest rooms within the estate to wait on the return of the Guardians. As we made our way towards the doorway, several fully armoured figures appeared from seclusion around us and stood rigidly to attention before their leaders. There were two or three of each style of armour which I'd seen on display earlier, showing me that each of the factions involved in this endeavor were being waited for. I was also strangely pleased that two giant warriors from Em's guard materialized amongst the group here, stepping from beneath their own veils, as well as the three non-descript men from my own staff.

So not everyone was billeted away waiting.

Em and I stopped walking at the appearance of the guards but we were quick to recommence our forward movement. All of the soldiers snapped to attention as we approached them, instinctively lining up perfectly into an honour guard for our arrival. There can't have been any planning between all of the people here, surely. Olympic synchronized swimmers wished they were that good.

Em marched on oblivious of the actions of the people around her but I tried to at least acknowledge what had happened around me. Seeing all of the wealth and opulence within another estate kind of reinforced the need in me to make sure the so called little people were treated as anything but. I hurried after Em as she powered on but at least nodded in the direction of every person who was lining our pathway.

Before we reached the main door, it had swung open and Mark was stood looking casually terrifying in the doorway, his arms behind his back to display a relaxed demeanor but I could tell that he was anything but.

"My Lord and Lady." He bowed but without his usual coating of ceremonial pomp and circumstance. What was wrong?

"If you would please follow me, I am afraid to say that the child has taken a turn for the worse. Mr. Christian is with her assisting the medics."

The gap between us had closed completely now and I could easily see the worry beaming from his eyes. They burned like beacons heralding the catastrophe next to his onyx skin. Mark was a man of few words, a giant pillar of resolute certainty in everything he was and did. If he was showing the level of concern that met my eyes, something very serious was happening.

Em and I surged through corridor after corridor, passing by the maze of doorways and rooms as we headed for the suite Maria occupied. Mark followed behind wordlessly sharing the tension Em and I now wore. We hadn't turned onto the corridor before the corridor we needed when we heard the first sign that Mark had been somewhat understated in his assessment of "taken a turn for the worse."

The sound which was piercing out in all directions threatening to physically damage any and all that dared get in its way. There was the most pure primal agony in that sound, showing the creator of it being both human and animal. And both were in violent pain. Even Em slowed her pace as she came into contact with the howling. Despite ourselves, despite the power and strength we both had at our disposal, neither of us wanted to get any closer to the sound. We both knew who was screaming and the reason behind the pain being felt but we were both reacting in a purely instinctual way. The most primitive sections of our brains were doing some screaming of their own, telling us not take another step for fear of befalling the same fate.

Rounding onto the final corridor, we were both confronted by a rolling wave of invisible magical energy. It was surging up the corridor away from the room and Maria within, in rhythmic pulses. I felt the similarity to what had been in existence when we had first been introduced to Em and wondered how this was going to affect us as we closed on it. That said, Mark had said Mike was in the room with at least one other person who wasn't as powerful as we were so they must be OK.

We arrived outside the door and both stopped. There were no guards of any kind standing as sentry. There didn't need to be. The screaming from the other side was moving in unending waves encompassing human and beast emotions. The owner of that sound was in the most horrific pain and it was down to us to be able to help her.

Before we entered the room, I looked at Em and it was clear that she was feeling the effects of whatever was coming from the room.

"You OK?" Aside from the instinctive need to make sure a colleague wasn't in pain, the thought that Em was being undermined by something was quite unnerving.

She creased her brow in concentration against the forces still booming from the room, and simply opened the door and walked in by way of answer. She wasn't going to let the matter of her own discomfort get in the way of her being able to do what she was expected to. Mark remained outside.

There was nothing in the world which could have prepared us for what was on the other side of that door.

The horror. The abject suffering. The brutality which was being visited upon the tiny frame of Maria was so far beyond what any human should have been forced to endure.

On the bed before us, four of Em's guards held on for all they were worth to a limb, making sure that the child they restrained couldn't spasm herself apart under the weight of those powers raging within her. Each guard remained fully encased within their suits of armour and by the look of the stances they were taking, each was having to really work against what Maria was doing.

Two medics, one I recognized as Llewellyn, the other I'd never seen before, stood at the end of the bed, held their arms out above the child and chanted loudly. Their voices were twisted in effort as they did all they could to be able to help Maria. They were creating a deep blue haze over her, forming a spectral blanket of buzzing energy which hung over the bed and lightly touched her skin. Sparks of the sharpest green leapt into the air at random points, looking like a strangely compelling fireworks display as the powers being loosed in the room fought against each other.

Behind the two doctors stood Mike, one hand on each of the medics heads. He too had enormous strain carved into his features as he added to whatever the others were doing. A halo of white light was beaming from the heads of the two medics as they worked, Mike's augmenting power creating the coronal discharge.

The waves of expelled power continued from Maria and tasted like electricity, like licking the points of a battery, but all over the body. Em and I could feel the power and it was making me feel sick, but by far the most awful piece of the image being played out before us was what was happening to Maria herself as she writhed on the bed.

The small child was being dismantled from within, fighting to maintain her sense of self as the Dragon power within her fought to overwhelm her humanity. She was straining wildly against the arms holding her down and screamed out every last vestige of her pain from the magics being cast over her. But that was still a picture I could have tolerated if that had been all which had been befalling her.

The clearest terror of what was taking place was the physical effects of the struggle. The Dragon she was supposed to become had been within her for weeks without there having been any way for it to have been released. She hadn't gone through an Awakening like the rest of the Guardians, instead being forced to endure the power while a decision was made. She'd been forced by inaction to become the temporary vessel of the so called sacred gift while The Circle had discussed and debated the most appropriate next step.

Thinking back to the time before my own Awakening, the pain and disorientation which had threatened to drag me deep under the ocean of insanity, it made it very clear that she was being dragged through the most completely hellish torture any human had ever been forced to endure.

Her flesh was being distorted by the energy within her, the shape of the Dragon pushing against her skin, fighting for a way out. At so many points all over her body, were cuts of various sizes, some partially closed but others fully open, blood seeping out to soak into the now bare mattress beneath her. Stains of several kinds spread out all over the surface of the bed and it was agonizingly clear for everyone to see that there was no way this poor child was going to be able to survive this horror for much longer.

Em and I stood motionless and just stared at what was before us. Mike looked up and nodded slightly to me by way of greeting, his face filled with the concentration needed to maintain whatever he was adding to the treatment of poor Maria.

"I'm afraid I won't be able to join you my lord and lady, my skills are required here to add to what we need to do to try and save the child." He was speaking from between clenched teeth but seemed to be oblivious to the sour waves of energy thundering out from Maria's body.

"And by the look on you two, you need to be away from what's happening here." Mike could recognize that both of us were both physically and emotionally affected by the suffering on one so young.

"Mark can fill you in but I'm afraid I'm needed here."

"Thank you. You all OK?"

"We'll see."

Not a good response but there really didn't seem to be a great more that needed to be said. My stomach was feeling more and more twisted as Em and I suffered through each of the power pulses from Maria so I knew I had to be out of the room. Mike returned his focus to the medical procedure he had been working on and I turned to leave. Em, though remained rooted to the spot, either unwilling or unable to break her eyes from the bed.

"Em. You coming?" Simple sentences seemed all I could muster. She didn't move.

"Em! Come on." More forceful this time but that was all I could drag together. I needed to leave this room. Em turned to face me and her face was almost as shocking as the tableau of pain on the bed. Her powerful demeanor was gone and had been replaced by the most unnerving expression of all.

She was crying.

That made me feel even worse.

Her resolute features had been criss-crossed with tiny waterways as the tears had wound their way down. There was no attempt made to conceal her sadness or to pass it off as anything other than the outpouring of awful emotion. She was at the mercy of whatever she was feeling and it was as clear as day that she wasn't familiar with any of the sensations she was experiencing and was without escape as the tumult continued.

Placing a hand on her arm, she stared up at me, eyes pleading for something she just didn't know how to name.

"Come on Em. We've seen enough here. Let's plan how we save her." I tried to be as consoling as I could, showing her that I understood and that I was going to make it all alright. She nodded back gently and headed to the door, her shoulders hunched and her arms crossed across her body. For whatever reason, Em had been reduced to tears and was now far from the warrior I'd first met.

Closing the door behind us, I moved us both quickly away from Maria's suite towards a study which was close enough to what was happening but far enough away that the power of whatever was going on inside Maria wouldn't wear us away. Mark followed behind without a word. He had dropped casually into step behind us as we made our way but he had immediately taken on the air of a soldier on high alert as we emerged from the room. He was prepared to do violence in any and all directions because Em was crying and I looked so washed out.

Arriving at the room I wanted, I could feel that the power coming from Maria was still too strong for us to withstand. We had to be further away still and quickly.

"Mark, can you carry Em please?" I had been feeling the sobs getting stronger as we'd walked but now they were starting to have a ruinous effect on our Messenger. I'd have done the carrying myself but I could feel my own body wobbling under the psychic attack. Wordlessly, Mark swept Em from her feet and cradled her gently as he waited on word from me. I couldn't risk a bridge jump, even a small one, feeling like this. We needed a sanctuary.

"We're going up to my room."

Climbing the stairs slowly I could feel the effects of the power waning with each step. Closing on the room, I was starting to feel a little better but still far from good. Eventually, we arrived.

Mark opened the ornate, heavy double doors and I guided Em inside. I thanked him with a glance and he nodded in response as he closed the doors behind us. I knew without fear of contradiction that he was taking up a guarding position outside the door, just in case we needed anything. He'd rightly assumed that if we had both been affected in such a way, something serious was afoot so he was going to defend us with his life if needed. That was more than just duty, surely?

Em was curled in a ball, laying in the centre of my bed. She had stopped crying on the way up the stairs but it was still clear for all to see that she was going through something unpleasant. The decoration of the study I'd originally aimed for was the familiar heavy dark wood and plush fabrics which had been in every other room I'd walked in in the mansion. All of the furniture was perfectly sculpted and positioned to somehow make sure that the maximum effect of stately wealth was reinforced without there being any confusion. My room was much less intimidating in its décor, having more muted colours and welcoming 'feel'.

Moving slowly across the room, approaching in as sympathetic a fashion as I could manage, I edged towards Em trying not to seem in any way confrontational. She remained on her side on the bed, hugging her knees up to her chest and doing her best to hide behind them, her own protective shield against the world. Her head was resting on her knees, her eyes hidden.

Kneeling down at the edge of the bed, I spoke as soothingly as I could muster.

"Are you OK Em? We're away from Maria now. I'm feeling a little better now we're away from her. How are you feeling?"

Em lifted her head and her eyes were a picture of emotional hardship.

"That poor child. What have we done to her?" The pleading in her voice whimpered for attention, begging for someone, anyone, to take the pain away. Tears were flowing freely down her face again and her face was puffy with the outlet of emotion.

"She's a tough nut. We need to get that power out of her and into the new Guardian before she loses her mind or spasms her body apart. We've just got to find the Drake Stone and use it as soon as possible." I was trying to remain as factually solid as I could in what

I said while being as positive towards the entire situation as I could, despite not truly feeling that way myself.

Em sniffed and juddered against the sadness which was washing over her. Her posture remained the same, clutching to her legs, making herself into as small a ball as possible. I just had no idea why she was crumbling like this. She had been utterly single minded in everything she did when we'd first met but she'd been getting more and more, not unstable, just, more tender. She was feeling.

Again, looking at her shivering form, listening to the sobs which were filling the quiet, still air of my room, all I could see was a person who needed help. She was dealing with something which she had no prior experience of and she was being beaten down by the sensations she was feeling. She had seen countless battles and from what I'd seen, was more than capable of handling herself in the depths of the most awful fighting but it was clear that her current predicament was new to her and was proving too much.

The anger at what was happening to Maria and what was, potentially by extension, happening to Em was bubbling inside me and I knew that I had to do something. Andrea had been feeling the same uncertainty before all of this and there had been very little I could do to help her. People around me were being hurt. I needed to crush something, to incinerate an enemy, to blast The Drake Stone free of whatever place it was secured and save the people around me from all the horrors they were seeing.

I could feel my clothes becoming tighter as my body began to spill over into the early stages of transformation. It was purely a reflex to my feelings but I knew I needed to act.

Em must have been able to sense what I was feeling.

She lifted her head sharply from its resting place on her knees and pushed herself into a sitting position and looked into my eyes.

"You're going to save Maria aren't you? You're going to re-claim The Drake Stone." She tilted her head in that familiar curious dog fashion and her pain was gone.

"You're going to take the pain away and save us all."

Her voice was suddenly resolute. There was no tremble there, instead it had been replaced with a sliver of steel. She sniffed again but for the final time. Then lunged forward, flinging her arms out and hugged me with enormous force, pressing her body to mine tightly.

I didn't move and for a second I swear I must have looked like I was a statue, stuck rigid in one position which didn't fit the hug, my arms outstretched as balance following her forward momentum. All I could do was wrap my arms around her and console her, again doing my best to be reassuring.

There was no hint of anything more than just reassurance from either of us. Em was hugging me in much the same way a child might hug their parent who'd made the monster under the bed go away, and I was no more than just the parent in the equation, protecting someone who needed my help.

For me, there was no purer demonstration of what a Guardian was.

The problem was that it was at that exact moment that the heavy doors opened behind us and The Elder and Andrea strode purposefully into the room, followed closely by Mark.

Judging by the expression on the two Guardians faces, I hadn't managed to convey the same sentiment as I had been feeling.

26

"UNHAND HER YOU ANIMAL."

The Elders voice screamed throughout every last space within the room and I swear it made a few more. Its piercing edges practically sliced into me and I couldn't help myself but recoil from Em, almost dragging her from the bed as I did.

I burst backwards and stood up with my arms spread, showing in one move that I had released the hug but was also not holding any weapons.

The Elder seethed but Andrea was worse. Her white hair was rigidly frozen into place and there was a cracking sheen of ice all over her body but her face was the clearest sign of her anger. There was unbridled fury smashing behind her eyes which were fully the grey colour of her Dragon form, her own transformation leaking out around the edges. And all of that fury was squarely aimed at me.

"Ladies, The Messenger is feeling the effects of what's happening to Maria. I tried to comfort her with a hug. That's all." My arms remained outstretched in an exaggerated show of submission but there seemed to be little sign that it was having any effect on either The Elder or Andrea.

Em slowly eased herself to her feet and stood next to me, possibly a little too close.

"Guardians." Her tone wasn't back purely to the usual resolute explosion which simply demanded obedience regardless of what was said but there was still a very clear sound of power in what she said.

"Anthony has been comforting me. Surely you can feel the effects coming from Maria. I have been affected somehow and he has shown me care and attention."

The Elder was far from happy but she was being spoken to by The Messenger of The Circle, a position she had held in such high regard for so many lifetimes that she couldn't do anything but bow. Andrea was far from convinced though.

Her hands were clenched tightly and even though the ice covering her body was receding, her eyes remained those of her Dragon and the barest hint of a snarl played at the edge of her mouth. She was calming down but not by much.

Em stepped between Andrea and I and adopted a more ready stance, casual yet still primed for action. Andrea subtly matched what she was doing, her eyes flitting from me to Em.

"Miss Thomich. Stand down your anger Guardian. As everyone within The Circle, he is mine and he has been giving me something I've never experienced before."

The Elders expression was whipped back to a snarl, Andrea was seething as ice formed all over an area about six feet around her and all I could do was close my eyes and hope I could protect everyone before my own anger at this ridiculous situation bubbled over. The spinning early warning system in my head cranked up and there was no longer any doubt that it was about to kick off.

Andrea hurled herself across the space between her and Em, her hands outstretched ready to attack in human form. At least she hadn't gone straight for the Dragon attack option. The Elder was a fraction slower but had already started to surge across the room at me, determined that I'd just been outed as defiling someone who was apparently The Circles version of holy.

All I had available to me was to stand and fight and somehow avoid killing The Elder or, as was more likely, being killed myself. And then try to stop Andrea before she could start her very own war with Em.

"In for a penny ..." and I began to raise my arms into some form of defence.

Have you ever been surfing?

If you have you'll be familiar with the sensation of being at the mercy of the water as you try and complete whatever move or action you want. At any second, your apparent mastery of the tidal forces can be turned upside down and you can find yourself at the bottom being held down by the energy of a suddenly riled and angry wave.

What happened next can only be likened to that sensation.

All of the senior members of The Circle were suddenly knocked on our collective rear ends as the fight was slapped out of everyone. Marks basso rumble of a voice was still expanding into the room, filling the space and threatening to push the walls down and that voice had been made a fist of order by my giant soldier.

"HOW DARE YOU ALL," had erupted into the room with a force of physical mass and magical will enough to stun all of us. The shadow of the words was still palpable in the room and was still echoing through all of our minds. All any of us could do was just stare at him. We'd been knocked off balance so fully that it was more shock than anything else that had poured cold water on what we had been up to.

I tried to think through the cotton wool in my head but whatever he'd done was slowing me down. The buzz slowly began to dissipate and it was only then that I could make out the details of what I was looking at.

In our collective thoughts concerning the plight befalling Maria and the effects it was having on the rest of The Circle, none of us had noticed Mark open the door and allow Mike in. Both men had watched as all manner of violence threatened to break out but had had the presence of mind to step in and stop what was about to unfold.

Mark stood upright but his legs now moved like they were made of water, waves of life flowing through them as he struggled to maintain his balance. His body seemed to be sagging under the crushing weight of weeks of fatigue following what he had just done but he was still standing, the concentration on his face exhibiting an anger I had never seen from Mark. Mike was stood behind him and to the left, his right hand resting on the giant chef's shoulder. He too had a pained expression on his face and the coronal shape around his head was still clearly visible, a fading image similar to what we had seen around the heads of the medics.

I blinked at them both and flailed my mind to find some clear water to relax into, the waves of confusion still waging war on my senses. I knew what I wanted to say but the words just couldn't find the path out of my head. By the looks on Andrea and The Elders faces, they were feeling much the same. Only Em seemed to be, not unaffected but certainly less than the rest of us. She looked up at Mark and Mike as she sat on the carpeted floor and her head was tilted in that by now all too familiar curious dog fashion.

She opened her mouth to speak but then stopped whatever she had intended to say. She looked utterly confused by what had just taken place, yet another sensation she had no experience of.

Marks legs finally gave out beneath him and the giant came down smoothly into a pile at Mike's feet. No steeplejack could have ensured such a clean demolition even if they'd tried. He struggled to force his body to answer what he wanted to do but the signals just couldn't get through. Mike moved his hand from Marks shoulder to settle on the top of his head and my protector lay still, an expression of not contentment but ease on his face.

Mike was still looking at Mark when he began to speak.

"My Lord and Ladies, please forgive our actions but we have more important things to deal with than petty squabbles." He spoke with casual authority which just seemed to compel your attention but I could make out, even in my disorientated state, that he was scared, fearful of the reaction to what he was saying.

"I believe I have more understanding of what is happening here from the child and by looking at the evidence which has presented itself. The Circle cannot pull itself apart. I beg of you, please forgive my outburst but it was necessary to avoid bloodshed."

"Your outburst?" questioned The Elder, shaking off the effects of what had happened faster than I could. "Surely it was your soldier who attacked a senior member of The Circle. Surely it is your soldier who has now shown himself to be a traitor."

What? Still struggling against the dead weight wrapped round my brain, things got a little more serious. I couldn't just sit here and let everyone threaten someone else.

"Lady Elder." This time it was Em who was speaking. Her voice was calm and strong again, a casual return to her more familiar demeanor, any trace of whatever uncertainty she was feeling before, now wiped away.

"Do you suggest we punish those of us who are willing to do anything they can to help us?" As before, there was no hint of emotion in her voice, no signal of an agenda she may have had, just the question, bare and unhindered.

The Elder was able to reason but she was still under the effects of whatever Mark and Mike had done.

"We have processes which need to be followed. The correct response to an attack from a member of our house is that the attacker is hung, drawn and quartered. Should we just dispose of all of the ways we have had for so many years? The correct response must be followed, there cannot be any excuse." She was speaking clearly but it was a voice coming from the shallows as she beat her way through the last of the casting affecting us all. I was still so far away from being able to speak it was embarrassing. Despite my best efforts I was still floundering in the deeps. Looking everywhere I could for any kind of support, I could see that Andrea was in a similar position to me but by the expression on her face, she was still bubbling her anger at everyone, but mainly me, despite whatever had taken place.

I was in trouble. There was nothing I could do to prevent the protagonists starting up again so all I was left with was watching as the mansion was brought down around us and who knew how many people were killed.

Em gathered in her composure and stood up. It was a controlled movement, one which showed that she was still feeling a residual effect from the magic that knocked her over but also one which could be interpreted as being the precursor to a mindless violence. She looked down at The Elder who was still struggling to stand and spoke from a strong stance of readiness.

"Lady Elder. We are far beyond the constraints of rigid rule. As a collective, we have to be able to move beyond the obsession with arbitrary decisions. I have seen so far that we have to be able to bend with the wind should it be needed. If we are rigid, we will break. The soldier you wish to discipline saved us from bloodshed. Would you destroy someone who stopped you killing your fellow Circle members?"

The Elder responded by purposefully standing herself, matching the intention of Em in her posture.

"I believe fully in The Circle and everything we stand for. Without rules to guide how we act though, we can descend into anarchy. I have been affected by what has just been unleashed on us but my memory of our laws isn't changed in any way. Are you sure that you yourself haven't been compromised by this attack? Your deviation from the correct path shows me that not only are you being attacked by the magics emanating from the child, but you have been tainted by the actions of Mr. Johns. He has been able to invade your mind as he corrupted the sanctity of who you are."

Both women were sure of their own position and it was clear to see that we were back to the brink of fighting. I had to get in the middle of this before it was too late.

"As I said before, I didn't do anything inappropriate." I heaved myself from the floor and zombie shambled myself between the two of them. My head was spinning, both from the impending attack threat and the magical hangover. Somehow I had to talk them down. Roll the dice now Anthony.

"I will not have my name, my mansion and my people threatened at the merest hint of a perceived slight. Lady Elder." Now for the big finish.

Straightening my back and leaning just a dribble of my transformation into place, my body grew at least a further three feet in height, wrecking my clothes but allowing my Dragon form to just show through. I lowered my head slightly and stared into The Elders eyes, as much stone rigidity in my glare as I could muster.

"Remember who you are and who it is you are threatening. This is my house and everyone is a guest of mine. Act like one or you will be subject to the same law you seem so intent on upholding on my man."

We can all remember that one moment in our lives when our argument on whatever point was both tungsten strong as well as being delivered in the most devastating fashion. That wonderful time where there was just no counter. This was mine.

The Elder stood with her mouth open, shock all over her features. She knew it. She knew she'd just been caught out utterly and there was nowhere for her to go. She bowed her head slightly and frowned as she accepted.

"You are finally learning the importance of the rules we have in our system. I'm glad it was I who taught you this valuable lesson. There could be hope for you yet." Relaxing her stance and her expression, she returned to an at ease stance and casually regarded us all.

I didn't take my eyes off her despite her apparent surrender.

"Michael. You were saying something about knowing more about this situation?"

Mike cleared his throat as he straightened his shirt, re-building his composure before speaking.

"The child is carrying the power of the Dragon line from our Argentinian guardian, that we all know. What I have just seen makes me believe the theft of The Drake Stone is entwined with more than just disrupting our ability to call another guardian."

"Explain."

Andrea was on her feet as well now and stood just behind me. There was a great emotion in her single word answer, an urgency which was uncommon for her to show. The raggedness in her voice was unsettling in contrast to her default icy calm.

"The Dragon energy of the child's line is that of Fire. It has a very familiar resonance, a singular finger print marking it apart from the other energies of The Circle. Indeed, within the Fire family, the power in the child is different to that which is within you Anthony. Each Dragon is a different power and that power is what will tear the child to pieces should we not recover The Drake Stone."

He stopped and looked at each of us, seemingly assessing what our responses were. He had to crane his neck to look up to me but it was enough to make him feel very little indeed.

"So? We are aware of this. What is it you think is further information you know?" Andrea had now eased passed me and carried a growing impatience at not knowing. The hulking form of Mark eased back to a standing position but there was no reaction from anyone to his apparent recovery, though he still looked a little shaky.

"When we were with the child, as we bound her utterly to a finite stasis, I could make out that Fire power all around and within her but that wasn't all. I could see a collection of other powers, other colours within the maelstrom of her suffering." Mike twitched his eyes to each of us again, this time trying to register our understanding. It was clear that none of us had quite grasped what he was saying.

"Somehow, Maria is having to fight against the power of more than one Dragon. Somehow, she is having to deal with other power being pushed into her. She was struggling against her own energy, the other she just can't handle for long."

I dropped out of my partial Dragon form and closed the gap to Mike. We all did.

"Do you know how this is happening?" Em spoke to Mike in her monotone but there was now no hint of social class being observed as there had been the first time I had seen them meet. She wanted information, we all did.

"I'm afraid I do not know my lady." She may have done away with the need to observe protocol but he hadn't wanted to risk it quite yet.

"Do you have any suggestions?" I needed him to continue analyzing the situation as it had presented itself to him. He had seen a level of information we hadn't been able to comprehend when we'd been in Maria's presence. He was the only person who would be able to provide the assessment of those details.

Mike considered his words carefully before speaking, struggling to line his thoughts up to a coherent image.

"The Drake Stone is a repository of Dragon energy. It is a perfect crystal of incredible power able to encase and control the most unbelievable power. If that power is being found around someone it shouldn't be, my only thought would be that it is damaged in some way and the power is leaking out."

That couldn't be good.

If the stone was damaged there was no telling what was going to happen to Maria. There was no telling what was going to happen to any of us within The Circle. I settled myself back in under the Sword of Damocles and pondered what to do next.

If the stone was damaged in some way there could be all manner of pain coming our way sooner rather than later. It could mean that we started to lose our power as the magical energy drifted out of the crystal and was lost to the atmosphere. It could also mean that someone was syphoning off the power to use themselves.

All in all, the possibilities could only get worse the more you thought about them or the longer nothing was done. We needed to do something immediately.

"Right guys." Now was the perfect time to start taking charge of the situation.

"Mike. Can you and Mark please bring us all some food so we can continue this discussion more comfortably. You are both invited to attend, your input will be vital." Both men nodded their agreement but Mark stiffened as he did. He was being invited to sit at the top table with his perceived betters and he just didn't understand what the correct thing to do was. They both turned and made for the door before I had continued.

"Ladies. We are now in a position that we have to identify exactly where we have to strike and how quickly or Maria will die and any number of hideous possibilities await us. We all have to now put away any anger or resentment and concentrate purely on the job at hand. Agreed?"

They all nodded, only Andrea taking a furtive glance at Em before she did.

Mike opened the heavy doors to bring refreshments for the impromptu war council and took a startled step back as the doorway was blocked by the slender frame of Leatherpants, back straight and his hands clasped behind his back looking every inch the high class regular. His skin suit seemed to glisten in the lights, taking on the familiar sheen you see on the skin of snakes.

"I hope I'm not interrupting your meeting. I had been aware of my lady's arrival here and was surprised I had not been summoned. Is everything as it should be here?"

He casually floated into the room, ignoring Mike and Mark as he did and looking solely at the people he saw as being worthy of his attention.

"Everything is fine in here. How long have you been outside? Didn't want to knock?" He was up to something, I just knew it.

He made his way past us all, not even stopping to answer my question, until he stood at the side of The Elder. He nodded a bow of greeting and then turned to face the rest of us.

"I merely wished to ensure that there was no danger to my lady before I entered. I had heard all manner of shouting and screaming and by the look of you," his scorn was blatant, "it would appear that 'fine' is far from the truth."

It was only now that I looked down at myself and realized what he'd meant.

I was nude.

Very nude.

I hadn't even registered that as I'd returned to my fully human form, the remnants of my shredded clothing had just fallen into frayed and torn heaps around my ankles. Everyone else had been just as focused on what was taking place as I had been so hadn't picked up on it either. That or they just didn't want to say anything.

Whatever the state of play, it meant that I was far from my ceremonial best. No time for self-doubt, just carry on regardless.

Jamming my hands on my hips and flexing everything just a little, I continued in as defiant a tone as I could manage.

"The actions in here have led us to the need to move decisively to resolve our problems. You should have come in earlier, you may have enjoyed what was going on rather than just listening at keyholes." I could feel the anger in me rising without any real effort, like he was reaching into the centre of my calm and giving it a really good twist.

"Mr. Johns." This time it was Em who spoke. Again she gave no hint of sensation in the words she spoke, instead remaining in the more familiar logic tone of hers.

"You did say that we should all put aside any anger and resentment for the purpose of dealing with this situation. I can feel the anger in you from here." She slowly slipped her arm around my waist and moved in very close to me.

"Please calm down." This time her words did have sensation behind them. I swear they did. She was asking me but with just a light glazing of so much possibility. I could feel that the fire in me was still raging but at least it wasn't raging at Leatherpants.

The change in me must have been clear as she quickly let me go and moved away to stand nearer the door. My skin felt alive with energy and I absent mindedly scratched at my neck in response. Everyone watched her move across the short distance but I was confident that I was the only one thinking what I was. I couldn't see beyond the curve of her hips, the strength and order of her whole countenance. She was baiting me, she must have been, just giving each step that extra level of sway to draw attention to her athletic form.

All I could see was her and my mind began to take me on a very vivid journey through the realms of future events I could just reach out for and have. I could just peel the skin tight uniform from her and we could really explore what each of us could do. Two hugely powerful beings challenging each other in a very new arena.

I have to accept that it was the Dragon growl which started the problem. I can look on the events and acknowledge that Andrea did the right thing. Didn't feel great though.

The sheets of ice formed all over me in a heartbeat and began crushing against me and forcing the air from my lungs and, quickly, the desire from my everywhere else.

The Elder spoke into the air before I started my response to what was going on.

"It would appear that all of the guardians are vulnerable to attack from whatever sorcery is being cast. Mr. Johns here is a confusion but he has shown that he can do what needs to be done even in the presence of his Fire. He has just shown that his power is now not fully within his control. None of ours is." Ever the public speaker, she let the vivid threat in her words hang in the air for us all to digest.

"Somehow, our power is being manipulated by another and from what has been disclosed here, I believe that I understand how. We need to move from here to be able to confirm my fears but I think that the truth has presented itself."

Leatherpants looked smug as she spoke, practically basking in the reflective glow of the words of The Elder as they made for the door.

"Where are we going now?" My teeth chattered as they strode away, my tomb of ice holding me firmly in place. The Elder didn't break stride or even show any sign she was addressing me as she replied.

"We need to get to Mexico as fast as we can. It is clear to me who we are being manipulated by and therefore, who has The Drake Stone. We need to pay a visit to the domain of The Tayne."

27

It took about twenty minutes to crack me free of the ice Andrea had brought into being around me. I could have just blasted through it with my own special brand of pyrotechnics but with everything which had taken place recently, I thought it wiser if I didn't draw too heavily on my Fire unless I really had to. Mark had been surprisingly gentle with the sledgehammer after it had been deemed to be too dangerous for me to risk getting myself out.

We all gathered in the same place we had earlier in the day, crunching the gravel of my mansions driveway, after we'd been served a rushed yet faultlessly exquisite meal which was the response to my request for a snack to keep us all going. How the people in the kitchen managed it was still a wonder to me. Did they do the same thing in the other estates? That would have to be a question for another day.

This time I was in my own armour as well. If my Dragon power was being affected in any way by who or whatever was in possession of The Drake Stone, I wasn't going to risk being killed before I could defend myself in my human form. I also only had Mike and Mark as my honour guard. It seemed to make more sense to me that whoever I had with me be willing to protect me from any and all threats, including magically warped Guardians. There were more than enough other soldiers hanging around to create a strong enough battalion of fighters without the need to throw any of my bodies into the pot.

"Why are we going to The Tayne?" I was getting impatient as we all gathered outside, not from any kind of Fire power coming from within me but just because I was wearing such a solid and delightfully ceremonial suit of armour which, despite the best efforts of everyone I'd dare let near me, just didn't fit properly. Having my one piece under suit practically painted on was bad enough but the armour just didn't feel quite right. Everyone had kept reassuring me that it was the armour of the Guardian of the house so would meld to my shape, regardless of who I was, a good trick if the Guardian is changed regularly, no need to create a new suit, but it still just didn't quite feel as snug as it should have done.

My protestations fell on deaf ears and I swear I could hear Mike calling me a big baby as I readied myself although I couldn't be sure of that.

The basic design was that of a medieval knight, large plates and jointed to allow some form of movement. It was also so much more than that as well. Swirls of carving depicting all kinds of fire covered every inch of the plate, showing to anyone who even flicked a glance my way what my power source was. It was made of highly polished, what looked like steel but there was a red tinge to the whole thing, again showing where I was starting from. It was far from being as artistic as the other forms of armour being worn by the other guardians but mine did look like it was several levels tougher. There were weighty spines running up the back and over my shoulders and the gauntlets looked like they were weapons first and protection later. Massive blocks of metal had been wrapped around my hands which contained more spines but also wickedly serrated blades as well.

Despite the beauty of the carving, the craftsmanship of the suit and obvious ceremonial function which my dress had to perform, it was clear to me that this armour had been designed for face to face combat. I was designed as Fire to make the best of my burning temper, by anger. This garb showed that my line had not been afraid to literally throw themselves into the melee of battle.

Top it all off with the brutality of my heavy helm, all horns and teeth, and you were left with in doubt that whoever was inside the suit was more than willing to go absolutely nuts.

The Elder had her honour guard around her and Leatherpants strutted amongst them, just to make certain they were all standing utterly to attention. Leatherpants was the only one without any kind of battle dress on but he didn't let that get in his way. He carried on inspecting The Elders troops despite being dressed for dinner rather than a fight. He continually straightened and adjusted his skin suit as he moved, seemingly maintaining the perfect countenance.

Knob.

As he walked and judged, The Elder was now taking on a more serene temperament. Gone was any kind of anger towards me or, anyone else for that matter. She was now more akin to a calm mountain lake, no ripples of emotion even hinting on the surface. She was speaking now with an almost ethereal calm in her voice.

"The Tayne were there weren't they? That weakling race were all around us during our fighting in Argentina. They were somehow able to greatly increase the magical power each one of their swarm had which resulted in them being able to bring down the shield wall. The Tayne are a ruined race who have raised their hands to a more powerful adversary. They will have the Drake Stone with their Queen, deep in the catacombs."

Andrea and Em stood waiting as well, Andrea with her soldiers and Em just standing with her arms folded. When we'd gathered here previously, the sun had been up and the day had been warm, a welcoming summer day in South Wales. Now, the sun was gone and we stood in the black of night, erratic shadows and indeterminate shapes running casually between all of the people there. It was probably the dark coupled to the threat implicit with the effects of whatever magic was being thrown in our direction, but I could swear that there was a level of fear whispering into everyone's ears that something unknown was waiting for them and they stood no chance.

Like I said, just the dark.

"We are all prepared." Andrea's voice called out into the still night air in the same tolling way she had always used. She had removed the raggedness from the confrontation in my bedroom and it was reassuring to have that familiarity back.

Despite every action which had come along, I was still desperate to speak to her to clear the air and reassure her. I wanted to hold her in my arms and take her pain away. And I wanted her to do the same for me.

"When we pass through our bridge gateways we will be walking into the heart of the lands inhabited by The Tayne. We Guardians will lead the way but each and every one of us will be open to attack. We have seen that The Tayne are not the most powerful of enemies but we can't afford to underestimate them." Andrea spoke from the stairs which led up to my huge great door and looked down on the gathered masses like a religious leader speaking to her gathered flock.

The Elder eased her way up the steps and joined Andrea.

"Our target is to beat a way to the centre of their lands, find their Queen and retrieve The Drake Stone. We will Bridge jump in at the edge of The Tayne realm and make our way to the Queen. This should be more than possible for a fighting force equipped as we are but there will be no Dragon support in this endeavor."

That comment drew a fluttering of half gasps and shuffled movement from the troops. In any other group of people that would almost be akin to a riot but these people were resolute to the point of fanaticism.

"There is a great power being wielded against The Circle and all of the Guardians are at risk of having their powers turned against them. We must jump in a distance from our target to avoid risking the Bridges being tampered with and losing us all. But never forget. We are all here to serve as are you and we will continue to do so even if we are suffering."

That last comment was an immediate salve to the Dragon issue and I swear that at least half of the gathered forces let out an audible sigh of relief.

Now it was my turn.

"We also go on a humanitarian mission." I was doing my best but I'm sure that the others just sounded more at ease in front of a crowd like this. Teaching a fitness class is one thing, delivering a battleground speech is something entirely different.

"We are not only re-claiming our lost property and re-forging The Circle, but we go to save the life of one of our family." Perfectly on cue, armoured figures parted to reveal Mark as he carried Marias rigid form from the house and waited at the top of the stairs. She had been placed in some kind of glittering ovoid shape, held weightless and motionless within and was carried by Mark in a hastily put together harness. Her eyes were closed but she was still showing a great deal of pained expression. Her fragile skin was raw and split and I swear her skull was oddly misshapen, although that could have just been a trick of the light.

She looked every inch the sacred backpack. Remembering the stasis comment from Mike, it would appear that she was just 'stopped' within the construct. Hairy, almost a forgotten issue for me to consider up to this point, followed behind also dressed ready for war. His armour was akin to my own, huge anger and violence implicit in the design. I still had to come up with some way of getting the power swapped over between them without leaving Maria to die.

"We go to save the life of the last in the line of Guardians who have been protecting the site in Argentina before that power and responsibility is passed to our newest member. Never forget that we all exist to save the lives of every single person on this planet."

There was a ripple of agreement from the crowd and I felt relieved that there had at least been some agreement to the point I wanted to make.

Andrea resumed.

"We are going to attack if we are attacked and smite any and all who try to stop us reaching our goal." Andrea finished her speech and raised her right arm before her, fingers splayed in a very dramatic fashion. The Elder did the same.

From behind me I recognized the telltale signs of their Cascade Bridges. The blue/white light washed over us all and I could make out the hum of the energy being worked. Ozone filled the air. I slowly turned and added my own power to the mix and the three rings of power hovered expectantly, waiting to accept the assembled army for their journey to the domain of The Tayne.

Em was the first of us to move but she was quickly followed by Andrea and The Elder. I hadn't been expecting the shrill battle cry to come from Em though as she streaked past me and hurled herself through the central bridge gateway. She was again in her all in one suit but now she looked more as if she were wearing something made out of plastic or metal rather than the figure hugging fabric of before. Segmented pieces of whatever material slid over each other as she moved, giving her the look of someone wearing a skin of armour rather than the more bulky suits the rest of us wore. Add to this the two metre, ornate sword which was suddenly in her hand and she looked every inch the berserker warrior.

"Close your mouth. Don't want anyone to trip over your tongue." Mike was next to me and spoke as low as he could to get his point across. Did everyone just think all I ever thought with was my – instinct?

I shut my mouth.

"That's better bach" and he followed up with that now welcome too hard slap on the back.

"It was just surprise at her shout and her get up. Nothing else." I tried but I could tell he didn't believe me. The snort gave it away.

In seconds Andrea and The Elder flashed past and all that was left was for me to take my turn and bring our forces after us. I didn't dare think any further than my whispered "In for a penny ..." before hurling myself through the gateway I'd opened up. I could hear the footfalls of my followers as I hit the boundary of the Cascade Bridge and then there was no sound bar the crunch of scattered leaf litter rather than gravel under each step and the sun was again hanging above us. No matter how many times you travel between time zones like this, stepping from night to day like you are walking between rooms is a singularly off putting sensation.

Only slowing my pace slightly, I did my best to take in all of the detail from around me, doing my best to be able to look everywhere at once in readiness for the attack which was no doubt just waiting to erupt. We had emerged onto a wide expanse of dusty ground, almost as wide as a tennis court. The terrain was incredibly flat and was utterly devoid of vegetation or plant life despite being in the wooded outlands of Mexico. From around me in the bushes and undergrowth of the area we were running along, there was no movement or noise save for the usual sounds which come from any wooded area in the world. Tiny life carried on regardless of my expectation of a computer game like attack as enemies of all kinds leapt out from behind anything that could have concealed them.

Already far ahead of me, Em, Andrea and The Elder were still powering on, making the most of the unhindered path they found themselves on, while behind me, I could make out the gradually increasing sounds of more and more armoured feet hitting the ground as our soldiers joined us on this side of the Cascade Bridge.

The final member of our group emerged from the magical bridge and I could feel the effort of the Cascade Bridge fall away. It hadn't been a mighty weight in my mind but the effort needed was noticeable as it faded to nothing.

I risked a short glance over my shoulder to check on the progress of the others following behind me to be immediately greeted by the appearance of Leatherpants, full Hive skin suit and associated bejeweled finery, sprinting effortlessly to draw alongside me. He was keeping remarkable pace. I'd like to think that I was being slowed by the amount of armour I was enclosed within but I hadn't been finding it that difficult to keep moving. He was fitter than he looked.

Returning my attention ahead of me I was confronted by the other guardians now stopped and all standing still at the edge of what looked like a substantial drop over a cliff of some sort. As gracefully and as artfully as I could, I slammed on the brakes and came skidding to a halt next to them, kicking up a wildly enthusiastic cloud of dust and gravel as I did.

Eventually, as the dust settled, I could see everyone clearly and no-one looked happy. They all wafted their arms around clearing my dusty exuberance from the air and looked at me with a mixture of disappointment and worry. It really was starting to get on top of me that there was always a mix of negative emotions on everyone's face whenever I did anything. No matter what I did it seemed that it was always going to be wrong. I was becoming the self-fulfilling prophecy. They expected me to do something wrong so anything I did was treated with ultimate suspicion and derision, minor errors being viewed in inflated terms.

"What?" My belligerence was breaking the surface at the accusations from the looks I was getting.

"I think that your fellow Guardians were thinking it a stroke of luck that you noticed that they had stopped their forward momentum before you threw yourself from the cliff edge here." Leatherpants was casually strutting around the edge of the drop, peering over the edge with a remarkable expression of contempt on his face. He kicked a stray black stone from the edge and watched absentmindedly as it plummeted.

I did my best to ignore him but his voice just seemed to get under my skin. I caught myself before I could act on the immediate need to rip him to pieces. My power was being manipulated from somewhere else and I had to keep my cool. Whatever was going on, me going off the deep end and attacking my own people wasn't going to help.

Taking a steadying breath, I exhaled the building anger and shook my head clear of any lingering emotion.

Leatherpants skimmed me with his eyes, obviously expecting some form or reaction but was quick to continue when said reaction didn't come. He continued to walk around his superiors while all the time looking like the prowling master, watching and judging the actions of his pupils as they were put through their paces.

All of the troops fell into defensive position around us, melting into the foliage despite their armoured attire. Even including the run, they were all looking perfectly fresh, not one breathing even slightly hard. It would appear that everyone was fitter than I'd first given them credit. I caught a glimpse of Mark easing into a defensible position with Maria on his back, shielding her from as much potential threat as he could. Just as the others, my giant colleague looked as if the effort of the run had been nothing to him. Hairy was a step behind them, also looking every inch the dutiful soldier but not wanting to move too far from Maria.

Mike casually took in all of the details of the surroundings as he moved through the crowd and settled himself at my side. He too was wearing a suit of armour but it was more lightweight that mine. It was still very much the medieval suit but there was a much greater feel of modern tactical gear. Smaller plates and less additional shielding had made him look more akin to a stripped down version of Iron Man than the knight of old the rest of us looked like. He carried the helmet under his arm and just looked at ease in the battle kit.

"Excellent flourish at the end there bach. I'd have given you a 9.5 for artistic impression." His voice was low to avoid anyone else hearing the jibe. I smiled under the helm and replied with a very Anglo-Saxon word of my own, again trying my best to not be over heard. After all, there were ladies present.

"What's the problem? Why did you stop? Aside from the cliff that is?" I tried to snap back to the business end of things and do my best not to embarrass myself with any questions.

The three ladies all remained looking out over the edge.

"The entrance tower to the realm of the Tayne is gone." Andrea's voice was slightly muffled by the helm she was wearing but it was still clear that this turn of events was an issue.

"Gone? Gone where?"

Em turned to face me and began to explain the details.

"We opened the bridges to this location because it would have allowed a clear path direct to the tower entrance portal to the Tayne's nest. There has always been a black stone tower at the edge of this cliff which will lead down to the catacombs below but as you can see, the tower and all of the settlements which have surrounded it have been destroyed." She dropped her eyes to the ground as she finished her explanation, showing that she had been affected by the details. Was she sad? I thought that she'd levelled out again following the events in my estate but it would appear that there were still a few little bumps in her mental fabric.

"So this will make the entry a little harder and we're up against the clock." I nodded in mock sage wisdom as I interpreted her meaning.

The Elder spoke this time but still didn't turn to face me as she spoke, the calm tranquility still wrapped around her voice.

"We will have to adapt our plans but that is not the concern. The tower has been destroyed but so have all of the surrounding settlements. All of the Tayne guards which were based here and who surrounded the tower entrance are now missing and all the signs of their existence would appear to have been wiped clean. Did you not feel that there was perhaps too much open space for a Mexican jungle when you cleared the Cascade Bridge?" She'd spoken in a very level tone, adding no emotion of any kind to the details she'd given. She hadn't needed to. They had said enough by themselves.

Looking back up the route we'd just followed I could see now that the edges of the wooded areas were showing the signs of coming into contact with a great heat. Whatever had been here had been caught in the blast of such an immense torrent that everything within whatever beam had done the damage had simply been vaporized. There was singeing and scorch marks on the trees and bushes beyond that but this had been a focused amount of energy, very little spilling beyond the intended target. Now I'd noticed the signs, I could make out the barest odor of smoky burning, the final remnants of the attack.

Whatever had done this had started from practically where we had jumped in. There was a clear wall of trees which were untouched by the devastation to show where it had started. It had just surged through everything ahead of it and demolished the tower as well. It wasn't a huge comfort to take but still, looking down I could make out that whatever it had been it hadn't destroyed everything. At least the ants were still marching around our feet.

"What did this?" It was a comment more to myself than one expecting an answer but Mike responded.

"Whatever it was, it's certainly far more powerful than anything we've seen from The Hive short of their masters and they're all secure. I don't know?" it may have been Mike who'd said it but as soon as he'd finished speaking I knew it was something everyone was feeling.

No-one knew what had done this.

Andrea turned and spoke to every member of our forces who had come with us, her voice carrying with a familiar authority.

"Our plan remains the same, warriors of The Circle. We now have a hazardous descent into the catacombs of the Tayne but there is no early warning system as you can see. When we arrive in the tunnels below we will continue on as we have planned to the Queen."

Body by body, our soldiers executed a tactical extraction from their hastily filled vantage points and formed up ahead of us. The ordered lines of troops all nodded as one. Either they hadn't been aware of the details or they just didn't see it as big as a concern as I did. Just focus on the job at hand Anthony.

Rolling my shoulders under the armour against the tension already bunching into my muscles, I took stock.

"How do we get down there now? I don't think flying us all down is viable if our Dragons are at risk. Any other options?" I felt my question was valid but Mike smiled back at me.

"You have a grappling hook in the right gauntlet of your armour. Magic after all."

I looked at my hand but couldn't see anything remarkable which was going to give away the presence.

"Great. How does that work?"

Mike didn't answer. He didn't have time. Instead I was given a beautiful demonstration from every soldier with us as they followed Em as she leapt from the cliff edge, turned to face the edge as she fell and punched out a massive piton of energy into the rock. I could feel the vibrations caused by the anchoring of all of the magic through my feet as everyone gave themselves over to gravity.

Andrea and The Elder joined them, creating their own thump, thump of impact.

"See. Easy. See you at the bottom." He'd replaced his helmet as he'd spoken and cast himself off the cliff edge, practically swan diving his way down. I thought that I'd have given him a 9.0. I felt the impact of his magical tether through the soles of my feet as he fell and now found myself alone.

No point being scared. Taking a steadying breath I hurled myself from the cliff and into the emptiness of thin air.

When you freefall, there is a split second where you seem to be suspended in the void, untouched by the pull of gravity. In that snapshot of reality, you can embrace the purest wonder of the world. Flight. As a Dragon, I'd held that moment for far longer than it would have been possible for a man without the aid of hang gliding equipment and it was liberating in ways I could never have expected. This, though, was not in any way the same.

That split second as a Dragon could last for minutes. That split second as a man encased in metal didn't even last a split second, I swear.

Reaching out my arm I willed as much power as I could into the casting of whatever facility was in the gauntlet and fired out a flapping magical rope which smashed into the rock face and held firm. The success made me catch in my mind just what a risk I'd just taken but thankfully it didn't stay long. First issue resolved but now I was acutely aware that the ground was rushing up to meet me. I may have been able to fire off my magical piton but I was still falling at the mercy of gravity.

And I panicked just a little bit.

All of the others were settled happily on the ground and were moving about freely, obviously none the worse for the drop but I had no clue what to do next. This was going to sting a little.

If I'd thought a little about what to do to slow me down I could have dragged together some power and moulded it in some way to be able to do some good. All I could do was just flail my arms and jibber as I scrabbled around my mind for options and none presented themselves. My Dragon was all I had. I knew that we were meant to be approaching with at least some level of stealth and that any call I made for my Dragon energy was fraught with the danger of having it back fire in who knew which way but as an alternative to the impending pancake, the risk was worth it.

Closing my eyes and picturing my altered form in my head, my concentration fluttering as the wind rushed past my face and the ground surged up to meet me, I was about to split myself from the suit of armour when I was quickly yet gently eased from my descent.

The rope of magic pulled tight and the weight was carried all over the armour without placing too much stress on any single part of my body and almost all of the speed of my fall was removed.

I landed cleanly next to the others in the dusty ground at the base of the cliff and the magical rope simply dissipated from above me, leaving me with my right arm reached to the sky above, almost asking the teacher to pick me.

"See. Told you it was easy." Mike's voice held a sliver of a giggle at my arrival and it made me snap my arm down to my side. I straightened my posture and strode purposefully towards him. Leatherpants remained fixed in his position at the mouth of the Tayne nest and watched me intently.

The rest of the group were already making their way down what remained of the stairway within the tower and into the subterranean world of the Tayne. Each member of our assault party was bristling with Magical force and implicit menace as they swiftly made their way down. Em was at the head of the advancing column, with The Mage and Andrea evenly spaced amongst the soldiers. I nodded to Mike and we took up our place within our forces. Leatherpants was the last to start the decent. Maybe he was starting to feel the exposure his skin suit represented so didn't want to be first into the fight. Business dress really wasn't a good choice for military action.

The stone cut pathway spiraled down at the edge of the tunnel walls. The depth of the shaft was peppered with areas where the stone walls had been removed leaving behind openings onto the world below the surface. The bright sunlight from above poured into the abyssal darkness but only penetrated into the area directly below the opening to the outside world. The deeper we went, the heavier the murk became until we reached the bottom and found ourselves in much cooler air and a landscape of whispering shadows, holding the threat of any form of concealment. Looking beyond the space we were stood in gave us no further clue as to what was going on.

The Elder, Andrea and Em all stood in the centre of the pool of muted sunlight as all of our troops repeated their deployment movements from the top of the cliff and melted away into the surrounding area. Mike and I strode towards the three ladies and waited. Leatherpants was quick to join us, slipping soundlessly behind our group, able to hear what could be said but without making his presence felt within the inner circle. Mark took up a stance a little further back from the centre than Leatherpants but was stood directly opposite him. He obviously didn't trust him either.

"Where to then ladies?" I tried to maintain a level of relaxation in my tone but that was more down to the fact that I was more than a little apprehensive about the whole situation. There was now an eerie hollow to every sound that skittered across the darkness, giving off the impression of a deserted tomb. Despite this, I scanned every inch of the space we were in for any sign of something which was likely to reach out and start causing havoc. The three ladies didn't bite at my casual comment, obviously feeling similar tension.

"Where are the guards?" Andrea was in the same stance as I was, looking in all directions at once. So was Em. The Elder was still her newly serene self but she was still at a loss to explain the absence of Tayne to at least be near us.

"Where are any of them?" The Elder added. "There isn't a single Tayne nearby is there Mr. Johns?" All eyes of the group swung to me. I didn't know. I couldn't see any further than anyone else so what did The Elder mean?

"Can you feel any threat from the area we stand in? Can your Dragon senses feel any impending attack?"

This time, when The Elder questioned me concerning a point that everyone else had deemed should have been the most obvious for all to understand, there was no callous rebuke or barbed comment concerning my ineptitude. This time it was just a question. One which was framed as coming from the caring teacher rather than the brutal task master.

And it worked.

My head wasn't spinning so there was nothing my Dragon was picking up as a threat. That didn't mean there wasn't something waiting to attack but it did show that my senses, as they were, were giving me the all clear.

"Nothing" I breathed and let my tension levels drop a couple of notches. "So, as I said, where to?"

"There is something very strange at work here." Andrea was still scanning every direction at once, doing her best to look nonchalant but not quite managing it. The Elder may have been happy to trust my Dragon instincts but it would appear that Andrea still needed a little more convincing. I couldn't blame her, what with everything that had been going on, I wasn't sure I trusted my Dragon sense either.

There was no sound coming from anywhere around us, the cool air was still and there was no sign of any movement from anyone or anything.

"Should we just continue on with our mission my lady?"

Leatherpants had spoken, clearly aiming his words at The Elder, but had remained casually looking around at any and all information that he could find. Casual step after casual step, he paced around the stone strewn area and just took everything in. His hands were held easily behind his back and there was an almost unnatural ease to his actions.

"I think that that would be the most appropriate course of action given what we can see here." The Elder was still speaking with that now familiar calmly even tone, any of the usual contempt for everyone else now a thing of the past. There didn't seem to be any further need to comment. Whatever had taken place here, we'd missed it and whatever it had been looked to have removed all of the enemy for us. We'd still need to keep our wits about us but all signs up to now were pointing to us being relatively in the clear.

"Onwards to the Queen it is then." Decision made, I was just keen to get the ball rolling so we could get out of here. Yet another underground stronghold wasn't my idea of a holiday location.

Without calling out to the assorted troops around the area we were stood, The Elder signaled with one hand and all of the troops just filtered forward and as one we all started on our way into the darkness, The Elder leading the way with Leatherpants close to her side, the rest of us following on without another word.

My first impression of the realm of The Tayne was that it looked very similar to the Mines of Moria from Lord of the Rings. The film version. That won all the Oscars. Not the cartoon. It was clear that The Tayne had been making use of a natural underground space rather than having had it excavated to their needs, but there were also a great many ragged structures intermittently spaced, oddly shaped and all ancient. Blocky building after blocky building huddled close to its neighbor, working as hard as they could not to draw any attention to themselves. There was a dusty coverage to the floor as we walked, either kicked up as a result of the collapse of the black stone tower or as a side effect of years of feet eroding away at the rock.

Our column of troops moved quickly but carefully through the cavernous area, each step heading us deeper and deeper into the murk. A number of our group cast light magic into the air and we were surrounded by a diffuse haze. We needed to be able to see where we were going but couldn't risk attracting too much attention to ourselves. As our route took us near to any of these tumbledown structures, a pod of our guards peeled away from the rest of us and performed a sweep, all the time on high alert. You see this sort of thing on the news and in films but nothing can compare to seeing it enacted in the real world by heavily armed and armoured soldiers who are there to protect you.

We slipped past hamlet after hamlet, all deserted and looking as if they had been that way for a great length of time. Each time the soldiers returned from their scouting of a building with nothing to add, no signs of any kind of life beyond the insects that make the subterranean world their home, no signal that anyone or anything had been there for a very long time, there was a palpable increase in tension. Already, the original plan we'd been working with was seeming to be obsolete. We'd planned for warfare and instead we were being greeted by a walk through a museum. There was nothing to see, nothing to confront as we made our way onwards but we still seemed to be taking longer than expected. The light that had been pouring down from the ruined tower entry was waning at an almost supersonic rate, leaving us truly in the depths of night.

"What the hell are we missing?" I was whispering as best I could to Mike who was still at my side. This couldn't be this easy.

"This is supposed to be a struggle, supposed to be a fight for all concerned but here we are, walking through the outskirts of their home without there being any signs of life let alone resistance. You got any ideas about this?

Mike shrugged.

"Sorry bach. I'm as mystified as you are. I'm still keeping an eye out but so far, this is shaping up to be nothing more than a training hike. About time we had some good luck."

The way things had been going, I didn't believe we could have this much luck.

I needed to know more.

I picked the speed up and headed for The Elder, passing Andrea and Em but knowing that they would have followed close behind, for no other reason than to see what I was about to do. Passing by The Elder and Leatherpants I turned and positioned myself directly ahead of them, forcing them to stop or walk into me. Thankfully they stopped.

"What do you want now?" Leatherpants very nearly kept the contempt out of his tone. "My Lord" he finished the sentence as an afterthought, knowing that he couldn't yell at me for fear of upsetting the rules of order. The Elder remained utterly blank to the question, still calm beyond words.

Andrea and Em joined me and I could see over Leatherpants shoulder that the troops had again managed to spread out without any word from us, back into their holding pattern. Scary good. Mark had again given the rigid form of Maria as much protective cover as he could and again, Hairy went with them, adding his own considerable bulk to the effort.

"There is something very wrong here. Where is everyone?" I aimed my questions at The Elder but she gave no hint of there being any kind of recognition that she may be required to answer.

"We all thought there would be a fight to be had but instead we're having a casual stroll. What's happened here?"

I hadn't meant it but I'd ended the final word with a Dragon growl as an exclamation mark. The ever present threat of attack was bringing my Dragon closer to the surface and add to that the potential manipulation from whoever had The Drake Stone and things were feeling a little odd.

I cleared my throat and repeated my final question. I just knew that everyone was paying minute attention to every word that was spoken as well as keeping alert for attack so I couldn't risk being anything other than ceremonially perfect despite the wider situation.

"Has your mind given us any cause to believe that there is any threat to us?" Leatherpants asked having readjusted his ceremonial mask. That huge smile of his was now back in place. The Elder remained impassive, eyes still glazed.

"I only ask in that you had agreed earlier, that the way you are able to identify any impending attack is via a trait of the Guardian form, your spinning mind. Has that trait alerted you to the presence of anything which could threaten attack?"

Now he tilted his head in that very curious fashion that Em had been using, innocent of everything even slightly approaching scorn. I could see Andrea and Em look at me, not accusingly but certainly eager to hear that there was something I was magically aware of.

But I wasn't.

"I can't sense anything and therein lies the problem wouldn't you agree?" I could feel my internal rage broiling away and did my best to channel it in a positive fashion. I couldn't afford to let Leatherpants control the discourse.

"We'd been aware of all manner of potential threats coming from this mission, all kinds of risk were waiting for us meaning we needed to plan for the most brutal exchange possible as we made our way to the Queen of The Tayne. Don't get me wrong here, I'm glad we haven't had to battle to the point we now find ourselves but surely I'm not the only one who's thinking this is a little too easy? My head flickered a couple of times but nothing actually happened. It only lasted a fraction of a second."

Leatherpants wrinkled his overly tightened forehead, plainly confused by my concerns. He continued to speak for The Elder.

"As I just said, you haven't sensed anything have you? We haven't seen any sign of anything even resembling a Tayne fighter and our progress has been steady, almost brisk, as we double check for every possible evidence that we have any enemies within striking distance of us. All of the evidence here suggests that something major happened to the encampment at the top of the cliff and that that same something had a knock on effect to events down here."

He was back in his ordered ceremonial groove, practically playing to the crowd as he laid out his points one by one. With minimal effort he had transported us back to that very uncomfortable moment in the infirmary in Freddy's estate in Argentina where he had been able to put me in my place just by stating facts. There had been no attempt to highlight any short coming or failures, no need for him to try any form of character assassination, instead he just relied on the resolute facts and they were more than enough.

Behind him, Andrea and Em were showing that they had had all of their support for me removed, Leatherpants casually batting away my ideas.

But he'd said we were making good time despite the loss of the light from above. We weren't making brisk anything.

"We're not making 'brisk' time at all. Where did the light go?" I wasn't going to let this go that easily.

Andrea and Em now frowned at me. I had to be careful pushing now, for fear of looking like a child who just won't listen. Despite the pain of what was taking place, you had to admire the skills of the smarmy little bastard.

"I am sorry Mr. Johns but non sequiturs are not my forte. Light?" Leatherpants didn't suddenly exude any fear or confusion at my question, instead he did his best to fold his plasticized features into a frown.

Fighting the building urge to roar, I tried to continue my point.

"We've lost the light from above. Look back the way we came and the sunlight coming in from above is gone. That means its night time. How can that be the case when we haven't been down here that long? You said we were making brisk progress but yet here we are, still away from the target but taking much longer than expected."

I left the statement hang in the air, hoping that it was going to cause everyone else to take it on and question. That didn't even vaguely happen.

"I am sorry Mr. Johns. I did not explain this tactical deployment to you but The Elder requested that I station a handful of troops at the entry way as a rear guard but also to cover the entry to the outside world. They have been casting coverage since we set off to prevent anyone being able to see the hole from above. I hadn't thought that anyone would be looking behind us so intently."

His tone was as devastating as any weapon strike. He maintained such a gentle tone of explanation as he'd spoken, letting me in on the details of what was going on in the way of any sage explaining a basic point to the would be simpleton. At least he stopped short of patting me on the head as he spoke.

Looking around at all of the faces looking at me, Andrea and Em showed clearly that they had fallen down firmly on Leatherpants's side, The Elder was serenely staring at all of us without even trying to add anything and even Mike was forced to shrug in acceptance. The Elder hadn't made any comment so had obviously ordered the move so all I was left with was the impotent concern that we were missing something when it appeared that I was the only one missing anything and that detail was a minor one at that.

Great.

Leatherpants straightened his jeweled tie pin and waited for any follow up comments. Despite my best efforts, none came.

"Excellent. Shall we continue now this basic issue has been resolved? The Tayne Queen will be more heavily guarded than these outskirts and may be fortifying her position as we speak." He spoke with his now all too familiar creeping passive aggression, letting all there see that he was calling the shots for The Elder but we were all left with the painful conclusion that he had been right.

We moved off again, deeper into the realms of The Tayne, again with The Elder leading the way but with Leatherpants an ever present fixture at her side, always bowing at commands that the rest of us couldn't hear and whispering to her his responses.

The more I watched them as our column marched on, the more suspicious I became.

We continued our progress into the ongoing darkness that was the Tayne homeland and the abandoned living quarters continued to greet us. All of the off shoot tunnels which led away from the main route we were following were given a thorough examination but all yielded nothing. Every single remnant of the occupants of this once thriving community had been mysteriously whisked away, leaving behind nothing but buildings and possessions.

Still there was no hint of threat revealing itself. Still there was no increase in revolution from my magical early warning system. Still, despite what should have been a very well populated city under the ground, there was not a single hint of any of The Tayne.

I could practically feel the frustration crawling up my spine by this point. This was ridiculous. Where was everyone? Why was it that no-one else could see that this was more than a little bizarre? Occasionally I thought that my mind was cranking up through the gears, building the spinning early warnings, but each time the sensation was gone before it came into being. Wishful thinking for the fight? Was my Dragon power just lusting for the violence?

Andrea drifted to my side and, in as subtle a voice as she could manage, whispered to me.

"You can't let Mr. Ward get to you. We all know that your powers are being attacked but he could be the only senior member of the group here who isn't being affected by whoever has The Drake Stone. We need to maintain ourselves." Her accent hugged her words and reassured me. Any previous anger had been draining until where she was now, almost back to her usual self.

My instinct took over. There was nothing my mind could do to prevent what I needed to do. Far away from my Dragon self, my own human desire for a connection with another swelled and I gripped her hand tightly, intertwining our fingers.

For a heartbeat that lasted for an eternity, we continued walking, two armoured figures showing the simplest form of affection. Andrea made no attempt to pull her hand from mine and for a second, despite every threat and concern that was circling us, I felt a calm I hadn't ever felt before.

It couldn't last. It just couldn't.

The Elder and Leatherpants continued their separated progress but, as if he'd somehow been able to stop time, Leatherpants had turned back to face us, about to deliver who knew what kind of speech or order, and his eyes just burned directly at us and our shared grip. Our hands flew apart in that all too familiar way we all know from our teenage years when you're caught doing something you're not supposed to.

Had we been lucky enough to come apart in time? Had that preening fool seen what was going on?

Tension spread throughout my body and I could sense from Andrea that she was going through the same thought process. We were both suddenly on the tightrope over a very high drop.

Leatherpants was quick to remove any hope he'd missed it.

He thrust out his right arm with an accusing finger and screamed in a voice far too high pitched,

"TRAITOR!"

Everyone stopped their forward momentum and just stared at him as he jabbed his finger at me and me alone. Andrea was sensible enough to edge slightly further from me, leaving me squarely in the cross hairs.

"You have defiled the sanctity of The Circle through your actions." His voice was still a squeaky trill but at least he'd stopped screaming. Our entire group was now turned to look directly at me, most obviously trying to work out what was going on but a few of The Elders troops just looking daggers, satisfied that the accusation from Leatherpants was enough to convict me, even if they weren't completely clear of what they had just convicted me of.

I had to think fast and somehow maintain control over the Dragon power inside me which wanted ever so much to attack him. .

"How dare you? How dare you accuse me of anything?" It was all I could think to do, go on the attack, verbally, and try to pull rank in any way I could. He didn't want to let go though.

"I dare, my lord, because you are breaking the laws of what you are. I just witnessed you moving beyond the bounds of the acceptable with a kind of physical intimacy towards another Guardian that cannot be excused. Do you deny this?"

"I deny nothing. There is nothing to deny, now be quiet and let's all continue in what we're doing."

I tried, I really did. Unfortunately Em didn't accept anything I'd said and just reacted.

She loosed her own scream of anger and swarmed onwards, not towards me but instead at Andrea. I could sense the roiling disgust she felt, she was back in the same frame of mind as she had been in the mansion when Maria's magic had been affecting her, all righteous fire and fury.

She crashed into the unsuspecting form of our Russian Guardian and they both thundered into the ground, kicking up a plume of dust as the fight commenced.

Em flailed her arms wildly and rained down blow after blow at Andrea regardless of her armoured exterior. Andrea, despite being taken off guard by the swiftness of the attack, had started by simply defending herself from the hammer blows from the women now sat atop her but quickly switched to working her own violence. She opened her mouth and spewed forth a blast of freezing white power directly into Em's face. The effect on Em was down to physics rather than magical power. The blast from Andrea heaved her backwards simply due to the physical force of the attack rather than the potency of the magical ability. It reminded me of someone being blasted away by water from a fire hose yet not getting wet.

Em crashed back against a pod of soldiers who were all staring at the unfolding events without truly understanding what was going on. They cushioned her fall as much as metal clad warriors could and she was soon back to her feet and heading back at Andrea, all thought of any kind of deference lost.

Blow after blow rained down from Em and sent splintered shards of the formerly ceremonial armour that Andrea was wearing spinning away in all directions. Each blow was accompanied with an animal shriek of fury which just tore at the rocky surroundings we all found ourselves.

Andrea reeled against the attack which she'd been thoroughly unprepared for, just doing her best to shield her head as much as she could as crushing blow after crushing blow continued.

In an instant, Leatherpants had signaled to a group of his troops, The Elder remained unmoved during all of the activity, not even noticing that anything was taking place, just watching on serenely, so the troops had passed to Leatherpants to command. Whatever the situation was with The Elder, it was clear that Leatherpants was going to be the one making the moves but would most likely make the most of the situation and push his own will on the soldiers. Maybe this was a play from The Elder to keep her hands clean? If needed, she could just throw Leatherpants under the bus if this action didn't work out. In an instant, they were surrounding me with various bladed weapons drawn and levelled at me. I lifted my arms slowly in a gesture of surrender, not daring risk any kind of aggressive response, an action wholly at odds with my inner voice.

"You will not dare infect this mighty order any longer." His words were hissing out at me with a huge smile on his face as he spoke. He had troops at his side as well, ready for any possible attack that I could have conceived, no wonder he was smiling.

Risking a quick look around the mess which had suddenly unfolded, I could see that I wasn't the only one who had been pinned down by the pointy ends of The Circle's armoury. Mike and Mark were both now surrounded and had both taken on a similar pose to me, although Mark still looked as if he was the one doing the threatening despite himself. Hairy had left his side and had joined Leatherpants at the head of the group, a look of smug satisfaction plastered all over his face. He carried with him the stasis pod which held the frozen form of Maria. Despite the weight which it must have carried, he hefted it about as if it were nothing more than a school backpack.

Members of every house were now pointing their weapons at me and mine and there seemed to have been fluid organization to get them all ready. I knew that they were an incredibly efficient fighting force despite the fact they had just been assembled for this mission but it almost looked as if they'd had prior warning that Leatherpants' outburst was coming.

The only people who seemed to be overlooked in this were Andrea and Em. The fight continued between them unabated as Andrea fought back, forcing Em back from atop her with freezing blasts of energy and her own swinging blows, her clenched fists now encased within massive maces of ice. A handful of soldiers had taken up a very loose ring position around them, intending to act as either protection or guard, I couldn't tell which but by the looks of things, I was looking to be the only culprit. Instead they all just carried the air of confused onlookers, unsure if they should intervene in any way but mesmerized by what they were seeing. I almost expected someone to pop out a mobile phone and begin filming them.

Leatherpants took a step forward and left The Elder staring into space. His soldiers came with him and he sneered his contempt without any fear of breaching the strict protocol.

"Your actions have plagued this mighty assembly for too long, boy. The Elder has been instructing me for the duration of this mission, that should you show your true colours, I should take the steps that need to be taken."

He was walking casually back and forth, but this time, his stride carried with it a much deeper swagger. Gone was even the barest hint of his usual adherence to what was 'correct' and in its place was a violent, seething confidence.

"It's been painfully clear to all who would see that you've been trying to crack apart The Circle. You are the one who's started all of these actions and you are the one who's now going to pay the price."

His words just held me in place and he locked eyes with me, almost daring me to be the one to look away. I was doing my best to keep a lid on my fury as he strutted about but I could almost hear my Dragon roaring in my ears, desperate to reach out and introduce itself to the situation.

Step by step Leatherpants moved closer to me, passing between the ranks of soldiers holding me at bay until he was stood practically touching his nose to my chest.

"Do you even want to try and deny what you've been caught doing? Don't you care for our mighty Guardian line or Miss Thomich, who you've sullied?"

"SULLIED!" My Dragon was getting nearer the surface and the roar of the word showed everyone that fact. The swords pointed at me all jumped slightly in reaction to my outburst but all edged closer to me in response.

Leatherpants stepped back a couple of paces. He kept that confidence in what he was doing but he clearly thought better of risking being next to an angry Dragon should it appear.

"What I think my lord wanted to say was that he was surprised that a charge had been levelled at him." Mikes voice was full of apprehension as he leapt into the conversation but I could readily make out his attempt to diffuse the situation as best he could, easing both sides away from the brink.

"Is that correct my lord?"

He edged gingerly through the various blades which were pointed at him and made his way to my side.

I took a calming breath and blew out as much frustration as I could. Keep it together for crying out loud.

"What I'd like, is an explanation of the details of the accusation. By your actions here it appears that The Elder has been planning a coup d'état. Not even our troops are this good." I gestured my arms openly to the soldiers around us.

"And I believe that I have at least the right to be accused by my equal rather than just a functionary like you. Is that correct, Messenger?"

"It is Anthony. You are the power here and will be spoken to in the correct way." Em was breathing hard and her suit was showing the effects of her fight with Andrea, dents and cracks wound around her with a casual abandon.

"Isn't that correct Miss Thomich?"

Andrea joined her and crossed her arms across her chest.

"It is Messenger."

Her voice was a frozen surety, showing clearly her resolute heart. Her own armour was pitted and spoiled following the fracas with Em but both of them looked to have at the very worse, put it behind them. At best they'd just be pretending it hadn't happened. Andrea showed no sign of the fight on her but her skin was a much brighter white than usual and her eyes were clearly the grey of her Dragon form. She was turning as well, her power being twisted as mine was. Whoever was pulling at the strings of power which were wound round The Circle was clearly having a very strong effect on us. The fight between Andrea and Em had erupted in an instant and it would appear had died away in the same fashion.

Regardless of the cause, two people who had been otherwise occupied when Leatherpants had made his move were now back in the frame.

The soldiers around us shuffled ever so slightly as the two women set themselves ready for the exchange, placing Leatherpants squarely in the cross fire between us. Leatherpants made no show of any fear or concern but his guards let their masks of certainty drop for that fraction of a second. It was the tiniest movement but it explained so much. These troops were loyal to The Circle first and foremost, meaning there was no malice or underhand dealing in what they were doing. Whatever was happening was being done under the banner of the greater good rather than being a private action from The Elder and Leatherpants.

The downside to this, though, was that I now couldn't just obliterate everything around me to get us out of trouble. These troops were doing what they had been ordered to by their superior for the good of The Circle so they were still on my side, even if it didn't really feel like it.

"The Elder has given order that she will no longer speak to that," he pointed out at me, as if there was any chance of confusion.

"I have been instructed to speak for my lady on this matter."

"Mr. Ward, this is unconventional at best but if The Elder has given this order to you, we must accept it." Resignation hung on Andrea's words as she nodded her acceptance of the situation, again gripped by what the laws of time demanded of her. The Elder remained unmoved from her vantage point, just looking on and taking in all of the details as they played out. Her attention was fierce but aloof.

Leatherpants smiled and bowed to Andrea. He knew he was back in the driving seat of the exchange, knew that he was able to use all of the shared laws of protocol to his advantage, and despite there being a flashing beacon of concern above it, no-one else did anything about it.

I swapped glances with Mike and he was just as non-plussed, shrugging his resignation at where we were. He knew the rules as well and knew that Leatherpants was getting up a head of steam.

I growled my frustration, mainly to myself, but I could feel that my inner beast was close to breaking free. Purely by instinctual accident did the sound come out but it was clear that all of the gathered members of our team that, despite holding the moral high ground, the thought of facing one of their Guardians in a fight was far from their desired plan for the day.

Leatherpants just raised his eyebrows on his too tight face and raised his arm.

"This is a clear demonstration that our latest Guardian is nothing more than a beast, given a charge but who is unwilling to consider anything but his most base instincts. He would threaten all of the gathered members of our most sacred order, simply compounding his actions as a Lothario."

"Get to the point Leatherpants. Facts please, not you grandstanding." I had to keep him on topic and do my best to regain my control. I 'was growling through the sentences in a far more Dragon tone now. It was all I could do to keep my body human and not burst the armour, any more than that was just a bridge too far. It didn't matter that I was being manipulated by an unseen hand, the swords all remained as constant threats. I swear some moved even closer to my throat.

"As you command my lord." Leatherpants grinned and bowed in my direction, adding a flourish of arm sweep to sell the point. He was pushing me and I could feel the adrenaline climbing through my every fibre as I held as tightly as I could to the animal inside me. His every action was just making me want, need, to let go.

"You have deflowered Miss Thomich, have you not?"

For a terrifying instant, the world just stopped. Everything became blasted in the horrifying glare of a truth exposed. I didn't understand how he could have known but that almost seemed irrelevant now. He had known and he'd just made sure that everyone here knew as well.

The intake of breath from a handful of locations amongst the soldiery highlighted exactly what everyone else there thought about the revelation. By the looks of things I had just been accused of the crime beyond all others. My face burned red and from behind Leatherpants I could see Andrea going through the same although any colour on her porcelain features stood out starkly. She dropped her eyes to the ground and only dared tiny flicked glances around as she checked to see who was looking at her.

The Elder remained motionless, her face blank of any kind of emotion at what her servant had just done. Soldiers I could see just looked stunned. They all gripped onto the job at hand by way of holding onto any stable base as their collective world tilted wildly. Em narrowed her eyes and frowned, tilting her head in that questioning manner of hers, no hint of violence forthcoming.

The silence just stretched on.

And on.

I just didn't know how to respond.

"So?" Marks voice startled everyone, including me, and all eyes turned to him.

Silence resumed.

My heart was crashing in my chest, adrenaline coursing and my inner animal almost free.

"So what if my two leaders have indulged in what you say? Why is that a bad thing?" He spoke slowly and with a real question in his voice. He didn't understand and was asking for an answer to justify what was happening. It wasn't a massive question but in the context of who he was and what he was doing, it was an atom bomb.

Soldiers turned to Leatherpants for a response. He, in turn, straightened his jacket and aimlessly stroked over his tie before responding.

"Why is this bad? Your question is the reason why it's bad. We all have a duty to behave within a set of laws as a part of who we all are. This thug has belittled us all by not being able to do what he should and that influence is spreading and growing like a cancer."

He paused and scanned the crowd, still adjusting his dress, as if his suit suddenly wasn't as fitted as it needed to be.

Was he nervous?

There was no time to find out.

From the enveloping blackness of this subterranean world, the unseen attack swooped in from all sides before another word could be uttered.

28

The Tayne warriors swept in on us without any warning in my head. They were already crashing in on the nearest soldiers to them and were clawing and biting against the armour, some of our troops being picked up and hurled against any rocky area available. Searing screams and shrieks came from the invading hoard, each a battle cry meant to unnerve and disturb. In that instant, all previous accusations of wrong doing were forgotten as the more pressing matter of our survival took precedence.

"How many of them are there? Where are the coming from?" Mike shouted into the mayhem swarming all around us as he slammed on his helmet and began drawing power into his balled fists to start his defence. His voice was high with fear. Already I could make out that his wasn't the only one. There were strangled calls in response but no-one could really give a definitive answer. It was only now that my danger warning system kicked in and started to spin. Better late than never but we'd been taken utterly by surprise and The Tayne were now ripping into us.

From everywhere there came the swishing and hacking sounds of swords fighting back but The Tayne were just battering on regardless, an apparent utter disregard for the health and safety of any of their number highlighting that they just wanted their prizes. Em, Mark and a few others had added their magic to our defence and were blasting at anything and everything which came their way while I made a bee line for the construct holding Maria. Hairy was still crouched over her, swatting away at anything that came near him but so far, they were both being left pretty much alone. Andrea joined me as we readied ourselves for the fight, our Dragon powers rising in readiness, potential risk to ourselves forgotten.

But the fight never came.

The Tayne just aimed directly at Leatherpants, bypassing what should have been the more prized targets of the Guardians and moving with an almost blurring oneness and balletic violence. Thinking about what was happening when the attack had taken place, they must have seen him as being the one in charge of us all and in classic military strategy, had aimed to cut the head from their enemy.

He was a prick but I'll give him his due, he was delivering a masterful display of defensive magic, burning through any and everything that came near him. His hands moved with an almost liquid grace of their own, blurring through casting after casting as he actually did something worthwhile.

The Tayne didn't let go of their attack. Their shrieking changed and a hooting replaced it. In an instant, more and more of the leathery monsters flooded over Leatherpants. The weight of that new attack began to change the balance of power.

Leatherpants started to grimace, that too tight face of his looking oddly stretched and misshapen as he did. His blasts continued to rip down attacker after attacker but now, some were getting through. The first sign was the long slice which appeared over his left cheek. Then one which opened up across his forehead. His flesh sagged limply from his face but there was no blood accompanying the wound. Instead, amidst the melee of the fight, I could see a dark second skin underneath. Whatever he was, Leatherpants wasn't human. At least that explained the remarkably long lifespan.

My instinct took over.

Leaping through the air at the mass of flapping horrors spread all over a member of The Circle, I just started swinging my arms and roaring. I smashed into the mess of bodies and let my beast go wild as much as I dare. Hooting Tayne were crushed and shredded, pulverized as I did my best to free Leatherpants from the bottom of the pile. The syrupy blood spattered in every direction as I continued until I eventually reached him.

I may have been coming to his rescue but that didn't mean I was going to be that careful about it. Taking a firm grip on one leg, I heaved him up and launched him back to where we had set up a defence of Maria. He landed on the dusty ground hard and slid past the readied form of Andrea, who was now standing with a fierce cold energy gathered in her hands. Next to her stood Em, Mark, Mike, Hairy and a handful of the soldiers. With Leatherpants clear and me heaving my armoured shape back towards them, they all opened up with as much magical violence as they could muster. All manner of wound was inflicted as the Tayne just took what was being thrown at them. And they started to move forward against it anyway.

The Tayne followed after the conniving Head of House and by sheer weight of numbers blasted past the attacks which were mustered. The hooting continued as they descended on Leatherpants again.

Power poured into that pile of flesh from every angle as the remaining members of the party attacked but it proved to be useless. There was a single scream from the bottom of the pile, a sound beyond humanity, one that came from the clarity of the animal part of a person. It was clear that Leatherpants was succumbing to an awful death at the hands of these maddened monsters. Even if we had been able to break him free he would have most likely perished anyway.

Didn't mean I wasn't going to try.

I snorted out black smoke and spat a flaming gob of saliva away and headed in. Mike did the same from the opposite side of the melee. I had absolutely no feeling of bonding with Leatherpants of any kind but underneath all of the layers of expectation, of protocol, he was a member of The Circle and as such was under my protection. Besides, after all of his showboating and general attempts at undermining me since this whole mess had started to unravel, I wasn't going to let him die without having the chance to expose him in front of my peers. We were almost at the mound of flesh when a greasy ring of power appeared around the group. That same corrupted ring of energy I'd seen on the battlefield was here. Ozone filled our nostrils as an eerie haze of yellow illuminated everything. Andrea was quickly at my side, as were the others of our group, prepared for whatever was about to come crashing out at us. Even Hairy was stood shoulder to shoulder in the line. But nothing further happened and in a second more, the ring collapsed under its own weight and detonated a howling maelstrom of energy as it did. It left me with a slight feeling of disorientation but I shook it away as the ring finally winked out of existence.

Most of the pile of Tayne went with it. As did what must have been left of Leatherpants.

All forward momentum had been momentarily stolen from us as we adjusted to what had just taken place. My eyes struggled to clear against the amorphous shape which was now hovering at the centre of my vision, the brightness of the enemy's bridge rendering me temporarily blind. My hearing though, hadn't been affected in the same way, and I could still recognize the scratching, scrabbling sounds of the Tayne stragglers who hadn't escaped through the construct.

We each smashed down on a remaining Tayne and held it in place and looked around to survey the wreckage as our eyes adjusted. There were bodies strewn all over the area. The vast majority of our assembled force was now gone, leaving behind a small band of frightened fighters. The creature I had pinned flapped its broken wings in a vain attempt to break free and its jaws reflexively bit out at me. I'd been up close and personal with more than my fair share of the winged beasties during the last couple of months but this one was very different to any of them I'd seen before. It was huge.

The creatures I'd seen each time The Hive had attacked the site in Argentina had been wispy and thin. They had been practically see through and hadn't ever been anywhere near as nasty as this thing was. A wingspan of at least twenty feet allowed the hulking body to fly. Whereas they had been the relative weaklings of the worlds I was discovering, these were much higher up the food chain. Its lumpy and distended form continued to struggle against my grip, still snapping out at me, spattering gobs of sticky hot saliva as it did.

What the hell had happened to these things and why had they just attacked us with that kind of ferocity? I knew it had been too easy getting here.

The Elder remained stood where she had been, still utterly unmoved by what was happening, her face still that blank emptiness. She just didn't care. My Dragon power was up and I wanted to know if she was happy with what she'd just made happen.

I was going to make her speak.

It was only then that Andrea called out something which made me stop in my tracks.

"They took the child."

Tightening my grip on the Tayne beneath me, I scanned round the area as best I could, hoping, that I'd be able to pick her out but Andrea was right. Maria's tiny casket of power was missing. It could only have been taken when we were all trying to protect Leatherpants.

"WHERE IS SHE?" I roared at the stricken Tayne, my armour creaking in protest as my body began to warp as my fury came closer to the surface again, threatening to break free. The Tayne's eyes just bulged in protest at the grip I held on it, its jaw still working but now as a clamoring, rasping for air.

I held that violence directed at it for a further heartbeat, allowing it to feel all the fear I could muster but also to give me the chance to control myself. I leaned down to it and repeated the question, this time with more white hot fury than I knew I could place on words.

The silence settled down on all of us and the tension continued to build. There were no other Tayne coming to attack us, the look on this one's face showed that clearly. It was terrified. It had to now understand that it was beaten. What it had to decide now was if it wanted to risk keeping its mouth shut.

"You have taken something from us today, beast." Andrea was stood behind me and loomed over the creature. She was imposing to me so I could only imagine what The Tayne was thinking.

I tightened my grip just to help it focus. It worked.

"You have invaded our lands and destroyed so much of who we are." Its voice came out in a constricted wheeze, placing emphasis on the wrong parts of the words as it spoke, forcing them out over teeth that seemed to be too large for it. But it spoke.

I released some pressure on its neck and beckoned for it to continue.

"Why would I help such a barbaric group as The Circle?"

Despite the horror of its form, its voice was a cultured velvet. Hearing without seeing its owner would have brought to mind a very different image of what was speaking.

Andrea responded.

"You have been attacking us in earnest for the last two months yet you call us the barbarians? How many of our people have your race killed? The Hive wish nothing but conquest and you speak of us as the murderers?" I could feel the freezing hatred in her words before I felt the temperature climbing behind me. She was angry and was struggling to control her own inner beast.

"We are not a part of The Hive. We have seen what the war between your factions has been doing and we have remained far from joining any side." Its own anger rose in response, an indignant belligerence spitting the words back.

"You have attacked us. You have murdered us. You have destroyed so much of who we are but The Tayne will never fall. You mutilated my people and now we have the chance to mutilate one of yours."

My anger took over. A vicious scarlet filled my vision and all of the rage of Fire took over for just a split second. The thought of Maria being released from that magic just to be ripped apart was enough to bring my Dragon side thundering to the fore. The Tayne fighter just immolated under my grip. There was no scream of pain, no call for mercy. In an instant it was just gone, just ash and ember.

"Em. We need to get to the Queen fast and tear that whole palace to pieces if need be. I will not lose Maria to this band of warped monsters."

Em nodded her agreement.

"ELDER." Now we were going to have a chat and I was going to make her see that she had been undermining everything we were in her slavish desire to always do what the process dictates.

"Are you even slightly concerned that what you've done has resulted in the deaths of all of these people? Your rules and regulations have meant you've probably just destroyed this link in The Circle. You've managed to accomplish something The Hive has never been able to do and you've even lost your head of house in the process." Andrea placed a warning hand on my shoulder, trying to soothe me, but I was beyond her help. I could feel the righteous indignation growing as each image of pain and suffering brought about by The Elder and everything she seemed to touch, built on the rage which I was already feeling.

"Come on then. Haven't you got anything to say for yourself?" I seethed with each syllable and my Dragon voice was now fully to the fore. Just standing before her unmoved form, I wasn't sure if I wanted her answer or not.

Her blank expression remained in place. Despite everything that had just happened, everything that had been happening and everything that she felt about me and my ideas, she remained as calm as a mountain lake. There was just nothing. Here, deep in the depths of the earth, following an enemy attack which had killed so many, but also her right hand man, she still couldn't stoop so low as to even acknowledge me. Until, eventually, she frowned.

"I have nothing to say to you."

What? The question detonated in my head and the fury was almost free.

"I do, though, have a question I need to have answered."

She locked eyes with each of us in turn, that relative serenity still in her expression.

"Who are you all?"

She couldn't have sucked the wind from my sails any more effectively even if she'd tried.

"What?" The question was very simple yet carried so much weight behind the words, meaning creeping on disguised as a basic query.

"I haven't got time for games now you're high and mightiness. You may not think you should have to speak with us but the needs of this mission will out-weigh your petty concerns. What have you got to say?" I asked my question again, more out of my own need to remain on firm footing but The Elder didn't let me find it.

"I'm afraid that I don't know who any of you are. I also don't know why I'm here or indeed, where here is."

"My lady?" Andrea pushed past me and edged towards The Elder. I could feel a very new tension in her as she did. The battle may have been swift and violent but it was something that she had at least been used to. She'd practically been expecting something to happen so when it did kick off, she wasn't wholly taken by surprise. The Elder and a mysterious case of amnesia were a different ball game entirely.

"Are you certain you've never seen any of us before? Have you been injured? Is that causing this loss?"

"The Elder looked lost and took a small step away from Andrea.

It would appear that she hadn't been involved in the planning of any kind of coup after all. But what the hell had The Tayne done to her? Had their version of a Cascade Bridge mangled her mind? It had made me feel a little confusion when it had detonated but I'd been right on top of it. The Elder had been the furthest from it yet she was the only one with any issues of memory.

Inside my head, my Dragon was still spoiling for a fight. Taking as steadying a breath as I could, I tried to remain focused on what needed to be done.

For just a little too long, we all just stood in the near darkness, confused and alone. The deaths of soldiers had been, at least on a sub-conscious level, expected. This mystery affliction was not and it was clear that everyone was suddenly very aware of their potential frailties.

"I think the mission remains the same." Mark's voice was quiet but resolute. It was oddly reassuring.

"If The Tayne have taken the child they will have no doubt taken her to their Queen. We therefore still require the same outcome as when we started, no?" Famously tight lipped, Mark had just shown his feelings on the topic. The fact that he had felt he needed to interject wasn't lost on anyone.

"I agree, but, are you sure that we should?" This time it was Mike.

"Being purely pragmatic, surely it would benefit us to return to the estate and gather a stronger force? Return and simply level this entire civilization. We'd be better served in the long run."

I knew he was playing devil's advocate but it was still an uncomfortable thought to come from him. I just wouldn't simply play the mission by the numbers. Human beings are always more than just numbers.

"No. We don't run for help. We mourn later. We don't stop to look into every doorway. We don't stop to inspect every shack. We just go now, straight at their Queen. We protect The Elder but we are going to get Maria back."

Feet shuffled on the dusty ground, showing clearly that no-one was certain of anything anymore.

"None of us will be safe if we just play percentages. The Messenger, The Elder, Andrea and I are all having our powers twisted so the faster we can resolve this the better. We have enough muscle here to do the damage we need to and get out safely. Em. Can you guide us in?"

She smiled wickedly in response and cracked her neck, freeing herself for more violence.

"I still have that knowledge," she responded.

Mike, though, added a single comment before we set off.

"If you had the full power of your Dragon at your control then I'd agree but without that there is a much greater risk. We still don't know who's able to manipulate your power. Just thought you'd like to know." He was beaming a smile as he spoke, just low enough so the others didn't hear him, and he replaced his helmet before clanking me, still just a little too hard, on the arm.

"Come on then team, we're travelling light. In for a penny......."

Em led the way and she led fast. The previously slow pace of our much larger fighting force was now replaced by the whole group charging on in the same we had when we first burst through the Cascade Bridges here. Our group was making short work of the journey and I was loving every step of it. My inner animal was still roaring around inside me, crashing against my mind, pleading to be let free to just destroy everything but this physical activity was at least helping it let off a little steam. Watching the rest of us moving on as well, I could only guess at the turmoil of magic in Andrea and Em but also in the fear in everyone else.

More and more ramshackle buildings rushed past us but there was never any sign of life that we could make out. Indeed, there continued to be no sign of any Tayne of any kind as we moved.

Lone shacks began to be replaced with larger groupings which in turn became villages. We were heading into the core of their civilization yet there was still no sign of anyone.

Unbidden, Em withdrew two dark metal sword pommels which had been attached to her suit at her hips and, with a mere thought, caused the massive blades to magically extend, ready for the fight. She continued to run without hindrance despite the weapons. We all followed her lead and drew together our respective powers and weapons. By her actions, Em had signaled that we were closing in on our goal.

"We are almost to their Queen's location? I can sense no life in the area bar her and a small group of creatures in her attendance." Em's words were almost lost in the rush of wind as we powered through the narrow streets of what had once been a thriving and busy city. As with every other location we'd passed through, there was still no sign of the previous inhabitants. All of the businesses and homes were alone in the dark. My rational mind took in the detail as much as I could muster but the animal in me was still scratching behind my eyes to break free and all it cared about was burning everything to a cinder.

"Can you sense the child with them?" Andrea asked. Her grip on the task at hand was obviously stronger than mine.

"Nothing my lady," Em's response was flat, matter of fact.

"Where exactly is the Queen?" I roared, Dragon now fully back in my voice.

"Ahead, approximately seven hundred meters." She gestured ahead with one sword. "That structure with the small turrets all over it. What do you want us to do when we get there?"

I bellowed out a battle cry from the Dragon inside and increased speed, passing Em and taking up position at the head of our party.

"Everyone," I called out, "follow me in, and pick up the pieces of anything I miss."

Each and every one of us has seen a cartoon or film or some such where a character just runs through a wall and leaves behind them a 'them' shaped hole. We all know that that doesn't happen in the real world but for me, at that moment, I knew I was going straight through what was ahead of me.

I can only guess but by the time I hit the outer wall of the Tayne Queen's 'palace', I must have been travelling close to thirty miles an hour. There was no consideration given to stealth or guile in what I was going to do, I just reacted purely on need, that pulsing desire deep down that calls to you and you have to do your best to quieten the temptation to listen. I needed to just tear my way into that place and rend flesh from bone. I needed to tear down the leader of The Tayne and unleash the kind of violence which would show to any and every other race of creatures who'd dare try to stand against The Circle that our response would be swift and terrible. I was going to save Maria and make sure those who had started out to hurt her, and all of us, were shown the errors of their ways.

My armoured shape hit like a bowling ball hammering into pins. My armour was already dented by use over the years, a much more functional suit than the ceremonial efforts of the others in our group, and it flickered through my head that maybe this was the reason why. Years of the Fire Dragon doing just what fire would do would take its toll on the finery and craftsmanship of any design.

I'd aimed at what looked like a doorway but it was clear that the doors were made of the same materials as the walls. Huge lumps of masonry flew ahead of me and a thick black dust billowed. The cracking and breaking of the stone swarmed into the various tunnels within the palace and I could hear them echoing away as they travelled. Despite the stygian blackness of the location, the palace was very slightly illuminated. Inside there were signs of the palaces use, furniture and what could have been called great wealth to a Tayne, but there was still no actual living creature here. I skidded to a halt and slammed into objects of who knew what construction, scattering them all over the area.

Andrea, Em and the others followed through the hole I'd made and rushed to my side.

"Subtle bach, really subtle." Mike spoke quietly from next to me through deep gasping breaths. He'd clearly been having to work hard to get here at the speed I'd forced.

I ignored him. Wave after wave of nauseating anger swelled in my head, each calling with such rotted sweetness for me to relax my faltering grip on my senses and just let the need to destroy take over.

Sullen clouds of dust were still filling the air, creating an almost physical sensation of the smell of the room. My eyes were tracking round hurriedly, taking in all of the information I could while trying to decide where I needed to aim my fury.

"Where's the Queen?" It was a call to the whole group. I knew that someone would be able to locate her for me. I could probably have done it myself if I'd really concentrated but my mind was in no mood for that. I just needed the fight.

"Fifty meters to the right. At the end of that corridor." It was Em's voice, again pointing the way without any addition of comment. She was back to her purely business based approach. Excellent.

I just reacted. Having been given the new direction I just tore off down the corridor in the direction Em had just signaled. I could feel the out pouring of heat from my magics being readied for the attack as I ran, each step was becoming slimy as the stone melted beneath my feet. I didn't care. Danger was nothing to me.

I again seethed through the doorway, sending pieces of it in all directions once more. And slid to a stop amid the falling debris and the liquefying stone. I was breathing hard, not due to any of the exertion but more down to the almost physical hunger I was now facing for the kill. Ahead of me in the high ceilinged chamber were seven stone carved cots, angled at forty five degrees to allow the occupant of each to see ahead in some fashion. In each one was a Tayne, but not anything like The Tayne I'd seen before or those we'd been attacked by earlier. Whereas we'd encountered the waftingly weak Tayne regularly before, and the monstrous beasts from the attack earlier, these were all broken creatures. They were all sinew thin but rigidly solid and wore an expression of twisted agony. They all bore the hallmarks of statues which were partially brought to life but which were now trying their best to move petrified limbs despite the futility and pain.

I didn't care. One roar and I was toward them, fire balling in each of my hands. This wouldn't last long.

"STOP."

It was a strange sound. One that I recognized as a word and one that I knew the meaning of but it still just flitted around the edges of my mind. I knew the voice saying it as well but couldn't place who they were.

"ANTHONY, PLEASE DON'T."

I was Anthony. Don't what? What?

I shuddered to a halt and looked around me, trying to place the owner of the calls. I was still breathing hard with anticipation, the lust for violence driving me almost to madness, but I could feel the question in my head pulling harder.

"Who said that?" I snarled into the darkness. This had better be good.

"Stop the attack Anthony. It's me, Andrea. They didn't take the child. They couldn't, look at them."

Andrea. I knew her. I trusted her.

Swinging my head to look down on the Tayne, still breathing like a ravening beast, I was able to see, now clearly, that these creatures were so far beyond the pain I'd first envisioned them to be in. This close I was able to see the haunted eyes, stretched by their own horrors but all unseeing. Their skins were all rotten, boils and sores erupted indiscriminately, pus and worse weeping out to stain their dressings and the bedding. But worst of all was the smell. There was just nothing beyond death. All of them were rotting, decaying despite somehow still clinging to the most slender sliver of life they had.

The fury in me abruptly dropped back to nothing. All of the maddened violence I'd felt was now clearly laid out before me as the product of a magical incursion into my own head.

Andrea ghosted next to me as I just stared down at the bodies of the Tayne, looking for all the world as if they represented the last of their civilization.

"They've been like this for too long to have been able to kidnap anyone. If they did order it then we'll need to speak with them first." She spoke soothingly, bringing me down from the power high until I'd regained enough of my faculties to be able to respond.

"What happened to them?" I still couldn't quite understand what had befallen The Tayne. They were never the heavy hitters of the magical fraternity but seeing them in this state was something else altogether.

"They were the first to be taken and changed."

We all span round to face what I'd left of the doorway, a massive hole replacing the original. Framed perfectly by my handiwork was a tall and slender Tayne, hovering gracefully and carrying a basket of wet towels. She had over her head, the orange/red crest which signified her regal lineage. This was the Queen of The Tayne.

"What do you mean, taken and changed?" Em was directly to business and took up a place between the Queen and the Guardians. "What have you done with the child you took?"

The Queen just narrowed her gleaming white eyes and fixed her gaze on Em.

"These are what's left of my honour guard. These were the strongest of us all but they were laid low by the hand of those who seek to enforce their will on others." She fixed each of us with her gaze as she spoke the end of the sentence. Her voice was akin to a cat mewling it's words with a cumbersome accent but, the same as the monster we'd faced in the tunnels, it was very clear that she was articulate and educated.

"And any child you have lost is nothing to do with us." There was a haughty snap to her comment and she drifted into the room, making her way towards her fallen subjects and ignoring the group of enemy fighters gathered around her.

She set the basket down next to the cot on the far left of the line, removed a damp towel and started to bathe and tend to the crushed occupant.

"Your majesty." It was Andrea's turn. "The Tayne have been a part of the fighting force which has been attacking us over the last months. A great many of our people have been killed by your actions and you have been complicit in the actions which have placed the safety of the whole world in jeopardy. Do you deny being an enemy to The Circle?"

The Queen tensed but continued to care for her fallen soldier, only the barest pause coming at the mention of The Circle. She finished what she was doing before looking back up to us.

"The Tayne are a peaceful race. We know that before the might of The Circle we are nothing but you should also know that The Circle is not the only great power in the world." Her words were angry, with no attempt to hide that anger.

"So you admit that you've sided with The Hive against us?" I leapt in and matched her tone with my own anger, the fire jumping back up inside me.

"I did not."

Pause.

"I told you there are more than just you for us to be afraid of. The Circle and The Hive have been fighting each other for so long, I swear you can't see the most basic points around you."

Interesting. What else? I used every inch of who I was, before I became the Guardian, to drag the anger back down. I needed control. Andrea took up the questioning.

"Are you saying that you weren't in league with The Hive? You were attacking The Circle with a different group?" I could hear the skepticism in her voice and could understand what she was talking about. I was still new to what was going on but so far there had been no time given to the topic of further issues than The Hive.

"I'm saying," the Queen continued, "that my people were indeed a part of the army which attacked The Circle. I'm saying that we were at no point aligned with The Hive and most importantly for all, we did not take part willingly. We were conscripted at first with promises of greater security and then with threats." She picked another towel from the basket and moved to the next cot, starting her ritual of cleaning and tending again.

No-one moved and the silence was deafening. Inside the giant chamber, which had once been designed with nothing more than a regal lifestyle in mind, now acted as a hospice for the fallen. And the races leader was now the sole custodian of the broken.

"These soldiers were the first to receive the gift from our would-be benefactor." The Queen spoke in a low tone of resigned loss, all the time watching as she moved about her latest charge. "He promised us such things." She dabbed at the corners of the mouth of her patient. "He came to us and gave us the one thing we could never turn away from. He offered us the chance for safety. He gave me hope."

She held the pause before continuing just long enough for everyone within earshot to understand.

"He promised to give my people the power to be able to defend themselves against foes from anywhere. We were to become a mighty army with the strength to be able to defend our way of life against any and all threats." The Tayne she was attending to, coughed a rattling, dry burst and moaned in pain as she ever so gently dabbed at the crusty wounds around his neck.

"All I've ever wanted for my race is its safety. I want us to all live, here, away from your petty wars." She looked sideways at us. "I wanted to have a people free from bullies." She turned back to her task, pausing yet again, on the final word of the sentence.

"But we were told that the only way for this to happen was to take part in the raids needed to re-claim the power that had been stolen by The Circle."

She shrugged her shoulders as she recounted the idea.

"I know how ridiculous it sounds now but we have been used and abused for so long by so many that the chance to save ourselves was too great an opportunity to let pass by." She still looked down at the Tayne in the cot and slowly smoothed over the cracked skin of his bald head, giving any form of care she could to ease the suffering.

"After the second attack he gave us what he had promised. His crystals slammed power through us, giving us such strength. These were the first to receive the gift and they became so powerful, so vastly strong. They could do so much more than any of us had ever been able, surpassing the very Gods in strength." Despite everything which had brought her to this desolation, there was still a vibrantly fierce pride when she spoke of what these soldiers had become. The rest of us remained still, not interrupting anything she said.

She moved to the next cot.

"I saw that power and all I could understand was that the bargain was true. We were going to free of all of you so I gave the word that everyone should be given this mighty gift as soon as possible." Another pause but it was clear that any pride she had for her people was fighting against her own shame. Her voice wavered ever so slightly as she finished, "I gave the order that damned my whole race." She dabbed and smoothed the latest living corpse.

She continued to move down the line as the silence just grew and grew until, "I actually said that I would be the last of the people who would receive this gift. My people deserved to have this strength far more than I did."

Silence returned, all save for the ever more labored breathing from the cots.

"It was after he had given to all people bar myself that he turned to me and said that he would require our help in attacking The Circle for a fourth time and that with our greater strength we would be of more value as fighters. I told him no, that we had fulfilled our bargain to him and his people and that we would not be taking any further part in any violence. He did this to my honour guard by way of warning." She held out her arm indicating the shriveled forms.

"He used his crystals to ruin these poor souls and leave them in this state. They just shriveled before our eyes at a single movement from him. I told him that he would have to take all of The Tayne before I would give him what he wanted. I was tired of my race being used." She looked directly out at us and we could see the tracks that her tears had made down her barely there face.

"So he did. He took all of us. Those crystals of his gave him the power to warp and destroy us but it also gave him the ability to control us. Control the minds of all those he had gifted. He just dragged my whole race away to use them as he wished." Her impotent anger in what had been done to her was clear but she still maintained the same rod of pride in her people.

Em moved forwards, her swords now retracted back to the pommels and stowed on her suit, and placed her hand on the shoulder of the Queen. The Queen looked as shocked as the rest of us with the simple display of emotion and empathy but bowed her head and placed her own hand on top of Em's. Through everything that any of us had experienced, through every moment of bloodshed and horror that been a fixture for everyone in the chamber, that single gesture from Em signified so very much. There was no adherence to what 'should', instead there was just the simplest gesture between two beings to signify the loss that was felt.

Andrea placed a steadying hand on my shoulder and I could feel the heat of my rage dropping back. Whether it was as a consequence of her inherent magics or from what she represented to me, I didn't know but it really didn't matter.

"Your majesty," Andrea spoke so softly into the rancid gloom. We will do all we can to be able to free your people from whatever hex they find themselves under. After that, if it is still your will, we will leave you be, here on your own as a people and do our best to keep you out of any future conflicts. You can call on us to your aid should you need it but I'm afraid that we must ask for your aid."

The Queen patted at Em's hand and moved gracefully away from her to face Andrea and me.

"What is it you want?" Her voice came out with the resignation that she was again in no position to do anything other than what was being asked of her. Andrea was going to be as gentle as possible but we needed answers.

"If you don't have the child who was taken from us, who does?" I leapt in, still not fully back in control of my faculties.

"I do not know. We are all that is left of the realm of the Tayne and I have been consumed totally with caring for all the subjects I have left." She again gestured back at the stone cots to show clearly that her focus was far from being that of a kidnapper. "I am afraid I know nothing of the child you've lost."

The answer made me angry, but not at her. I just couldn't believe that we were losing further ground on rescuing Maria. There was no deception in her. She just didn't know. Andrea took over following my outburst.

"Who was it that did this to your people? How was it that such power could be given in the first place but warped in such a hideous way?" She was still hard on the case of facts. She was asking the questions that needed to be answered to give us any hope of success rather than what I had done, just chasing the latest cause. Cold pragmatism against fiery passion.

"He never gave me his name." The Queen's cultured voice was hard. "He came and went through this palace as he wished, arriving without my calling. He just walked into my chambers and made his offer without preamble."

"He didn't give you any indication of who or what he was? Did he have anyone or anything with him when he came to you? Is there any information you can give us about what he was? A demon? A man? Anything?" Despite keeping her voice the same calm level, Andrea was pleading as she spoke.

The Queen considered for a second, then answered.

"He was a man but like no man I'd ever seen before. He looked so much like a man to be classed as one but there was; something more to him. He felt calmly threatening in my opinion. He was never openly hostile but there was always a sensation from him, an intangible violence under that cultured exterior of welcoming. Even more so than any malice I felt from you when you first entered here." She was looking at me as she explained and that singular point was something which needed no explanation. Whoever he was, he was either a wonderful confidence trickster, able to make people believe that he was a terrible threat or he was the power that he suggested. Both were dangerous for different reasons.

But where did that leave us? So far all we had was he was a mysterious stranger who either had immense power or at least the ability to make it look like he did. It may have been a new player on the field but at least if he was a man he could only come from a certain number of places.

Without there being any signal that anything had changed, The Elder spoke this time.

"How was it he was able to give you such power? You said he needed you to help him in an attack against The Circle and that he'd be able to give you the powers he promised after the attack. That would suggest that he didn't have them to give in the beginning but acquired them during the fighting, would it not?" She looked between all of faces that had turned to face her. She hadn't said a word up to this point and I'd almost forgotten about her.

"I'm sorry. I didn't mean to speak out of turn but that did seem to be the next logical question." She just looked around us all with her eyebrows raised in question. She may have lost all of the details of who any of us were but she still had full control of all of her reasoning skills. The conversation stopped at her interjection. None of us had even considered that point. My mind had been set on one of two options but the details looked like they fit somewhere in between. I opened my mouth to disagree with The Elder out of sheer belligerence but stopped. She'd never liked me and had been a part of a group trying to have me killed but that didn't mean that she was wrong about this. The Queen looked like she was taking the same route of thought.

Whoever he was, he'd needed help breaking into the fortress in Argentina for some reason. Whatever he was after, he knew he was going to be able to use it to deliver an enormous amount of power to the Tayne in payment for their help but also that he was going to have the ability to control them should he need to use them again.

But if that was the case, why attack again? Why risk exposure when you've already got what you came for? The question was limping around at the edges of my head as it fought against my animal rage. The conversation continued without me.

"You said he was using crystals to give your people the power he had. What did he do?" Andrea kept to her methodical probing but it was obvious now that she was feeling a level of excitement. It was an almost tangible sensation crackling around the chamber as we all joined the train of understanding.

"He brought with him a small casket full of glowing fragments of crystal. None were fashioned or worked, they were all raw from the ground. He took each of my people in turn and forced a fragment against their head. It glowed and he said it was done. We were skeptical at first but when the changes started to happen, I brought everyone through as fast as I could." That final thought checked the previous positivity. The Queen was again confronted by the fact that she had, in her mind, damned her people.

Perfectly on cue, it was at that moment that one of the ruined Tayne rasped out an arid cough, reinforcing perfectly what was running through her mind. It broke the atmosphere between us all and the Queen hurried to the aid of her pained subject.

"I'm sorry but I must tend to my people. Please leave us. I thank you for the offer you have given us but there isn't anything further to discuss." I started to protest but Andrea cut me off sharply.

"Thank you my lady. We will leave you in peace."

That left us at an impasse. We didn't have any way of finding out anything further and the Queen had nothing else to give.

The same Tayne continued to cough horribly and was joined by one of its comrades. Both sounded in agony, as if the sheer act of living was wrenching at them in an attempt to break everything they had.

What could have done this to them? It all pointed to the fact that whoever this person was, he'd managed to pull off an amazing heist and steal from under the noses of The Circle.

Andrea and Em turned to leave the room and The Elder serenely looked between everyone there, obviously still quite some way off the full understanding her stolen memories could have given her. Hairy and Mark stalked out looking equal parts dutiful soldiers and crazed Goliaths. It was only now that I noticed just how huge Hairy was but he was hanging his head as he walked and every inch of his demeanor was that of someone who was fighting back tears.

Mike caught me looking. "He's lost his chance at the power of The Circle. With Maria gone, there's no way to Bridge to him. All of his life he's been told that the role of Guardian is a sacred calling and he's just missed the passing of the mantle. Another soul who's lost."

My anger rose again at the thought that the potential death or torture of a small child was being mourned as nothing more than the loss of a job. The Tayne had been decimated, he'd not. They were nothing alike and the way Mike was able to see exactly what was going through that oaf's head was like needles on my skin. The parched coughing of several ruined soldiers in their stone cots from behind us just made it worse.

I started to stride towards him and the red was gathering at the corners of my vision, the coughing still ringing in my ears as I went, when I realized that the coughing was no longer coughing. One by one, gently at first and then gathering intensity as a new voice joined the chorus, that hideous hacking cough was steadily being replaced by a cruel laugh.

Turning quickly to face the alien cackling, I was greeted by the rictus grins on all of the faces of the patients. Their bodies were still contorted by pain and that same pain was etched ever more clearly on every face, but now they were all emitting a hissing demonic laugh.

"No no no no. Not these poor souls as well?" The Queen was backing away from the cots and had dropped the basket of towels she had been tending the sick with.

"What is this? What's wrong?" My voice held an element of squeak as I spoke. I was getting slightly more used to the effects of monsters and the like coming to kill me but that noise coming from those beings, coupled to the reaction of the Queen left my bravery sadly lacking.

"It looks to me," chimed The Elder from the entrance to the room, "that whoever it was who did all of this to The Tayne is starting again."

The laughter continued as, one by one, each sallow face picked out The Elder in the low light of the chamber. Every one of them had tears rolling down what was left of their faces but the smiles and the laughter remained. It was the Tayne on the far left who spoke first.

"Yessss," it spat, holding the final 's' for far too long. "I am returned."

The Queen was hurriedly backing away from the stone cots and was whimpering as she did, making her way back to take up position behind me. Mark, Mike and Hairy were quickly at my side and they all snapped their power to a ready posture, coloured energy forming in their hands as they balled their magic for any attack. I did the same, though so much of my magic was already near the surface, it didn't take much.

The Tayne who had spoken leaned itself forward, sitting upright and leaning forwards, a gesture of threat despite its crushed form. The laughter continued from the others and as my eyes flicked across each of the faces in turn, I could see that the tears on those faces were those of such sorrow and suffering. The Tayne knew that they weren't in control of their actions. They knew that they were being manipulated from afar and they were experiencing both a physical and a mental anguish. Their tortured bodies were being forced to act despite being ruined and they were being forced to act against their Queen. These were the honour guard of the Queen, her personal guard. I thought of what Mark was like around me and any possible threat and was easily able to see what these fighters would have been sworn to. Being wholly unable to prevent what they were doing towards the one person they had been sworn to protect was probably a worse pain than that their skeletal frames were undergoing.

"Who are you and what do you want?" Andrea was stood next to the Queen and asking from slightly behind the wall of prepared violence between them and the cots.

The laughter increased slightly, mocking the question just for being asked. In the light which was produced from the actions of my soldiers, the faces of all of the crushed Tayne looked even more nightmarish. Shadows and eerie shapes danced across features and the walls, adding to every inch of menace.

"Silly little girl. You've spent far too long in your ivory tower haven't you?" the same Tayne spoke. "It hassssss taken me some time to be in a position to be able to do what so badly needs to be done." The other Tayne continued to laugh but the shriveled form on the far right now lurched forwards and forced itself out of the cot and began shuffling and stuttering towards us. There was a sudden intake of breath from behind me as the Queen watched on in horror as another member of her personal guard was twisted and controlled like a demented marionette.

"I asked who you were and what you wanted," boomed Andrea into the cackling group of Tayne. "Answer the questions." She was in no mood for games and I was in complete agreement.

"Come on sunshine. The lady asked you a question. Show some manners and answer her." My animal was back screaming away behind my eyes and the sentence was again issued forth wrapped in the roar of my Dragon. Whoever he was, he needed to know just what was going to happen if he didn't play ball.

The laughing dropped down in volume but continued, that same insane twittering and sniggering. It was like they were all in on the joke and we were the cause for their amusement, but the shuffling

Tayne continued to approach and the speaking Tayne continued to speak.

"I'm here to create a new power. I've shown the world that The Circle, the once feared and revered Circle, has become fat as they ruled. I have shown the world that the Guardians are no longer the horrors to be feared. I've killed you and stolen from you and I've done it with only the aid of the weakest members of our world." The shuffling Tayne stopped and gestured around with his spindly arms to highlight just how weak they were.

"As for my name. You all know me. I've been within your group for years and years and years, building my strength and waiting for the right time to present itself to me to strike back." It leaned even further forward at the conclusion of the sentence and leered at The Elder, licking its split lips as the laughing returned in earnest.

It was all that was in the air for a long time and as the words sank into each of us and we all came to the same conclusion. Beneath the tortured body uttering the words, the owner of the voice was clear.

"Mr. Ward?" Andrea's voice was high and unsteady. The shock of realization.

Leatherpants.

We may all have been thinking the same thing but that didn't mean that a betrayal of this kind could be taken lightly. I had always thought that the guy had been a first class pain in the ass but it had been drummed into me that everyone in this group had given their lives for the good of the human race. Remembering Wynne in my estate and now Leatherpants here, it was beginning to look like that shared adherence to the central strength of the cause, the foundation bedrock of The Circle, was cracking under the weight of time.

"How could you? The Circle is your sacred place in this world. We all share the same duty." Andrea was pleading with him through his many possessed avatars, and then added "Look what you've done to all of us. To these poor creatures."

The laughing stopped.

Feet shuffled on the dusty stone floor as we all waited on what was to come next. The removal of the laughter from The Tayne left the chamber hollow and the silence seemed to echo around us, trying to fill the void itself. When Leatherpants Tayne spoke this time there was a new malevolence in what he was saying.

"I have done something bad? You believe that I have somehow stooped to depths of pain that have never been visited before in my dealings with The Tayne?" Cold. His voice was cold.

"I have done nothing other than what has been shown to me time and time again within the ranks of The Circle, have I not? I acted in the interests of the greater good." Creakily, another Tayne heaved itself from its cot and began to inch across the space between us. Mark stepped between me and them and the azure light in his hands grew in intensity. Leatherpants Tayne spat out a contemptuous snort.

"You still protect that little fool. After all of the loss he has been the overseer of?"

Silence. Mark just maintained the ready position but I stepped in front of him. If Leatherpants wanted to have a pop at me, I'd be more than happy to let him.

"Ah, the little boy wants to play with the nasty man," his voice was razors and they seemed to be slicing through all of my calm and control. My Dragon was climbing.

"Well then. Come on," the niceties were over and all of The Tayne creaked upright and shambled forward like the zombies they practically were.

"Don't hurt them, please don't hurt them." It was the Queen pleading as I set myself for the fight.

"They're being controlled by this person. They are not willing."

"Fine," I roared out over my shoulder. I could feel the humanity of what she was saying in the back of my mind but it was being loudly shouted down by my almost free beast.

"Come on then Leatherpants. Here's your chance to have a crack at a Guardian. One at a time or all of them at once? What you prefer?" He may have wanted to slap me but I was pretty keen to do the same to him. My smile must have shown perfectly as I felt it spread wider than usual, coupled with a fraction of facial transformation.

"All at once it is then," spat from Leatherpants Tayne and the cackling laughter started up again from all of them as step by tortured step, the crippled warriors of The Tayne lurched and stuttered and became an irregular line of formation.

"Relax everyone," I snarled, "I'll look after this," and I stepped forward, fixed my helmet in place and smashed my armoured fists together, all the while growling my intent.

"Little boy will attack these poor weak creatures? You won't hurt me though, just them," Leatherpants spoke from behind his puppet wall but I didn't care.

"I'll still want to hurt you though. You just won't be able to hurt me, remember that child." There was a playful quality to his voice but one that had nothing to do with pleasant actions. He was pondering the best way to cause maximum agony.

"These creatures have worked wonderfully for me and they should have been rewarded fully for the sacrifices they've given. These warriors, if that's what you can truly call them, deserve to be afforded some level of protection as they act as my fist against you, don't you think?" Leatherpants Tayne was almost speaking to himself as the others continued to laugh.

"So I gift them all protection. Enjoy them."

The laughter stopped abruptly and all of the Tayne snapped to a rigid form of attention. Previously bent backs now stood rod straight as the screaming started. Each of the bodies which had been left emaciated by whatever had been done to them began to convulse and bulge, to expand and morph as whatever magic Leatherpants had at his disposal surged up in all of them and began a new horror.

We all took a step back out of sheer surprise.

The Tayne remained motionless as they screamed their new pain out, just unable to break free of what was happening.

"Please stop this. I'm begging you, stop hurting them," the Queen sobbed from behind us but the actions of Leatherpants just continued without showing any sign of ceasing.

"What's happening to them Mike?" I couldn't just stand and watch this.

"Not sure, but I'd suggest that Mr. Ward is probably going to do something awful to them. I don't even know what to suggest to stop this." He was shouting over the agony and soon the awful sound was being joined by an awful smell as all of the Tayne lost control of themselves, expelling whatever meagre sustenance they'd had recently. I shook my head to try and clear my thoughts against that building Dragon but I couldn't hold it all. My Fire was climbing at

311

the injustice of the pain being given with so little consideration to the consequences.

My armour began to creak and buckle as I grew. Plates and joints cracked and pinged around the chamber like popping chestnuts in a fire. I didn't care and for the first time in what seemed like an eternity, I let go of all of my mental controls and let the beast take me.

The red veil descended over my vision and my metal suit was ripped apart as my Guardian Dragon surged up and out until I was stood with my hunched under the slightly too low ceiling of the stone cavern. The horns on my head scrapped against the rough surface above me and I was forced to pull my wings in as close as possible to stop them being damaged in the confines of the room.

I dropped down onto all fours and roared with all of the joyous release of being my animal self and loomed over the seven Tayne. In that instant they all stopped screaming and for a heartbeat I considered that Leatherpants had stopped whatever he was doing because he'd been confronted by a Guardian but that hope didn't last long. The Tayne all started laughing again, but this time there was a gleeful chime to it.

"What's so funny then Leatherpants?" I needed to keep calling him by that nickname to try to show him that he was nothing more than a joke to me but I was also fed up with that awful laugh.

All of the Tayne spoke in unison in reply, all in the same voice.

"You will learn eventually, fool, that true power isn't just turning into that Dragon of The Circle. You will learn that I have the true power because I can take that power from you. You will learn respect for me because I have your whole order in the palm of my hand."

The laughter broke out again but this time when the Tayne began to contort, there was no pain shown from them. They all began to move and stretch in ways I recognized all too clearly. Their limbs dislocated and grew. Their skin changed colour. It started to turn red. The understanding hit me at the same time as my own pain, plunging directly into the back of my neck akin to a burning scalpel. There was no early warning from my spinning head, just the sensation of a white hot needle being plunged into me, and I was driven to the floor under the weight of it.

"ANTHONY!" Andrea and Em screamed the same time I fell, just as Mike called out "MY LORD!" I could feel all three rush to my side and prepare to offer some form of defence although none were sure of against what. The light of their prepared magics cast further strange shadows as they crowded to me. The laughter continued from the Tayne but now it was being driven by growls rather than their usual voices. When Leatherpants Tayne spoke again, sneering at me as I lay crumpled against what was pinning me to the floor, I didn't need to see what had just happened.

"You see boy? Do all of you see?" Clutching my chest, I forced myself to look up at him, the tiniest act of defiance I could muster. This time, the shattered body of the Tayne warrior had been altered. It was far from being the emaciated husk it had been. Now its body was full rather than sunken. Its muscles rippling and tight rather than withered and its eyes now opened into the deepest abyss of purest hate. The Tayne may have still been the same height as it had been previously but now it was the Tayne version of my own red Dragon, armoured and prepared for the fight. It looked at me and its lips peeled back from the array of sharp teeth into a wicked smile, nothing but crazed contempt leaking out.

"I told you, didn't I?" Leatherpants strutted back and forth as he looked down contemptuously at who had just given him the power to transform as he did.

"This," he gestured at himself and then to the others who were still stood rigidly to attention but were now all altered to Tayne/Dragons. "This is the truest power. The power to take what you want, what you need. What could you do to stop me?"

I bit out at him, purely on animal reflex but he was more than able to evade, smoothly sliding back and away from me, and continued to taunt us all.

"There really isn't anything that you can do now to stop whatever whim happens to cross my mind. I've managed to signal the whole world, on this plain and every other existence, that the once mighty Circle is nothing more than a bloated caricature of its former self. You've all grown fat on the comforts of power, slapping out at whoever you chose to deem an enemy." Leatherpants Tayne abruptly stopped parading himself and swiveled to face all of us.

"Just consider what I've just made happen. I have utilized the weakest of races to over run your defences and kill Guardian after Guardian. I've been able to steal from you, from the heart of your own stronghold and I've been able to empower the weak with energies from the Guardian here. I haven't even needed to delve that deeply into you all to take what I wanted. Just small pieces here and there. The occasional twist of what you all see as so mighty." His voice mocked all of us with each word. "And yet, still not one of you has even attempted to do anything other than stand and stare. I can control you all. I can control everything."

His logic was flawless but his grandstanding had snapped everyone out of the fug which was over us all. Everyone around me opened up with a magical blast at either Leatherpants Tayne or the other group, doing their best to subdue rather than destroy. All of the Dragon Tayne, Leatherpants included, blurred into motion and there was a starburst of bodies as they all cleared the blast zone and headed off in different directions. The firing followed after them all, tracking in all directions as the newly energized Tayne responded to the commands of our treacherous former member.

And as they did, I began to notice the tiniest of relief from the pain which was pinning me to the ground. It started out as barely more than a hint of lessened weight but soon, that icy agony was falling away at an incredible rate.

"Hold your fire." The order came from Em. "They're not attacking us, they're trying to rile us." Her huge swords were back in her hands at the ready as she scanned over me as well as the enemy before us all. The outpouring of magic abruptly stopped and everyone considered the words.

"Why aren't they trying to do more damage?" questioned Mike, glowing magical violence still held in each hand, he watched on as the Dragon Tayne all continued to swoop and dive in an aerial ballet designed to avoid any attack that could come their way.

None of us knew but Em was right. There was no attempt coming from the Dragon Tayne to actually strike against us. They all just seemed content to loop and twist in a bizarre fashion without doing anything to us.

"Looking at the way that the fight has progressed so far, it would appear that in this instance, they are relying on members of this unit to be the power source of what they're doing. Mr. Ward even pointed out that no-one had attacked him. It would appear that he was asking us to." The Elder's voice was flat, still nothing more than her calm logical assessment of what was playing out before her.

"Your reasoning is sound my lady," added Em as she continued to stare on at the Dragon Tayne as they still didn't attack outright. The pain which had accompanied the metamorphosis of the Tayne was now faded to nothing so I pushed myself up to a standing position and assumed as much of a ready position as I could manage without actually reaching into my Dragon power as preparation for the fight.

Em turned back to the rest of us as the display continued.

"My Lord Anthony. You have had your power taken and gifted to these creatures. I believe that you will therefore have the power to cause an error from Mr. Ward. In any coming fight, we will all be fighting against your power. Who of us knows you better than you? I would recommend that our other Guardians refrain from joining the fight in their own Guardian form for fear of them being drained as well." She looked between Andrea and The Elder but neither gave any kind of indication that they'd even heard her. To be fair though they were standing still rather than attacking so that was something. Em looked back to me and continued. "Use the knowledge of your own struggle against the power to strike against him."

She made sense. I began wracking my brain for options and we all readied ourselves for whatever it was I was about to do.

Finally, the Dragon Tayne seemed to pick up on the fact that we were just watching rather than reacting to what they were doing. With the calm organization which synchronized swimmers train for years to attain, they all dropped from the air and landed in a single line before us, snarling and roaring as they flexed and pulsed. One of their number slowly edged forward but I could recognize Leatherpants behind the features of this monster even before he spoke.

"What's the matter Leatherpants?" I couldn't give him the chance to start on the front foot. "Not strong enough to actually do anything except flap about?" I was back at my diplomatic best, doing my utmost to keep the snarl from my voice but replacing it with as much laughter as I could risk. I could still feel that anger in me, that fire that fuels me, still being twisted by the outside force we now knew was The Elder's former Head of House, but I did my best to cling onto the human side of my mind. I needed to stay away from my Dragon power and instead rely on my own intellect. If the fire I had was being used by the creatures before me, then that meant that they would have the perceived weaknesses of it as well as the strengths. They may have had the huge physical power but they also had the short fuse to go with it. That had to be my point of attack.

All of the Dragon Tayne spat out small gobs of fire and screeched their anger behind Leatherpants while he spread his wings as far as they could go, intent on intimidation of some kind. His growl was growing as he cast a look of utter hatred at us.

"You need me to power you don't you? You've told us that we don't understand real power but I'd say that you're just taking things that don't belong to you. You're just a petty thief who's done well with the things he's taken. All in all, not really that powerful." I stood up as tall as I could muster and gave my own wings just a little stretch just to highlight the differences between us, me the full size Dragon of The Circle, him a corruption of a broken victim.

Leatherpants just roared. There wasn't any build up to his outburst. There wasn't a single word uttered that was human. All he did was bellow and reach out his hands to the other Dragon Tayne stood behind him. They all started to shudder under his control as he forced them to react to his wishes.

"That didn't take long. I thought he'd be tougher to push around than that." Mark spoke loudly and his words were like pouring lighter fluid onto the fire within Leatherpants. My giant general was always economical with his words but that didn't mean he had nothing to say.

Leatherpants went mad.

He was utterly unfamiliar with the power of the Dragon he was manipulating and it was already starting to overwhelm his mind. Leatherpants Tayne reached to the others and began to drag all of the power from their bodies. Their roars turned to screams as their own fragment of the Dragon power was removed by force, leaving them hollowed out and as crushed as they had been when we'd arrived. All of the red energy from the other six members of the Queen's guard flowed outwards and drifted to Leatherpants, wrapping around him with a crimson vapour trail and sinking into his skin.

As it finally ended its migration, the bodies of the Tayne fell to the ground and lay still. It was easy to see that they were all now dead as their bodies had all collapsed into wholly unnatural positions, fragile bones breaking and paper thin skin splitting.

Stood before the death, was a trembling Leatherpants, his head rocked back and his eyes bulging at the forces of primal magics now fully within him. He looked almost euphoric.

"Still want to destroy me?" He spoke into the air without dropping his attention back to all of us but I assumed he was still talking solely to me. "I dare you to try now."

It was a clear call to action but even despite all of the strings he was pulling on me, I knew I couldn't just kill him. He wasn't the one actually stood before me. He was just the demented puppet master forcing the body of this poor Tayne soldier to do his fighting for him. Unfortunately, that realization wasn't shared by the whole group.

Mike just roared his own battle cry and heaved himself forwards, magic unloading all of the time as he did, and hurled himself at Leatherpants, clearly intent on tearing him to pieces.

"WAIT! NO!" was all that any of us could say before Mike landed on Leatherpants and was confronted by the reality of fighting against the power of a Guardian. Leatherpants just let Mike land on his chest, absorbing the impact easily and without any sign of effort. Oddly, all I could see in my mind's eye was a footballer controlling the ball on his chest before volleying it on.

The fire roared back up in my head in reaction but as soon as it did I could feel that same icy needle, again in the same spot at the back of my neck and I knew that further energies were being taken. I dropped down onto one knee under the pain of the latest draining and looked on as Leatherpants launched Mike far across the chamber to smash into the left most wall before clanking to the ground, armour and no doubt bone, broken. He didn't move. He hadn't needed to volley him.

"I've so much wanted to see what the reality of the power of a Guardian is truly like. I can see why you all protect it so fiercely." His voice had travelled further into the rumbling growl of the Dragon as he flexed and straightened his fingers, admiring what he was now in command of.

I was back to my feet in a slow, deliberate fashion and just stared back down at him.

"Come on then sunshine. You want to see what a REAL Guardian can do with that power? Come and have a go." My own Dragon voice wrapped around as estuary an accent as I could muster, channeling not only the monster but also the cockney gangster.

I could sense the others moving back and away from us, aiming to remain out of the impending fight while doing their best to make their way to the stricken Mike. I snorted out twin blasts of flame in a display of my own readiness to fight.

Leatherpants just looked up at me and smiled. A smile of cruelty and malice.

Then he began to grow. Steadily at first but soon he was rushing up to a matching stature to me. Finally looking eye to eye, Leatherpants wasted no time in commencing his attack. He just opened his mouth and blasted me square in the face with a volley of searing flame.

I staggered back and dropped my face away from the force of the attack. There was no risk to me from the flame, Fire Dragon after all, but it felt akin to getting it in the face with a jet of water from a hose pipe. Annoying yes, fatal, no.

The jet was held for longer than I would have ventured but as it dropped away I could hear an almost erotic pleasure coming from my foe. He panted due to the effort but also with so much more feeling. Opening my eyes and shaking away the effects of the fire, I could see that Leatherpants was stood with his mouth open, slavering tongue hanging down as a torrent of saliva ran out to spatter on the floor. His shoulders were now more hunched and his eyes were wild with the power he'd taken.

"So. Much. Power" he panted before loosing another jet of fire at me, this time hitting me squarely in the chest but again causing no damage.

"Oh come on. This will get really dull if all you're going to do is breath on me." I could see that all I had to do was do all of those wonderful things that wound me up to get any sort of reaction from him. I followed that up with a snort of my own flame into his eyes. He did exactly what I'd hoped. He stopped his attack and dived forward, dropping his head out of the way of the missile before it could land.

He'd been ignoring the detail of what he'd taken. He'd been so obsessed by the power of what he'd stolen he'd given no thought to the practicalities. He was still thinking like a man who was vulnerable to fire rather than something which was able to make the primal force do his bidding.

He quickly regained his balance and heaved out yet more flame as he closed the distance between us, his wings pulsing reflexively as he did. I again let the fire wash over me but this time I decided to make my own act of aggression. Leatherpants kept his burn going as I strode forward, balling my right fist before smashing him right on the end of his snout. Magical energy and eon's old power had to give way to the simple effects of physics. The lengthened bones within the face of a Dragon are nowhere near as strong as the armour plated wrecking ball of the fist that I'd hit him with. His nose cracked and collapsed under the force but his flame continued, splashing out at all angles as shock took over his actions.

I hit him again.

This time I'd lowered my aim and drove my fist into his throat. I was fighting like a man, not wanting to reach into the power of my Dragon too deeply for fear of giving Leatherpants any more of who I was. I was also fighting dirty. The flame abruptly stopped as I crushed his windpipe and for a blissful second, the look of utter bewilderment on his face was intoxicating.

I swung again.

And again.

And again and again and again.

His face and body took the force of a true Guardian of The Circle and he was being introduced to what true power really was. I could feel that I was winning and my violence surged inside me. I had him at my mercy and I was crystal clear on what I was going to do to him.

"Where is ssssssshhhhhhhhhhh." My question died on my lips as I was shuddered back to the reality of the fight. That icy needle was again being driven into my neck and this time I just crumpled under the weight of the pain, all the air stolen from my lungs, my legs turning to water. Again, there'd been no signal from my spinning early warning system, I was just hit.

I hit the ground hard. There was no attempt to break my fall, I just wasn't able. I just fell into Leatherpants and slammed into the stone floor.

"What was that you were asking?" His words were garbled thanks to the shattered features of his face but the contempt was still there, ringing at perfect pitch. He spat out blood and what I could only assume was a tooth or two. Stretching his back and extending his wings, he enjoyed the power flowing into him. He was gloating.

I just couldn't help myself. I just couldn't. His face and the implied smirk behind it was just too much for me to control. I just heaved against the agony in my neck and drove myself up and against him, crashing him backwards as far and as fast as I could manage. I didn't care that he was probably going to leach even more energy from me, I just needed to unload as much anger as I could. The squeak in the back of my head from my rational mind was easily drowned out by the howling of my monster and I didn't care if I was being manipulated into feeling the way I did, I was just going to attack.

We hit the wall hard and mighty slabs of masonry rained down around and on us. Cracks extended out in all directions behind the warped version of my Dragon and I could feel the structure shaking in warning. The pain remained but I was moving further away from being able to feel it. My own animal was taking over.

"I said. WHERE IS SHE?" There was barely any human left in my words, the beast now in control. Leatherpants let out a stuttering half laugh as we grappled with each other in the almost complete darkness. When he spoke, the words were still mangled but were clear enough to comprehend.

"The child? You're still concerned for the child? How typical of The Circle. I've done so much to fracture you and all you're worried about is the vessel. You still can't see beyond keeping your own position in this world and you call me the monster."

More loose stone fell onto us and bounced away as I just locked eyes with Leatherpants. He was a power mad lunatic and his assessment of the situation was driven by his own demented standards but to the outside world, this was the only reason we were doing anything that we were, the continued survival of our own grasp on power.

"I don't care about the vessel. I care about a frightened little girl who needs to be protected." I forced my rational mind to take over despite the call of righteous indignation at my motives being questioned. Leatherpants frowned but remained silent. The falling stone continued but was now down to just the small fragments. The tension remained as we both just stared at each other, seemingly caught in an impasse of will.

I wasn't going to prolong this anymore.

With as little finesse as I could manage, I just pitched my head forward and slammed a head butt at the centre of the ruined Dragon face before me. I was going to just rip the body to pieces and see what Leatherpants was able to do from there.

Leatherpants, I'll give him credit, was learning. Rather than ducking away from the impending blow or protecting himself in some extravagant way, simply turned his head slightly. It wasn't actually his body that was going to be damaged by whatever I was about to do but that didn't mean it would be prudent to let any and all injury take place. Protecting some of his ruined snout, and as more rock and dust fell onto us from above, he took the force of my attack on his own horned temple.

As I hit, there was a thrumming crack which echoed around the chamber, far beyond anything it should have been able to do, and a pinpoint beam of purple energy speared through the murk, first against my face then away against the far wall. Leatherpants just stood rigid. His previously tight grip on me was stolen away and his limbs just held in place like a statues, his eyes glazed and fixed on nothing, his mouth fixed open. He'd totally been stolen from the moment and I could recognize that the warped Tayne body was now free of his control. More tellingly for me, the pain in my neck, that which had been tearing away the power I had and giving it to another, vanished.

Reluctantly releasing my grip, I warily stepped back, my fists still raised in readiness at the uncertainty before me and watched as the light emanating from Leatherpants steadily waned to nothing, leaving behind the hollowed out form of the Dragon he'd been, lifeless and suddenly limp. It crashed forward and shattered on the floor of the now ruined royal chamber. Slowly at first but still quickly enough, the loss of the energy from the construct resulted in the collapse of the Dragon form. The meat of the body altered and twisted back into nothing more than a mangled lump of flesh, a far cry from what the Tayne soldier would have been. Looking at the destroyed matter I could feel the roar of victory coming to my lips but it was never given. I was looking down on the dead body of a Tayne warrior who had been abused by someone who had thought they had the right to do it and had been left to perish as Leatherpants withdrew his control.

My fiery anger swirled in my mind but I could see that it was more than that. Leatherpants hadn't withdrawn his power from the construct, he'd lost his grip.

"What happened?" Em was immediately stood next to me, back to her probing ways, already trying to understand everything about what she'd just witnessed. Andrea was quick to join her and they looked on at the still settling remains of the Tayne.

The Queen of the Tayne rushed past the others and began to weep at the remains of her most tortured guard. I just stood and stared down at the agony she was feeling and, rather than it fanning the flames of my fury, it instead dowsed water over it, leaving me with a hollow empathy for her loss. All I could feel was the understanding that she was blaming herself for the suffering and destruction that had befallen her race, justified or not. She'd been driven utterly by the desire to protect her people and do her best to remove them from under the boot heel of whatever power decided to kick the weaklings about. I could understand the need to protect those around you, the feeling that family is more than just shared blood. I could remember Mike crashing against the wall of the chamber and I shared her connection to those who were deemed to be beneath her.

My rage dwindled and with a little concentration, I sank back away from my Dragon form and returned to my more familiar human shape. I was naked but no-one paid any attention and no further comments were made.

"What did you do to him?" asked a familiar voice from beside me. Mike's calm voice was usually a balm to whatever slight I was getting angry at but now, understanding what the Queen was feeling,

I was suddenly incredibly glad to have my Head of House back at my side.

I slapped him on the shoulder, far too hard considering what he had just been through, and despite the armour, he winced at the impact.

"Good to have you back with us," I said, holding as much machismo as I could in my voice. He half smiled and I could feel a mixture of emotions boiling within him.

The Queen continued to weep and Andrea and Em had gone to her side. By the looks of things, Andrea to console and Em to investigate the corpse as much as she could without looking ghoulish.

"What the hell were you thinking, just charging at him like that?" My question to Mike was framed seriously, there was no other way to do anything, but it was quickly followed by something to lighten the mood.

"You may be wearing a suit of armour but that doesn't mean you're anywhere near as hard as I am." He snorted his response and rubbed at the back of his head, reflexively showing where he'd been injured without saying anything. For that second, he was ashamed that he'd been so forward and I was far too glad he was OK, far beyond what was going to be appropriate for a master and his servant anyway. The Elder interrupted us.

"Is it over? Is that thing dead?" Her words may have been relatively callous but her tone was nothing more than questioning. She wanted to know what had just taken place and she was far from being concerned about the sensibilities of those involved. The Queen didn't take well to her question.

"THAT THING WAS ONE OF MY MOST TRUSTED GUARDS." Her voice was wavering as she screamed her anger. She was now nothing but a raw nerve of sorrow.

The Elder blinked and did the last thing I would have expected. She apologized.

"I am sorry your majesty, I meant no disrespect to you or you fallen subject. I merely enquire after all of our safety against a further attack."

The Queen was still breathing hard and sobbed with each breath but her eyes showed the anger there for The Elder was fading quickly. She was angry at herself.

"I am not to be addressed as 'Your Majesty' from now on." The Queen's voice was low, a flame kindled partially by the hatred of what had happened to her but mainly by her loss. The words of The Elder must have stung.

"From this day, address me as Haras. I am alone now, the last of the Tayne. Only a monarch with subjects can be called 'Your Majesty'." She straightened up and faced me directly.

"I have lost everything because of the actions of one power hungry maniac attacking another and using my race as a tool. I say to you, Guardian of The Circle, your group is equally culpable in the fall of my proud and ancient race. I will do my utmost to spread the word of what has happened to us and your role will be exposed to the light in a way that has never been."

The tone of her voice was painfully clear and deeply resolute. She'd meant each and every ounce of venom she'd spread over her words and it had all been levelled at me. Her fury would have been bad enough if I'd been clothed in my suit of armour but being on the receiving end of that while utterly nude really showed that the Tayne weren't completely helpless.

"Your Majesty ….." I started to respond.

"MY NAME IS HARAS!"

Taken aback, I corrected myself as quickly as I could.

"Haras. I offer my, our, sympathies for your losses and beg that you don't act too hastily. We weren't the ones who did this to you."

"This, maybe not but this is the latest in a long line of actions concerning The Circle which has befallen my people with pain. Actions from yourselves or by those you battle as they attempt to fight you. Your group are at the centre of the world in matters of destruction and don't even look at the ants you crush along the way. This latest catastrophe just means that the ants were used against you and you helped squash them all."

She was breathing deeply and had a burning scarlet hatred for us all.

"Now get out of my realm." The final sentence was almost a whisper and was as sharp as steel.

There was nothing more to be said.

Andrea bowed her head and began retreating from the wrecked cavern. Em and The Elder followed, as did all of the others until it was just Haras and I who remained. Mike had collected up the pieces of my armour as he left so there was at least a chance I'd be wearing something soon.

"We will leave you and we won't return but never forget, *Your Majesty,* not all of your people are dead. You said they'd been taken away."

Her anger just blazed in her silence.

"I am more than just The Circle. I am looking for the people who brought us to this place and I will make them understand the error of their ways but I will do my best to return your subjects to you."

I walked away with as much regal dignity as I could muster before turning and adding, "I won't come to you again but, in the future, should you require anything from me or The Circle, I'll be more than willing to listen to you. The Circle is changing so now we pay attention to everyone, even including the ants."

29

Walking into the still deep gloom outside, I was greeted by quizzical expressions. Each of the remaining force just stared and showed that they all felt that the final lead we had been clinging to had been snatched away. I walked slowly towards them all and could feel a weight on my back which was beyond every loss I'd felt up to this point. I could see that Maria was lost and there was nothing I could do about it.

Andrea was the first one to speak.

"It would appear that all possible avenues have been exhausted in this venture. We should return to the mansion in Wales as soon as we can to inform The Mage and the rest of The Circle of the outcome so we will be able to prepare our next line of defence. I would suggest that the site in Argentina is razed to the ground and an outpost garrison set up over the prison to allow us to at least maintain its charge."

"I will take The Elder back to her estate and explain what's been taking place. They will need to have the entire estate 'cleansed' before we can proceed with any kind of confidence that Mr. Ward left us no more surprises." Andrea spoke with re-discovered wintry surety. She looked at me with a hard expression and I could see that there was no chance of persuading her into any other course of action.

Reaching for The Elder's arm, she took a tight grip and jerked her to her side and began gathering in her power to open a Cascade Bridge. The Elder frowned at the sudden hostility and was about to protest at the treatment but Andrea gave her no chance. She snapped her grip down hard around the upper arm of The Elder and before any of us heard the scream, we could all clearly make out the crunching crack of bone.

The Elder, as you'd expect, screamed. I think it was equal parts shock as it was pain but the end result was the same. Her knees gave way and she collapsed to the floor, her fingers raking uselessly at Andrea's hand, trying in vain to release her grip.

Everyone took a shocked step forward towards The Elder before stopping at the situation before them. No one knew what to do. Em was the first to re-gain control of her speech.

"Miss Thomich. May I ask what it is that you are doing to The Elder? Has she done anything which would warrant this kind of behavior?" Her head was tilted back in that familiar canine fashion as she just took in all of the detail that was before her, trying to understand what all of the pieces of the puzzle meant. Andrea's eyes were arctic stone but somehow now burned with a fiery anger as well. She looked hard at Em as she spoke.

"We've pointed out that the estate in Argentina needs to be destroyed because of the breaches there. You accepted when I pointed out that we needed to do the same in China yet find it hard to comprehend that we have been betrayed by The Elder."

She was breathing deeply as she spoke, as if she was almost unable to maintain any control of her emotions. I needed to get involved but being naked in this situation is more than a little off putting.

"There has been no proof that there has been any deception from The Elder. She doesn't even have all of her mind yet you feel that she is to blame for a great wrong?" Em continued.

Andrea shook The Elder just to highlight the control she had of the situation, causing a fresh scream to join the bubbling whimpers which had been coming from The Elder. I couldn't help but wince at the fresh agony.

"Mr. Ward was able to affect the almost total defeat of The Circle and the theft of The Drake Stone. He has been in the service of The Elder for over a thousand years and you are suggesting that The Elder had absolutely no prior knowledge of what he was truly doing? She is either complicit or she is incompetent."

"Andrea," it was my turn now. I edged closer with my hands raised to highlight the fact I wasn't going to attack her with a concealed weapon, although I had no place to conceal a weapon even if I'd wanted to.

"The Elder has been the truest member of The Circle for the longest time and there has been nothing new which would suggest that she had done anything." Andrea shook The Elder again.

This was going to be tough.

Andrea was now glaring at me with a venom I'd never have expected from her.

"We've tried to do things the way you suggest. You were the one who was keen to abandon the old ways and do everything in your power to keep us from them and look at where we are now. We've lost everything we were looking for and are now at real risk from The Hive. The Messenger here says that you are not involved in the treachery but you have allowed it to flourish just by confusing the issues as we discover them. You need to learn the duty we all have."

Gobs of spittle flew from Andrea's mouth as she spoke, more emotion in her than she was able to control.

"HOW DARE YOU!" Now it was Em who was joining the fray, stepping beyond me and practically squaring up to Andrea.

"Anthony has been resolute in doing what is right all of the time and has given all he can to be able to resolve the theft. How dare you go outside the rules of The Circle, the very crime you are charging others of."

I could feel the anger coming from the two women even without the use of magical energies. I couldn't let us pull ourselves apart here. Gesturing at Mark for help, I edged between the two warring women and tried to ease them apart.

"We need to stop this. It's now we've got to be one team, not pull ourselves apart. Enemies on the outside remember?"

It didn't work.

I was facing Em as I did my best to speak to them both but I'd made Andrea angry.

Andrea just roared at me. Even though she was still very much human, the roar was purely that of her Dragon form. She was totally losing it.

Letting go of The Elder, she lunged forward and swung her armoured arm at my head. I was stuck. If I turned and attempted to defend myself, then I'd have to let go of Em which would probably mean that she'd just make a bee-line for Andrea and the resulting fight would probably have one of them dead. On the other hand, if I stayed put restraining Em, then Andrea would just cave my skull in. Yes that would probably mean Em would be released and then the fight again but more importantly, it was going to mean the end of me.

I did all I could do and braced myself for the impact, aiming to move my head at the very last minute so at least I'd try and take the impact on my shoulder. My eyes closed and I waited for my spinning head to signal the best time to dodge as much as I could.

And I waited.

And waited.

When I finally opened my eyes and risked turning around, still holding Em back from the fight, Andrea was stood with her arm raised in attack but now it was held in place by Mark, high above her head. She was struggling against the grip but was having very little luck.

Turning back to Em, I shoved her hard away from the conflict and ordered her to remain out of it. She didn't look happy but at least she listened, bowing her understanding even though her eyes glinted with purple fire.

Turning back, Mark still held Andrea firmly in place. The Elder was still crumpled on the floor just behind them cradling her crushed arm, doing her best to remain motionless to both reduce pain and avoid drawing attention to herself.

Andrea struggled but had no effect on her captor. To highlight the point, Mark lifted Andrea from the floor by her arm and brought her to his eye level.

"My lady," he spoke, no hint of emotion in his words, "This is my 'no' face. Stop your violence."

She shook her head as if to free herself from the effects of a clouding of her mind then just stared daggers at me.

"Get your animal to let me down." Her voice was frozen solid and there was no doubt that she meant every ice covered syllable, the same purple fire glint showing in her eyes as was in Em's.

But it wasn't exactly the same.

It wasn't in her eyes like it had been with Em. It was only in one and it wasn't even in that. That purple fire was coming from the side of her nose, merely reflecting the light onto her eye.

As I stood in the gathering gloom, rubbing at the back of my neck, an important piece of a puzzle I hadn't really known was there, stared me in the face and suddenly I understood so much of the what's and the how's.

That glow. That fiery power wasn't coming from Andrea or Em. It was The Drake Stone.

What the Tayne Queen had said about her supposed savior rubbing crystals on her subjects screamed its relevance. How the hell had I missed it? That was how Leatherpants had been able to reach out and control the Tayne. Through The Drake Stone pieces he'd inserted into them. That glow was coming from The Drake Stone, a piece of which had been embedded in all of us and it was the power of that stone which was being used to twist us.

That was how we'd been attacked and drained of our powers. That was how we'd been manipulated by Leatherpants. He'd stolen the Drake Stone and had split it into the tiniest fragments and placed them on all of us. That was how he'd done it all to us. He'd been able to use his position to do all the damage without having to resort to the more traditional fighting. I didn't know the specifics of how he'd been able to do it but he'd had the free run of everywhere within The Circle for so long he would have been able to do it at any point.

Thinking hard back through the details of everything which had been taking place, that same glow of power, the tiniest of all signals of the true cause of our problems, was clear for all to see. It was only now, in the stygian depths of the realm of the Tayne, that the tiny ember was able to burn so obviously. Every time Em had behaved in a strange way, every time her persona had changed, she'd been in the presence of the warping power of a Guardian who was silently being attacked.

I'd figured it out.

Now all I had to do was talk Andrea down.

Edging slowly forward I signaled to Mark to lower her down but I could see that he was still ready for action, just in case she decided to lunge forwards.

"Andrea." My hands were far from me, exaggerating my already wide stance. "This isn't you. You're being controlled from outside." She snarled at me but didn't attack.

"We've known that we've been on the receiving end of some kind of magical attack during the whole of this but I think I've just worked out how they've been doing it."

Her lips were peeled back to reveal a furious, snarling set of teeth but she still hadn't attacked me.

"We've all been expecting there to have needed to be some kind of physical contact to be able to take the power from one being and give it to another. That's what happened to me when I was fighting Tyus and The Zarrulent. But there has been physical contact with all of us without us even knowing it." I pointed slowly at her face as a way of highlighting what I meant.

"You've got to admit that you're acting very strangely, not like you usually do. Add to that, there's a tiny glow coming from your face. That glow has been coming from everyone when they've started to behave in a way that was beyond what they should have been doing. That same purple colour is what comes from the Drake Stone. That was why Leatherpants could control all of the Tayne and I'll bet that's why there was that beam of purple light before his Dragon construct fell. The power was broken free after I hit him and the crystal fragment was broken."

I risked a look at The Elder on the floor and then back to Andrea. Both were considering what I had just said. I could only hope that they were going to agree with my logic.

"If that is the case my Lord," Mark was still looking hard at Andrea but was speaking to me. "Should we not remove the piece of crystal?"

"Good idea. We need to take the pieces out from all of us."

Now The Elder chimed in, her voice shaken but still determined. "But how do we determine who it is who has been affected in this way?"

Despite the fact it had come from our amnesiac compatriot, the clearest example of someone who had been affected, it was a good question. It was a fair bet that the sharp pain I'd felt during every incidence of my own power being drained from me had been caused by the presence of the crystal shard and I could clearly make out where it was on Andrea but how were we going to check everyone else?

"I can determine this fact." Em spoke from behind me and walked forward to take up a place beside me.

"We can all use the energies in individual shards to highlight the pieces of the stone that are in all of you and locate their whereabouts. I would also suggest that it is not just the Guardians who have been affected in this way." Her voice was calm again but I swear I could

331

pick up on some primal force of nature roaring from inside her. My mind was suddenly filled with amazing images of challenging her and battling with her hand to hand, tooth and claw, of tearing her clothes off as she did the same to me. I could just feel the deepest animal heat from her.

"My Lord. We must move quickly before you are lost to the effects of this devilry." Mark was speaking loudly and was edging himself and Andrea in my direction. Shaking my head I pushed the vivid pictures of Em away from my mind's eye and did my best to focus. I could only hope it had been the expression on my face that had alerted him to the rising Fire power in me rather than anything else more 'apparent' which had been rising.

"Mike," I called to my Head of House. "Can you hold Andrea securely while Mark completes what needs to be done to The Elder and me?"

Ghosting next to me, he replied in the affirmative, and in a blur was behind Andrea, gripping her tightly to hold her in place. A coronal discharge ringed them as she fought against him and he poured all of the power he had at his disposal into keeping her from unravelling completely. Both their white hair reacted to the static and began to come alive.

I relaxed slightly but ran to Mark. I waved my hand at the back of my neck, hurriedly signaling where I thought the fragment of crystal was.

"I could feel the pain here and I've had this incredible need to scratch the area since the last attack in Argentina. None of us ever noticed there being an issue because Leatherpants was only taking small pieces. It was only when he was removing my Dragon energy that it hurt. Must have been too much to control. Be as gentle as you can but cut the thing out of me."

Mark didn't wait.

Andrea screeched out against Mike but just couldn't break free of him. He'd bound her arms to her side and hugged her close to him, giving her no chance to maneuver. Even as Mark set himself, I could see the strain on Mike's face as he chanted all the magic he had to contain a Guardian. My own anger was rising fast at the image so Mark was running out of time.

My focus on Andrea was broken by the sharp pain of field surgery. His blade was terrifyingly sharp, and without any pressure, slipped easily into my neck. The sudden pain kicked at my anger and it rose faster.

"Hurry it up," I said through gritted teeth, "I'm losing it."

The red in my vision grew and I could almost taste the Dragon roar building.

But in an instant, that anger was gone.

My vision returned to normal and the rising monster was returned back within me. The power of my Dragon was back under my sole control, leaving me safe in the knowledge that my mind wasn't being messed with. The pain in my neck remained as a sign of what had just been done but I was now free of the warping control of Leatherpants and The Drake Stone.

"I have it my Lord," stated Mark from behind me.

I took a steadying breath to truly savor the feeling of being free of the uncertainty but as I blew it out, before I was even able to turn to thank Mark, still surrounded in the dark by the other worldly shrieking of Andrea and the danger of our situation, still unsure of what the next step was going to be, my mind swarmed with a nauseating tidal wave of images and sounds and I was driven to my knees under the weight of what I was experiencing.

"ANTHONY!" Even from within my mental prison, I could hear the violent call of Em as I collapsed and I could make out the indistinct sound of her footsteps coming closer.

Before she could arrive at my side, despite everything that Mike had been doing, Andrea broke free, throwing him off like a discarded jacket to crash away from her and releasing herself to recommence her violence against anyone she wanted but which was far too clear was going to mean me.

"What happened? What did your servant do to you?" Em was in my ear now. Her voice was again twisted to her own anger, a response to what was still coming from Andrea no doubt but she sounded so far away, like she was calling to me from across a great valley. I was doing my best to hold myself together but as each second passed, my mind just continued to fill with contradictions on my memories. I shook my head against the effects but I was being confronted by my very own spot the difference competition as situation after situation was replayed but with some subtle, some more blatant, variations. Our walk through the estate in Argentina changed details throughout, the time spent in my own mansion became different, as did almost every memory in my head. My head filled with hundreds of new pictures, all feeling like the shared memories I'd seen before. They had all come through the eyes of the Guardian but so many of them, despite having me involved, felt like they had come from someone else.

I hadn't registered what was going on around me, I hadn't been able, but I could assume that the noises I could hear were as Andrea roared and smashed into Em, and then them both crashing away from me. They screamed and I could make out the sounds of magical energy being discharged and of metallic crunching sounds as they fought against each other with a ferocity that, despite not being able to truly witness the details, I was glad wasn't being aimed at me.

Then as fast as it had hit me, the maelstrom of memory started to slowly become rigid. There were empty voids in my mind but I was already able to see a clearer outline of the wider truth. All of the confusion about what was happening just collapsed away. I stood up as quickly as I could and took in as much of the detail of what was taking place. The memories I had of two of almost everything, including my time with Andrea at my flat.

"Mark. I need you and Hairy over there to subdue Andrea and do the same surgery on her as you did on me. The fragment of stone is here." I gestured to the side of the bridge of my nose to give him a place to start.

"And you?" He queried back.

"I'm going to stop Em before she kills Andrea."

We attacked in unison, but with more noise than actual malice. Andrea and Em remained locked in something which could loosely be called a wrestling grapple when we approached them and they were, happily, taken utterly by surprise.

Hairy and Mark crashed into Andrea and dragged her away from the conflict. Em watched her be swept away which allowed me to wrap my arms around her and carry her away from the others in the group. I could hear the anger in the air from Andrea as I moved but Em made no attempt to break free from my grip. After thirty or forty feet, I stopped and lowered her down before me.

Her breath was hot against my cheek and it was clear that she had been fighting very hard against Andrea as she breathed deeply. I stepped back from her slightly and watched her warily, knowing that in a split second she could unleash all kinds of terror on me and be heading right back to the fight.

"Are you OK Em?" I asked with as much certainty as I could muster. I knew I was stood before a hurricane. Em's eyes remained fixed on mine and her eyelids lowered slowly, hooding her gaze.

"What do you think? Did you think that I felt OK?" Her words were practically dripping with suggestion, honeyed and offering the chance so many would have killed for. To add to the effect, she slowly moved her hands down her sides to her hips as if reaching out to guide my opinion.

"That wasn't what I meant," I nervously giggled. "I want to make sure you aren't injured or being affected by the magic that Leatherpants has at his fingertips."

She sighed and slowly ran her finger down my stomach, lingering slightly on my naval. "You want to care for people, don't you? You want to care for me."

Oddly for me, thankfully, but oddly, my brain took over.

With my Dragon power being twisted, I probably would have agreed with her about caring for her and taken my first step down a very slippery slope. Happily, now devoid of Drake Stone control, I was able to recognize that that would have been great fun to start with but wouldn't end well. I reached down and gently took her hand from my stomach and lifted it before me.

"We need to remove the fragments of The Drake Stone from all of us. We need to be sure that our powers aren't being manipulated by any outside forces to be used against us. Can you help me with that please?"

She smiled and dropped her gaze to the floor. She kept a firm hold on my hands as she did before she eventually lifted her eyes to meet mine, now with an expression of resolution on her features.

"I am The Circle. As Guardian, should you require my help I will gladly give it. I can feel the effects of the magics being manipulated in all of those affected and that is what had caused me to act in such an, unusual fashion." She paused as if to gather herself and that resolute expression became gently coloured by a new emotion. Regret?

"I must apologise for my behavior my Lord. I will do what is expected of me and will submit myself to the judgement of The Mage when this mission is concluded."

She was doing her best to resist whatever effects the swirling magical power was having on her but that meant that she was holding on tightly to the rigidity of the rules as her anchor. Which meant that she was going to report herself as someone who is an enemy of The Circle because of her actions. Her anchor in this was looking like it was going to drag her under the waves and drown her.

"I'm not asking for that, I just need your help to get through everything. You won't be submitting yourself to anything while I have a say in it."

She smiled sadly and squeezed my hands tightly before releasing her grip and backing away steadily, looking over my shoulder as she did.

As I turned I came face to face with Mark, Hairy and Andrea. They all moved with a steady confidence which suggested that their minds were at ease, free of the effects of Leatherpants. Looking at Andrea's face, I could see the small incision on her nose where the crystal shard had been removed. A very small trickle of blood was making its way down her face but she seemed to be utterly unfazed by it.

"How are you feeling," I enquired gingerly as Andrea approached. She may have been under the control of an outside force but still, she had been the one doing all the damage.

She blushed, her cheeks colouring barely, but on her porcelain skin, it was akin to a vibrant scarlet on the rest of us.

"I have had the piece of the stone removed and am now again in control of who I am." Her voice was back to her usual calm certainty, all business and no emotion.

"Lady Messenger. I must beg your forgiveness for my behavior. I have attacked you on more than one occasion and for that I am deeply sorry. I was driven to distraction by the poor behavior of Mr. Johns."

Em just bowed ever so slightly. "I was not blameless in this my Lady. I was beyond myself because of the power around us all." Direct and to the point, as much control as possible back in place.

Andrea nodded her agreement and the issue appeared to have been resolved between the two of them. The comment about my behavior was a little odd though.

"Besides," added Andrea, "I still carry some of that effect with me." She raised her hand to lift some of her white hair and it was only now that we could all see the pinkish red flush at the ends. A small reminder of the Fire based rage she'd been facing as it had been poured into her.

Mark and Hairy flanked Andrea, stood back a respectful distance so it was clear that the effect of The Drake Stone had been removed.

"How are The Elder and Mike?" Now the problem with mentally warped Guardians had been removed, the next concern was for our wounded. Andrea had thrown Mike away during the fighting so we needed to be sure of the extent of any injuries he had sustained and The Elder was far from being her usual self.

"I found Mr. Christian and he was perfectly fine," explained Mark, his deep voice again filled with a reassuring authority. "He is continuing the removal operation on the others having done what was needed on us." He lifted his trouser leg to show a small incision point on his shin.

"Excellent. How did you know where to look? Hurting you as well?"

Mark lowered his trouser leg before explaining.

"Mr. Christian was able to use the pieces of the stone from yourself and from Miss Thomich to locate any further pieces on anyone else, as The Messenger explained. They will all be here shortly, when he has completed the removal." Mark was back to his old self, all formality and deference to those he saw as his superiors. Looking at him now, hugely menacing yet totally muzzled by perceived rules, his recent behavior also showed all of the hallmarks of one who was being twisted by the furious rage of the Fire Dragon. He may not have been screaming and shouting about what was going on but his comments and actions, answering back and slapping down petulant Guardians, really stood out as being far from the norm. Seeing as how everyone else was reacting because of their own changes, his must have just made him want the ground to open up and swallow him whole.

We all stood in silence as we awaited the others from our group. Hairy was barely a wordsmith at the best of times but he seemed to be taking the quiet man act to almost new levels. Everyone just looked like they were recalling the drunken antics of the previous night and were just too ashamed to admit to anyone that it had taken place.

My mind was, fragment by fragment, steadily being reassembled and I knew that everyone else was going through exactly the same process. Confusing and bizarre images would be filling everyone's minds as individual pieces of their whole memories returned to their rightful places. The only positive to add to the situation was that at least Hairy had given me use of his flourishing cape as the barest attempt to cover my nudity.

Eventually, The Elder approached us, followed closely but at a respectful distance, by the remaining members of our armed forces. She cradled her broken arm before her but gone was the pained and frightened expression and demeanor. Instead, in their place, was her more familiar posture of utter authority and aloof certainty. Her face was etched with that all too familiar visage of displeasure with everything around her. As she closed in on us, I could make out a very small incision across her chin. Looked like Mike had been extra careful when conducting the surgery there. Probably a wise move.

She stopped and just stared at all of us in turn, finally landing on me. Her face didn't change but I'd swear that there was so much emotion buried there.

"How are you feeling Lady Elder? Do you know who we all are?" I tried to be as gentle as I could but I was already preparing for her eruption at me.

"I am back to the whole I have needed to be for the duration of this mission." She stopped speaking and just held my gaze. There was just the bare bones to her response. Nothing else. It looked as if she needed to say something else but there was no sign she was actually going to do it.

"Great. It looks like we're all back to who we need to be." All I could do was move ahead with what I had in mind.

"I think I know how everything was done and I'd expect that everyone else is beginning to put it all together now we all have our memories back." Small nods from everyone showed agreement.

"But we are still no closer to understanding where the child has been taken or what they intend to do with her." The Elder spoke fact and nothing more. Previously she would have used every word as an opportunity to highlight the flaws in anything which I was putting forward but now there was just the bare reality. Progress?

"The Elder is correct," now it was Andrea who spoke. "We do now have a clear way of ensuring the removal of the control of Mr. Ward but we are still utterly without knowledge as to the next step we should take to bring this whole situation to a conclusion." Again there was no emotion added to what was being said. She just had to rely on the clarity of the facts as they were presenting themselves.

Everyone else around us had the same expression on their faces, one of simple rudderless not knowing. I just knew that now the twisting play of Leatherpants had been removed from all of their minds, they'd returned to their original selves, which meant that they'd all reclaimed that rigid hold on the rules they were all supposed to be following.

"Don't worry team, we're not beaten yet." I had to do something to get the morale back up.

"We've never needed to know why Maria was taken. She's only been missing a short time and, yes, we don't know the reasons behind the capture but all we have to keep in mind is we just need to get her back." The same expressions remained.

"From what we can all recall now, and what we were told by the Queen in there," I pointed back towards the palace we had only recently left, "Leatherpants had taken The Drake Stone following one raid on the estate but he attacked again. Why would he attack again if he'd already taken The Drake Stone? Why would he go through all of that again if he'd taken what he was after?" Still blank looks.

"Because he was after the child all along."

Still blank looks.

"Surely there can be no greater prize than The Drake Stone in all of this?" The Elder was questioning my logic, but at least still without her disdain for me. "Why would anyone take such a vast reservoir of power and that not be the purpose of his mission? We've all seen the damage that he's been able to do with The Drake Stone in his possession. Why would Mr. Ward want to claim anything further than that?"

I blew out a breath and replied.

"I don't know but whatever he's up to must be worth it. It has to worth the enormous risk of going through all of this, of going through all of the work to get access to The Drake Stone and then to keep going. Don't forget that he would have needed to do the same thing to The Mage as to all of us to make this work, that can't have been an easy task."

The blank looks remained but they at least seemed to be a little less blank. All of the people around me were all doing their best to come to terms with a set of facts which didn't fit into anything they'd ever seen before and the only person who had any kind of map to these unknown lands was me. No wonder they looked ill at ease.

"If he had been able to infect The Mage in the same way as he has all of us, wouldn't he just have removed the power directly from him? He is more powerful than all of the Guardians, why not aim for him?" Em's question was spoken flatly but was still valid.

I considered her words and prodded the ideas about. Why wouldn't he? If you had access to that amount of power surely the Guardians mantle would seem like a waste of time? Unless he couldn't take the power from The Mage?

"Em, you said The Drake Stone was used for the storing of Guardian power, Dragon energy. The Mage isn't the same as the rest of us so maybe it wouldn't do the same thing to him?"

"But why would Mr. Ward want to lead all of us down into the land of The Tayne just to take the child." Andrea was asking this time and I swear it felt as if she was doing her best to tear my ideas down rather than trying to find the truth of the situation.

"He probably wanted to be able to make his move for Maria away from our strongholds and then have us either tear ourselves apart down here or have his Uber-Tayne do it for him. The longer for the theft to go undetected." My words carried their own anger in response.

"But that also means that the longer we can keep the charade going that no-one has heard from us the longer we are likely to have to rescue Maria. If there's no hurry it's likely that Leatherpants will be more relaxed about his plan so won't be rushing. That means we have to be very quiet when we get back to the mansion and not 'free' anybody else, including The Mage." I'd followed the logic chain and had come to a very risking location. Could we risk just leaving it to ourselves and not spread the word of removing the shards of crystal?

As each person considered what had been said, it was Andrea who reached another, starker conclusion, faster than the others.

"But this doesn't bring us any closer to being able to locate where Mr. Ward or the child are now? We may have been able to decipher some, if not all, of what has been taking place around us but we're still without the knowledge of the next step." The Elder may have been less angry about what I was saying but it would appear that Andrea was taking her place. One problem at a time.

"We don't know where they are now but we have the tools to be able to find them. We get back to my estate, you get changed into less medieval attire and I put some clothes on, and we can pick them out quickly and get the rescue mission underway." The wolfish smile on my face must have given everyone some indication that I was feeling positive and that seemed to lift a little of the somber mood from all of us. As I opened the Cascade Bridge back to Wales, everyone who ran through had a much more determined look on their face.

At least that was something.

30

There was daylight when we all stepped through to Wales, showing we'd been gone for much longer than we'd first thought. I'd opened as small a bridge as I could into the comfort of my bedroom. I knew that the door would be closed and no-one would risk entering the room without my knowing so it seemed to be the only place available for all of us to gather and plan our journey to rescue Maria. I didn't dive in the shower despite really needing it, instead dressing as much black clothing as I could find which would be appropriate. Combat trousers, boots and a turtle neck jumper and I was ready to go. The others all began to take off their armour as quietly as possible and I fished out as much clothing as I could find for them. Em was the only one who didn't accept what I was presenting.

After the attack which had taken place in this very room, I'd requested there be a comprehensive first aid kit left stored here along with a small clutch of weapons. Happily, my stash of snacks was enough to provide us with some much needed fuel, even if the others were more than a little wary of chocolate gummy sweets. Clothing, weapons and medical care were all in the one space so we could keep our arrival away from prying eyes.

In less than thirty minutes, myself, Andrea, The Elder, Em, Hairy and Mike were settled in chairs which had been pulled up around our makeshift table, my bed. I'd invited Mark to join us as a vital part of the war council but he was resolute that his place was outside, standing guard. When I'd tried to protest he just fixed me with that resolute stare of his and told me, "This is my 'no' face" before closing the door gently. I think he was trying to be funny. The other surviving soldiers just stood to attention back at the walls of the room and got back to doing what they were familiar with.

Taking my place at the table, I picked at a few pieces of the enormous pile of food which had been assembled for us all. We'd all been in need of something to eat and time was of the essence but I was still shocked by the volume of provisions which had been discovered. I really needed to stop snacking this much. Despite my body needing fuel, I was also far too wound up to be able to eat. Surveying the scraps of food which the others were aimlessly considering, it would appear that they were feeling the same.

Back in my own estate, surrounded by the familiar and now being fully clothed, I was ready to begin what needed to be done. Dressed now in more tactical attire than armour, I was ready.

"I know that this is going to be a difficult task for everyone but I need you all to trust that I know what I'm doing." Everyone just sat still and listened.

"I said once that we'd been worked out in how we'd been doing things. That was true. The Circle has been doing things the same way for so long, everyone, friend or foe, knew exactly what we'd be doing at each step of the way. That in itself was the greatest weakness we could have inflicted upon ourselves. We're predictable."

The expressions around the table showed that there was clear comprehension at what I was saying. Andrea just watched me with no emotion showing but her head was nodding gently, as was Em's. The Elder was the only one who wasn't meeting my eyes but she was clearly struggling with the realities of what had been taking place, but she too was showing her agreement. Her arm had been wrapped in, well something more than bandage but not armour, and it was glowing steadily. Llewellyn, my head medic, had said it was akin to living splint which could allow a broken limb to still be used as it healed. Looking at The Elder, it was already clear that the bone was mending.

"To start with, they kept attacking the same house. They didn't fight hard, they fought smart and each time, we lost the Guardian as we defended the prison. But they never wanted to break the prison, they were always aiming to end the Guardian and then 'miraculously' be repelled at the last minute. What this eventually gave them was the power of the Guardian passed into the weakest possible vessel, Maria."

Everyone frowned as I pushed on through the details as I saw them.

"Maria couldn't control the powers inside her, which was why we were all summoned by The Messenger to Egypt. We needed to choose another person to take her place in The Circle and have the power transferred from her, therefore bringing The Drake Stone into the open."

I sipped slowly from a goblet of water and did my best to maintain my balance on this high wire I was trying to traverse. No-one else spoke though. Until.

"Why would anyone go to this much trouble to take The Drake Stone if it was then going to be used as nothing more than a tool to reach the child?" Andrea probed at my logic for the first time, that silent anger still on her face.

"I don't know. We can all see what happened now though can't we? The power being syphoned off all of us wasn't the only reason The Drake Stone was valuable was it? Em said when we first gathered here to run this mission that when The Drake Stone was first discovered all testing on it was stopped at the word of The Mage when he discovered that it was able to store Dragon energy but I think that it's capable of so much more. Mind control."

"Again you are reaching towards conclusions." It was The Elder but her words were still without anger. She was testing my logic. I needed to show her I was right.

"We can all see that Leatherpants and whoever he was working with did the same thing twice. We've all got our memories back so we all now know that we did the same things twice. We travelled to Argentina to investigate what had taken place but in the first version, we went with Leatherpants with us. It was the version where we went without him that we could remember, the second trip. Every situation in this house that we've been going through was the second time we'd done it. Each time it was so Leatherpants could move us around to the positions he wanted."

I sifted back through the memories of what we'd been doing and hanging before my mind's eye, in each and every situation, Leatherpants was newly present in so many recollections. He was always there. Always smiling his too wide smile and always pulling the strings.

"Surely he would have just taken us all to pieces if he had the ability to just steal away our memories? He must have had all of the members of The Circle controlled in this way so what would be the need to go to all of this trouble?" The Elder spoke to the gathered meeting but at least they were valuable words. She seemed to have forgone the sneering derision of me but she was still smart.

I pondered the question before answering with a question of my own.

"How strong is he?"

No-one answered. Em tilted her head in her usual fashion so I could only imagine that she didn't understand the question.

"If you're strong enough to do the damage, you do it, no questions asked. If he was the all-powerful monster we're all worried he is, why not destroy us all himself? Why, of all of the races out there who he could have used to destroy us, did he choose the relative weaklings that are the Tayne? In every choice he made, he went for the same type of option."

Everyone just wore they're frowns of worry and confusion.

"Not one of you has ever played poker have you?"

Silence as the frowns deepened.

"He's been bluffing all along. He's throwing possibly the world's biggest dummy. Everyone in The Circle is used to things happening in a certain way. We're the big gun so we're used to getting our own way through the use of intimidation or through force, and it's been that way for so long that no-one looks for anything else. He just made us behave in the way that he wanted, expecting attacks to come in the way everyone was used to, before undoing us with a new tactic. All we did was think that he had vast power because of the results not because of the evidence we were being presented with. He made the Tayne do his bidding by force because he dangled the exact thing they've ever wanted, freedom and the strength to resist the bullies, allowing him to take control. His misdirection has allowed him to take what he's been after, not huge magical ability."

Silence followed as everyone digested the words.

"The logic is sound," stated Em into the silence. I took the continued lack of comment as a wider agreement in what I'd said. Em spoke again though.

"That still doesn't give us a reason why the child was taken from us or where she is currently being held."

The silence remained but now it seemed so much more pressure filled on the inside of it than it had done a second before.

"He needed both The Drake Stone and Maria, that was the point. I think he's going to try and use The Drake Stone to remove the power of our Argentinian Guardian and transfer it into himself. He's been next to possibly the most awesome power on the planet for hundreds of years and has seen so many other people be granted it while no matter what he does, he just can't get close. He was openly dismissive of me despite the 'proper' way he should have behaved. Deep down he just wants to sit at the top table with the other Guardians."

"That isn't possible," Andrea was direct with her assessment of my theory. "He would need an enormous amount of power to be able to complete something of this kind. We are only able to do it as we have all of the Guardians to pull from. Where could he possibly find that kind of energy?"

I thought for a second but the answer was clear.

"The Tayne," I answered somberly. "He's going to use them as the battery for his little spell."

This time the silence around the room was serrated as well as heavy. No-one dared move for fear of being caught by what the facts meant.

"He couldn't be that mad?" asked The Elder, fighting against her own shock to give the words sound. "He wouldn't bring about the genocide of a whole race just for the power of a Guardian?"

"Look team, the truth is that whatever he's going to do is not something we're likely to want to happen. Now this is where we have to find him and destroy whatever he's doing. We've got two races of people hanging in the balance now."

"But how should we expect to locate Mr. Ward?" Em was standing now but her head was tilted again so she was unsure what the path to take would be.

"Mike removed the shards of The Drake stone from all of us and he was able to do it by following the link between the pieces. They've all come from one stone so they all behave the same way, magically speaking. That means that we can use those pieces to locate the rest of the stone, wherever it is."

"My Lord," it was Mike speaking softly, back to his more familiar place as feeling on edge even being at the table. "I was able to use the linking magic only because I had one piece of The Drake Stone to place near to another. I was able to create the link only because I was able to bring the pieces so closely together. We aren't in a position to do that with the rest of the stone." He spoke strongly but there was a hint of fear wrapped in the words.

I just smiled.

"We have the perfect weapon to use in this situation which will give us what we need," and I banged my hand on the bed hard.

Behind me, the heavy doors opened and Mark walked in carrying a heavy old chest. Setting it down on the bed before me, he nodded curtly to everyone before turning on his heel and marching back out, the ever ready soldier.

Around the bed, more confused expressions.

"What weapon have you brought us? What have you seen which none of the rest of us have which can save us?" The Elder was again stating fact but she was now just looking for the answer. She obviously didn't like being in the position of not knowing.

Across the table from The Elder, Andrea nodded her head and spoke just as I opened the lid.

"He has Banus Stones."

"All we need to do is channel the power from the fragments of the stone we have, into the stones of the map, and we can locate the remaining pieces."

I wasted no time in laying out the marker Banus Stones and, using a small piece of adhesive tape, attached the shards of The Drake Stone to them, one on one. I'd like to think it was at least magical adhesive tape but no-one else seemed that impressed.

When I'd finished doing what I needed to, I asked Em to use her power to create a map of the world in the bed, akin to her display when we had first set out. She complied without any hesitation and the surface of the large bed warped and buckled as outlines of land masses and oceans formed themselves. She was careful not to disturb the Banus Stones as she worked what she needed to and soon the world was laid out before us.

I handed control of the actual casting here over to Andrea. She was far stronger than me in terms of direct control of magic but she was also the one who'd shown me this method of finding anything so I thought it wiser to let her lead the way.

One by one we all placed our hands flat on the edge of the bed and waited for the command to begin.

"I need everyone to focus their attention, their power, on an image of The Drake Stone in their minds." Andrea spoke with wintery calm but it was clear to see that there was a deeper emotion driving her. We were all feeling it and knew that we had to find out where Leatherpants was.

I closed my eyes and summoned the image in my head, pumping as much detail into it as I could muster. I imagined the same purple hue burning within it as I'd seen crisscrossing Em's suit when she was using the maximum level of energy she could. I added the sensation of the sharp piece that had been carved from my neck and the cold stab which had come from the effects it had had on me, all the time willing more and more power into the picture.

"Excellent. Keep adding more power," spoke Andrea as the scraping sounds of stone on wood began to etch the air. "They're moving, keep going."

I risked a look at what was taking place. Each of the people involved were utterly motionless and had their eyes closed, each with a slight crease in their foreheads as will and focus built and built. Mike looked the most affected by the process but that was to be expected, he wasn't as strong as the rest of us. The bed had taken on the appearance of a game of Risk being played by two invisible men. Stones slid drunkenly around the fabric map. Closing my eyes again and taking a resolute breath, I pounded my power at the image I was holding in my head and the scraping noises grew in both volume and speed.

Until all of the stones stopped their journeys, settling at the points that they were heading for. Everyone held their attention still, all of us maintaining the energies within the construct for fear of losing our one and only lead.

Andrea broke the silence.

"It is done. We have the location of The Drake Stone."

Everyone else opened their eyes and took in all of the detail before them. Around the map were tiny piles of dust, dotted on various locations supposedly signifying a piece of the whole stone. Looking at them it was clear to make out that they all corresponded to our very own prison sites, including here in Wales. The Banus

Stones had been broken ever so slightly to leave some kind of marker on the smaller concentrations, while the main pieces gave the stronger location.

And it was easy to see they were all pointing to the same place.

One by one, all of the stones had arranged themselves into a tower which reached well towards the high ceiling of the room we were in. They were all balanced rod straight and there was no hint of any wobble in them. They were held in place as if by a powerful magnet, unflinching in the show of there being one location where the whole of The Drake Stone remained.

"Turkey?" My geography had always been a little sketchy at best.

"Very good," said Em, indicating I wasn't quite as bad as I'd thought, "This is a great concern though," she finished with a large dose of apprehension added to her words.

"Concern? What's in Turkey?" Back in the dark.

"That looks as if he has taken The Drake Stone to Gobekli Tepe in southern Turkey. It is an ancient temple site which was unearthed very recently. Archeologists from all over the world are very interested in the site."

"OK. So what's the problem? Lots of people to avoid when we do our thing?" It was unnerving to see Em look so concerned.

"Not at all. I'm worried that Mr. Ward may have found something else at that site. You see it wasn't always called Gobekli Tepe. Generations ago it went by another name and if Mr. Ward has set his camp there, he may really be able to unleash an almighty havoc. He's based himself at the ruins of Bress Tal."

31

"If he's taken The Drake Stone back to its original home, there must be a wider reason to what he's doing. We must move immediately."

Hearing the details she just had was enough to break the almost paralyzing hold that had been wrapped around The Elder. As she spoke she jumped to her feet and strode for the doors. Everyone else followed her, releasing the power from the bed and the Banus Stones all collapsed.

She powered through the doors of my bedroom, the rest of us trailing behind her, looking like she was aiming for the main lobby area. Mark had spun from his position of guard as we had all left the room. His presence at least stopped her carrying on into the house and exposing us. She reached into her pocket and hurriedly punched keys into a small phone. It was answered before there was a chance for it to ring. Chinese words poured down the phone with a vibrant urgency and although I had no clue what had just been said, I could tell that she was setting something terrible into motion.

"What are you planning Lady Elder? We can't let any of the other staff here see us." I was nervous but her sudden haste made me even more so. I was trying to remain as calm and respectful as I could as I probed for answers but I was sure it just sounded like I was being facetious. She replied while still running through her own plans.

"I am going to have the entire site razed. I'm going to have so much power sent there from so many locations that when the dust settles, there will be nothing more left than a smouldering crater."

"What!?!"

"The Drake Stone and the child will likely survive what will take place but I will make sure that the treachery of my servant will be remedied."

This wasn't good at all.

"I don't think that that will be the best course of action available to us." I needed to bring her back from the edge without there seeming as if I was just calling her plan stupid. Maybe I really was learning how to talk to people in the correct way? This time, it was Andrea who responded.

"We need to cleanse every sign of what has been done to us here. The Elder is going to do the right thing by taking decisive action." She'd spoken from behind me but her words showed me clearly that she was angry about something. Very angry.

The Elder snapped her fingers and the soldiers who'd been silently in the room with us were immediately at her side.

"Get back to my temple and prepare yourselves for a fast jump and to bring every ounce of doom down on our enemies." She gestured purposefully and the troops all jogged through the Cascade Bridge she'd brought into existence. They were heading back to China to gear up for something awful, towards the expanse of grassed area I could see beyond the event horizon of the Cascade. I had to stop this.

"Elder." I was still trying to hold onto some level of control as I spoke but I was now throwing my own authority into what I was saying, rather than coming across as begging. I needed her to see me as an equal. "We can't just revert to type. We need to be smarter."

"Are you suggesting that my plan to remove the enemy from existence is foolish? You think that I am feeble minded?" Her eyes were glittering with a familiar surety, leaving me somewhat back to where I'd started.

"I'm saying," I began, hoping to avoid too much conflict, "that Mr. Ward has been working all of the time with the knowledge of what actions will be coming next. He knows our plays so he's set to defend against them. If we just revert back to what has always been the 'correct' thing to do, we're just going to be playing into his hands. We need to do something different."

She did at least consider what I'd said. She narrowed her eyes as she pondered what I was suggesting but Andrea broke in before The Elder had a chance to respond.

"What would you have us do in the situation?" That anger was rising in her voice, even higher now. "Would you suggest an elaborate attack? Surely you wouldn't be suggesting that just this small band do the job alone?" Her venom was more than a little off-putting. I just didn't know where it was coming from. I'd been reviewing my memories as closely as I could since I'd had them returned but I just couldn't see what the issue was.

"I'm saying that we have to evolve our thinking to be able to survive. Elder, will you continue to prepare whatever it is you are going to prepare, but don't pull the trigger yet. Yes Andrea, I am suggesting that a small force could be able to complete the operation and that's mainly because Leatherpants isn't expecting it. As long as we can keep the Tayne away from him then the casting can't happen. Simple."

This time, it was The Elder who broke through the conversation.

"I will do as you say Mr. Johns, but I will only refrain from unleashing the power I have for as long as it takes to prepare what needs to be done. I will give you that time to be able to resolve this 'quietly' before I will unleash our more familiar 'loud' response." I swear I almost fell over. How far had things come that now it was The Elder agreeing with me and Andrea was the one looking down her nose. Andrea turned to protest but caught the words before they came, The Elder's expression showing that she may have been willing to listen to me but that didn't mean all of the old hierarchy and order had been thrown out of the window.

Nodding my thanks to The Elder I turned to face the others.

"We're all ready for what we need. We're all kitted out to fight and we all have the weapons to do what we need to." Serious faces remained. "Look, when you actually look at how our fighting takes place, all the armour, all the ceremony, all of it shows that we haven't moved on. When it really gets down to the bare bones of the point, all we need is ourselves and our magic. We're all either Dragons or wizards, why do we need the armour? We are all we're going to need now, so let's go and save one of our own and give Leatherpants the kicking he deserves."

Em smiled and brought that sword pommel of hers into her hand. Mike, Mark and Hairy cracked knuckles, necks and who knew what else as they brought their power up to readiness. Following them, we all headed back into the room. Andrea was quick to join me but she didn't have words of encouragement.

"We are merely allowing them time to complete their plan. The correct course of action for us here would have been to destroy the site. The delay here could be fatal to millions of people, those people we're sworn to protect."

"I know we're taking a risk but the population of the planet begins with that one person. I won't let Maria just be forgotten under the guise of the wider picture. Besides, the Tayne are most likely there as well. I told the Queen that I was going to bring her subjects back to her."

The expression on her face showed that consideration of the Tayne had been furthest from her thoughts. There was no more time for argument so without any further words, I brought the Cascade Bridge to Gobekle Tepe into existence as The Elder took hers back to China. I was aiming to arrive some way from the location itself so as not to alert anyone to our presence, rescue Maria before the power-mad Leatherpants could do what he was going to and get us all out without any further loss of life. Taking a deep breath, I led the team, my team, through.

It was a clear, cloudless sky as we came through and we were surrounded by open land in all directions. The sunlight meant we had less risk of being seen due to the glow of the Bridge but it also meant that we were going to be more likely to meet locals who were out and about doing their normal day to day activities. Happily, I'd included a healthy piece of solitude in the construction of the Cascade which had meant we'd been delivered to a delightful spot in the middle of nowhere.

Around us were rolling hills and very little in the way of anything else. "Where are we?" Andrea was still impatient.

"I don't know exactly but we're close enough." Positivity as always.

"We could have used a map but you left all of The Banus Stones with the crystal shards back in Wales. Not a good start." Andrea was really impatient now and I could see that even Mike was noticing the change in her.

I puffed out a resigned sigh and was about to bridge jump back to pick up the ancient map when Em spoke.

"The power from The Drake Stone is in that direction," and she held out her arm to signal off to the west of where we were standing. Her eyes were narrowed as if in concentration and judging by the power which was running in tiny patterns all over her suit, she was working hard to make that determination.

She relaxed her effort and the purple power on her suit winked out. She drew a breath and began walking off in the direction she'd just identified, knowing that each of the rest of us were going to be hot on her heels. Andrea huffed but joined the rest of us. I needed to at least attempt some kind of reconciliation with her.

"You've done this more than I have," I started, trying to remain as conversational as I could for fear of stoking the newly kindled fires within her. "How long are we likely to have to complete this before The Elder does her thing?" Andrea remained staring ahead as she walked and I could feel the boiling heat of her anger even without the aid of my own magical ability.

"The Elder will be attempting to bring the powers together on her own rather than with any other members of The Circle so it is likely that it will take hours rather than minutes as it would usually. Probably should have considered that before deciding that this was the correct course of action." She was biting with every comment and there seemed to be nothing I was going to be able to do against it.

"Thank you my lady. I will have to make sure we hurry." I gave as stock a reply as I could and just left her be.

We walked briskly for close to an hour, each of us doing our best to hurry while also looking as nonchalant as we could should any locals see us, before Em finally signaled we were approaching our destination. I'd been getting more than a little concerned that we were just going to burn all of the time that The Elder was giving us to affect the rescue, just arriving at the location. Em pointed ahead indicating that the low sound we could all recognize coming from beyond the far off hills was the target we were here to intercept.

"What's our next step? We are running short of our allotted time." Andrea asked angrily, showing she'd been having the same thought.

"Now," I started my response, doing my best to just stay focused on the job at hand. The last thing I needed was to have everyone see me react to Andrea's very obvious misgivings about my ideas. "We need to see what their up to. I need to get close to them as quickly as I can without being seen. Lady Messenger, can you assist me with this task please?" I'd hoped that by addressing Em in the more formal title would at least make Andrea see that we were all on the same side. Her grimace showed it hadn't worked. Thinking quickly, I added,

"Can you help us with this task please?"

Em just nodded her agreement, understanding what I was asking, before adding, "Everyone will need to be very close to me as we approach the site. I will only be able to cast my concealment so far and with this number of us it could become very crowded within the shell. We must also be aware that this place will be very different to the house in Argentina. When Mr. Johns and I moved through that estate, we weren't running the risk of tripping any form of magical trip wire. Here, there is a real possibility that Mr. Ward will have countermeasures in place for this kind of approach." It was a somber thought but needed saying.

"I thought you said that all of the planning of what we're going to find has been based around the old tactics of The Circle and that we would be able to be victorious by doing something unexpected?" It was Mike asking but he'd only just beaten Andrea to it. At least he'd made the question seem interested rather than accusatory.

"We can't assume anything at all. All of the evidence suggests that I'm right in what's going to happen but I can't guarantee anything." Again, I had to admit that there was a chance that I was going to be found out to be wrong and we were all going to be on the wrong side of this fight. But that chance didn't mean that we were.

"I know that we're all going to walk into a fight and that there's a good chance that we're going to be beaten. Leatherpants has shown that he has been able to out-think everything about all of us but now we're ready to go outside his experience. This is going to be our best chance." My voice wanted to crack so badly but I managed to keep the rod of surety pressed firmly in place, even if I didn't feel as confident as I was sounding. I just couldn't let my fear out.

Everyone nodded and closed in around Em. The violet light of her power sparked into the familiar trails over her suit and that familiar weight of her power enveloped us, rendering us invisible and intangible to those who may stumble on us.

Moving as fast as we dared, it took us eleven minutes to reach the top of the nearest hill to the site of Gobekle Tepe, formerly the stronghold of Bress Tal.

What greeted us was quite startling.

The valley below us fell gently down towards what looked like a writhing and swelling grey sea. Waves of energy frolicked through the surface of whatever we were all looking at and moved all over the entire valley floor. It was only as I focused my attention on a specific area of the swelling sea that I could make out the constituent parts and I recognized the bodies of emaciated Tayne filling this whole valley. They all seemed to be moving with a singular energy, creating motion as if part of a much greater whole. Gone were the much larger creatures we'd seen in the caverns in Mexico but we were now face to face with a very concerning fact. They may have been back to their more familiar form of the playground weakling but they would be more than able to overwhelm us just by sheer weight on numbers. Yet another reason that Leatherpants had chosen this race as the ones to bring onto his side of the fight.

Em hadn't stopped her forward momentum as my mind had been working and we began our decent down the hillside towards the mass of bodies. I couldn't see anything beyond the wall of creatures so wasn't sure where we were heading.

"Can anyone see anything ahead? Can we see more than just the Tayne?"

Em's response was almost reassuring.

"The location of the power in this valley is coming from directly below the central point of the Tayne. I am heading in that direction. It did seem to be the quickest way to reach our goal."

She was right but that didn't stop me feeling as if I'd just had a very basic point explained to me. Somehow, I'd managed to lead us into the fight but had quickly been overtaken in terms of the details. That just made me worry that maybe the experience of the others in The Circle was more valuable than I'd given it credit. In any case, it was too late for doubts.

We all continued on, shrouded by the magics Em had at her disposal, down into the valley, easing into the Tayne as easily as we would have walked into the sea, passing through their bodies without them having any kind of awareness of us. The sensation of sickness which had come when Em and I had passed through the doorway in the mansion in Argentina was missing this time. I could only assume that this was down to the fact that the Tayne were far from being the same level of power, even in their current numbers.

Internal cross-sections of bodies passed us by with each step and soon our tiny little bubble of power was totally submerged in the fleshy mass.

"How much further do we have to go?" Andrea was impatient and I could recognize on her an expression of desire to cut loose and start fighting. I could recognize it as something which I'd worn on more than one occasion as I waited on the edge of unfurling my own Dragon form but it wasn't something I was familiar seeing on her. Of all of my traits for her to pick up.

"We are almost at the focal point of the energy on the surface," responded Em, again just answering the question on face value, but her voice was shaking slightly. I risked a slight glance at her and saw that the effort of what she was doing was starting to really push her reserves. The energy surged all over her suit and judging by the huge number of competing vapor trails snaking all over her, she was having to really push hard to be able to take us all through the Tayne bodies while maintaining the shell. More time constraints.

"The surface?" Mike asked.

"I can feel the power coming from ahead but its true location is beneath us. When we reach the centre of the valley, we will have to break through to whatever is beneath us." The exertion remained but her tone remained as matter of fact as it had ever been.

Em was true to her word and within another minute she signaled for us all to stop moving.

"We are now at the lowest point of the valley. The Drake Stone is below us, still another," she closed her eyes to concentrate, "eight hundred meters below us, and a little to the left of our current position."

"Excellent. Can you 'phase' us through the ground like you've been doing with the Tayne?" Time for me to take some level of control again.

She wiped the sheen of perspiration from her forehead and closed her eyes again, power again bursting to life on her clothing. The shell we were all enclosed within began to sink into the ground, blades of flattened grass suddenly clear of the magics being wielded and inside Em's boundary. The upper surface of the dome lowered as well.

But we didn't.

The space above us rapidly decreased as the shell penetrated the ground but we weren't going with it. Instead we were trapped on the surface with the power Em was using closing in to squash us.

"WAIT! WAIT!" It was Andrea's voice and there was a clear tolling of desperation despite her still evident anger. Thankfully, Em listened.

"You aren't taking us through. You're going to kill us all like this. What's wrong with you?" I could feel the accusation from Andrea as a sharp blade and couldn't be sure that what she'd said hadn't been, at least in part, aimed at me.

Em took a long breath and brought the shell back up from the ground and settled back into the position it had been in, though I swear that as it came to rest, at least one of the Tayne in the swarm outside registered some level of awareness of us, and turned to stare very hard in our direction. I had to put that fear out of my head. We were who knew how deep in these creatures and Em was the one standing between them and us. What was wrong with her?

"You OK?" I asked, hoping that there was nothing more wrong than a mis-judgement of the number of bodies she was being asked to transport. Her response was far from encouraging.

"We are too many. It is too much for me to complete. I cannot phase us all through the ground to the cavern below." Her teeth were gritted and now I was really looking at her, it was clear that she was straining hard against the casting. Another Tayne turned their attention towards us. I still knew that inside this construct that we were all totally gone from the reality outside but if Em was getting tired, what then?

"Don't worry, I'll blast us in." Time was against us so a decisive move was called for. Taking a deep breath and raising my hands above my head, despite the cramped conditions, I prepared to bring down a hammer blow of energy and break us a way down. Andrea grabbed at my hands and shoved a hand over my mouth, breaking my concentration.

"You can't just punch everything," she snarled, her anger still boiling under the surface. "We do that and all element of surprise is lost. This small a team needs surprise, remember?" I had to concentrate. I'd made the big play about doing things differently but as is always the case, it's very easy to suggest different ways when you haven't actually got to deliver on what you suggest.

"Good point. Em, can you take us back to the surface of these Tayne and bring us through in smaller groups? Two's and three's instead of the whole group at once?" Em swallowed against the effort before replying but it was Andrea who spoke.

"We are against the time it will take The Elder to bring together the power needed to destroy this whole area. Taking several trips is hardly productive is it?" Her voice was a severe blast of frozen air and her eyes had glazed their translucent Dragon tone. Even as she breathed at us, frosty clouds billowing, it was clear that she was losing control.

"We need to stay focused on the job at hand. I need all of us to work together. Andrea, whatever it is I've done that's making you this angry at me, you're just going to have to put it aside until this is finished. Look at the big picture will you?"

The words stung her like a slap to the face, they were a direct and blatant rebuke before all of the members of this team and that simmering anger of hers split the surface. Her fists balled and were rapidly encased in massive chunks of ice which she then started to swing wildly in my direction. Everyone dived for cover, as much as they could within the confines of the magical sphere Em was still holding together.

"You are such a risk to us all," she screamed as she plunged onto me, smashing those massive blocks of heavy ice down with no care for the consequences. I knew that this wasn't her, that there was something more going on so I couldn't risk anyone coming to my aid and causing this ager to escalate any further.

"Leave her be everyone, she's just venting. I'm OK." Nobody moved so they must have heard me so I was left with nothing but my own defence as the appropriate response. "You are causing just the disharmony for us that it has been feared."

Em was the only member of our team who was still standing but her posture and visage showed that she was now really struggling to maintain the shell we were surrounded by. Beads of sweat which had broken out on her forehead were now becoming almost constantly pouring rivulets of water and the pulses of violet power which chased themselves around her suit as she controlled the energies at her disposal were now looking far from the ordered and controlled flashes of brilliance they usually were. Instead they were jagged and dim.

As Andrea continued to vent her anger, I could make out a terrifying extra detail behind and all around us. Whereas previously, the Tayne outside had been writhing and squirming over each other with next to no awareness of anything let alone specifically us, now though, they were all beginning to turn and move, to force themselves away from the magical shell until they'd formed a clearing of their own, all staring intently at us.

I had to stop what Andrea was doing.

Waiting for the first second when both of her hands were away from me, I lunged forward and up and took as tight a hold on her frozen maces as I could. She reacted in exactly the way I expected and her violence erupted even further, snapping against what was holding her as she battled to free herself.

"Andrea. You have to stop this. You're going to bring the shell apart. You have to calm yourself down. Just breathe." It was all I could think to do. I couldn't risk just attacking her, that would most likely just bring her Dragon fully out and that would mean death to most, if not all, of the people in here. For an achingly long time she just locked eyes with me and stared violence down at me. All movement ceased and all of her attention was brought down to a pinpoint on the end of my nose.

"Do you think that I wish to be acting in this way? I do not understand this feeling but I can only react to it." Her accent was still the same but her voice was changing, leaving her humanity to become the beast. She was losing it but she didn't understand why.

Why wouldn't she know what was taking place? Why was she so willing to just erupt if she didn't understand why she was doing it? I was still holding onto the ice blocks when she screamed again and brought even more ice into being around her fists, sealing my hands into the constructs.

"Andrea, you're not yourself. There must still be a piece of the Drake Stone on you to make you act like this. That's why you don't understand, you're being manipulated."

I was doing my best to hold a level tone as I spoke, showing that I wasn't there to fight her and hoped that what I was saying would get through the haze of control coming from the shard of crystal we'd missed. In response, Andrea heaved me from the floor and smashed me against the wall of the shell, our frozen grip proving to be incredibly powerful. The impact made my teeth rattle and I could feel the air get blown from my chest. The wall of energy around us was hugely strong but now there was a slight stickiness to it. All around us, the Tayne all lurched at the impact, expecting me to fall through to them. Some of the weakest they may be but in these numbers, there wouldn't need to be any violence, they'd just have to envelop us. Andrea slapped me against the shell again and Em winced before dropping to one knee. I couldn't just do nothing, we'd all die. I'd have to fight back.

Andrea shoved again but this time I shoved back, cancelling out her effort. Calling into my fire power, I quickly melted away the ice holding me to her and jumped forward, grabbing her in a bear hug to hold her arms down at her sides. We toppled over backwards and I landed on her, though the impact did nothing to stop her squirming or snapping at me.

"Em, are you OK? Can you hold this together?" I needed to get us out of this fast but that question just enraged Andrea even more, bringing even more fight from her.

"I'm losing the shell. I can't get us through or out. Please my Lord, help me," Em pleaded, anguish in her voice as she begged for he superior to come to her aid.

I did all I could do and pulled together as much power as I could and forced a Cascade Bridge into existence but it was too late. The light was still flickering into place and the familiar ozone aroma was just a suggestion on the air, the tug of tidal energy coalescing but not whole, as the shield of power surrounding us cracked and fell apart. There was some feeling of coalescing power but it just didn't feel strong enough. The darkness which was the ocean of Tayne above us poured in and there was nothing more to do.

32

I was alone in the dark.

I could hear far off noises, diffuse and nebulous but I was totally enfolded by an impenetrable blackness. Was I dead? I could make out different smells warring for attention, some pleasant, some decidedly not and if I was dead, I would have thought that I wouldn't have been laying on a dusty stone floor when I came to.

Easing myself gingerly into a sitting position, I risked bringing fire into being, gingerly to begin with, just so I could at least see where I was. Flame blossomed in the palm of my hand. I was in a room, no bigger than my bedroom in my flat in London. The floor was bare stone, pitted and imperfect and the walls were high and dug directly from the rock. Above me, there was more proof that there had been very little aesthetic consideration to my location and by the looks of things, there was no door. I couldn't see any fused stone anywhere which would signify any recent activity but aside from the tactical concerns of my current position, I was interested in the sheer mechanics of how I'd been placed here. Had I jumped myself here?

Standing up, I risked raising my light a little more and the flame which had been dancing happily in the palm of my hand climbed higher and became more intense. My original assessment of the room wasn't expanded but at least there was more detail for me to make out.

I was stuck, but on the plus side, I assumed I wasn't dead.

With just my light source to keep me company I took stock and wondered if I'd jumped myself here in the attempted escape. If that was the case, where was I but also where were the others? I slid my hand over the surface of the wall and tried to glean any information which could help me. I felt a rocky wall. No magical or mystical insight came and all I was left with was the awful possibility that I somehow jumped myself out of the collapsing shield bubble into a solid piece of stone somewhere. For all I knew, I'd travelled twenty feet from my original point and was just below the surface but I could also have been on the other side of the planet. Add to this the fact that if I was sealed into a block of stone somewhere, I'd be using up the air in here at a rapid rate. In short, I needed to leave.

Stepping away from the wall, I began to concentrate my mind with an image of home, readying to create a bridge and leave wherever I was when there was a tiny fizzing hiss from behind me. Spinning to face the noise, my concentration broken, I located a small stone on the floor. There was nothing else, just a loose piece of rock. Moving my hand closer to it to provide maximum illumination, I recognized the smooth surface just as the fizzing started again. I leapt back and away, shutting off the flame in my palm. It was one of the 'devices' Em had shown me in the vault in Argentina, the ones that open portals to places and didn't react well to magic close by. That meant that wherever I was, I'd been put here by someone rather than me doing it. My immediate situation hadn't changed but in that second of understanding, it certainly felt more perilous.

Whoever had put me in here had also made sure that I couldn't do anything magical to ensure my release. That meant that there had been a prior level of planning as the stone weapons, although not said by Em explicitly, had seemed to be unlikely to be available to any and every one. I still didn't know anything about where the other members of my team were and I had been quickly captured and every part of my strength nullified. Suddenly very perilous.

Sitting in the dark, unable to risk calling any magic to me for fear of the little pebble of doom in here with me, I had to try and rely on my other senses. Nothing at all would be gained if I just let the thoughts of what had most likely happened to everyone else float to the front of my mind. I had to push away the fear for them all. For Em, Mike and even Hairy but most especially Andrea. I just couldn't let the thought of losing her climb any higher.

I reached out and found the nearest wall and began to sweep my hands back and forth across its ragged surface. From there I did the same across the floor but nothing more than rock was forthcoming. Next, I sat in what I could identify as the centre of the room and just listened. To start with, all I was able to pick out was my own pulse and my breathing but as I remained in the same position and just did my best to relax, I thought I could make out the most muffled of sounds coming from off to my right. More than just sound, they had shape and purpose to them. My heart rate jumped in excitement and filled my ears but as I calmed myself again, and shuffled in the direction I thought it was coming from, yes, I could recognize the barest of sounds, tiny and weak but unmistakably there.

Hands to the wall again, this time I could make out the slightest ringing vibration as that sound travelled through the stone to me. Without having a starting point I'd just waved my hands past that tiny signal from beyond but now it was clear to feel. And it was growing.

As each second passed, the vibration grew and grew and grew, bringing with it first a slight buzzing sound which grew to become a more clattering, cracking howl. Reflexively stepping back and away from the growing sensation which was now shaking the floor as well as the walls and no doubt the ceiling of my little cell, I pressed myself as flat as I could to the far wall and kicked the magical pebble towards the vibrations, shielding myself as tiny fragments of stone and dust fell on me from above.

The explosion of stone didn't come. The force coming closer built and built and I was close to making any kind of magical attempt to repel whatever was approaching when, through a splitting, roaring crack, a tiny light spread over me. The stone hadn't blown towards me, instead it had been sucked back towards whatever was moving in. In that hanging fragment of time I was treated to the sheer blandness of the cell I'd been held in. It was just a roughly hewn box, suitable for any number of mundane tasks but created with the minimum of care.

That, though was where any possible relief abruptly stopped and the pebble, which had been buried under a small pile of the debris which had broken free as the wall was breached, proved that whatever was coming was using magic of some kind, and it erupted in a swirling plume of blue/white power. I'd seen the result of one of these things going off once before and recalled the detail that Em had given me about what was going to happen to anything nearby. I tried to call together as much power as possible to create my own Cascade Bridge but there was just no time. The gargantuan pull from what was before me reached out but before it could grasp me, it was quickly wreathed in a bright purple shell, severing the force utterly. The power continued to buck and swirl but it was impotent before what was surrounding it. In a few more seconds, it winked out and the purple shell went with it.

I was still rooted to the spot with the expression of shocked terror on my face when Em walked through the gap she'd created and stood over me. Her face was blankly calm, back to an almost familiar posture of indifference to her power but now her skin was a much deeper shade, closing on the colour of her bodysuit and was akin to polished crystal. Her features moved despite this solidity and her eyes were afire with the blaze of violet flame.

"My Lord. Are you well? It would appear that our captors were unaware that I can control the energies within the defence stones they left with us." Her head was tilted again and her voice was that usual flat enquiry. For her, it would appear to be just another day at the office.

I just hugged her.

One of my team was still alive and she'd just been able to break me out of the deepest hole. That knowledge was such a balm to me, that I wasn't here alone. Her posture was stiff and her skin cold and hard but, as she hugged me back, tightly, the humanity returned to her, softening her as we embraced.

"I thought I'd killed everyone." I'd spoken into the top of her head as we just stood there together, her short hair smelling nondescript yet pleasant. "Where are we? Have you see any of the others?"

She just held me for a further second before easing away slowly and looking up at me. "We are within the boundaries of Bress Tal but I have only been able to locate you. I can feel that the others are still alive but I cannot pinpoint them. It feels that there is something shrouding them in the most part."

They were alive as well. I needed to hug Em again but kept a grip on myself this time. I just nodded but didn't hide the fact I was happy with the information.

"So now we need to go and find them. Just point the way and I can jump us in." Everyone was safe and time was of the essence. Swift action was needed.

"I would suggest a more cautious approach to our comrades," Em replied, her head tilted. "We are unaware of the defences that Mr. Ward has at his disposal and it would be unwise to assume that he hasn't taken steps to stop us taking the easiest possible route in. I would recommend a more low key approach."

I needed to keep my enthusiasm in check. No matter how relieved I was that everyone was still alive, it most certainly didn't mean they were out of danger. I had to stay focused on why we were here and not totally lose sight of the tactical details of what we were trying to do.

"OK fine. Makes sense." I closed my eyes and tried to feel out with my magic and locate where anyone else could be, friend or foe. I hadn't been able to send my mind out beyond the tomb I'd been left in and now, with the walls cracked open, I was still blind to what was going on around me. Em had said that she was able to recognize the fact that everyone else was still alive but that there had been some kind of attempt to shroud them yet there was just a blank space out there to me. I couldn't find anyone, friend or foe. And I swear that I could still hear those same whispered, far off voices, just out at the edges of my senses.

"It looks like you'll have to direct us in. I can't see anything beyond this room. I can't sense anyone."

"Very well my Lord. Please follow me."

Em turned and marched from the ruined cell and into the low light which was beyond. I followed, doing my level best to channel every ninja movie I'd ever seen and make as little sound as possible.

The walkway we were in was made of the same stone as the cell but there appeared to have been a great deal of architectural care used when this space was created. It may have been the same pale stone but here the walls were covered in the most exquisitely carved reliefs of all kinds of animals and plants. As we moved quickly, lifelike figurine after lifelike figurine passed us by, their dead gazes seeming to follow us, silently regarding these two interlopers. All I could think about was my experience with the Wraiths in my own mansion, peeling themselves from the walls to attack in any and all ways they could. Shadows coming to life was one thing but stone creatures, and a hallway full of them like the thing in the vault in Argentina, that wouldn't be good at all. I closed the gap with Em just in case.

Hallway after hallway sped by as we moved through the underground fortress. The further we went, the less well preserved the decoration became. What had started out as opulent design had still been in place to begin with but it had been worn down by the effects of time or possibly the touch of a million hands, each taking a miniscule piece with them. From there, any proof of previous civilization drained away and the areas we travelled through became more akin to the naturally formed underground spaces, haphazardly fitting into the spaces left by the living rock itself. Em made no attempt to slow her pace as she went though. At each junction she just marched in her chosen direction without even the barest hint of hesitation. Her power was flowing through her suit as she lithely moved, spilling out a violet light as the passageways darkened so it was clear to see that she was pulling on the magic she had within her to be able to find the way.

"How are we doing?" I asked quietly, wanting to know if we were at least getting close to where we needed to be.

"We are closing in on the location where I can feel the echo of the people we came with," was her rather perfunctory response. It was also very loud.

Looking around me like some kind of frightened animal, searching for the predator, I shushed her before asking, "Shouldn't we be doing our best to stay out of site or sound of the enemy?"

She stopped and looked over her shoulder.

"We are within the libraries of Bress Tal, or what once were the libraries. I know where we're going and have been constantly checking for the approach of anyone as we've moved. As yet, there has been no sign of any person or creature at any point. We are alone."

"Alone?" We couldn't be alone here really, could we? "Are you sure? There must be people here with Leatherpants." She considered what I'd said before saying, "Didn't you yourself say that he was far from the world shaking monster everyone else was thinking of him? Besides, he has an entire race of people acting on his every whim. He's got more than enough resources to be able to do what he's done up to now. How do you think you were placed in the cell in the wall?"

I started to reply but stopped short. It was all true. Now Em was beginning to use logic to be able to work through the details ahead of her. I did consider just becoming my Dragon right there, if

Leatherpants was on his own, but even I could see that it would still be wiser to keep that particular card close to my chest. He would still be under the impression that the fragment of the Drake Stone he'd given each of us was still in place.

Nothing more was said as we resumed our trek.

As we travelled, I was continuously doing my best to reach out and 'feel' what was going on around me, to recognize any fragment of the people who were down here in the way that Em was able but there was just nothing for me. In every direction there was nothing. As we made our way through what were now incredibly damaged pathways, the spaces long since having foregone the description of rooms, my rational mind was just letting me know that trouble was getting closer.

Picking our way around fallen rock, Em held up a hand in warning and we both stopped and eased our way back against the stone walls as best we could. Ahead of us, where the floor had been once, was now a gaping chasm. Em edged up to the rock edge and her suit glowed again, casting more light around us. The rock walls glowed back, ever so dimly but uniformly across the whole space, bringing a detail to everything beyond us.

Across its vast distance, the far side of the space was so far away as to be almost out of sight. Below and above us continued the theme of a raw emptiness. There was just an enormity to what had taken place here, so far beyond anything which I'd seen before, and I could just recognize from everything here, this vast nothing had been created by something other than simply the greedy hands of time.

"What is it? Can you see them?" I couldn't make out anything specific but the area I could see was such a tiny fragment of the whole as to be insignificant. The same voices were still just out there at the back of my mind and gave an even eerier feel to the place. Em blew out a breath and just shuddered.

"I would have thought that after all these years, these thousands of years, the stain would have faded." She was just looking around the void and her voice had softened as she spoke.

"Stain? What do you mean?"

"Bress Tal was overrun. These libraries of wonder were at the most great risk and the creatures of The Hive were storming every part of this beautiful city". There was an almost wistful quality to her words before she turned to me and spoke with more force. "These streets were filled with happiness once, calm and at peace. We used to play here as children, here where there used to be a fountain which was always so achingly, wonderfully, clear." Em waved an arm out at a space just beyond the edge of the chasm and a tear fell to the floor.

She was remembering being here. Not the passed on memories of former Messengers, she'd actually been here when the place fell. There wasn't any magic to the knowledge, I could just see it in her that she was in pain.

I went to her side and lightly placed my hand on her shoulder. What was she saying?

"Em. Were you here when it was attacked? Did you see the city fall or are you calling on some kind of shared memory?"

She sighed and put that thought away, the memory of huge pain, back into whatever locked place it had just come from.

"This once great city was destroyed in such an awful way, and yes, I was here to see it. When it had become clear that we had lost the city, that the operation to remove our artifacts of wonder, of healing and of power, was not going to be enough to save everything, it was decided by The Mage that not only would we flee the city, but we would destroy it utterly as the enemy swarmed in on it." The tear that had fallen had been a part of the sadness of her previous memory but now she was recalling something for which she had equal parts pride and shame.

"As so many of those Hive monsters flooded through the streets, it was decided to detonate one of the Infernura Rods, a much larger version of those little stones, to prevent them taking any more than they already had. As you can see here, the blast radius on that device is monstrous," she casually waved her hand at the space behind her, "and it was left to me to detonate it, even knowing that there were still thousands of people within the danger area."

"That must have been awful for you. You were ordered to destroy everything, but remember, you were ordered to do it. For the greater good. What would have happened if The Hive had taken all of what was left?" It was all I could think to say. Try to absolve her of all of the horror she could feel. Her back straightened and I could sense the resolution in her.

"I was ordered to do such a thing because we had to safeguard the whole population of this world but having to stand in the centre of my home city as the eruption blossomed, having to watch so many people be ripped to the place outside, to Yondah. I watched this city be immolated from a point inside the fire. I stood safe and watched as everything around me was cast away, in the name of the greater good."

"From inside? You were in the centre of the blast?" It must have been all she could do to keep her mind in one piece after seeing that. But how did she manage it?

"You've never spoken of any kind of detail in your past before. Why now? Why tell me now?"

Em took one final sweeping view of the wreckage which had been her home before turning back to me and slowly undoing her suit. There was no allure to her actions, she was being purely mechanical. Her movements were almost awkward as she eased the suit over her shoulders to reveal her upper chest.

"This is how." Again, purely mechanical.

In the centre of her chest, framed by puckered and scarred flesh, was an irregular chunk of purple crystal. It was a part of The Drake Stone. A massive part. Its surface was scratched and pitted and the power which emanated from it was just infusing her skin, glowing and pulsing with that otherworldly light.

"I am The Circle. I have the power of every Guardian within The Circle at my disposal. That is how I was able to defeat you so easily when we first met." My jaw throbbed dully at that memory. "This stone fragment was refined specifically to serve as a way for The Mage to extend his reach to defend against The Hive. I have never spoken of it before because I have not had the memory of it prior to this point. It is only now, that Mr. Ward is manipulating the powers so very close to me, that he does so with the body of The Drake Stone instead of a tiny piece, that those memories are returning to me." She stopped for a breath, as if preparing herself once again for a further revelation of horror.

"With this much of the Drake Stone within me, I have been happily impervious to the effects Mr. Ward has been employing to twist us all to his will, yet another reason that knowledge of this fact was so jealously guarded." She must have been able to sense my emotion at the way she was being so matter of fact with this.

"In the beginning, the Mage decreed that those memories should be taken from The Messenger for fear that should they be captured, a vital part of who we all are would fall into the hands of the enemy. The Drake Stone had been in Bress Tal for generations before the Hive attack which caused the city to fall and none of the previous Messengers knew anything of the way they were granted their power because the memories just weren't there. If the one person with the stone doesn't know it, it is that much safer."

She finished her explanation and re-clothed herself, all the while locking eyes with me.

What the hell do you say after that? She'd done an almost unspeakable evil in the name of good and had had her mind 'adjusted' so she wouldn't be burdened by it. What could anyone say after that?

I stuttered limply, just so utterly lost to what was being revealed. Em held my eyes with no hint of anything other than the simplest thoughts on our mission in her mind. She was just trusting that everything that had happened, the destruction and then the taking of it from her mind, had been the correct thing to do. There just wasn't a right response.

"The stain I spoke of is the shadow of all of the lives which were burned away here when I detonated that device. All of the life force which was taken from this world has been burned onto this plain of reality, like the sun does to your eyes when you look directly at it. I can still feel all of them."

My follow up question was lost even before I asked it. Was that the reason that my own sense had been so diminished since we arrived here, the static of a thousand deaths?

Em continued,

"But now we don't have the time to be able to dwell on the past. Our arrival here has been discovered so we now need to move quickly." She was now privy to more memories and they were all weighing on her.

"The power here is alive because of the presence of The Drake Stone. That stone is so strong that it's charging the echoes of everything here but to do that safely, Mr. Ward must have found or already had possession of an object The Mage created when he first studied the stone."

"Great. Something else that's going to kill us?"

"No. It was the suspension matrix that The Mage built to be able to allow others to manipulate the power of the stone. He controlled the stone's energy so others could study without the fear of death. As Guardian, you should have some kind of memory of either it or its image."

Half closing my eyes, I pulled up the memory landscape of my shared heritage. From next to me, Em explained the basics of what I was looking for and quickly, a single image roared to the front of my mind. It was an ancient parchment drawing, one which was being laid out on an old wooden table. It was there for the barest of instances and then gone, but, as I slowly rewound the image, the detail became clear.

It was made of a dark stone, arranged in tight rings around the Drake Stone, forming something which looked oddly like a birdcage. On each of the stone pieces were carved shapes, glyphs and runes. Some I recognized from the rocky cavern below Neath Abbey, glyphs of power from the Dragon guardians, but most of them were new to me. As it sat before my mind's eye, I considered the awesome power this thing must have been able to manipulate and why there was just a single picture of it for me to find. Why had my line seen anything to do with it only the once through all of the ages?

"Do you have it?" Em was still all business, her question planting me back on the correct course. I'd have to ask about my own memories at a later date.

"I think so. Looks like a stone birdcage with symbols all over it." Not quite as impressive when I described it.

Em slid next to me and spoke softly into my ear.

"That matrix will be able to aim the power of the stone but also give the user the power to manipulate it fully. By moving the bands to different positions, different combinations, that stone will be able to do almost anything."

"How did he get his hands on it in the first place? Surely anything with that kind of ability would be a vital tool to have around? Unless the Mage brought The Drake Stone himself, surely that cage would have been needed to get the stone out of Bress Tal?"

She sighed.

"It was held in the vault in Argentina, along with The Drake Stone, should it ever be needed. I would assume that it was stolen to allow Mr. Ward to remove the stone."

Well at least that answered that question.

Shaking the image away I looked at her, hoping she would be able to give me more information. Instead, she was looking far from military as she stared at me, her lips parted slightly and her eyes smouldering. I swear the air around us grew thicker as we just stared into each other's eyes.

Thankfully, we were dragged back to reality. Away beyond where we could see, but close enough that there was no mistaking what it was, a harrowed scream sliced through the dusty air. But there was more than just the sound. What came with it, riding the waves of steel sharp noise, was a concussive blast of agony. It landed hard on Em and I and despite the numbing of my magical senses, I could feel the depth of utter anguish that was travelling with it.

It was Maria screaming out in utter desolation. Leatherpants had opened the stasis shell she'd been held in. That could only mean that he was preparing to commence whatever casting he'd been planning. Em and I just bolted.

We followed that beastly sound and all of our thoughts of subtlety and stealth were forgotten. I didn't dare become my Dragon for fear of showing Leatherpants that we'd removed his little control too early. Instead, as I ran, I created an image of Maria in my head, sat between the two halves of an opened Easter egg, giving myself all the anchor points I'd need to Bridge jump to her. The Cascade flickered into being before both of us and we sprinted through without the barest hint of concern as to where we may be ending up.

Em had her sword in her hand and her Drake Stone powered suit was pulsing wildly with violet fire. I carried living flame in both of my hands.

That little girl wasn't going to suffer anymore.

33

We burst through the event horizon of the bridge and immediately recognised that that scream was far from being the only thing wrong. The Cascade Bridge, a construct which had been the mainstay of our transportation as a group was usually nothing more than a doorway but now, due probably to the close proximity of the magics that were being set free, it had taken on a more sinister and grasping quality. The forces within that ring had started to bleed from the construct and those fingers of power greedily tugged at us as we passed through, as if wanting to hold us to them. I could feel a far greater resistance from the energies, as if there was now a thick film over the entryway which needed to be pushed through and split to allow passage. Happily, the sound of pain carried from Maria had created enough urgency in us that we didn't give the Cascade the chance to take a firm hold on us. If we'd been walking through, well, we hadn't.

Pushing the oddity of the bridge from my mind we scanned every direction we could, doing our best to take in all of the detail of where we'd arrived. We came to a skidding stop and did our best to correct the plans we'd deviated from as soon as we'd heard the scream from Maria. Wave after wave of nauseating energy flooded over us in the same way it had back in the mansion in Wales, stunning us both into inaction.

We were stood at the centre of what was vaguely a clearing in all of the rough debris in the ruin. On all sides were huge mounds of mighty stone, all well over thirty feet high. And practically mounted on four of those mighty stones, akin to a line of macabre trophies, were Andrea, Mike, Mark and Hairy. They had all been stretched to the farthest reaches of their limbs before their hands and feet had been set into the stone itself, pinning them without the slightest hope of creating any kind of leverage, all their heads lolling forward in unconsciousness.

I just roared at the site before me. My inner demon gave vent to the immediate brutality which rose from a stirring in my chest and had there been even the slightest chance of Leatherpants not seeing us then that was gone amidst the growling call.

A serpentine cackle slithered through the air from our right and above us, daring us to turn to face it. I obliged with as much venom in my eyes as I dared, still holding tightly to the lead on my Dragon.

On top of that rock stood Leatherpants, carrying the now familiar expression of assured superiority and utter displeasure, looking down his nose at us. He radiated that usual arrogance and contempt for people he saw as being less than he was but now, a hungry malice was burning behind his eyes. His skin suit was still in place, despite everything, but now its previous immaculate precision looked to have been marred. By the attention of the Tayne which had attacked him? Where once there'd been defined lines of tailoring, now it looked as if every thought of care had been long since forgotten. Ragged flaps of suit skin stuck out, not torn but grotesquely misshapen and warped and there was a dullness to it where there had previously been an imperious sheen. He moved languidly but not because he was disinterested, more that he was content to be sat at the very height of readiness and so was murderously familiar with the sensation.

Maria was next to him.

She couldn't provide any risk of either escape or attack but Leatherpants had had her hands and feet sunken into the rock itself, just as he had the others, anchoring her solidly to the side of a boulder. Fragments of the magical shell which had been encasing her were strewn at her feet.

But despite that, she heaved against her bonds and screamed. Every possible human degradation seemed to be pouring from her as her previously ruined body was now warping and pulsing as all of the magic inside her now looked as if it was on the verge of breaking free. Set next to Leatherpants' other hand, mounted within that stone ringed cage, was what was left of The Drake Stone. It had had chunks taken from it at random points across its surface leaving behind scars and gaping wounds, revealing the brighter power within. The previous version I'd seen had been the construction Em had created from the surface of the table in my estate in Wales but what was here was far from the smooth beauty it had been depicted as. It had been corrupted for the cause of that grinning maniac. And he just didn't have the slightest care.

"Mr. Johns, Lady Messenger. How wonderful that you've arrived, just as the Bridging will be commencing. Almost like a marriage, this sacred process really does need witnesses. I hope what I've done to the Cascades didn't disrupt your trip too much." Leatherpants rested one hand on the head of Maria, causing her screaming to drop slightly, all the while stroking idly at her hair as his razor voice taunted us. With an effortless flick of his hand all of her screaming vanished. She was still roaring against the same terror as before, but now, through whatever he'd done, the sound was just gone.

My mind was swimming before the energy coming from Maria but I needed to hold my rational thought process in place. He'd proudly admitted that, even before we'd arrived, he'd done something to our powers. The virtual sickness in the construct we'd used to cross great distances. Somehow, the Cascade Bridge was under his control. I felt sick and as if the floor was swelling under my feet. Em was the same and her glowing energy sword had faded, the hilt now dropped to the ground and she swayed under the assault from Maria. She was still standing though. Trying hard to make it look as if I was just taking in the details of the area we were in I risked the question to Em.

"You OK?" She nodded curtly and swallowed against the discomfort.

Leatherpants noticed the discomfort from both of us immediately.

"Just another problem that The Circle has been doing their best to conceal for all these years. You can't control the power that you're wielding can you? Not really. You taunt the energy and do your best to make it do your bidding but, you stole it from those who were due it. That's why there's always such a dire need to affect a timely transfer if one of the mighty should fall." That over wide smile of his was pulling even tighter and there seemed to be a cracking at the edges of his mouth. The wound I'd seen on his face when he'd been surrounded by the Tayne in Mexico was still there but it showed nothing more than leathery darkness under his human skin. No blood that I could make out, more akin to a tear in his mask.

He caught me looking so I pushed the point.

"Not looking that good up there Leatherpants. Skin doesn't seem to be holding up that well after all these years. It doesn't mean you're not a real man if you moisturize you know?" My mind continued to roll over the tides of power coming from Maria, forcing me to throw all of my concentration into keeping myself together, my rage being chipped away. In response his smile seemed to widen even further, cruelty and hatred showing clearly now.

"Just let everyone go and then you and I can try and work out our differences." I smiled as sarcastically as I could manage, spreading my arms widely. I had to push his buttons to get him to move from his planned route and it did seem that I'd been more than able to wind him up, even when I hadn't been trying.

His eyes narrowed.

"Come on. That's the point isn't it? You think you're better than me and just hate that I've got all the best toys. Don't you want to prove that? Just have a crack at the weakest Guardian who managed to defeat the big monster despite not being worthy?" He licked at his cracked lips and his jaw clenched reflexively. I was having an effect.

"You are very perceptive, dog. I would very much like to show you what can truly be accomplished if you actually know what's happening around you but I feel that there are others who would like to speak with you first." He reached up to his jacket and caressed the crystal there at his lapel, and breathed out a chant of some kind. Immediately, from far above us, there was a distant crack followed eventually by a huge chunk of stone crashing to the ground less than a hundred metres from us. The next sound began as something small but quickly grew as more and more voices added to the first. A mass of the Tayne which had been in the valley were now pouring through a hole in the cavern roof and were spilling down to us here. Every possible shape of the creatures descended, calling and baying as they came, summoned by Leatherpants and his little mind control crystal.

They all settled into a circling cone of living matter directly overhead, circling us in a perfectly ordered holding pattern, just waiting on the word from Leatherpants to attack. Looking up at the primed army of horror, I could see expression after expression of pained hatred. Every Tayne which passed by overhead knew what they were doing. They were all acting as puppets rather than under their own control. Checking on as many of them as I could, again and again I saw them seething with anger towards not Em and I, but Leatherpants for making them do yet another task when all they wanted to do was go home.

They were going to attack me but they were in practically the same position as Maria. Each and every one of them was doing something they didn't want to and were being dragged through agony by another.

I could feel the fire building in the pit of my stomach. Blazing rage was kindled and growing.

Leatherpants' voice pierced the gloom and brought the fight into focus.

"My dear clown. The Circle is dying and I will be that which is left when it finally withers from the branch. I will be a worthy owner of that power." He was smiling again but his sharp teeth were bared and he salivated almost uncontrollably.

He absent mindedly stroked the jewel on his jacket as he said, "I will enjoy the show of you being ruined at the hands of these weak things." His smirk continued to show his madness. But it also showed something else. He didn't know that I'd removed the piece of the Drake Stone from my neck. He thought he was going to be able to control me to inaction as he brought the Tayne down on me.

"Mr. Ward," started Em, her face grey under the strain of the waves of power in the cavern. "Please stop what you are doing. You've seen what The Circle stands against. You've seen the war we're all fighting. Please let us continue to keep the world safe." Her voice had lost some of its edge but she was still a commanding presence. Leatherpants' eyes widened at her pleading.

"War? What war? All The Circle have ever done is conquer. A stolen power and a violent desire to hold control." He paused before adding, "I think you should see what it means for you to be at the position on the food chain you truly inhabit as a species."

He whispered a single phrase under his breath and all of the Tayne just stopped their circling, and hovered above us, each distorted set of eyes trained solely on Em and I. His fingers stroked lazily at that crystal pin on his lapel, an almost unconscious act to soothe and placate.

"I hold the power to control the Cascade, to control all of The Circle, in my hand. I control everything you could possibly be able to bring to bear on me." His tone crackled with a hideous confidence, unafraid of anything. "Now, these little things," he gestured to the Tayne, "should show exactly why you should be afraid of me." His eyes bulged with anticipation and more gobs of saliva fell from his withering face, spattering the floor at his feet.

"I have the ultimate power to be able to make a race do my bidding. They can't not, even if they so very badly desire to resist me." The Tayne just flapped above us and all eyes bored down.

There was nothing else for it. He was going to bring them all down on us and unless we were ready for the attack there was going to be no saving anyone. I couldn't risk it. Whispering as loudly as I could, I asked Em, "If I take the Tayne, can you handle Leatherpants? Get The Drake Stone out of that frame? I'll make as much mayhem as I can and keep the Tayne away from him so he can't kick start his Bridging but you need to give that asshole the beating he so richly deserves."

Em just nodded quickly once. I didn't wait for anything further.

My fire blossomed in my head and in seconds, the giant red Guardian of The Circle stood on the field of play. I blasted out a contemptuous shot of smoke from my nostrils and just waited for Leatherpants to acknowledge what he was up against.

Leatherpants didn't even react. The Tayne though showed clearly that they were aware of what was before them. Not a single one moved but it was painfully clear to see that they could all recognize that they were about to come into direct contact with a most dangerous foe and they'd all much rather just turn and head back to Mexico. But they couldn't. Despite that screaming terror, each and every one of them was locked onto the task at hand at the control of someone they'd been betrayed by.

These were potential allies.

"TAYNE WARRIORS," I roared into the cavern. "I know you act at the will of this creature here." I thrust out an accusing finger at Leatherpants just in case. "I will defend myself against attack but I will also be trying to free you." Their wings were still beating but there was still no other sound from them.

"I have promised your Queen that I will return you to her but I will need your help to do this. When you are able, tell me where the piece of crystal is on your body and I'll do the best I can to free you from his spell."

There was no further warning but Leatherpants must have just realized that I'd given the Tayne a vital piece to the puzzle of their freedom. As one, the Tayne just fell from the sky and began to crash down onto me with huge force. Reflexively, I threw my arms up to shield my face and then spread my wings as much as I could to spread that protection as wide as I could. At my feet, Em roared out her own scream of defiance and sensibly dived away from me, doing her best to escape the column of falling bodies as she brought together her own energy into that magical shell of hers and she vanished from site.

With as much force as I could muster, I heaved my tail through the rapidly growing, seething pile of flesh at my feet and scattered the bulk of the Tayne in a wide arc away from me. Hundreds of bodies were lifted away but they were soon replaced as more and more Tayne fell limply from the sky, almost as if their strings had been cut. Roaring all of the time, making it impossible for Leatherpants to look away for fear of missing my collapse, I brought my tail back through the pile of bodies and began to kick and swipe at the Tayne, doing my best to simply keep them away from me. Avoiding being buried by the weight of numbers was my first priority as images of the 'sea' which had been above the ground came to mind.

Back and forth I slapped my limbs, shoveling away truckloads of the creatures in each movement but, even after mere seconds, I was already up to my knees in the lifeless bodies. I needed to get out from under the flow before I was buried.

Dropping down onto all fours, I hurled myself forward, bursting through the meat torrent and, still holding my wings in as much of a shroud as I could manage I sailed away from the initial point of attack, again, still roaring. Opening my eyes, which I must have closed on sheer reflex, I had to take in as many details of what was taking place as I could as I was not only expecting the falling Tayne to follow me but I knew I had to give Em the best chance to play her part.

I'd been turned round in my efforts to defend myself from the Tayne and instead of finding myself soaring over the fallen rock which had been ahead of us, I instead watched in shock as the platform which Leatherpants had been stood with Maria flew past underneath me. By the look on his face, he hadn't been expecting me to do that either. I considered taking a swat at him with my tail as I passed overhead but he was still standing practically on top of Maria. There was no way I could risk hitting her. Instead, I just sailed over them and unfurled my wings to their full span and glided away, banking around to my right to circle back towards where I'd just come from. I wondered if Em was OK.

As I turned back to the fight, the previous cascade of Tayne had ceased. Now, rather than them just falling to the ground to swamp me, they had all started to head after me. Quickly. I hadn't noticed earlier but the giant mutant Tayne that we'd been attacked by in Mexico had been held out of the first assault. I'd been engulfed by hundreds of the smallest and weakest members of the Tayne but now the chase was underway, the bigger, stronger monsters were taking their turn. The first thing for me to do, which was probably going to be the easiest really, was just outrun them. All I had to do was stay ahead of the crowd and hope that Em was going to be able to somehow overpower Leatherpants and free the Drake Stone and then Maria, which she needed Hairy for at the very least. It may have been the easiest thing for me but it wouldn't actually achieve anything in terms of freeing everyone else and saving the world.

Thumping my wings hard I headed further away from Leatherpants, out towards the nearest edge of the blast radius cave which had once been Bress Tal. The Tayne followed behind, fast. There was a deep hooting as they came, feeling akin to the bugle blasts of a fox hunt. Oddly clear that it was me who was the fox. I was red after all. Ahead of me the wall closed rapidly until, with a subtle change of weight, I was banking left and gliding with my belly just feet from the rock. Still, the Tayne followed me in a single column, closing the space between as fast as they're bodies could allow. I needed to get the crystal shards out of them so I could get down to the real business here. Time was running out for Maria because of the power in her but also for all of us thanks to the impending attack from The Elder. No matter which way you looked at it, I didn't have time for this.

Changing tack, I headed up, beating wings hard and lifting myself high up the side of the cavern. As expected, the Tayne adjusted their course to follow. I climbed as hard as I could and hoped what I was planning wasn't just as stupid as it sounded in my head the second time I ran through it. Nearing the roof of the cavern, I folded my wings back into my body and allowed gravity to do the rest.

Falling backwards I was quickly aimed nose to nose with the onrushing creatures. None of them even altered their course. They all just continued to soar straight for me, Leatherpants obviously content to just have them smash into me and bring me out of the air by sheer weight of numbers. I narrowed my eyes as we neared impact and picked out the two Tayne I needed.

When we met, I had my arms outstretched and took a firm hold of two of the Tayne mutants before pulling them in close to my chest as I ploughed through and scattered the cloud of bodies. Opening my mouth as I went, I blasted out as strong a gust of air as I could manage. I knew that fire could only be used as a last resort so instead I wanted to just clear them out of my way. Tayne tumbled and sprawled in all directions and that same hooting filled my ears as I hammered on.

Smashing through to open space I quickly set off in the opposite direction, leading the Tayne back towards Leatherpants but with some minor surgery to perform on my way. Transferring the Tayne in my left hand to instead be gripped tightly in the claws of my right foot, I raised the other close to my face and roared at it, "Where did he put the crystal on you?" Its face showed it knew what I was after though it was raking and clawing at my hand in an attempt to break free, no doubt being pushed by Leatherpants. It mouthed something but with the air whipping past as I flew on as hard as I could manage, it was lost. Pleading for it to try again I held it closer to my ear and this time, despite the wind, the snapping of its jaws and the risen fear in both of us, I could make out a gentle, single word. "Arm."

I manipulated it as carefully as I was able but my need for speed was quickly overtaking the desire to be painless. First one arm, then the other, I searched and watched the reaction of the creatures eyes. Eventually it was clear that it was signaling the inside of its right forearm.

"I'm sorry about this but I'll be as careful as I can."

It screamed. I'd tried to be gentle but I was still aiming to just scoop out a lump of flesh rather than extract the shard. The tip of my claw had been intended to only take the top layer of flesh at most but with all the other distractions going on, I pushed too hard. Thick blood was quick to appear and begin running down the arm of the Tayne. I could feel the syrupy liquid spattering against my chest and stomach as I flew and could only imagine what the other Tayne must have been thinking from its location in my clawed foot.

Then the bucking of the Tayne in my hand stopped. It was still making a noise of some kind but it was still now. Was it bleeding out? Taking as drastic a step as I dared, I blasted a column of fire out to my left and held my claw scalpel out into it, superheating it. It glowed with incandescent light and without any warning to my patient of what was going to happen, I did my best to stop the bleeding by placing the heated claw into the wound I'd just made.

This time it *really* screamed. Its warped eyes widened to the point of bursting as it just roared in agony. But soon it wasn't agony in its eyes. It was weeping, as you'd expect, but it was happiness there now.

"Oh my Lord, thank you, thank you, thank you." It now had a strong, determined voice which was easy to hear. It was free of Leatherpants.

"No problem," I replied needing to get to the next part of the plan.

"Can you do the same thing to your friend back there?" It flexed its arm where I'd done my work and took stock of what it could do.

"I can my Lord," and it just squirmed free of my loosened grip and fell back to my foot, gripping to my leg as it arrived before getting straight to work on its compatriot.

Looking back as it went about its task, the swarming hoard of Tayne still under the control of Leatherpants were now nearly on top of me, their leading numbers slavering at the effort they had been expending to catch up. My first instinct sent me tumbling down to skim along the ground, hoping that the change would at least give me a chance to come up with what I was going to do next. Down they came after me and immediately it became clear that I wasn't going to be able to outrun them but now I didn't have to contend with a fall from great height when they did catch up. The hooting and screaming continued but it was now all around me as the living cloud began to draw ever nearer.

"You done yet?" I roared back to the single Tayne I'd freed. There wasn't any kind of response but when I risked a quick glance in their direction, to my horror, I was in time to see the two of them leap clear of my foot and head straight up as fast as their wings could carry them. They were running. My roar was born of pure frustration but if I made it through all of this, I'm sure I'd be able to understand why they did it. It did, though leave me without the original plan of attack so as I skimmed the ground with the swarming Tayne following almost at touching distance, I knew I needed another way out.

Ahead of me, the clearing Leatherpants had set his little base up within was now being well lit from something inside. A yellow light was pulsing up and out from within the bowl of rock and the closer I got, it was obvious that it was coming from Maria. Shaking my head against the ever thickening mental fog which was all around me, I powered on over the top of the glow and tried my best to take in any of the details, risking dropping as much of my speed as possible.

Leatherpants was still stood next to the prone form of Maria and despite the speed I was travelling at, I could see that he was gloating at me. He gripped tightly onto the framework surrounding the Drake Stone and slid the different bars around like he was manipulating a massive combination lock. Maria was still shackled to the stone and her voice was still being suppressed in some way but her agony was clear. The warm yellow blaze of light was blasting in all directions from that poor child but, even with such a snatched glimpse, I could tell far too easily that there was nothing soft and pleasant about it. The light wasn't just glowing from within Maria, it was pushing through her, forcing against that which was binding it. That light had weight, it had mass. Time seemed to slow to almost a standstill as I passed and every stark detail of the pain being inflicted was burned onto my eyes. It was breaking her.

But it was also breaking the others buried in those stone blocks. Even as I arrowed through the thick air, I could see that Leatherpants was already commencing his own Bridging, despite my running of the Tayne on a little wild goose chase. That yellow glow was coming from Andrea, Mike, Mark and Hairy as well but rather than it pushing against their skin as if it were trying to break free, instead it was being drained from them, being pulled from a place way beyond just the physical, as if their bodies represented a piece of paper between two magnets, just getting in the way to no effect. The freed power swirled and washed throughout the small area, practically relishing the freedom beyond the flesh but it was being drawn towards the caged Drake Stone, no doubt to hold it ready for Leatherpants to affect the transfer.

There was no sign of Em anywhere as I passed overhead.

In a heartbeat, I'd cleared the site and the Tayne were all still following me, giving no suggestion that Leatherpants had changed their focus.

I couldn't maintain this kind of action. I wasn't achieving anything just by running away from all those things that were chasing me. All I was doing was running the clock down which was just going to kill Maria. As I flew, all I could see again was the fact that Leatherpants had planned for just this eventuality. He'd correctly predicted exactly how I'd go about trying to slow him down and had made plans to let me think I was doing something all the while he had something totally different in mind.

The first spindly pressure broke my self-pity as the first Tayne finally reached out and took a grip on my tail. The shock of which caused me to push harder on the speed to get away from what was behind me, purely listening to reflex. As I flew on, I shuffled through as many ideas as I could fit in my head, trying to conjure some clever way of being able to out flank or out think Leatherpants before he could claim the power of a Guardian for himself but nothing was sufficient. Every possible idea I could come up with would no doubt have some kind of elaborate counter move from him which would again leave me defeated. All of the people I'd put in harm's way would be lost. Mike and Mark had followed because that was what they'd been expected to do, Hairy because he was going to become something he'd wanted for years and Andrea ...

Andrea.

I could picture her laying lifelessly on that stone altar of his, all of the life pulled from her leaving nothing but a grey and wizened husk and my mind roared. My Dragon self screamed inside my head and thundered its balled fists against the cage of my mind. In all of this, in everything I'd been doing throughout every action within the Circle, I'd been trying to always keep my beast controlled and not go outside the 'proper' way of behaving. All the time, I'd been trying to resist the urge to just go on instinct for fear of doing something wrong or leaving myself open to some kind of attack. My power was manipulated in the realm of the Tayne so it became a liability. All of the time, that preening fool had been keeping me in his arena.

That realisation made me smile with an almost maniacal glee. Don't over-think. I just had to make a mess of his little spell to start with and then go from there. No people to leech the life power from, no Bridging. I was still going to be doing my best to save every Tayne warrior out here but I knew what chefs the world over said about breaking a few eggs so couldn't get hung up on it. As long as I was mathematically 'up' at the end of the day, we'd call it a win.

I angled myself to my right and banked into a massive arc, swinging my giant Dragon back the direction it had come and casually let my mind relax away from my human self and allowed the beast to come out and play.

"In for a penny ..."

34

The Tayne all followed on after me with that same detached zeal. The single creature which had managed to land on me had climbed up along the ridges on my tail and had seemed to be making a beeline for my wings. On its own it wasn't going to be able to bring me out of the air but that didn't mean that I shouldn't be taking steps to remove it.

As I'd hoped, the cloud of bodies didn't follow the same circuitous turn I made, most of them instead just altering their direction to intercept. My first task was to get passed them.

I was going to just fly straight through them. My massive, armoured bulk would act as the perfect battering ram and I'd be able to minimise the death toll rather than just burning my way through. I was going to tear my way through that swarm and make my way back to Leatherpants and save the day.

When I hit the first of the Tayne, all I could comprehend was the burning need for combat. I was being driven by that fire energy and I was going to make sure that these things were going to feel the fullest force of what a Guardian of The Circle could do at close quarters. The impact of something the size of my Fire Dragon would be bad enough on its own but when the object doing the impacting is also swinging heavy limbs with serrated claws, the likelihood of getting injured climbs rapidly. Tayne bodies exploded away from me like water parting to welcome a diver's entry. The hooting continued in some far off quarters but they had mostly been replaced by a more deep rooted panic at the fight they were all tumbling into against their will.

I kept on pushing on, my wings beating as hard as I could make them, all the while I was snapping and biting at anything which dared get in my way. Inside my head, my Dragon was screaming and roaring in an animal ecstasy as it just tore through any and all flesh that dared to get in its way. My human mind sat casually on the sidelines and watched.

Still moving forwards, the cloud of bodies was showing no sign of being dissipated as more and more of the tiny winged creatures flocked in on me. I was still pushing as much effort into my momentum but I could feel that my wings were getting really heavy, beyond simply being fatigue. Back inside my head, my human mind called out, 'They're going to bring you down in the same way as in Argentina.'

Argentina.

They'd done the exact same thing when they'd attacked in Argentina. I'd overlooked the basic point. The Tayne weren't attacking me, Leatherpants was. I stopped my wings dead and folded them back as best I could. I could recognise the clumped Tayne around my limbs now they were folded away, stopping me moving as fluidly as I would have liked. I couldn't shake the image of being covered in blood-leeching ticks at the sensation but this wouldn't last for much longer.

There was no grace as I fell out of the air but when I hit the dusty rock surface, I tucked my shoulders under my body and risked as huge a forward roll as I could.

Lifting from the floor of the cavern as I bounced from the rock, I did my best to roll hard onto the full expanse of my back rather than just hit on one point, thereby spreading the weight of the collision, but it also gave me the chance to just use gravity to crush those Tayne clinging like limpets to my wings. The crunching sound their bones made, coupled with the shrieking and squelching sounds of the death of those Tayne baited my monster again and my fury flared behind my eyes. Scarlet rose back into my vision and as I came up to my feet, I clawed into the stone floor to anchor myself for any impending attack.

The Tayne didn't hesitate in their response. A handful of the creatures had survived our landing and those who were still able to move began to power through the remains of their companions which were now slowly oozing down my back to spatter in pools and mounds at my feet, all of them aiming at my head. Others which had been lucky enough to avoid the initial engagement began to rise in several tendril bodies in the air, forming together for a combined attack, no doubt guided by their far off controller wanting to solidify their power. I scanned quickly, violently, around me and tried to keep all of them in my eye-line. I was stood on a relatively shallow fissure in the ground, as wide as any major motorway but flanked by more large black stone chunks.

I was calling the shots here. Rather than let the Tayne / Leatherpants dictate how this was going to play out, I was going to go on the offensive. Picking out the best possible option, I settled on the boulder nearest to my right side, one the equivalent size of a normal family car, heaved it from the ground and with as much shot putter power and skill as I could channel, I launched it at the largest of the Tayne clusters which was directly ahead of me. It sailed through the inky atmosphere and the Tayne just held their position and watched it come. It hit the centre of the cloud and passed effortlessly through, the eddying air causing the tendrils constituent parts to scatter. There would have been Tayne bodies caught by that rocky missile but the tendril was forming again in exactly the same place. I swear it was tilting its head in the same way Em did when she was trying to work out the nuance of something.

Roaring again, I wrenched another massive lump of stone free and took aim at a different target, this time the tendril on my left hand side. As I framed my intended victim and prepared to launch my missile, that ever present hooting sound which the Tayne had been making since the very start of this chase began to grow in both volume and location.

I stood at the ready with my boulder weapon and did my best to understand what was taking place around me. Where was the extra sound coming from? Was it just a trick of the cavern that made sound echo oddly? I swiveled around three hundred and sixty degrees as I scanned and checked for any kind of sign that something else was about to attack me and it was with a sinking heart that my eyes finally settled on a point back towards where Leatherpants was still working his magic.

High up, above the rough terrain of the cavern floor but moving closer at incredible speed, was another vast cloud of Tayne warriors, hooting and screeching as they came. There was a brief second that not even my animal mind couldn't quiet comprehend what was taking place. Where had these Tayne come from? I'd thought that all of the Tayne had come through the roof of the cavern at the call of

Leatherpants. It hadn't even occurred to me that I was fighting against a fraction of the total force rather than the whole.

I just stood and watched, rock still hefted and ready for action, as a mass of Tayne several magnitudes larger than the one I was currently facing off against spread out to fully fill my eye line.

As the distance closed in a dizzying clutch of breaths, I let my monster do the talking. I expelled two volleys of flame from my nostrils and unleashed my rock in the direction of the newcomers. It whirled gracefully through the air but this time all of the Tayne were fast to evade it, swooping left, right and up to leave a perfect void for the stone to pass through harmlessly before it crashed apart on the cavern floor. The Tayne just kept on coming. Starting to panic, I took hold of another stone and loosed it at them but despite the one I'd chosen being greatly smaller than the first two, the extra speed had no effect on the Tayne. They again just shifted from the path and carried on.

I was out of options. I couldn't use a Cascade Bridge and just jump back to Leatherpants and the others, but even if I had, the Tayne would just follow me back there and I wouldn't be able to do any kind of fighting there if I was continuously having to run away before coming back. Leatherpants would just surround himself with a wall of the Tayne and I'd be stuck again. I'd have to truly fight fire with fire, regardless of the number of Tayne I destroyed.

Digging my claws deeply into the stone below me I lifted my arms into as much of a ready stance as I could muster. Roaring and snapping at the Tayne all around me, I lanced out a jet of flame at the first tendril I'd been faced by, rapidly followed by blast after blast at the others tendrils and then towards the onrushing horror. Readying myself for the impact and violence, I bellowed out my defiance as the new wave of Tayne closed for the kill.

But they missed.

Rather than just swamp me with their vastly superior numbers, they just peeled past me or shot overhead and began ripping into the tendrils of Tayne warriors instead. The violence which erupted everywhere was startling because of the sheer surprise value it had come with. Hoots became chittering screams, clicking and clacking as Tayne fought Tayne around me, all thought of attacking me gone. Em must have beaten Leatherpants down and taken control of The

Drake Stone, compelling the Tayne to come to my rescue. Blowing out a mightily relieved breath, I just stood and watched in awe as the now Em commanded Tayne struck a ruinous blow against their Leatherpants controlled kin.

But wouldn't that mean that Em would be in control of these Tayne as well so wouldn't need to send anyone to rescue me?

Perfectly timed as the panic filled my chest, the Tayne I'd performed that surgery on earlier swooped down before me, landing clumsily before prostrating itself at my feet.

"My most powerful Lord, rescuer of the Tayne race, please forgive my retreat. I explained what had happened to us all to the one you sent me to free as you did me and we thought that freeing the rest of our clan would give you more value than just our freedoms. Please forgive me mighty one." Its voice had started as a purposeful call but as it finished speaking, it had become much more reedy and pleading. It had given amazing help to me and having seen how all thought of warfare practically brought them all to a standstill, the actions of bringing a Tayne army to my aid was bravery far in excess of any I'd been able to see up to this point. I couldn't, wouldn't, let that fact go unnoticed.

With as much pomp as I could drag together, I responded.

"I thank you greatly for what you've been able to do here. I thank you and so does The Circle as a whole."

It lifted its eyes from the floor and seemed to consider what I'd just said. The slightest crease settled in on its misshapen forehead but I just didn't have the time to ease it through the strange lands it was traversing, trying to work out if I was truly thanking it.

"What is your name please? I will not forget what you have done for me today." Again, make it sound authoritative.

"I am Greyas, Handmaiden to my Lady Queen." The voice came immediately, almost relieved to be in the familiar position of dealing with someone thought of as a better. Greyas bobbed her head in as formal a gesture as she was able but her swollen frame was moving in ways that she just wasn't familiar with. Since she'd been warped by Leatherpants, she'd almost completely lost herself.

"Thank you Greyas, but I must now move to end the one who did this to your people." She bowed shockingly deeply again before, with much more grace than I would have thought possible from that mutilated frame, and she took to the air and headed back into the fight which was still raging all around us.

There was no way I was going to risk the flight back to where everyone was, I just couldn't risk that I'd be too late. Instead, I concentrated on the picture of all of the people in that central hub of power, back where Maria and all of the others so desperately needed me, and brought a Cascade Bridge into existence directly ahead of me. I just had to take the risk and step across the path through Yondah. Rolling my shoulders and readying myself for the worst possible conflict, I snorted and charged through as fast as I could move my giant frame.

I'd felt the nausea of the energies in the place when the bridge had opened but as I passed through the gateway, I was almost driven to the floor by the diseased energy which was swirling in all directions, whipping and bucking against any and all attempts to cage it. My senses filled with an enveloping pressure that dulled everything, leaving me to struggle to even identify where I was jumping myself. The sticky, cloying mass within the Cascade seemed to adhere to every square inch of my body and for a terrifying second, I thought that I'd been held solidly in place. Happily, the grip from within the ring of power faltered and I was able to escape back to the cavern.

Ahead of me stood the rocky platform that Leatherpants had set up what was going to be his seat of new power, still with him frantically wrenching at the casing frame around the Drake Stone. Its runes and symbols pulsed with an oddly cadenced beat, as if showing that whatever he was doing was only partially correct and more subtle than I'd first considered, but that he was getting closer. The yellow light was growing in intensity as more and more power was drawn from all those around Leatherpants and the Drake Stone was beginning to pulse with newly reclaimed life.

There was no sign anywhere of Em but Maria was still next to him. Her tiny body was splitting and breaking away but I could see that now the very edges of her where starting to dissolve slowly, as if burning away to dust, drifting through the air. The power within her was destroying the vessel that wasn't prepared to hold it. She wouldn't be able to hold on much longer.

Leatherpants' eyes were wild with mania as he manipulated that cage device. Different segments of the runes and glyphs were scorching with life as he moved and moved the blocks within the arms of the cage. Maria reacted to some of the actions, bucking and writhing at some and sagging at others, while I could feel the not so subtle alterations in the atmosphere as he went about his business. I roared and spat fire at him on pure reflex. Considering that Maria was still trapped next to him, the flame splashing against whatever kind of energy barrier he brought up in defence was a huge relief. He didn't take his eyes away from the Drake Stone despite my arrival. He was utterly engrossed with the thought of taking that Dragon energy.

Maria was still coming apart under the weight of the power in her but now I could see that all of the others were in just as much danger. The energies were still being dragged from them but now the effect of that theft was written deeply on all of them. All of their features were wizened and sallow, their skin hanging limply on what was being left behind. Every ounce of magical power was being taken from the four people who'd come on this mission with me, hollowing them out for the brutal insanity of Leatherpants' jealousy.

My Dragon took over and I just threw myself headlong at Leatherpants. There was no finesse in my thinking, just the desire to be the righteous deliverer of retribution for what he'd done to all of us. The shield of energy he'd raised ahead of him stood firm as I slammed into it. Sizzling fingers of energy danced across the shield in response, bathing Leatherpants in a flickering blast of light. That did make him look up. He took in the detail of the Dragon trying to break its way to him with a detached air, as if he were just lifting his eyes from his labour for a break. That indifference added more fuel to my fire and I rained down blow after blow on the barrier, roaring and growling for all I was worth.

"Ah, the animal returns." He turned back to the caged Drake Stone and resumed his dextrous manipulations. "Keep on banging if you wish but you aren't strong enough to break through. It's the same as that which surrounds the prisons you seem so obsessed with defending, with just a tiny addition from me. No Dragon will make it through." I didn't care and just unloaded my aggression on that wall but, despite every effort, it remained in place and resolutely powerful. Leatherpants lifted an eyebrow when I finally admitted defeat and took a step backwards to reassess my plans, all the while breathing deeply.

"I told you, you mindless beast." His words were like rods of steel being slowly inserted under my giant claws. "No Dragon will be able to cross the shield."

Had he just given away a secret? No Dragon was going to be able to cross the threshold he'd brought up but did that mean something other than a Dragon would? I looked around the area I was stood in until I settled on to what I was looking for, balled up my fists and began to batter away at the nearest edge of the huge boulder opposite where Leatherpants was. After several impacts, a section of stone as big as my head was cracked away from the rest to land at my feet. In one smooth movement, I'd lifted it from the floor and using every ounce of knowledge I had of the shot putt, I swiveled and launched the stone at Leatherpants. I'd aimed as far away from Maria as I could so if this did work, it at least would only hit that grinning loon.

The massive rock tumbled through the air before hitting the shield hard and splitting in half with an ear shattering clack which made me wince. The shield was still very much in place but the impact had at least caused the ground to shake wildly, jarring Leatherpants and causing the Drake Stone cage to lurch on its platform. It was only thanks to the steadying grip of Leatherpants that the thing didn't topple over but that was as much effect as I had had. My shoulders sagged. I couldn't help it. I was being out-thought and I just couldn't see a way to break the hold Leatherpants had on everything which was going on. Dust and smaller fragments were still raining down, the remains of the previous missile strewn at my feet. I just stalked back and forth amidst the rubble and fumed my anger at my impotence while my enemy was almost within my reach behind his spell cast haven. He could have been on the other side of the planet though and I knew there was nothing for me to be able to do. Looking at Andrea and the others just shone an even brighter light on that awful truth. In sheer frustration I slapped away at the fragments of stone on the cavern floor with my tail, just to show that I could at least affect them. The pieces flew away and crack-crack-cracked on the shield as their big brother had done, but this time, a couple of the larger pieces didn't stop there.

Rebounding from the blockade, they fired away directly at where my four comrades were trapped. I watched them ping through the air and waited for the impact on the shield surrounding my allies. Instead, I was greeted by a startling sight. The rocks drove deeply into the stone above Mike and cracked it perfectly down behind him, breaking him free of his bonds as it did. I hadn't even considered the fact that they wouldn't have been protected and it would appear that Leatherpants hadn't even considered the fact that I might make any kind of attempt to save my friends first before Maria. That said, aside from some very dumb luck, he'd been right.

In an instant, his limp form slumped away from the others embedded in the stone and fell to the ground in an unordered pile of limbs. Coupled to that, a vast segment of the swirling energies in the air were wrenched away from the whole to return to the donor who'd given it up. That power was absorbed back into Mike, akin to him taking in a mighty restorative breath.

The effect on the remaining cloud and on what Leatherpants was trying to accomplish was instant. The runes and sigils of the cage structure which had been glowing as they'd been moved all winked out at once bringing to mind so many eyes all blinking closed at once in fear and disgust at what they were seeing. The Drake Stone flared once before losing the building light back to the ether and Maria's scream lessened by a degree as some of her power was restored to her and the energy cloud was quickly returned to the others as well, inflating them all with returned life.

Leatherpants was driven back in shock at the sudden change from the subject of his attention. He hadn't shown even the barest hint that he was even aware that anything had been happening outside his immediate sphere of attention so the jarring of the power at his fingertips must have been shocking in the extreme. He was fast to regain himself and from behind his wall of energy, which was now crackling through with an energetic ripple, almost warping under an unseen force, his eyes burst alive with a sickening hatred.

"WHAT ARE YOU DOING?" He screamed and screamed out at the one who'd just undone what he saw as being his right. My own anger was still close to the surface but I needed to nudge him over the edge into madness before trying to do anything. I just couldn't risk him having the tactical advantage.

"Sorry shorty. You really do need to ask permission before taking someone else's toys. If something doesn't belong to you, you can't just take it." I needed him to be so consumed with the desire to hurt me that it would at least give me some time to do something. I still wasn't sure what that something was going to be. In response, Leatherpants growled wildly while dragging his hands through his lank red hair, his eyes rolling back in his skull. When he brought his hands away, they held clumps of his hair which he'd not just pulled out, but had uprooted with ragged lumps of flesh still attached. That made me gasp silently. He stood there shaking, every sinew of his body just tensing to almost breaking point, his eyes still turned inwards as the nausea in the air seemed to grow even further. Was Maria approaching meltdown? She was silent now but her body was still breaking and dissolving.

I was about to risk a dive for her and the Drake Stone when Leatherpants snapped his glare back down on me. He'd been an arrogant, power mad arse since I'd met him and there had never once been the suggestion that I'd got that assessment wrong but his eyes showed now that he was something so very much worse. Both of his eyes seemed to have been punctured and had dribbled down the lapels of his suit. In the space they'd inhabited, there now appeared the eyes of something else. Two golden orbs, devoid of pupils of any kind, peered out from that degrading face. In that instant, I knew that I was looking at something very different from what he'd been mere moments ago.

Leatherpants took a purposeful step forwards back to the cage surrounding the Drake Stone, and raised one deliberate hand to brush ever so delicately over the jewel pinned to his lapel.

"Sorry sunbeam," I called out. "I think the Tayne are all but done with you and your mind games. Hadn't noticed that they haven't come to play since I got here?" My own confidence was building at his apparent oversight. His golden eyes, unblinking and somehow serpentine, remained fixed on me as his long fingers left his lapel to instead perform rudimentary moves on the central arm of the cage surrounding the Drake Stone. As he moved, he spoke, and his retort was unexpected.

"Tayne? No Tayne." His voice was altered now, as if something had finally been released. It was much deeper, far more confident and much more venomous. Gone was the small man standing up to claim what he wanted. In its place, his voice was angrily confident, intelligent yet bestial. The fingers worked again and I could see what he'd meant when he dismissed the Tayne as his weapon.

From a point next to him on the rocky platform he'd based himself, one which had been empty a mere second earlier, with a scorching fury ablaze all around and murder etched through every sinew, walked Em.

35

She just flowed forward, passing Leatherpants without a glance, all of her attention focused on me. What was she doing? Why hadn't she just slapped him down when she'd got close instead of now aiming her ire at me? Step by step she continued to move towards the edge of the rocky ledge they were standing on, closing on the shield wall that had been brought up. And without breaking step, she passed through as calmly as if it hadn't existed, before jumping down to the floor of the cavern before me.

That's why she hadn't been able to bring Leatherpants down on her own. That's why I hadn't been able to see her doing anything by way of fighting. Somehow Leatherpants had been able to tap into the chunk of stone in her chest and use the same trick to control her. And she was showing that she was going to tear every inch of me from every other inch of me under the control of a lunatic. Despite the huge size difference between us, I edged back away from her as she slowly, deliberately strode over the pitted floor of the cavern towards me.

"Em. Can you hear me? You don't want to do this, we're on the same side remember?" My giant taloned hands were raised in as clear a gesture of non-conflict as I could muster but there was no response from Em as she just kept coming closer. Her suit was again more of a crystalline whole that being of fabric or even plates of the stuff. Her skin had a subtle purple hue and looked to be as hard as her clothing but in her eyes, where she had once had so much strength but suffused with a naivety, was now pleading dread. She was going to kill me but she was watching on as it was going to happen, locked away inside her own body. Back on the platform behind her, I could see that Leatherpants was back at work with the Drake Stone and that that diffuse yellow glow was rising again.

"Help me my Lord." Her voice was stretched thin and pleading, giving me yet another person who was hurting because of the choices I'd made.

I didn't have time for this.

All I had to do was make certain that I gummed up Leatherpants' spell, everything after that would just have to be a plus at this point. If I could save everyone else, catch the bad guy and make sure I didn't die along the way, I'd love to know what more was expected of me.

Em didn't let me consider my options any further. She just blurred into motion and, even before I'd been able to register that she was going to attack, I'd felt an immediate, crushing grip close on my left leg before I was heaved away from where I'd been stood with a strength far beyond anything I was expecting. Em. She's thrown me relatively flat so there was going to be no way I'd be able to right myself and extend my wings before I hit the ground so I'd have to make do with as comfortable a crash landing as I'd be able to fashion.

My attempt at comfort didn't work. I just skidded through stone outcroppings and towers, all the while trying to keep my fragile wings as tightly clasped to my back as I could. Slamming my right hand at the ground as hard as I could, I was able to pierce the stone surface with my claws and slow my momentum enough to at least get me back on my feet. As quick as I could, I tracked my eyes all over the available landscape and did my best to pinpoint Em as she no doubt closed in on her next attack. Nothing moved. There was no sound for me to lock onto as a cue of her whereabouts and the only thing I could smell was the dusty air which was still billowing all around me. And then there she was. She shimmered into being before me, at the zenith of a running leap, no doubt from within her cloaking bubble of energy, and she had her right fist balled ready to pulverize me when she landed.

I reacted on pure instinct. I'm not a fan of wasps and other buzzing insects, never have been, and I react in the same way whenever I encounter one of them. I bypass rational thought and just start to flail my arms about by way of protection. As such, seeing something much smaller than me suddenly appear on a collision course with my head brought out the old fears and I just struck out with both hands as I tried to protect my face. I managed to swat Em away and she was thrown away from me to land beyond a large mass of fallen rock to my left. She was being controlled by that creature just as we all had but to see her, almost the ultimate innocent in The Circle, was just beyond anything I could allow.

"I'm Sorry Em," I boomed after her. She had to know that I was going to do everything I could to help and that I wasn't trying to kill her. "I'm going to need your help to be able to stop this. Just answer the questions and I'll do the rest." There was no response to start with, the air remaining charged by tension but that tension was quickly cracked as I heard her reply, "I will. Please help me." The sound was moving ahead of me now, showing just how quickly she'd been able to brush off the landing and get moving again, but her voice also showed me something else. As Leatherpants controlled her actions, she was crying.

My monster climbed up behind my eyes and the scarlet which swam across my vision became that of righteous violence. He was hurting yet another innocent. The pictures of Maria and the others, of all of the Tayne and now of Em being corrupted because of one madman stoked the fire of my animal perfectly and fire erupted all over my back, my arms, my wings, everywhere, chasing itself around my body as it spread. I just roared and roared and roared at the utter injustice of what was going on and poured all of my fury and hatred into the flame, the raging inferno surrounding me melting the stone at my feet until I was sunk at least a foot into the molten magma.

I hadn't even registered that Em was even near me before she slammed my jaw with another of her ever so delightful hammer blows. My spinning early warning system was still useless against a foe like Em. My mind blurred as the pain of the impact exploded from the point on my jaw. My knees turned to water and all of the energy being channeled into my display of rage winked out, extinguishing the flame of justice I'd been waving about. I fell hard and slapped into the ground a sprawling mess. I took in a handful of hurried breaths, doing everything I could to keep myself awake and hoped that Em wouldn't just turn and pounce on me in my current position. Blinking my eyes back to focus, I felt sick but needed to get to my feet. The effort that required was almost greater than anything I'd been forced to endure but drunkenly, I brought myself back to my feet, eternally glad for the existence of my tail to aid with my balance.

Em lay on the floor before me and as my mind continued to fight its way back to full power, it was painfully clear to see that the reason I was still breathing was the effect the fire had had on Em. In Wales, on the night we first met, she'd hit me and sent me to the canvass with little to no effort. Here, she'd had to pass through the wreathing flame which had been dancing all over me. She'd still landed an amazing shot but her tiny form was now blistered and scorched by the effort. My knees gave way and I crashed down over her, dreading what had happened.

I spoke as gently as I could to her. "Em. Are you awake? Are you OK?" She opened her eyes from within her seared face and the tears continued to flow.

"I am my Lord. Please forgive me for attacking you. I am trying to fight what is being done to me but I just cannot."

"Shhhh. No apology needed. How is he doing this? You said you were immune to that kind of attack." I did my best to balance between the need to show I cared for her well being and the need for information. She closed her eyes again, squeezing more tears to tumble across her overly pink flesh. She didn't open them again before her arms spasmed wildly. I jumped at the unexpected movement, thinking that she'd just want to remain still but as I took in more detail of Em I could see that, ever so slowly, the skin on her face and hands was starting to heal. The open wounds were steadily retreating, as un-marred skin grew to take its place. She was healing, no doubt thanks to the energies coming from the Drake Stone. Which meant I didn't have long to be able to speak with her.

"Em. How is he controlling you? I need to know how to break you free."

She spasmed again but this time over her whole body.

"I don't know how he did this. The fragment of the stone I carry is big enough to be able to function on its own, separate from the whole. The only way possible to affect this kind of control would be to return it to the whole but that hasn't happened, look for yourself." Her eyes darted downwards at her burned clothing where the stone, pitted and scratched, was clearly visible through a hole.

"That was how he did it," I boomed into the air as Em flailed one arm at my face. All of the time, I kept forgetting that Leatherpants had a very set way of doing things. He relied on the same tactics all of the time. "He didn't need the whole stone, he just needed a sliver. The scratch on the surface of the stone was how he did it. He put that into the body of the Drake Stone and that was enough."

Scrabbling to my feet, I called over my shoulder as I took off and headed back towards the centre of the cavern, "I'm sorry Em. I have to leave you here but I know what needs to be done. I can stop his casting." Em didn't respond but her body kept on twitching and bucking as the link to what Leatherpants had in mind was slowly being repaired. I had a very shaky idea what I could do to stop the spell but there really wasn't any guarantee that it was going to work. Didn't mean I wasn't going to try it.

In seconds I was closing on Leatherpants again and the sight that greeted me was even worse. Mike had been returned to his bondage on the side of the stone but it looked like now, Leatherpants was beyond trying to remove the power from everyone concerned in any way other than the most brutal. The sickness in the air was making my mind wash away but it was coming from everyone now. Each and every person was just screaming against what that monstrosity was doing to them. Each face was being contorted and the agony washed out in all directions as a twisted greed for power went steadily about killing them all. I struggled against the waves of magic detonating all around the cavern and just aimed myself rather than trying to land. What I had in mind didn't need any kind of finesse. Coming down with as much force as I could muster, I brought my hands swinging down like a mighty hammer, and drove then hard into the rock that my friends were locked to. There was no shielding in place despite the tactical risk. Yet again, I'd been quick to think that Leatherpants was almost all-knowing in how he was fighting but in reality he was still sticking with plan A. He didn't have a plan B.

The thunderous crack of the tearing stone filled the whole giant cavern as I demolished the would-be prison for my friends. I'd put safety second as I'd come down on top of them, knowing that all I needed to do was disrupt what was taking place to be able to stop Leatherpants taking his prize. Lancing hot pain ripped through my legs and back as I hit the ground too hard and my hands went immediately numb at the impact with the unforgiving stone before me. I tried to stay on my feet but I just couldn't control my legs with the agony through my thighs so all I could do was try to avoid landing on those people I was trying to save. The rock was blown apart under the weight of my impact and the entire cavern reacted like there had been a minor earthquake, walls shuddering and the floor bucking in waves.

Laying on the ground, I just couldn't move. Sensation below my waist was quickly washing away, I could barely breathe and by the look of my hands, I'd broken all of my fingers as well as most of the bones in my hands. But the shattering crack of stone and what sounded like glass, followed by the scream from behind me was the greatest painkiller.

The point of my less than subtle dive bomb was to cause as much movement in the ground as I could and shake the Drake Stone over. Leatherpants had set the thing on what looked like a ceremonial rostrum but it was less than secure. I'd been able to shake it badly when I'd hit his shielding with the boulder so all I needed to do was be more aggressive with the force I used. I laughed to myself at the thought of that freak missing his chance but my revelry was quickly halted by the needles of pain spreading through my chest, causing me to cough at the dry air. Gathering myself again, I became aware of movement from the platform, then I felt slow footsteps passing across my shoulder and then my chest until Leatherpants, his golden eyes so hate filled as to be overflowing, stood on my chest and just stared down, bringing to mind the image of a hunter posing with his fallen prey. In his hand burned a massive chunk of glowing purple crystal, The Drake Stone. He held it without any protection now as it seared away at the flesh to fill the air with a dank foulness.

"Sorry sweetie," I coughed. "Looks like I'm the fly in your ointment. No Dragon for you today." I closed my eyes mainly out of exhaustion but if it meant I was thumbing my nose at him then so be it. But he just laughed.

"I have Dragon today soon," he spoke coldly, as if he was unsure how to make the words. My eyes opened slowly and I tried my best to judge what he was saying but he just thrust out his hand and Maria just flew through the air to him. He caught her nonchalantly and held up the Drake Stone piece as well. Hunks of charred meat fell from the bones of his hand as the raw energy within the crystal ate away at him. Maria was as good as gone. He face had been wrenched into a permanent howl of anguish and her eyes just stare, fixed ahead. Tiny motes of glowing energy still drifted away from her showing exactly how much of her tiny human self had been destroyed by the energies warring inside her, giving the sickening impression of her coming apart under the effects of a brutal solvent.

"I don't think so Leatherpants. No-one's going to get out of here." My voice was cracking slightly as I spoke the words. In everything I'd done since coming into The Circle, there had always been the thought that I'd be able to get away from what was happening. Even as I'd fought against The Zarrulent there had always been that tiny little voice in the back of my head that just always pointed out that I was going to be fine. No matter the problems, everything was going to work out in the end. Hell, this whole crisis of trying to save Maria from being Bridged had come about because I thought I knew better than everyone else who was saying she had to be sacrificed for the greater good.

Laying there in incredible pain, I'd made the choice that no matter what, I was going to stop what was happening and save the human race but that none of us in the cavern were going to survive. I'd realised that there wasn't a way for me get around every little problem that was being put in my way so all I could hope for was to just make good on stopping the bad guy in his dastardly scheme. I'd hit the ground knowing that I needed to do as much damage as I could and my own safety was forfeit, as was the safety of the rest of us here, Circle and Tayne alike.

Leatherpants just grinned at me.

Our attention was broken by the blinding flash of light from above us and as we both winced against the pain, we could see a massive Cascade Bridge hovering towards the roof of this once mighty cavern. The blue/white energy in the ring was so much more than usually appears and I could feel the burning static even from this far away. With his control of the Drake Stone broken, it looked like whatever he had been doing to the bridges was broken as well.

"Told you," I chided him. "No-one gets out."

He smiled down at me before adding, "My sister burning this place from the face of the Earth. She's never done that before you know." He was confident of how to speak now and again brandished the Drake Stone fragment before me. He knew what was coming. That wide smile of his remained and as the mighty blast summoned by The Elder speared into the cavern and into the stone in his hand, all I could think was, "Bastard had a plan B after all."

36

The energy that came through and down at us was monstrous. There was no other way to describe it. It crackled and burned the air as it roared down, a blazing column of golden energy at least ten feet across, set to detonate and erase everything here from existence.

The energy blast landed on us directly and for the barest second, I could feel myself being ripped apart at the tiniest level of my being. Every atom was being shredded under the weight of the cleansing fire but in an instant, it was passed and I was still laying crumpled on the floor with Leatherpants and Maria stood on my chest. The energy swirled around us yet had no effect on us at all. In the eye of the magical storm, the air was calm and still but looking at Leatherpants, it was clear to see why.

He stood hunched against the hammer blow of the energy which was all being absorbed into the burning hunk of Drake Stone in his hand. His face was caught in a pained rictus as he struggled against the forces impacting all on the one spot. Maria was still hung limply in his other hand but the burning of her had started again, light coming from within her towards the stone.

I tried to move but I'd been pinned down under the weight of that blast. Focused on Leatherpants, I was held in place as if by one giant, smothering hand. All I had available to me was a drunken swing of one of my battered arms and with all the power I could muster, I swatted at him as best I could. He didn't even flinch, as if the impact had been nothing more than that of an insect. He just kept his arm raised against all of the roiling power surrounding us and drew that power into what was left of the Drake Stone. He was going to use the destructive energy from The Elder to kick start what he needed to happen. He'd had another option available to him because he knew what course of action The Circle would use, of course he would, being the Head of House for The Elder. But why had he called her his sister? They weren't related.

I risked another swing and the result was the same, nothing so much as dented his concentration on the casting he was attempting to weave. Next I spat a gout of fire which had the same effect but made my head spin wildly. I looked around the space hoping to find some way to interrupt what he was doing but there was just nothing. Andrea and the others were still buried under the rubble of the stone they'd been embedded in and there was no hint that they were even still alive after what had been done to them, the Tayne were a huge force but they were on the other side of the power wall which had encased us, as was Em, if she was OK.

On my chest, the weight holding me in place wavered and then wobbled, weakening and pulsing as something changed. Leatherpants was straightening his posture against the force of energy and the golden light shell surrounding us had begun to flicker. At oddly spaced intervals, stone shapes became visible on the far side of the boundary before the power noticed the breach and filled in the gap. He was pulling all of that power into the stone. He was winning. I had no other options so just poured everything of me that I could drag together into one final throw of the dice. I rolled my shoulders and slapped out with both of my arms at the same time as I lurched my body as far off the ground as I could manage, hoping to repeat the same results as before by just shaking the footing of the enemy. This time it had an effect.

Leatherpants wobbled and stumbled as the last of the power in the cavern was consumed by the stone. He fell backwards, flinging Maria away as he worked to maintain his balance and in that very instant, I could see a sickening change in his face. The human element of Leatherpants' face followed after the child, a look of snatched longing on what was left of the features whereas the darkly monstrous element of the face looked away from the child, as if there were two distinct creatures in the one body and they were going after different things. Heaving myself to one side, doing everything I could to track the movement from Leatherpants as he fell, I landed on my side before ponderously toppling onto my front and watched the creature who had been ripping at the belly of everything I was now a part of, clamber jerkily to his feet.

He straightened himself in sudden cracks of movement until he'd finally reached his full height. His gold eyes were now aglow with more power than before and I could feel quite easily that he was burning hot with all of the energy The Elder had sent his way. His head turned towards me and those golden eyes sparkled in the low light, and I knew that he was going to kill me. He took one step towards me, his shoulders bunching in readiness as he prepared himself to strike out, but then he faltered and took a step towards where Maria had fallen. He stopped statue still after this single step and his brow furrowed deeply, as if he was confronted by a great puzzle. What was he doing?

"I think it's time to end our arrangement Mr. Ward. I thank you for what you've been able to do but your services will no longer be required." Leatherpants was talking to himself as a now vile grin etched itself over his face, one which belonged to something interested in only the worst things in the world. There was no further warning before Leatherpants began to scream. A high pitched squeal filled the air, like that of a wounded pig, and the skin suit which had been as much a part of him as his arms or legs, began to bulge and squirm. The Drake Stone thudded to the floor and continued to glow as a warning of the danger it posed.

It took me longer than it should have done to be able to understand exactly what was happening but as the jacket split up the back, expelling a jet of slimy material to settle in the dust of the cavern floor, I caught on. The animalistic scream continued as a wizened lump of flesh began to slowly protrude from the tear in the back. The flesh thing grew as the hollowed out skin hung down as if a discarded pupae, until with a slurping sucking sound and an eruption of noxious smelling fumes, the flesh suit landed in a pile on the floor, sloughed away and discarded, and the meat object within fell backwards to writhe on the floor in a puddle of its own filth, retching and gurgling.

Bile rose in my throat at what I'd just seen. It was hideous and rooted me to inaction. It was then that the skin suit moved on its own. First lifting one arm and then the other to reach out before it, as if exploring the ground like a mollusc of some kind. I just lay and stared at the horror as that prized skin suit ever so slowly began to inflate and slither its way to a standing position, growing slender bony hands and feet tipped with long curved claws, and worst of all, a mutated head which brought to mind any number of long since forgotten nightmares, until it was stood before me, all elements of tailoring lost, the complete living creature which was as much a corruption as it was a being. The skin had reclaimed its sheen now, all the previous damage forgotten and there was a power within the limbs which made me sick. Its enlarged gold eyes fixed me with their malice and it took a shuffling step towards me.

"What do you think?" it drooled out at me in that deep resonance, stretching some letters and squashing others as it did. "I'm not feeling myself you see but I've been waiting so very long for this." The steps continued, each bringing it closer to me but whatever it was, it was taking its time to savour every second of what was taking place.

"What the hell are you?" I wheezed from my prone position on the cavern floor, doing everything I could to be able to move but getting very little traction. This walking oil slick was revolting and inspired nothing other than the desire to run and hide from it. It considered my question but the shameless brutality in those eyes made it clear that there was never going to be a chance to reason with it.

"I am a newborn," it replied, almost mockingly. "I am a shadow of the whole, a crossing of creatures. I am the life within flesh of The Hive." The mention of the Hive twisted my stomach tighter than bow string. If this thing was a part of The Hive, where had it been hiding? But I could see where. In plain sight.

"You're a part of one of The Hive demons, aren't you? That suit of old Leatherpants was the skin of The Elder's charge so kind of makes sense that it would have power of some kind still in it. So that's what you look like." The creature's face split into a sneer and it took another step.

"Indeed. For someone who my," it flicked its head towards what was left of Leatherpants as he continued to struggle on the floor, trying to live, "associate, felt was beneath contempt, you seem more astute than I would have given credit. Though I stand here not my usual self, but instead a bastardised version of the power of the original and the energies wound through the man there." It took another step closer, bringing with it an odour which was almost solid it had that much of an effect on my senses. I jerked again but just couldn't find enough energy to move. It cackled.

"I've waited for so very long to be able to walk free and not be wrapped around such a weak excuse for a leader." There was real hatred in those words. "That insect," it pointed out a monstrous finger at Leatherpants, "is nothing but the result of power by association and fear. He is a tiny man who thinks on nothing but attaining more power so all I had to do was whisper what would bring that power. He even thought that all of this had come from his mind." Its eyes glittered as it took another step. I still couldn't move.

"You seem to be having trouble rising. What a surprise." Arrogance touched the words and it tilted its head in a gesture similar to that I'd seen on Em but this time it was nothing more than a threat. My mind scrambled against what it had said, trying to understand. It had seen me do all of the damage to the stone altar so must know I'd hurt myself. Why was it so confident?

"You must have been fighting so very hard, using up so very much of yourself, before this moment. Much like there was someone wanting you weakened for some reason." The tone hardened with the final word and it licked its split lips and salivated as it closed on my face.

I panicked. I tried to blast fire at it but all I got was a small jet of fluffy white smoke. The creature was shrouded for a second, I was so glad to not see its hideous face, but it wasted no further time. It burst through the cloud with speed fueled by madness, its skeletal arms out, grasping as it came, and its huge mouth opened to reveal rows and rows of tiny yellow teeth. Leaping over my snout it landed on the bridge of my nose, clamping its claws into my flesh as easily as if the armour of my Dragon skin had been nothing but tissue. A pain which was far beyond the minor wounds, bolted around my head and my skin felt as if were being flayed away. I roared in surprise, then agony, as it sank its teeth in and began to gorge itself on me.

My roar became a terrified wail at what was being done to me. That thing was latched onto my face, less than three feet from my eyes, and was feeding on me. It slurped and suckled at the wound it had made on my snout and there was a numbing sensation of cold spreading quickly beneath my skin as it did, reaching out over an ever widening area, and my eyelids began to sag. I tried to call for help from anywhere, the Tayne, anyone, but all I was able to do was mumble, my mouth was just too heavy to control. The thing on my face laughed at my efforts without stopping its feast. It was gorging itself on me knowing that it had nothing to fear. I'd burned all of my fuel when I'd been fighting Em and it knew that, having been the one controlling her. This thing had manipulated me again until all I could see was the one option which would put me out of action and now it was going to drain me dry like some starved vampire before starting out against its next victim. Pure, animal panic set in at the realization that I was going to be eaten.

The burning detonation on my face slapped me briefly away from everything, shock taking over before the panic rose again. I did everything I could to blink away the swimming colours before my eyes, leaving me to make out that the creature was now separated from my face but nowhere to be seen. It had left behind a jagged wound on my face which was already grotesquely swollen but the beast wasn't still attached. Where was it? What was it doing? Oh God, where was it?

Then it was there. At least a hundred yards from me and crouched next to a large fallen piece of the cavern's roof. Within the dark flesh were the only points of any light, those two golden eyes, looking out accusingly and tormented by hate. But it wasn't looking at me. It was looking into the air. Had the Tayne come to help me? Were we all going to be saved?

There was another detonation of purest white as a bolt of energy zeroed in on that thing, lighting it in silhouette as huge swathes of rock were vaporized all around it. That blast couldn't have come from the Tayne could it? Even with all the energies they'd been given they weren't that powerful were they? Another blast came down but this time, spearing down after it on wide wings of the purest white light, came Em, her whole body suffused with that same energy setting her aglow. My world slowed as I drank in the heart wrenching beauty that Em was. Huge power but carried by one so fragile. She touched down gently and the energy which made up those giant wings fell to the floor to be dragged behind her like an over long train on a wedding gown. She scanned the area that thing had been in but there was no sign of it, living or otherwise. Eventually deciding that there was no immediate danger, she span and ran to me, concentration and worry on her face.

"My Lord. Can you move? Are you able to fight that thing with me?" Her voice was again holding that surety of purpose that she'd had from the very outset. Looking at her, I was speechless. I wasn't in great shape to say that much anyway but seeing Em descend from the sky like that was just so beautiful. All of the Dragons had the ability to fly and my memories of Andrea swooping and diving, her white sheen in balletic motion, were to be cherished always but Em seemed to be so much more than all of us. Her human form was still strong on those wings of hers but it was the wings themselves which did so much. They weren't physical. I couldn't reach out to grasp at them but I imagined that they would feel like a smile from a loved one, warming you to relaxation. Em evoked so many pictures in my head with the effortless way she moved, the certainty of her every fibre and the desire she had to fulfill her duty, that she was very much the stereotypical guardian angel.

I'd been feeling more and more woozy as the creature had been gorging itself on me but my head was clearing a little. Em checked the wound site quickly and expertly but gave no indication that she'd discovered anything either way when she'd finished. Instead she stopped to check around us, watching for the return of the thing. So pleasantly as well, she was idly stroking at my face as she did which just infused me with the knowledge that everything was going to be alright, that she was going to look after me, after all of us.

"I will need your help to defeat the creature," she continued, all business, sticking to the terrain she knew as her hand still drifted over my jawline. "I will never be enough to do this alone, my Lord." She finally turned her eyes up from the job at hand and looked into my eyes. Her other hand joined in the action and I could see that she was pleading with me. She was in need and she was looking to me to save her. My inner fire blazed at her call. I had to try.

With an almighty effort, I planted both of my ruined hands hard on the floor and with as much violent purpose as I could find, drove myself upwards. Somehow, I moved and moved fast. My arms felt strong and I was starting to recognise the sensation bleeding back into my legs. Bringing myself carefully back to my feet and leaning into the support created by my tail, I regained my full height, brushing away loose lumps of broken stone which had covered me and stretched out my wings by way of emphasis. I could also move most of my fingers now, though very painfully. I'd been feeling too sorry for myself laying on the floor and letting that thing eat from me. I'd let that creature dictate the terms and now I was going to put that thing back in its place. Growling and snorting out smoke, I could feel my aggression returning and my low charge became a thing of the past.

"Where is it?" I was going to rip that thing apart now I was back on my feet. I'd show it what it could expect in return for that sucker punch of sucking on my nose. Em rose slowly before my eyes, her vast wingspan outstretched but not moving in any way, as if the sheer presence of the wings was going to be enough to propel her.

"The last time I saw it my Lord, it was retreating beyond that far ring of stone." She pointed away out ahead of me and I was past her and heading towards the location in a flash. I began marching but as my humanity continued slipping away I dropped to walk on four legs, the animal taking over as I closed on what I was hoping would be a brutally violent end for my quarry. Reaching the point she'd indicated I just clambered all over the stones, employing all of my senses to try and pinpoint our enemy. The stink of it was still fresh on the rocks and I could taste its presence all around me. It was close by and that knowledge just pushed me on with more intensity.

"I can taste it Em. It's here somewhere," I called over my shoulder as I foraged through the landscape. Em was approaching but I didn't hear any response if she gave one. Instead, the ground began to shift under my feet, lurching one way then another. I gripped tightly to my footing, hunting for the cause of the upheaval while still doing my best to hold the attention on that thing. I wasn't going to lose that oily fiend, not when it was so close.

The brilliant white blast from Em broke my attention on the hunt for the stain thing. It fizzed past my head before detonating and sending a shower of scorching lightning in all directions. The spinning in my head forced my mind back to the more human as I recognised exactly what my body was telling me but was just too slow to do anything about it. The ground shattered under my feet and tons of rock and stone erupted from beneath me to be flung away in all directions. Em had fired to delay the creature as it had made a move to attack but hadn't been able to stop it. I had begun to turn away from the little thing when I actually glimpsed it. It wasn't the little stain anymore. It had grown.

Now falling towards me, its spear tipped fingers raised to rake at any part of me it could find, it had become a vast block of warped flesh, still with those same golden eyes alight with venom beyond measure. It was as least as big as I was but it's blackened skin seemed to warp the very light around it, extending and expanding its appearance in hideous new ways. On its back were what looked like they could have been wings or maybe should have been wings but instead they were horribly malformed. Jagged shards of bone protruded from those bizarre appendages creating nausea in any who would see them.

The giant slammed into my side and sliced through and down my flank effortlessly, spilling my blood all over the floor of the giant cavern. There was so much strength in the blow that its claws were driven into the stone floor. I yelped in pain and clutched at the tear in my flesh, all the while attempting to back away from it, keeping my wounded side away from further injury. The thing had sprawled on the floor after its attack, relying on brute force and gravity to be able to do the damage. Now, as I retreated, it began to move forward, dragging itself with those mightily muscled arms to reveal that, as those would be wings had been, its legs were a ruined stump, useless and corrupted. I could make out the detail of what should have been feet and claws spaced around the lump of meat it dragged. As it lumbered forwards it felt as if it wasn't finished growing. My hand went reflexively to my snout. Rubbing at the wound made me retch. This thing had not only been eating me but using me to fuel its transformation. It slathered and clacked its jaws as it closed in on me, heaving its breath all the way.

Em opened up again from behind me, blasting gout after gout of energy which 'whoompfed' into the chest and shoulders of the brute as it advanced. Each impact burned into the blackened mass, cooking off charred lumps of foul muscle and tissue but the thing just kept on coming. I added my own fire to the bombardment, beginning with a wide spray of flame before concentrating it down onto a single rod of white hot death. Even under all that fire, it just kept on moving.

I was still retreating but it closed the gap quickly and slashed with its right hand, aiming for my head. This time I'd been able to see it coming and reared up on my hind legs, avoiding the downward thrust, but this time it didn't fall totally flat. Bracing itself on its left arm, it wavered before reversing the swipe and driving those claws skywards, hoping to split me across the stomach. I continued to back pedal but the deformed arm was stopped prior to connecting with me, held in mid swing by Em, sending the slap of flesh on flesh through the oppressive air. She'd dispensed with the artillery and switched to hand to hand combat. Gripping tightly with her arms, her skin and suit turned to shiny crystal, her wings came alive as ropes of pure light, shooting around the hand of the creature and crushing it to a pulpy mess, the sound of the bones shattering clear to hear. It didn't react to the injury, as if pain just didn't exist, but began to bludgeon at the ground with that wrecked arm, smashing Em down again and again. After several punishing blows it just raised its arm before it and took in what it had done to Em. Those pure wings of hers were still mostly wrapped around the limb of the bulk but her previous magical armourment of glinting crystal had been cracked and broken in so many places. She was still gripping tightly to what was left of the things arm but she was showing the effects of the fight.

"Lady Messenger," it drooled at Em. "You do not appear to be yourself today." It brought its arm even closer still to look almost eye to eye with Em.

"Have you been giving yourself to this young Dragon?" It was a good job I was red or anyone would have seen me blush at the accusation. I had wanted that several times but I'd put that down to the actions of this monster. Em just tilted her head in that usual, disarming fashion but before she spoke it was clear that that gesture was now very different.

"A little, but as one of the High Guardians of The Circle, he is due anything he should possibly desire. He has power given whereas you just take it." Her voice was as hard as diamond, cutting and slicing an accusation. The bulk angered into an incandescent rage and hammered Em into the ground hard, creating a small crater with the force of the impact, before gouging out a massive handful of rock from the floor and hurling it at me. I tried to catch it, I would never be able to avoid it, but it hit with the force of a high speed train and I was forced to the ground clutching at my chest, gasping to retrieve my breath.

I was on my knees and could only watch as it began to metronomicaly, deliberately smash at Em's head with its free hand. Crash after crash came down on her and despite the effort she was giving to break free of the stifling hold of the stump of the thing, she was powerless to avoid the attacks. She may have been shrouded in a crystal hard shell but there was no way that it was going to be able to withstand every bludgeon. The splintering sound heralded the fact as a huge crack opened in her armour, directly across her face. I stood up and took a step forwards in anger but the next blow landed. As the hand came back up, I could see the blood smeared across her features, standing out starkly against her pale skin. Her eyes were closed and her previously anchored grip was relinquished. My anger screamed behind my eyes at what that thing had just done to Em and all pain was forgotten.

My vision turned scarlet as my hatred blossomed and I screeched out my anger. Its eyes darted from Em to me and it drew itself taller whilst freeing itself of the bonds around its hand and sending Em wheeling through the air, away, like a discarded shred of rubbish. I heard her thump into solid surface, more shattering sounds and the barest yelp as she did, then nothing.

My pain and injuries were forgotten. Bounding on all fours, I covered the distance between us quickly to throw myself into the thing. I smashed it with my shoulder before driving my clawed hands and feet into its fleshy stomach and ripping and clawing for all I was worth. The pain in my hands was terrible but I just didn't care. I could feel warm liquid spilling from it as chunks of meat wore torn free and I was going to rip this thing to pieces. But there was no sign from it that I was even causing any damage. Instead, it just began to flail its arms at me, attempting to sweep me away from it like nothing more than an annoying hovering insect. The blows were artless but incredibly heavy. I'd risked remaining for as long as I could to continue the attack but I knew that I couldn't weather every blow it rained down.

Instead of continued raking, I forced my hands and feet against it as hard as I could and drove myself away, blasting it in the face with flame as I left to cover my departure. Its arm came down where I would have been and slammed down to the floor, shaking everywhere with the impact. With as many quick beats of my wings as I could manage, I dragged myself into the air and just held my position above it. Those yellow eyes just stared up at me, their anger almost a physical force capable of pulling me down. My chest felt tight and the pain which had been stabbing at me like needles to my side was now just a hazy memory. The blood was still flowing though.

"You are a confusing creature boy," it shouted up to me. "So many see you as being the fool, nothing more than a problem to be endured, but I can feel a much greater strength in you." It shuffled itself forwards slightly, the crushed hand leaking all sorts of battered flesh as it did which added to the slick forming as more and more material leaked from its side.

"Why are you trying to kill me?" It was such a simple question and I couldn't believe it had asked me.

"Why d'you think? Look what you've done to the Tayne, to The Circle. Look what you did to Em." My snarl bubbled up without aid at the thought of Em being injured. "Are you telling me that you won't try to do the same, or worse, ever again?" I snarled and waited for whatever warped logic was coming.

"What if I do? Shouldn't I do it?" It still held me with those golden eyes as it sludged its way towards me, its tone one of idle curiosity rather than anger.

"Why not? You can't just kill or enslave people just for the fun of it. If you can't see that, it's a good thing they locked the rest of you up." It stumped forwards again.

"I can't kill or enslave, but you can? Don't forget, I've watched for years as The Circle has jealously hoarded its power and done everything it could to keep people in their place. You've just heard what The Messenger of The Circle, a hugely powerful member of your cabal, felt. That you could have whatever you wanted for no other reason than you are you. Unquestioning devotion is not a virtue to build any form of group. The fact that we are having this conversation suggests that you've at least considered what I'm telling you." Onwards again. I shook my head to clear it and remember that this was the bad guy. That thing may be pointing out truths but that didn't make him right. Below me, the words continued.

"You don't look that well you know and all those people working on your side have done is try to kill everyone here, regardless of affiliation. You'd have hoped they would have been more concerned with your safety."

I just hung in the air with my wings beating rhythmically. Again, I was face to face with one of the worst of the worst and all it was saying that The Circle were far from being the paragons of virtue that everyone was making out. Was there even the slightest chance that was the truth? I was feeling sick and my body was beginning to shiver.

I didn't have any further contemplation as simultaneously, my head began to spin and a vice was tightened onto my right ankle. With terrifying speed I was dragged from the air to crash in a heap on the rocky ground next to the Bulk. It had used my consideration of its words to edge closer to me and bring me down. It boomed with laughter as it slammed my head against the ground several times, cracking one of my horns off and I was sure breaking several of the bones in my face. My head was still spinning but I was sure that it was down to concussion rather than warning. It closed its face to mine and spoke with a rotting meat breath.

"Little one. It's always the young who are the most idealistic." That breath made my eyes water and, with the utmost violence it could muster, it shook me like a rag doll to highlight that it was in control.

"You must learn the truest fact. Everyone is like that, no matter where they come from or what excuses they give. The strong will always conquer the weak." It was a stark statement but I wouldn't believe that that was all the world was. "Now, I feel ready for a refreshing of the energy inside me," it pondered before dragging me along behind it at a far greater speed than it should have been able to move, back to the ruined altar area.

37

I was groggily aware of where I was but I was trapped within a body which was still bleeding, badly. I'd burned through my reserves of energy and was now at the end of any spare power I had set aside for a rainy day. There was just nothing left. I could dimly make out the familiar location where I'd at least freed my friends from the torture of this lunatic but as I was dragged along, I could feel that nauseating power burning like a dying flame. Maria's energy was still aglow like a dying ember but there was just so very little of it left. The fight was gone from her as the energy had been drained into the air. I didn't know if there was any way to save her or reclaim the power but I just couldn't do anything.

Eventually, I stopped moving and for a blissful second I remained still on the floor and just breathed. It only lasted for that second before I was jerked into the air and smashed into an unforgiving wall of stone. Half opening my eyes, it was all I could muster, I found myself face to face with the suit thing. I'd been locked to the stone in the same way the others had been and looking around, it was clear that I wasn't alone. I could make out Leatherpants, or what was left of him, now sat leaning against a nearby stone, as if resting after a monumental effort. His previously slim frame looked emaciated and pale. There was no muscle tone on him, instead he carried the look of nothing more than a skeleton covered with skin. His eyes bulged as he watched us, that longing envy still burned onto his expression.

A little further from him, lay Maria. She still had the faintest glow coming from her but she was practically mist on the air she'd come so much apart. The tiniest of breaths escaped from her but nothing else.

My mind span in warning just before the balled fist of the creature smashed into my face, sending so much pain running through my body that I almost passed out.

"Now, Guardian. I'm going to take more energy from you," and it slammed a balled fist into my side, and into the huge wound it had opened up. Oddly, the pain was more manageable but when it removed its hand, I could feel something left behind. Trying to look down at what was being done, the booming voice explained for me, to drive my fear again.

"You can feel it can't you? The Drake Stone burning your flesh from the inside." Despite my agony, I snapped my head up to try and prove to myself that the Bulk was lying. There was no sensation other than the weight of the stone in my side but that didn't mean that it wasn't coming.

"The stone is a mighty vessel," it continued, its voice becoming more and more cultured, more precise, with every passing syllable, and wholly at odds with the body it was coming from. "It stores the power of magic within it and now, it will be drawing that power out of you." The burning still hadn't started but still. I weakly jerked against the rock I'd been sunken into purely as a show of defiance, to show that although my fire may have been low, it wasn't completely extinguished. The Bulk frowned as if confused by my movements.

"I do so love the surety that comes with what you all are. The Circle. The Tayne. Any number of other races as well. All of you are so very keen to embrace a saviour. I've been able to do everything I have because I was allowed." It moved in to me and inspected my side, narrowing its eyes at what it saw. "Everyone is so desperately in need, so scared, that they will bow down to anyone stronger than them. You all wanted to have the certainty of knowing what to do." It pressed its own nose to mine, pushing our faces together. "Instinctively, you all want to be ruled."

All I could do was slam my head into it with as much force as I could, adding a slight twist to slash across the warped features with the jagged piece of my horn on my right side. At the very least I'd been able to open up another wound on my enemy but there had been precious little real force behind what I'd done. It just held my gaze from a slight distance.

"What's the matter ugly? Not going the way you'd hoped?" My ability to annoy was my last weapon. "Stone not warming up yet? Maybe you just need to give it a shake, or change the batteries?" The Drake Stone hadn't begun to do any of the things I'd just been told it would and I knew that the Bulk knew too.

"You know that performance anxiety can do all kinds of things. This ever happened to you before?"

With terrible speed, it slammed me across the face with and open handed slap, the impact of which filled the whole cave we were within. The shock of which stole any further comment from me. Reaching out to me, I screamed in pain as those needle claws probed into my side, delving into my flesh in search of the Drake Stone. With a sickening, sucking noise, the chunk of crystal was pulled free and the Bulk examined in closely, ignoring my blood, which was smeared all over it.

I couldn't speak. I could barely gasp in air the pain was that bad in my side. All I was able to do was try not to sag as exhaustion overcame me. The Bulk just turned and examined the Drake Stone with a scientific attention to detail, pouring over every possible fissure or tear on its surface as it tried to understand what had happened. No matter what it did, the stone remained inert.

The Bulk just growled. A sound which held so little of anything which could be reasoned with, it blew renewed life into my fear. My shoulders tightened and my back straightened purely in response to what that noise was going to mean.

The Drake Stone fell to the ground, a now useless relic of that thing's journey. The Bulk watched it fall with contempt, as if it were a mere minion to be scalded for failing at a simple task, before slowly turning its eyes to me. The gold seemed to become sharper with each passing second, slowly slicing into me as a precursor to what that thing intended to do next.

Speaking through clenched muscles in its jaw and with brutality draped over the cordial vocabulary, the Bulk approached me again.

"It would appear that the energies which were absorbed into the stone to free me from that spatter of humanity have destroyed what abilities it held." It breathed deeply as it fought to hold onto an infernal rage.

"I could feed from you through the echo of the stone but that is lost to me as well now." Its functioning hand balled and straightened reflexively as it spoke, still never taking those golden spheres from me. My eyes darted around, desperately looking for something, anything which could come to my aid.

"Which means that the only way for me to do what needs to be done and correct this monstrosity I've been marooned in, will be to rip, that, stone, from The Messenger before using what's left of that child to make me what I need to be." The staccato delivery made it even worse. I knew what was going to happen but I couldn't do anything about it. I spasmed against the bonds again but I was too weak to even crack the stone. The Bulk kept its face close to mine and its decaying breath poured over my senses, another display of its control.

"When I've done what I have to, I'll return to you, boy. I will show you what The Hive has at its core and, who knows, I may even make clothing of your flesh for my servants."

"You will not so much as harm a scale on his mighty frame," detonated into the tension. The clarion voice rang like the tolling of a bell of the mightiest purity and it caused the Bulk to wince and flinch back away from me. I recognised the voice and knew it couldn't have come at a better time. Turning my head as far as I was able, I could see Em suspended in the darkness above me, those glorious wings of hers outstretched and casting their cleansing light everywhere. Her face, though, showed that she was badly injured. Blood was congealing but that didn't hide the fact her left eye was swelling shut, she had multiple lacerations and what looked like a horribly broken nose. She was still shrouded in her crystal armour for the most part but now it was hugely damaged in so many areas, spidery cracks reaching to almost every part of it. The Bulk noticed too and sludged forwards again.

"And now you threaten when you are so very far from capable of actually delivering on the threat. That seems unwise little one." The voice was one of concern but was used as a threat.

Em ground her teeth and it was only now that I really looked beyond the injuries, that I could see the strain she was under. She was standing before a vastly stronger foe as she fought with herself, doing everything she could to hold herself together. Her voice, which I'd heard as a pristine explosion of authority, had been fractured, held together by will. Both of her fists were closed and the knuckles white with the effort. She was struggling to do the minimum. She was going to get herself killed to protect the Guardian.

"You can't Em," I pleaded with her limply, begging that she would listen to the order of her master. "You can't throw your life away, please. Now more than ever it's you we've got to protect." She tilted her head. "It's not me, it's you. You're the one." My pleading was left to just hang in the air and I could feel both of them watching me as if expecting something further. Em spoke next but her voice was now cracking.

"My Lord. Both you and that thing have made a very grave miscalculation of me." She turned back to face the Bulk. "You have both deemed to speak of me as a singular. Little one, that I am the one to be protected. I am afraid that this is very far from the truth." Silence became silence became silence as the tension expanded. What the hell was she talking about?

"You see," she continued, "I am so very far from being alone as to be the tip of a mighty spear," and with that she relaxed and expelled the breath she'd been holding onto, let her hands fall limp, and withdrew all of the power she'd been holding into the wall of cloaking of hers to reveal a swarm of fast moving, screeching and hooting Tayne, all blazing onwards at the Bulk with a fury so far beyond anything this race had ever mustered that no-one would believe who hadn't witnessed it.

The Bulk was powerless to resist.

The Tayne, still so hugely warped and corrupted, simply relied on gravity. There were so many of them that they didn't need to do anything else but crash into the monstrosity in a torrent of flesh and claw. The Bulk just screamed. It had shown that it was able to withstand the pain of anything which was thrown at it but now it was being defied. Its plans were openly being mocked, and by those who it had deemed to be nothing more than the weakest of the weak and a race to be bullied. The Tayne, in contrast, were ferocious. Not a single one of them did anything but attack. There was no hint of cowardice, no uncertainty in their actions or fear. Each and every one of them was finally taking the chance that their whole people had been wanting to take as they stood up for themselves.

The Bulk swung at the mass of Tayne with both arms, again relying on brute force as its only option, but the Tayne were able to surge around those massive limbs in a torrent which was already forcing the creature back. After each impact on the Bulk, the lucky ones just speared away in any direction they could to re-join the melee. Those who weren't so lucky littered the cavern floor around the Bulk having been no match for the pulverising force that thing could inflict. I watched on with a kindled ember of pride that in all of this, no matter the outcome, at least I'd helped the Tayne.

As the fighting continued, animal warrior calls filling the air, Em lowered herself before me and started to punch her way into the stone holding me in place. It crumbled apart and I crashed to the ground, unable to hold myself upright without help. Em was quickly to my side and whispered into my ear.

"My Lord, can you hear me? Please, you must be alive." Her voice was pleading to the ether, begging that the Guardian was alive. I opened my eyes to show her the good news but still wished it had been because she'd wanted 'me' to be alive rather than just the Guardian. She exhaled a giggled breath of relief and hugged at me tightly.

"I can't move." My body was smashed. "I've used up what power you gave me." She blushed slightly, though still strongly enough for me to recognise under all the blood on her face, probably at the perceived slight of daring to assume one of her superiors was in need, and looked away. "I meant no disrespect my Lord. Just to provide you with the greatest chance of victory." More admission that she was still willing to defer to the special few. The Bulk roared from behind her and she span to face it, arms raised before her ready to fight. Mounds of fallen Tayne littered the small space we were in and the stream crashing into the Bulk was diminishing almost visibly. It was winning. The Tayne, though vast in number, just weren't doing enough damage. Despite their effort, their sacrifice, they just didn't have the tactics to be able to defeat an enemy like that.

I planted my right hand to the floor and did my best to rise. I just had to help the Tayne. I couldn't let that thing win but more importantly, there was no way I was going to let it destroy the entire race in the process. I barely moved a foot from the ground before all of the power washed from my arm and I crashed back down. Em turned and was back to my side.

"Do not try my Lord. You are in no position to be able to defeat that brute." I tried a second time to stand but had the same result despite her request. I was here to fight. Em spoke more forcefully the second time. "My Lord. I've been doing some thinking of my own. I have devised the perfect response which will achieve all of our goals." She smiled wolfishly before adding, "We can save the child."

My eyes must have lit up at the possibility of finally being able to rescue Maria. That had been the driving force for everything I'd been doing up to this point. That was why I'd dragged everyone around with me on this quest and for so long it had looked that she was going to be yet another victim.

Em ghosted from me, her wings of energy being quickly drawn back into the fabric of her suit and doing her best to always keep the Tayne swarm between herself and the Bulk. Travelling with the ease of movement of a cat, all stealth and liquid grace, she made her way across the area towards the crushed rock which had held the others for the casting Leatherpants had been weaving. Roar after roar filled the air from the Bulk as it continued to thrash at the cloud of angry creatures which were still attacking for all they were worth. Eventually, Em reappeared from the mound of broken stone, but she carried with her, slung over her shoulder limp like a bag of sand, Hairy. She returned the same way she'd come to drop the big Argentinian next to me. What was she doing?

Next she rushed to scoop up what was left of Maria. The light had been extinguished from her and she looked as if she were breaking apart like wet sand. Motes of her spilled through Em's fingers as she cradled the child to her chest, moving as fast as she could to return to where I was. She carefully eased Maria onto the floor next to the still unconscious Hairy. I just watched on with a worry building.

"What are you going to do?"

"I'm going to bring all of the energy of the Guardian back a single point, remove it from the child fully, and give it to our new Guardian." She sounded almost giddy as she shook out her hands in preparation.

"You will most certainly not." I was ablaze within my Dragon body and although unable to move, I wouldn't let her do that.

"We haven't come this far to simply conduct a Bridging. That isn't going to save the child, it'll kill her." The din around me didn't stop her hearing but her face didn't show the expression of being rebuked. She just smiled slightly.

"Please just watch and all will become clear."

And with that she drew in a massive breath before reaching out her hands, one towards Maria and one towards Hairy. The effect was instant. An incandescent blaze of purple light exploded into being around the three of them, forming a shell of energy. The Bulk, now under attack from all angles, flashed towards the light and was fast to recognise what was happening. An orangey yellow light was lifting from Maria to flow directly into Em. But that wasn't all. That same light was forming all around us, that light which had washed away from Maria was now being dragged back to her, back to Em. At the centre of her chest, visible clearly through her suit and armour, was a purple fire coming from the remaining piece of the Drake Stone as it was used to channel all of the energies Em was using. The energies in that stone burned away at the suit above it as she worked.

The Bulk screamed and howled as it tried to beat a pathway through the Tayne. They in turn had started to use a more coordinated attack and instead of the single fighters attacking in a close space, now they were truly working together. Marveling at what was happening around me, I could see groups of Tayne linking and locking arms over shoulders and shoulders to backs to become a single solid force before hurling themselves into the Bulk to drive it back. Hit after hit went in as they engaged with wave after wave of repulsion and forced that thing to retreat from what it was attempting to reach. I couldn't believe it. They were scrummaging the Bulk away.

Inside the shell of power around Em, the golden yellow light was swirling and billowing as more and more of it was drawn in until, finally, the last fragment entered the shell and Em was able to drop her head and relax as she allowed the power to pass through her, through the Drake Stone, and into Hairy. His eyes flashed open the instant the first tendril of power touched his chest, his back arching in involuntary spasm and a howl of a beast emanating from him. Amidst the Tayne, the Bulk howled out as well, clearly recognising the fact that it was being beaten to the punch, and began to increase its wild flaying to reach its goal.

Inside the shell, the power dimmed as it was pulled through Em until the darkness returned and Hairy was left limp on the floor, his body twitching at the residual effect. The shell collapsed to reveal that, her power now gone, Maria was fading away.

"Save her please!" I begged Em as my own humanity took over and my Dragon form gave way to a return to the human. Laying on the floor, naked, I pleaded again and again, trying to rouse Em from the slouch she was now in. Tears rolled down my face as I did and there was nothing I could do about it. The Bulk laughed. Beyond the mountain of Tayne who were fighting like experienced warriors, the Bulk barked out a laugh.

"She's done what she needed to do hasn't she? She didn't listen to you and your plan of saving the child. She just followed the rule of The Circle. Protect the power." I didn't have the chance to respond before Em lifted her head and for the briefest of moments, locked eyes with me. I could see a deep sadness in her for the first time and, unexpectedly, a single tear fell slowly down her wrecked face. In that silent second, she smiled that sadness, before plunging her fingers into her chest, surrounding the Drake Stone in an iron grip, and ripping it from her flesh. A wave of low sound spread out in all directions and Em's shoulders rolled forwards under a great weight, her hand clutching the Drake Stone falling to the floor and beginning to blaze with angry heat as the power of that crystal began to burn away at Em. The Bulk and I both screamed but Em just slammed that stone into what was left of Maria for all she was worth.

The stone floor cracked beneath the child and a howling wind climbed up to gale force everywhere. The Tayne were scattered in all directions and even the Bulk was slammed away against a huge rock pile. Sitting in the eye of the hurricane, there was a relative stillness but the energy in the atmosphere put my teeth on edge and made my throat constrict. There was a static which twisted at you, a power so vast and timeless that it was clear that no-one would truly contain it. In that space, I watched on as all of the lost energy of Maria was rapidly reassembled around that heavy piece of crystal. She had an expression of pure serenity on her face as it did, as if she were finally coming home. Finally the hurricane lost a fragment of its energy. Then a piece more. Maria was solid again but remained laying on the floor. Hairy was struggling to his feet next to her with an expression of pained awe all over his face. Em also stood, gingerly before stumbling slightly. Hairy was there to steady her and nodded as she straightened her back.

Turning to me, her face was still just as damaged as it had been but now it looked as if she'd aged. Not that she was suddenly covered in wrinkles and had grey hair, but there was a haunted experience in her eyes. She carried herself with the weight of a thousand regrets and it was that which stole away her youth.

"What do you think to my solution?" She spoke as she approached where I'd propped myself against the stone. I tried everything I could to say something but I just couldn't. There was a gaping hole in her chest where she'd been forced to remove the stone and she was so very badly injured.

After an age, I asked the only question I could. "What did you do?"

She kneeled at my side, taking my hand in her remaining hand, the Drake Stone having destroyed the other, as she did. "I Bridged the child, but before she was lost I transferred the mantle of Messenger to her. She will be the one to take on the role from now." She breathed shallowly as she explained the point.

"I wanted to save everyone," I protested, the tears still falling. "I didn't want to save one at the cost of another." Em smiled.

"That is who we are. We can want but we must always return to the core of what we are charged with. The greater good." Her voice was tender, reassuring despite the situation. She stroked my hand as she looked at me as if she were consoling a distraught child.

"Now, please stand up," Em ordered. I had no idea how I was going to be able to do that, my body had been drained. Yet when she heaved against my arm, dragging me to my feet I was able to steady myself and remain upright. Looking at her still stroking my hand, I understood what she'd done.

"You've just given me the last of your power haven't you?" I hadn't intended the words as a rebuke but I just couldn't contain my emotion. She stopped stroking and smiled.

"The greater good, remember," she replied before letting my hand fall.

From the far edge of the arena, bubbled an angry cackle. The Bulk lumbered towards us and mocked us with its razor blade hatred. We both turned to face the thing and I raised my hands to fight. Em just watched it casually, not the slightest hint of emotion on her face.

As it ponderously advanced, I became quickly aware that I was naked so wouldn't be the most imposing figure in a fight.

"You see Guardian? When everything is said and done, all the actions of The Circle are, are attempts to protect its position, its power." It kept advancing slowly and it wasn't immediately that I could make out any of the details of it. When I did, I could see that the Tayne had done a huge amount of damage. It was covered in slashes and tears in so many places as to look more hole than skin. Fluid was pumping out of all of them to stain the floor in an ever growing river of gore that also contained chunks of flesh and internal organ that the thing was dragging behind it. I wanted to be sick. That horror had become so much worse than it had been originally. Mangled and ruined it may have been but it was still moving towards us. Clasping onto Em's arm, I turned to run. I had no idea where we would be able to go but I knew we had to try to escape. Em remained rooted to the spot despite her ever growing frailty.

"Come on. We can get away from here. I can jump us out. You gave me enough power for that." I was pleading again but seemed to have the same effect as before. Em just watched the Bulk.

"You're right my Lord. You have enough power for one Cascade Bridge but not yet. We can't leave that thing to escape. I'm sorry to say that the final part of my plan to defeat this brute and restore The Circle needs one more thing from you." Now she turned to face me, and I could see that the life in her was fading away. Without the Drake Stone to sustain her, she was going to die.

"Anything for you Em. Name it." I straightened my back and accepted that she had made her choices for the good of the whole. She'd done what she'd done because she believed in what she was protecting. I would play the part of her superior to give her as much gratitude for what she'd done as the set standards of decorum would allow. She nodded curtly once.

"I would like one kiss from you my Lord."

The Bulk wheezed its approach but there was no other sound to interrupt this moment.

"I cannot recall ever having engaged in such an activity but since we met, I've been able to feel such a passion coming from both you and Miss Thomich towards the other that it is something I feel that I should have the chance to experience at least once."

There were no further words needed. I just lightly cradled her head in my hands and pressed my mouth to hers. She gasped lightly at my touch but responded in kind. She was tentative in her movements, but let herself loose within our embrace, allowing herself to feel the pure humanity of it all. The kiss continued for as long as I dared allow it and when we separated, Em's eyes were sparkling.

"I can see now why she feels this way for you." I blushed at that comment and switched my attention to the brute approaching us. As I did, the Bulk roared its intentions, shattering the mood which had been surrounding us. Raising both arms above its head, it surged forwards, slamming those crushing hands into the ground and cracking the stone as it did before raising again for the death blow.

"I envy her, to have you," Em shouted above the roar of the Bulk, "But I have always, and will always, act for the good of The Circle. Please help the child in her role." And she ran towards the advancing monster as fast as she could, throwing herself directly at its ruined side. The Bulk ignored her but as I watched her fall through the space before our enemy I could make out her hand held out before her, a small pebble held in her fingers.

With simultaneous impact, she slammed into the blood soaked flesh and snapped the stone apart. That remaining fragment of what she'd called an Infernura Rod erupted into a maelstrom of swirling power and a doorway to Yondah. Em was engulfed immediately and her body was burned away before the might of the energy in the explosion. The Bulk reacted to the detonation in terror, trying for all it was worth to escape away from the crushing force of the tiny would be black hole. Screaming now, lumps of flesh were torn from the Bulk and taken through the construct Em had unleashed. I could feel the huge pull of the thing as it burned, taking more and more of that mountain of flesh, hungrily devouring all that it could lay its hands on. Small rocks and some of the fallen Tayne were sucked towards and through that hellish gateway, as was the limp yet screaming almost corpse of Leatherpants, the real Leatherpants, Mr. Ward. He skidded along the floor on his back before being lifted and rapidly consumed by the energy, feet first. He'd abused his position for years until he'd made a deal with the devil which had cost him his life. His eyes never stopped spilling hatred at me as he was pulled apart.

The screams from the Bulk moved through being animal until there was no sense in them at all, until all of the matter that had been a part of it had been minced to nothing and taken from our reality.

With a final strangled scream, the energy finally turned in on itself and collapsed, and the cavern seemed to have been emptied of all life. The emptiness just hovered everywhere and my senses struggled to adjust to the now lack of stimuli. Em's final sacrifice had shown huge bravery but also that she was looking at the bigger picture. People looked to her to behave in a certain way and they would have relied upon it, in the same way that she looked at me in a certain way and would have been reassured by that constant surety.

Blowing out a large breath, I knew that I had to get everyone home and in the best condition I could. I turned to face Hairy and Maria but as I did, my eyes passed over the ruins where the others had been suspended, and stood on top of a ragged stack of stone, red flecked hair hanging free on either side of her beautiful pale face, stood Andrea. My heart leapt in my chest and I took a step towards her but she held up a hand, stopping me dead.

"I saw you," she growled through clenched teeth, anger alight in her. "I saw you kiss The Messenger." I began to stammer my response but she cut me off.

"I watched as you did exactly what everyone has said you would do." I could feel the waves of anger coming from her even from across the arena.

"We need to get everyone away from here now. Please let me explain what happened after we're all home," I pleaded and yet again, it had no effect on the mood.

I gave up.

"Very well. I'll return everyone here to Wales, that's the last bridge jump I can make, but I can ensure that no-one will have to remain there for any longer than they have to." I donned the verbal cloak of the aloof Guardian as I spoke. I just had to get everyone home and if that meant behaving the way everyone thought I was going to then so be it. Bigger picture.

38

After about an hour of hunting through debris and other detritus of the battle, Mike and Mark had been freed from beneath the fallen rock they'd been buried under and Hairy was up and about but was already feeling sick to his stomach as his new power fought inside him in the same way it had for Maria. I tried to consider just how she'd been able to withstand the punishment she'd endured as I watched Hairy struggle almost immediately. Maybe she had been strong enough to take her place in The Circle despite her age? Maria remained blissfully asleep on the cavern floor where Em had worked on her. Her tiny frame had been ripped apart and then blasted back together but the wounds on her face were already healing to scars as no doubt the rest would in time. The Drake Stone sat in the centre of her chest. The puffy flesh surrounding the crystal a violent red after the trauma of its insertion. Hairy, showing a tenderness beyond expectation had draped his shirt over the child to preserve her modesty and stood guard despite his own discomfort, watching over her with a reverential ferocity. Rounding up as many of the Tayne as we could find, it appeared that they had lost over half of their population in the attack on the Bulk but there was a new feeling of pride in those who remained.

When the Cascade Bridge snapped into existence, it felt like I was being hit in the head with a hammer, such was the strain it put on my depleted reserves. Holding that construct in place for as long as I could, the survivors hurried through the portal and back to my estate in Wales. Mark and Mike had gone through first with Andrea and Hairy, who carried Maria in his arms like she was made of glass, to explain the impending arrival of what was likely to be viewed as a dangerous enemy in the form of several hundred Tayne. Happily, Greyas, the Tayne I'd operated on, had survived the fighting despite breaking one of her arms and was keen to act as my liaison to the rest of her people which meant that they could all be quickly dealt with in a controlled and ordered way.

Stepping through myself, and letting the hold go on the Cascade made me dizzy so I ended up in a heap on the lawn area at the front of the house. Servants and staff of all kinds buzzed around administering any and all kinds of help they may be required to offer and as expected, I was attended to more quickly than anyone else. Messages were passed on to be spread throughout The Circle explaining how to locate and then remove the fragments of The Drake Stone which remain on those affected and what had taken place in the ruin of Bress Tal.

Eventually, after very many hours and the setting of the sun, the Tayne were settled into any and all possible room in the mansion and were treated as the guests they were. I'd given word that anyone doing anything less than treating them as dignitaries would have me to answer to. Which left the rest of us in the infirmary under the watchful eye of Llewellyn. The head of the medical team was respectful but firm in ensuring everyone stayed put, and even Mark, who had been sure he was fine and needed to get back to work, settled back into one of the plush beds. Maria was still motionless but I'd had her placed in the bed next to mine.

Everyone continued to fuss around us, making sure we had everything we could have possibly wanted, until finally, and partially down to the shoo-ing of Llewellyn, they all left, dimmed the lights and left us all to rest. I needed to speak with Andrea as soon as I could but I knew that there was no way she was going to even look at me. Her features were hardened ice but inside that frosty exterior, a fire of rage was burning. I just lay there staring at her, willing for her to soften and at least register that I had something worth hearing. Opposite, Mike just gave the slightest shake of his head before closing his eyes. Even he could see that there was nothing I was going to be able to do. Restless sleep it was then, leaving me alone with my memories of this latest sacrifice from a member of The Circle I'd grown close to.

The following day I awoke to chaos.

As I came round, I could hear raised voices beyond the closed door to the room and I had a sensation of frustration bleeding to me from whoever was outside. I sat up to find a vast platter of meats and fruit on the table next to my bed and I was already shoveling great handfuls into my mouth before I was even aware that the other beds in the room were empty.

Hurriedly wrapping myself in the robe which had been laid out for me, I marched through the door and into the starkly white corridor beyond, puffing out my chest for all I was worth to reinforce the image of the mighty Guardian. Outside there was a startled collection of faces all turning to me at once, chief amongst them, Mike. I could recognise other members of my staff but it was Mike who was suddenly hugely on edge.

"Mike," I greeted him but left a level of question in my tone. "Good to see you up and about. Where is everyone else?" I needed to know what enough to put him so on edge was. I really was happy he was OK though. The other members of the group subtly edged away from Mike, as if hoping to stay clear of the no doubt impending explosion of rage. Straightening his already straight shirt, he cleared his throat before responding.

"My Lord. The Elder has been here this morning." He didn't add any further information before I roared out, "WHAT!" quickly showing my feeling of what had happened.

"She's taken all of them hasn't she? That woman just waltzed in here and took Andrea and Maria away from me. Where is she now?" My eyes were shrouded in a vibrant scarlet and I could feel the monster inside me, freshly renewed and recharged, screaming to be let loose.

Mike didn't look at all ruffled by my out-burst but the others all looked as if they would start crying such was the ferocity of my rage. Straightening his shirt again, he continued.

"The Elder was here to inform every one of the latest Awakening. You are required in Argentina as soon as possible so Mr. Blanco can take his place amongst The Circle." All business with strong attention on protocol. A perfect display of exactly how the Head of House should speak to his master. I grunted a response and stopped. What was wrong with me?

"I'm sorry Mike. That was uncalled for. Thank you for that information. Where is Maria?" I softened my tone this time and hoped that I hadn't been too out of line. Mike seemed to relax a little before answering.

"She was taken by the Mage's Guard when The Elder was here. They will be presenting her at the Awakening as the new Messenger." Then he leaned in to me, close enough that the others with him wouldn't be able to hear what was said.

"And I think you may be in a little trouble again, but what's new there?"

His conspiratorial tone relaxed me despite the content of the message. If he was speaking in that way, at least it meant that I was still in his good books despite my outburst.

"When do they want to have the ceremony?" I asked, again back into the show of perfect behaviour between the master and the subordinate.

"As soon as you are ready."

"Excellent. I've got one tiny errand to run before I leave for Argentina but it won't take any time really."

Twenty minutes later, I was stood on my gravel driveway holding a large Cascade Bridge open to an underground city in Mexico. The Tayne surged back through to their home and I did my best to thank each and every one of them as they passed me. Greyas was the final Tayne to leave and she bowed deeply to me before heading for the Bridge.

"Before you go Greyas," I stopped her and beckoned for her to stay a second. "I look to you as one of the bravest beings I've ever had the good fortune to meet and I thank you for not only your people as a whole, but specifically to you, for saving me and The Circle." I gave her a deep bow of my own and held my position facing the floor for a count of five. When I righted myself, her expression was one of shock and she had tears falling down her lumpy cheeks. None of the affected Tayne had been returned to the form they had been before Leatherpants and his devious plans. The changes remained even without the power of the Drake Stone fueling them but not one of these creatures seemed to mind. Maybe they felt that they were wearing these new bodies as a badge of honour having survived.

"My Lord saviour. You have been the first in our history to fight for us. We have had others fight against us but mainly fight over us but never for us. How could I not give everything for you?" We both smiled.

"When you get home, please inform your Queen that I am sorry that so many of your kind were lost during this fight and that should she need anything, any help at all, from The Circle, to contact me here." Greyas didn't move, still shocked to stillness at the conversation she was having.

"She asked me to never return and I won't. But I am offering my hand in friendship if she so desires. The Circle is not as it once was." We both bowed cordially to one another and she flashed through the gateway to her home.

Sighing, I hoped that I'd done everything I could to make a friend. I felt the need for some good news following all of the continued struggle I'd seen during my time within The Circle. Even we were looking to exact violence on us.

My next task was to honour Em. I'd already prepared the small stone myself and it was smooth in my hand as I walked across to the open expanse of the mansion's grounds. I turned it over and over between my fingers as I closed on the memorial crater. Standing alone on the lip of the water filled hole, I just breathed deeply and said a silent thank you to yet another fallen warrior, before hurling the latest name into the depths. There had to be change to how The Circle acted. I just couldn't let the old ways remain.

From there, now with a new fear, I opened up my own Cascade Bridge to the buried prison site in Argentina. All of the others who were going to be a part of this latest ceremony, Mike, Mark and a select handful of my military personnel, were already there and when I arrived I was quickly ushered through the crowd of gathered people to take up my place within this mighty hall, in a huge ring under a floating block of black crystal. Inside that crystal was the Hive demon, trapped in a magical version of amber. I hadn't had any of the detail explained to me about what it was or how it was being held but it was only now that I realised that I'd never been told anything of the specifics of the way The Zarrulent had been held either. More questions just piled on and made the water even murkier.

The Awakening proceeded in the same way the others had here but this time there was a new family line to be inducted. At the signal of The Mage, Hairy finally became a Guardian of The Circle as he transformed into that huge fire Dragon I'd last seen Freddy wearing. He roared and screeched as he became the beast, a much more intimidating version than poor Freddy had been, before standing resplendent as the latest link in a constantly re-forging chain. I wasn't even paying attention to what was happening, this was all so familiar to me having seen an almost constant repeating at this site in the short time I'd been a part of The Circle. All I could think about were the injustices I'd witnessed and Andrea. In all of this I could just feel the need to hold her and be held in return. She'd become a mainstay of my life very quickly and I just couldn't see my life without her. Seeing her again, in her full majesty as her white Dragon, made me want to just run to here and try to explain.

"GUARDIANS OF THE CIRCLE."

I was jolted back to the here and now in jarring fashion. It was The Mage calling out to the gathered masses in the cavern to leave, that what he had to say was only for the ears of the Guardians. Everyone bustled from the cavern quickly but precisely, and remembering what Mike had said back in Wales about me being in trouble, I prepared myself for the inevitable showdown.

"My Guardians, I thank you for the continued work to remedy this breach in who we are". There was the barest collection of growls in response. "And I thank those who were instrumental in the defeat of a traitor within our ranks. Miss Thomich, Mr. Johns and Lady Elder, your sacrifices will not be forgotten." More low growls came from the other Dragons but my temper was bubbling. We hadn't done the sacrificing, Maria had been removed from what could be considered her birthright after the kind of torture that would break anyone and Em had sacrificed herself to destruction to kill the Bulk. All I'd been able to do was watch on as it happened. The Mage continued to speak as my thoughts swirled.

"We have been weakened by the actions of the one from within us who chose to forgo our sacred duty and attack us. I believe that The Elder knew nothing of the treachery within her ranks, as she was so badly affected by the mental control of Mr. Ward." The Elder remained stony faced at the description of her being a victim. "We must now move to reclaim our rightful power within this world lest another force attempt to defeat us." The growls were now growing louder, being conducted expertly by The Mage. I also couldn't believe that The Elder was going to escape without the barest of rebuke. She'd been more than a little keen to mete out justice when there had been the chance that another estate had been infiltrated. Em's calm voice ran through my head, as if answering my unspoken question, "The greater good."

"Now we must remind the world what the true power of The Circle is. We must destroy the Tayne utterly in response to their unprovoked attack of us and send a message to any other creatures who feel reckless enough to want to rise up against us." The room erupted as the frenzy took hold of everyone. My own snarls of dissent were almost lost amidst the din, but only almost.

"GUARDIANS! One of our number has expressed a different sentiment." The Mage's tone changed and the implicit threat wasn't lost on me. He'd effortlessly focused all of the attention in the cavern on me whilst also letting everyone know what he thought, and yet again, despite having the best of intentions, I was underground and surrounded by angry monsters.

I didn't stand on ceremony, or wait for any kind of signal to speak.

"The Tayne were instrumental in the victory. They only attacked us when they were all acting against their wills thanks to Leatherpants and the bloody Drake Stone. They were helpless and you want to punish them for that? They fought with us as soon as they regained their free will. They should be allies, not cannon fodder." I was clenching my teeth against the fury which threatened what was left of my ceremonial poise. Surely they wouldn't.

"Yet this is what we have always done, Mr. Johns." Now it was The Mage's turn to speak through gritted teeth. "You have served The Circle with great passion since assuming the mantle of Guardian, including saving me personally, but it would appear that you still have a great deal to learn regarding the finer points of our protocol." I was about to respond with exactly what I thought of the protocols when, thankfully, I was interrupted.

"WAIT!" A new voice crashed through the cavern and each and every Guardian looked around to locate the source. From deep within the shadows at the far edge of the cavern, a tiny movement flickered and a shape began to approach. Mouths dropped open as the shape entered the light and made its way to the centre of the gathering of Dragons. Clad in a purple bodysuit and walking with purpose and authority, came Maria. She strode into the centre of us all and stood before the Mage, her arms clasped behind her back.

"I believe that Mr. Johns has made a valid point concerning the complicity of the Tayne. They were all controlled by Mr. Ward so should remain blameless in this." She was still a child but she was now so much more than that.

"I witnessed what they did in Bress Tal and they should not be punished for it." Silence covered everyone, as if preventing them from uttering a sound. The Mage narrowed his eyes and considered her words, ignoring completely the fact her body was just six years old.

"And what of the wider message this act would send other races who wish to conquer us? The truth doesn't matter, only what races perceive."

"But let the Tayne spread the word that we were merciful. Should we not evolve in our dealings if that were to give us a stronger outcome?"

The Mage stroked at his chin and pondered what Maria had just said, the creases around his eyes pinched in concentration. I couldn't have said it any clearer than she had. I don't think anyone could have said it clearer than she had, so now it was down to the Mage. We didn't wait long.

"Lady Messenger, you have presented a valid point, though poorly delivered. I agree. Sparing the Tayne will have a chance to do some good and any risk to The Circle by not wielding our might against them can be dealt with swiftly should it arise. But I will expect for them to be very grateful when they speak of this in the future." This time there couldn't have been any doubt concerning the threat in his voice.

Maria nodded once, gave me the smallest hint of a smile and without any further comment or discussion the matter was concluded. Just like that. The Mage had just accepted the word of Maria when mine was worth so very much less? I knew that she wasn't just a child but my anger still blossomed at the casual way I'd been cast aside. She may have been the new Messenger but still, we were both involved in the fighting.

"Is that it? Are we done?" I just had to get out of there. Looking across at Andrea, hoping that we could at least try to speak with each other, I found her heading towards Hairy's Dragon. He was only a fraction shorter than me but was a great deal more armoured. I couldn't take my eyes from her.

"We will be concluded when I have returned to Egypt Mr. Johns. We have another matter to discuss." The Mage paced towards me and the energy crackling around him was the vastest thing I'd ever encountered. With each step, the pressure from him grew and although I wanted to just jut my chin out in defiance, even I could see the need for calm. I bowed my head in capitulation.

"Excellent." The wall of force evaporated. "Miss Thomich will conduct the first training for our newest Guardian as she did for you. She made it possible that you would be able to do all of things you now can even despite your lack of knowledge of The Circle so will be more than capable of guiding Mr. Blanco in what he has to do." He turned away from me and all I could do was seethe. He'd made sure that I'd been put into my place and he'd done it with the rest of The Circle watching. Hairy the Dragon stood and just stared into space, seemingly oblivious to what was going on but Andrea stood next to him and folded her arms across her chest. This would have to wait.

"Gathered Guardians," began the Mage. "We now arrive at the final issue for the day." He was back to the cordially polite tone and there was no hint that there was anything out of the ordinary going on.

"We must now welcome the latest Messenger to our service. A former member of the Guardian line at this very site, this child has been granted the role of acting as my direct vassal." Maria had remained in the gathering of Dragons and acknowledged the various glances as they came. I didn't dare look but I could feel her eyes pass in my direction. The Mage beckoned for her to approach him. She obliged and he settled his hand onto head.

"This is a very important part of who we all are and has never been shared with any of the previous Guardians but I feel that I must grasp the chance opened to me." A blaze of purple energy erupted from under his hand and wreathed Maria in a cloak of light.

"My Guardians. The destruction of The Drake Stone and the arrival of this new Messenger show perfectly that our own magics can be twisted against us. What remains of the stone is simply to hold The Messenger together as a living embodiment of all of The Circle. To be the righteous fist of my will beyond." This didn't sound good. The light continued to burn.

"I have conducted this rite for every preceding Messenger and the details of what has taken place show that it is beyond vital that I continue to perform it." The light exploded, leaving one of those floaty blobs before everyone's eyes. Maria seemed unharmed by what had just happened, so at least that was something.

"To safeguard all of humanity and protect each and every one of the people who serve us, I am forced," he looked me dead in the eye, "to remove so much of the detail of this child's memory of the life she had before." Maria turned slowly around and took in all of the giant Dragons looking down at her. There was nothing. No reaction. She just took in all of the detail as if she were looking over her toy collection.

I'd known what he was going to do. I'd been told that it had happened to Em so I knew that it would happen again but I'd just stood there and let it happen. I'd stood by and watched on as the child I'd risked my life to save was 'corrected' by one of the people who was supposed to care for her. But it was just her. No-one else. The Messenger was now the only one who was going to have to lose any memory for the good of The Circle. I was starting to understand more clearly why my uncle had needed to live apart from it all.

"Gathered Guardians." Maria addressed us all and her voice now somehow seemed flattened and toneless. "I am The Messenger. I am here to serve all of you as we protect the world from the threat of The Hive. For the greater good." The words were a knife in my chest and while the others growled their agreement I was left hollow. Maria, now imbued with the power of the crystal in her chest, looked in my direction and frowned, then strode to me.

"Guardian," she stated to me. "Are you well? You seem to be angry beyond what a Fire Dragon such as yourself would normally be. Is there anything I can provide for you?" I'd never had the chance to speak with her before all of this had happened but now, face to face with a new Messenger, it was clear that Maria was gone.

"No thank you Messenger." I choked on the words, their enforced propriety.

"Very well", she said before bowing and turning away. But she stopped and turned back to me.

"I am sorry my Lord, but have we met before today? You seem, familiar to me." Hope flashed through me. Was Maria, or at least something of her, still in there?

"I don't think so Messenger," fell out despite every tiny piece of me roaring in my ears to explain the truth. "What is your name?"

She frowned. "I am The Messenger. I have no further name." My heart broke. There was now another name to be cast into my memorial.

"Well I can't call on you as Messenger." I smiled weakly. "How do you feel about being called Em?"

About the Author

Owen is a fan of all forms of storytelling and enjoys books, film and TV, as long as there's something compelling going on. He's worked in different roles over the years, but has always had the spark of creativity lurking in the back of his mind. A Welsh rugby supporter, he lives in South Wales with his wife Joanne and they are protected by their loyal guard cat, Baggins.

Visit Owen Elgie on Facebook, Twitter, and Wordpress.